FALLING INTO GRACE

Ellie Meade

PROLOGUE

It has been eight months since the event that changed my life forever. I try not to think of it, but in the darkness of the night, it creeps over me. I watch as the alarm clock shifts to 2:38 a.m. It should be no surprise to me; I have not slept since he has been gone. I am a robot. My body goes through the motions of each day, but my heart and soul are still in the deepest shades of black. When will I snap out of this? In that instant I go back to the moment I lost him. I stand in the shadows watching, as I'm told my future is no more.

CHAPTER ONE

October 2012

The morning starts like all the rest. I roll over to realize that we are once again going to be running late. I kick the blankets off my satiated, exhausted body and for a brief second look over at Chase's side of the bed. What we did last night was so good, I wish I could be doing it again right now, but I have to get the kids ready for school. I walk into Ella's room first, and she is starting to stir.

"Good morning, sunshine," I sing as I open her blinds.

"Stop, Mommy, I want to sleep," she says as she pulls the blankets over her head. She is grumpy already, but this does not shock me. My beautiful baby girl is like fire, and she is only five years old.

"Well, lovey, you have to get up if you don't want to be late to school," I say.

"Fine," she says in a snarl.

I roll my eyes as I exit the door and walk to Hunter's room. He is the most beautiful boy when he sleeps and unlike his sister, he wakes up happy and smiling. I open his door and he shoots up.

"Good morning, Mommy," he says as he leaps out of bed to greet me with a huge hug and warm kisses on my cheek. He makes my heart melt every morning.

"Get dressed quickly, or we are going to be late again."

Not worrying about him following my directions, I go back into Ella's room to make sure she hasn't gone back to dreamland. Much to my surprise, she is getting dressed in the outfit we picked out last night. I have discovered we are better off negotiating the outfits the night before so we aren't screaming at each other in the morning. *Good,* I think to myself, *this morning is going to be an easy one.*

I head downstairs into the kitchen to start breakfast. It's not a great breakfast, I think as I pour Rice Krispies into their favorite bowls, the ones with straws coming out the side. Before I can finish, they are coming down the stairs completely dressed. My beautiful babies; I was blessed with twins, one boy, one girl, or as Chase would put it, two birds, one stone. I go to the fridge and take out strawberries; this will have to do. I slice them thin and put a few in each bowl, making sure they each have the same amount. Lately breakfast has been an eating contest; I rush them to eat faster so we won't be late. As they are taking their last bites, I grab their bowls and put them in the sink.

"OK, time to brush your teeth." I'm on their heels as we head into the downstairs bathroom. We all quickly brush our teeth and wash our faces.

"All ready for school?" I ask.

"If we have to," Ella whines as she rolls her eyes. She is a mini me in every way, and she is going to be the death of me in the latter years. I can just feel it now.

"Get your shoes on and let's get in the truck. Move it!" I shoo them out the door and go back into the house. They forgot their backpacks, so I grab them and sprint to the truck. I check them in their booster seats, then hop into the truck. I start the engine and roll down the driveway. It's a fast ride to school, and they lean over to kiss me before they jump out the door.

"I love you," I yell after them. Ella rolls her eyes, giving me the look of *you're embarrassing me, Mom,* but Hunter, my sweet Hunter, yells back, "I love you too, hot mama." I laugh. Chase rubs off on him in every way.

I thank God I'm off today. I need a day of rest after working all weekend at the hospital. Unfortunately my day off will be spent cleaning. Chase is an amazing husband and father, but cleaning is not his thing. The moment I walk into the house, I check the dishwasher to see if it has even been emptied since I turned it on Saturday morning. Much to my surprise, it has been emptied and reloaded. *Good*, I think to myself, he is capable of doing things, but I know his game all too well. He likes to pretend he can't do anything so I have to do everything. He has been like this forever, but every now and again he surprises me.

It doesn't take much to please me. I enjoy all the small things. When Chase washes the dishes after dinner, it's like foreplay to me. I like to watch him stand and clean each pot with those rugged hands of his. Oh, those hands. I snap out of it, laughing at myself; he can distract me without even being here. I walk over to the counter and turn on my iPod, and then I turn my new Bose speakers on and connect them. Bluetooth and wireless connection is the best invention ever! I need music to clean, so I turn the volume up and flip on my favorite cleaning mix.

I push through the kitchen in no time, and move on to the adjoining family room. I fold all the blankets and start to launch the toys, that are all over the floor, into the toy box. It is a little game I play: How many in a row can I get in before missing one? I throw a remote-control car, and it hits the wall, leaving a big dent. Shit! I run my hand over the dent to see how deep it is. Then I hear the sound I should have run from, the sound that would change my life forever.

CHAPTER TWO

I walk over toward the door, peeking out the window to see who the hell would be knocking at my door at such an early hour. It's the police. I think back to my conversation with my neighbor just days before about a break-in a few blocks over.

"How the hell can this happen? We live in a good neighborhood," I had said to her. The woman was not home, thank heavens, but they stole all her jewelry and a few other novel items. I open the door to be greeted by a calm and handsome man.

"Mrs. Winterfield?" he says, to my dismay.

How the hell does he know my name? Why the hell does he know my name?

Suddenly I see Chase's best friend Kevin's car pull into the driveway like a bat out of hell. I don't think he even stopped the car when he put it into park, as he jumps out of the car like a rocket. My heart suddenly drops. *No, no, no.* What is going on? I step back into the house.

"Come in," I say in a whisper, taking another step back.

"There has been an altercation involving your husband, Mrs. Winterfield," he says gently as if he is talking to a child. I fall to my knees, because I can feel the void in my heart already.

I go numb. The room is suddenly spinning around me. I have never had this feeling before. I feel like my arms and legs have fallen asleep. I stare blankly at the floor and begin to count the floorboards. *What the fuck is happening?* I guess Kevin is reading my face because he begins to tell me what happened. I can't do this now, I have to get away from this. I get up and walk away. I begin to run through the house, out the back door, and onto the patio. Kevin follows right behind me.

He grabs my arm and yells, "Stop." He grabs too hard, and I feel pain shoot down to my wrist and back up again.

"Chase was inspecting a new building this morning that we bought." He looks down and I can see his tears.

"Is he dead?" I don't recognize my own voice, and a part of me already knows the answer. He nods. My heart sinks, leaving my insides throbbing. I can't breathe, and I feel my wounded heart sink deeper. It's the kind of sadness that immerses your stomach and leaves it all to ache. I'm broken. I plummet down again; it feels like a free fall off the top of the Empire State Building, then it landed right on me, crushing me beneath it's weight. Kevin gets down to my eye level and continues.

"We were told it had been cleared and condemned yesterday." He stops and I vaguely remember them on the phone last night talking. Chase—all business, with one hand in his pocket and the other holding his cell. He is sexy as hell, with long legs and broad shoulders. Then I shudder. He *was* sexy as hell. It starts to hit me that he is no longer here. I can no longer touch him and get a returning touch. I start to shake, and my breathing seizes.

Kevin starts again, choking on his words. "He was doing a fast sweep. You know how he is."

Yes, I think. He likes to touch and see things before he knocks them down. It hits me again like a wrecking ball: he *liked* to.

"He went in while we were talking. I heard yelling in the background and then the phone went dead. I tried calling back, but he didn't answer, which isn't like him. I was only a few minutes away. I wish I would have called the police sooner." He stops and I look up. He is crying.

The detective steps in, and we both jump. I have completely forgotten he was here.

"Ma'am, your husband was attacked by a man named Wesley Fisher."

I know that name. Why do I know that name?

"He is wanted for the murder of two police officers from two nights ago." That's why I know the name; it has been all over the news. I remember seeing his mug shot in one of my patients' rooms. The thought of this makes me shake once more. Feeling nauseated, I pull my knees to my chest for some kind of protection. I can't hear any more. I can't do this. I want to yell "Stop!" I want my life back. I want to keep cleaning my house happily and peacefully.

"He was hiding out in the building, and your husband—uh, Mr. Winterfield—must have spooked him." He looks down at his feet.

Kevin looks up at me. "I was too late. It's all my fault. I woke up late and was running behind. I should have been there."

I jump a little and devastation deepens inside me, twisting my insides, making me want to vomit. "When I got there, I ran straight to the third floor where he said he was before the phone went dead." He shakes his head at the word. *Dead.* The feeling inside me is horrific; I can feel the bile rise in the back of my throat, burning everything in its path. My insides feel like they are being shredded apart even more.

"He was lying there with blood all over him." He stops and looks at his hands. I can't believe what I'm seeing. I hadn't noticed the blood still on his hands, shirt and pants. His head is hung low, and he is trying to hold back more tears, but it's apparent he is reliving this all over in his head. The look in his eyes says it all. I can see the twister spiraling around, destroying everything in its path.

"He was still alive when I got there. I held his stomach and called the police, but it was too late when they got there," he breathes.

"Hannah." I startle at the sound of my name. He grabs my hands and holds them, sitting directly in front of me.

"I'm so sorry. This is all my fault."

"No," I say, but I'm not sure he heard it. I can't find my voice, and I don't want to find it. He pulls closer to me and with that, the feelings inside of me crest. I can't be touched. I don't want to be touched; it will hurt. My heart and soul are damaged beyond repair. My heart has been shattered into a million pieces, and I can't pick them up to put them back together. I move back. He can tell I'm still in shock, so he doesn't move any closer.

"Ma'am?" Shit, why do I keep forgetting the detective is here?

"If it's any consolation to you, your husband didn't go out without a fight. We apprehended Mr. Fisher shortly after we arrived. He didn't make it out of the building."

I look up sharply. "I hope that bastard is dead." The words surprise me. Well, truthfully the words don't surprise me; it's the tone that surprises me. It's a mixture of rage, resentment, and sorrow.

"Mrs. Winterfield, I can arrange to have you brought to the hospital to say your good-byes." I look at him as if he is speaking a language I don't understand.

"Hannah, let me take you to the hospital." Kevin stands up, reaching out his hands.

I can't move, I can't breathe, and I can't do anything but stare. He shakes me out of my head spin by picking me up. I don't fight it. He carries me into the house and sits me in a chair at the table. I sit and look down the hallway into Chase's office. It wasn't even twelve hours ago that I was watching him on the phone with Kevin. What could I have done to change all of this?

"Detective Campbell, would you mind giving us a police escort to the hospital?" *Campbell. A name to the face*, I think. He never introduced himself, but then again he never had the chance. "Yes, sir." He turns and walks out of the house, mumbling something over his radio.

"Do you need anything, Hannah?" Kevin asks, kneeling down in front of me. He looks disheveled, tired, and aged. I place my elbows on the table. My face lies in my hands as I rub my fingers over my eyes; I feel the tears run through my fingers. What is happening?

"Let me get my bag, then we can go." It takes all my strength to stand up and get some balance. I look around and remember it's probably still in the car. I have a horrible habit of leaving my purse in the truck, along with the keys.

"It's in the car. Let's go." He follows me out of the house, and I reach into the truck to take my purse out. I see my cell. There is a missed call, and it's from Chase. My heart drops. Fuck…fuck…fuck… Why did I leave it in the car? I could have spoken to him. He needed me and I wasn't there for him. I should have been there. I'm on the ground, sobbing uncontrollably, and I can't breathe again. I realize I will never hear the sound of his voice again. That deep, controlled sexy voice that liked to tease me at all costs. It's gone, and it will never be again—much like me.

CHAPTER THREE

June 2013

I roll over and stare at the clock; it's 3:21 a.m. I smooth the covers beside me and sit up, tucking my knees to my chest to hug myself. It has been eight months since he touched me last. I lie back down and close my eyes. *Sleep,* I tell myself. Who am I kidding? I don't sleep, and it shows. The dark circles of black surround my once-delicate eyes. They used to be a bright-green; now they look murky, like moss that grows on rocks in a stream. I have lost a lot of weight. I joke as I always do when I think of this, that I'm on the dead husband diet. Why am I so fucked up? I roll over once more, trying to get comfortable.

I try hard not to think when I go to bed each night, but I'm engulfed the second I get into bed. What could I have done to stop this?

October 2012

Kevin somehow gets me into his car. I have no recollection of this, but there I am in the passenger seat of his car. He'd just got the Mercedes earlier that week and had come over to show it off. I am thankful he is going fast as he follows Detective Campbell. It feels like it's taking an eternity to get to the hospital, but we arrive. Kevin pulls right up front, steps out, and runs over to my side. I haven't moved or spoken since I realized I was in the car. He opens my door and takes my hands; I don't have the energy to protest. I'm up and moving before I can respond. His arm is around my waist, holding me up and steady. He throws his keys at the valet and keeps walking, not waiting for the stub. We are at reception before I can comprehend it. Everything is so blurry. My surroundings are a huge haze.

"How can I help you?" the receptionist asks sweetly, and I hate her immediately.

"We are here to see Chase Winterfield," Kevin mumbles. "He was brought in this morning by ambulance."

"Sorry, sir, I don't see him in the system." She types for a little longer and soon loses her color. "I'm sorry, sir, he is in the morgue… Umm, please take that elevator to the bottom floor. You will exit the elevator and take a right; it's going to be the second door on the left." She sounds methodical as she speaks.

I lose her at *the morgue*. She hands Kevin two stickers and looks at me apologetically. I am once more pushed to walk. He takes the lead, and Detective Campbell and I follow. I feel like a lost child. We walk and wait at the elevator. My life is in slow motion. When the elevator chimes and opens, a bunch of people pass by, busy in their thoughts. We step in and he takes my hand, interlinking his fingers in mine. He quickly presses the button, and we are both jarred and start heading down.

I remember what Chase used to say about holding hands this way. "It means our souls are touching." I can remember him saying this, thinking *he just wants to get into my pants,* and yes, he did just that. He was in my pants and inside me that very night. I long for that feeling again. The door has opened while I'm deep in my thoughts. Before I realize it, we are at the door of the morgue. I can't do this, and before I know it, I'm on the floor again, sobbing. The dreadful feeling is back. Someone is taking my heart out by sticking his hands down my throat and pulling it out. I can see Kevin's shoes. They are perfect with no marks on them. They must be new. I'm back on my feet and wrapped in Kevin's arms. He is the only thing keeping me from falling again.

"Jesus, Hannah! Can you tell me when you are going to fall? Look at what you are doing to yourself." I look at my arms and see bruises on my forearms. I feel nothing.

Kevin slowly opens the door, and I want to run; I want to get as far from here as possible. I can't do this. I can't do this. I can't do this. Please. I don't want to go in there. This is a dream, this is a dream; this must be a dream. I feel like I am screaming, but it's only in my head. Kevin puts his hand on my back and holds on to me in the anticipation of me falling again. An older man looks up from his desk, and I can hear Detective Campbell's radio say something. He nods at us and walks in front of us.

"Sir, I would like to see Chase Winterfield's body. His wife needs to do an ID for me." These words stab at my chest.

"Of course. Mrs. Winterfield, I am sorry for your loss," the older man says as he steps from behind his desk. I read his badge. His name is Dr. Benjamin Clover. He gives me a nod with sincere eyes as he goes in through a door, and I feel like my body is being filled with lead. *I can't do this* runs through my head again, on repeat. I stiffen as he comes out moments later.

"I am ready when you are, Mrs. Winterfield." His voice is easy. Kevin starts to walk, and I grab his hand to stop him.

"I have to do this alone," I whisper faintly.

He stops and looks at me. I can see the pain in his soul. I can see it because mine is worse. He steps to the side, leaving me on my own to get my balance back. One foot in front of the other, painstakingly I walk. Slow and steady. Soon I am in the room and the door has closed behind me. I'm alone with Dr. Clover. I see him and I am suddenly frozen. I can't do this. I want to run out of here and never come back. I want my life back. I have this battle in my head for a few minutes.

Dr. Clover doesn't say a word. I bet he deals with this on a daily basis. He is patiently waiting for me to come over. I finally walk over, and Dr. Clover lifts the sheet from his face. I weep. The sounds coming out of my body aren't as loud as they are on the inside. My soul is empty and everything is echoing throughout my body. I hear Dr. Clover say he will give me a minute, but I struggle hearing him.

I climb on the table beside my husband. He is cold, and his eyes are closed. I lay my head on his chest, and cry. I run my hand down his arm and hold his hand with our souls touching. I sob, and I have no idea how long I have been here, but it doesn't matter. I want to stay here as long as he will be here. I need to hold him; it will make him better. With my head on his chest, I don't feel the rise and fall of his breath. I don't hear his heartbeat, and I don't feel his warmth. He is gone and will never be here again. Fuck. I cry harder than I ever have before. My heart is racing and the room is spinning.

"Come back to me," I whisper in his ear. "I need you. The kids need you. How am I going to do this without you? You need to come back to me, please," I plead with his lifeless body. I run my hands through his hair, and my sobs grow louder.

"You need to wake up, baby. Just wake up. You told me you would never leave us. We haven't done anything we wanted to yet. We haven't watched the kids grow up and graduate. This is all wrong. You're supposed to be here with us. Chase, I need you…don't do this," I croak. I'm on top of him, begging like I have never begged before, but this is a battle I have already lost. He is gone and he is never going to come back. I just want him to sit up and wipe my tears away and tell me this was all just a sick, cruel joke, but he doesn't.

I understand death. I understand I can no longer feel his heartbeat, the heart that pushed the blood through his veins, but I never thought I would be on the receiving end of this tragic news. I never thought it would be me having to deal with death.

"Hannah." I hear Kevin say my name and feel his hands on my back. I can't move. My body has been filled with lead after my heart was ripped out of my chest.

"Detective Campbell needs my statement down at the precinct." He is in pain as well.

"Leave me here. I don't want to leave him." I wrap my arms around him tighter. I want him to hug me back, but it will never happen again. I just want him to sit up and hold me. I look at him.

"Wake up, baby; I need you to wake up," I plead with him, but he's gone. He is really gone, and I will never have him to hold me again.

"Hannah, stop," I hear Kevin say. "I can't leave you here; we need to go home. We have a lot to do." I sit straight up. Shit, what was I thinking?

"What time is it? I need to get the kids from school." Oh, the pain is back in my chest, looming over me, stabbing into my deepest depths. I would rather the lead feeling.

"I took care of all of that. I called your mom, and she is going to get them and bring them back to her house." What?

"You called my mom? Did you tell her what was going on?" I think I'm mad, but my voice is still small.

"Yes, I told her. I had to. She wanted to talk to you, but I didn't want to put that on you. I told her not to tell the kids or even give them a hint something was wrong." He is all business right now. His phone buzzes, and he takes a quick glance at it and presses the ignore button. "Please, Hannah, I know you don't want to leave, but it's not good for you to stay here all day." He is trying to get me to leave and I don't want to.

Dr. Clover comes in the door. I slip off the table without letting go of Chase's hand. I look down once more at his face and kiss every one of his fingers. "I love you," I whisper, and then I kiss his lips. I step away from the table, and Kevin steps over, resting his hand on my shoulders. I start to walk with the help of Kevin guiding me forward. Before I realize it, we are out of the hospital in the crisp air. It is October and the leaves are starting to change.

CHAPTER FOUR

June 2013

I roll over again; it is 5:59 a.m. I get out of bed, wander into the bathroom, and take a shower. The water feels good on my body. I got this feeling back about a week ago. I'm starting to feel things again, which is kind of a relief. After the shower I wrap my hair in one towel and my body in another. Walking back into the bedroom, I drag my feet before and slumping in front of my vanity, taking the towel down and rubbing my hair dry. I haven't done anything to my hair except pull it back wet since he has been gone.

For the first time in eight months, I take out the blow dryer and begin to dry my brittle hair. It looks like shit when I finish, so I turn on my straightener. I can see the red light blinking, showing that it is heating up. I section my hair and begin the lengthy process. When I look at the clock again, it's 6:51 a.m. The kids will be awake soon. I find a pair of clean scrubs and get dressed. Glancing in the mirror, I realize, I have to go shopping for new clothes because everything hangs on me, but today that doesn't matter. I am getting it together this morning. Quietly, I go down the stairs and head straight for the kitchen to turn the kettle on, then begin taking all the ingredients out to make breakfast. Waffles should make them happy, I think, as I begin to crack the first egg.

Both Ella and Hunter have taken the news better than I have. It makes me feel like I failed as a mother because they are stronger than me. They have been my strength, telling me every day that they love me. I live for nothing but them. I see Hunter out of the corner of my eye and bend down to pick him up.

"Good morning, sleepyhead." I smile and he smiles back.

Ella follows shortly after. She runs to me quickly and jumps into my arms.

"Mommy, you look pretty today." *I do?*

"Thank you, baby! Do you want breakfast, lovey? I'm making waffles." They both look so happy today. I pour the batter into the waffle iron and close the lid. Excitement twinkles in their eyes as I get the chocolate syrup out of the fridge. I mix them both a glass of chocolate milk and place it on the table in front of them. I see the light flash green and the waffles are done. I make them each a plate and watch as they inhale their food. We finish up breakfast, and they go back upstairs to get dressed. They are back, before I finish cleaning up.

"We brushed our teeth already, hot mama," Hunter says, giggling.

"Oh, you did, did you? Let me see." They both open their mouths, showing off that they actually did a good job. To show my approval, I nod and laugh. They are my world. I would not have been able to move on if it weren't for them. I look them over to make sure they are all ready. Backpacks are already on their backs, shoes are on, and their faces are clean.

"OK, let's move it out the door." I drop them off at school and become a robot. I head into work with nothing on my mind. I sit down in my office and check my messages.

"You look good today, Hannah." I look up, and it's Michele, my boss in the doorway.

"Thanks. I did something with myself today. It's been awhile. I thought it would lift my spirits," I confess.

"Well, it agrees with you. You look like yourself again. If you need anything, I'm here." I have heard that every day for the last three months.

I took five months off after Chase died. I couldn't bear to see the world after it crashed down around me. It feels good to be back in the land of the living again. Slowly and steadily, I have begun to feel again.

"Oh, Hannah, I had to do emergency heart surgery early this morning; could you check on my patient for me? I have to go. I'm late for a parent-teacher conference." Dr. Michele Mitchell is one of the top cardiovascular surgeons in the state. I'm her physician's assistant.

"Sure, no problem."

"I told the patient's family about you and that you would be monitoring her today. Thanks, Hannah. You're the best." She gives me her big smile, then disappears out of sight. When I finish checking messages, I make my way down to ICU to see our patient. I say good morning to the staff, then sit down and go through the chart. Victoria Grace, sixty-one and widowed. I feel the pain and swallow. I read on and collect the info I need. I wonder if her family is still here, and yes, they are. Three men sit around her, making a fuss. She rolls her eyes and stops when they meet my eyes. I recognize the sadness, and I think she might too.

"Mrs. Grace, I'm Hannah Redman, Dr. Mitchell's PA. I will be monitoring you today. How are you feeling?" I ask as I walk over and take her hand.

"I would be better if they would leave. They are the reason I am here. They drive me crazy." She is fire. I love the attitude right away. *I'm going to like her*, I think to myself.

"Gentleman, could you please give me a moment with Mrs. Grace?"

As they leave, she sticks her tongue out at them. I almost laugh.

"Now, how are you feeling? Are you in pain?" I read her monitors and everything looks perfect. She is one strong woman.

"I feel as good as I can for just having my chest cracked open. I just want to get out of here. My sons are driving me nuts." Her voice strains, and I can tell she is tired.

"Do you want me to tell them you need rest?" I ask, tempting her. "They can wait in the waiting room and give you a few hours."

"If you could do that, I would give you my firstborn." She has a sweet look in her eyes. I feel like she is reading me, like she can see the matching pain in my eyes.

"No problem, Mrs. Grace. I will make sure they leave you alone for a while so you can rest."

"Please call me Tori. Mrs. Grace is my mother-in-law," she snorts, looking uncomfortable.

"OK, Tori. Get some rest and I will be back later to check on you." I walk out of the room and head into the waiting room. The three men stand as soon as I walk in the door. They are all well dressed in black tuxes. They must have been at an event last night when all of this happened.

"Is my mother going to be all right?" the first one asks. He is the tallest. He has to be at least six foot four. Their builds are all the same. They have wide shoulders, long arms and legs, and beautiful blue eyes.

"Yes, she is doing great, but she needs her rest."

"Aiden," one says, and the one who just spoke turns his head.

"Let's all go back home and shower and change, and we can come back later."

Aiden stands his ground. "Someone has to stay in case anything changes. John, call Sam and have him drive you and Shane home. I'm going to stay. I'll go later when you come back. I don't want to leave her like this." Aiden is the oldest and it shows. He is protective and loving. He reminds me a bit of Hunter.

"OK, Mr. Grace, but if you're going to stay, can you stay out here for about an hour? Your mother has fallen asleep, and she needs her sleep to get better." I feel like I'm talking to a child.

"Yes, ma'am," he says, slightly shocking me. *Ma'am?*

I extend my hand. "It's Hannah. Nice to meet you." He extends his giant hand and wraps it around mine. "If you need anything, please have the nurse page me. I will be back in about an hour."

"Thank you," all three say in unison.

"You're welcome." I nod and leave the room. They are all so good-looking. Good family genes. I smile as I walk away.

20

I make my rounds and find myself back in my office, where I stare at the picture on my desk. Chase looks so good. He has a grin on his face that I know all too well. I miss him and I feel the hurt once again. I stay staring at his picture for a while. After my picture gazing, I get up and head to Mrs. Grace's room; it has been over an hour, and I said I would be back. When I walk past the waiting room, I see Aiden isn't there. I hope he isn't bothering her. In her room, I see she is sound asleep. Aiden is at her side, holding her hand. I start to back away, letting them have their moment, but my eyes meet Aiden's; I look down.

"Thank God she is OK," he says. "She had us all worried last night." I look back at him, meeting his gaze. His eyes are fixed on me; I feel like I can't move in his stare.

"She is a strong woman, and she is doing better than expected." I see the hope in his eyes. I try to comfort him as much as possible. "All signs point to a full recovery." It is true; she is doing incredibly well for just having open-heart surgery. "They are going to move her down to another room later on today."

"Thank you, Hannah," he says. I like the way it rolls off his tongue. For a split moment, I realize that I think he is cute. I blush and walk out of the room. One of the nurses runs over as she sees me leaving. It's Jane. She is sweet and young, maybe twenty-two.

"Hey, Jane, what's up?" I ask, looking at her. She is all disheveled.

"Have you met Mrs. Grace's sons? They are gorgeous. I couldn't even talk, they are so good-looking." Her face blushes to a bright pink and I instantly look away.

"Yes, I guess they are good-looking, but I haven't noticed." I smile, and she can tell it is a total lie.

"Very funny, Hannah. I wish I had a poker face like you. Nothing makes you flustered." We both laugh. I'm slowly getting all the feelings back, although laughter is still forced. Hunter and Ella can make me laugh, but it's only because I can see Chase in their eyes.

Dr. Mitchell is making her way over to us. I glance at my watch and notice it's about four o'clock.

"How is Mrs. Grace?" she asks as she sifts through charts.

"She is doing great. Her sons were driving her up the wall making a fuss over her. I got them to leave for a bit and she slept. She looks like she feels better." Michele looks up.

"So you got to meet her sons?" One eyebrow goes up, inspecting me as I stand at the doorway.

"Yes, I made them leave the room, then told them they have to let her rest." She looks at me, proud.

"What did they have to say about that?" she prods.

"Nothing, two left and one stayed." I turn, ready to leave.

"Which one stayed?" she asks, teasing.

"Aiden." I smile.

"Oh, so you're on a first-name basis with him?" I turn to her before I leave.

"Dr. Mitchell, I have great bedside manners." I grin and walk away. I am getting my sense of humor back as well today.

"Have a good night, Hannah. I'll see you tomorrow." I go back into my office and get my purse.

I am heading out when I see the two other brothers walking back in. They stop me as I walk past them.

"Hannah," one of them says. I stop and smile. It is John, and I can't remember the other one's name.

"I'm Shane Grace, Victoria Grace's son. This is my brother, John." Yes, Shane. I remember now.

"Yes, I remember," I lie.

"How is my mother doing?" John is the shy one, I can tell. He looks down, then at his brother.

"She is doing very well. She is a strong woman. Go up and see her." I try to reassure him she will be fine.

"Thank you. I appreciate everything you and Dr. Mitchell have done." Shane's hand is strong around mine, as he shakes my hand.

"I had nothing to do with the surgery; it was all Dr. Mitchell." I nod at him and they walk off into the hospital.

When I get home, the kids are at the table eating dinner; my mom helps me out on the days I work. I now work three days a week. This week I chose to cluster them together to get it over with, and the kids have nothing going on this week, so I can. They are all smiles as I walk into the kitchen.

"Did you guys have a good day at school today?" I ask, playfully running my fingers along the top of Hunter's head.

"Yeah, I guess," he says, looking down.

"What's wrong, baby?" I get the feeling of hurt again.

"Nothing ice cream won't fix, Mommy." He looks up, happy again.

How can I say no to this face? I have been having a lot of trouble saying no to them since Chase has been gone. I have taken the role of both mother and father. It's been hard; I never realized how much I needed him. My mom stays, and we all have ice cream. When we finish, my mom says good-bye to the kids, and I walk her to the door.

"Sweetheart, you look good today," she says as she tucks a few strands of my hair behind one ear.

"It wasn't that bad today, Mom." I look down and sigh.

"I guess each day is different." She kisses my cheek, then walks out the door.

The night goes fast. I clean up dinner while the kids watch TV, and then it's bath time and bedtime. We sit in Ella's room while I read to them. When I finish, I tuck Ella in and follow Hunter into his room. I pick him up and squeeze him tight. We go back and forth about who loves whom more. I let him win, but I know my love is greater.

I find myself in Chase's office. He set up the treadmill for me after I had the kids. I would go in there once the kids were asleep and run while he worked. It was fun; he would tease me about the way I ran, and I would make fun of him about the way he typed. We would always end up on the floor together, wrapped in each other's arms after powerful lovemaking. I stand and gaze at the floor. I need to run. I get my sneakers on and start. I run until I can't anymore and think I just might sleep tonight. After my long run I shower and try to relax. For a while I sit on the big chair in my room, staring at my bed. I need to sleep, but I know I'm not going to. Finally I give up and get in bed.

CHAPTER FIVE

I lie on my back, thinking, *I need to stop this. I don't want to go there.* Suddenly I'm there.

October 2012

I made it home and walked into the house. I never got to clean, and I'm sure everyone will be coming through the doors any minute. When I stress, I clean. I go right into the bathroom off the kitchen and start to clean. Once I'm done there, I go into the den and finish what I started. I move back into the kitchen to collect the garbage. Cleaning calms me, even though it looks like I'm in a frenzy running around. I take the garbage out, and when I come in, I collapse onto the floor and weep. *What the hell am I going to say to Ella and Hunter?* I wonder. *How do I explain this? What am I going to say?* I hear Kevin in the office talking to someone. Suddenly I hear a car pull up. It's the kids. I stand up quickly, knowing I can't be like this when they come in the door. I need to be strong. I need to be OK. I need to do this for them. If I fall apart, they will too. I gather all the strength I have left and wait for them to come in. I see the door open, and in run my two beautiful kids.

"Mommy, Mommy," they yell. I put my arms out and pick up both of them. I needed this, needed them around me. I smell their hair. It's the scent of lavender. We split, and they run into the kitchen. Ella spots Kevin first.

"Uncle Kevin," she screams as she runs and jumps into his arms.

He needs them as well. I can see him hug her extra tight before putting her down. He does the same with Hunter.

"Where is Daddy?" Hunter asks, looking behind Kevin. He thinks Chase is hiding because he always does.

"Daddy, where are you?" Hunter and Ella split up and start the hunt. This breaks my heart, and the pain lunges deep in my chest. I start to gasp for air.

"Guys, Daddy isn't home. Come in here." I don't recognize my voice, and I don't think they do either, because within seconds they are by my side. I bring them into the den, and we all sit down on the couch. They know something is up because they both pile on my lap. *Breathe*, I tell myself. How the hell can I tear their little delicate world to pieces?

I breathe again. "Mommy loves you very much. You know this, right? "They both nod at me.

"Well, Daddy..." My voice cracks. Tears swell up in my eyes. "Daddy had to go to heaven today; he was asked to be an angel."They both look at me in shock. I know they understand the whole heaven thing. Hunter is interested in God and where he was born and Christmas. *Christmas*, I think, and the pain gets worse. They are still looking at me, so I talk again.

"Daddy was given a very important job as an angel; he will be looking over all of us. But we won't be able to see him anymore because he will be living in heaven."

Hunter gets up and yells, "I hate God! I want my dad back." I let him have an angry moment. I understand. I have had many today. Ella is still very still. I can hear her breathing, but she won't move.

"Ella, lovey, you OK?"

"Oh, Mommy, I want Daddy back." She turns and buries her face in my chest. Hunter is back at my side, crying into me as well. I can't help but start crying. Kevin just stares—I'm not sure at what, but the mood is heavy in the room. I can't bring myself to tell them how Chase died. When they get older, we can talk about it, but not all of it. I dread the future already. I don't ever see myself telling them the way Chase really died; just the thought of it makes me sick. This is the worst day of my entire life.

June 2013

I roll over and realize that the next few weeks were the worst weeks of my life, with every day equally just as bad as the next. It's a quarter after two, and I'm still not asleep. I get out of bed and walk down into the kitchen. I need water; my mouth is dry. I need to get my mind off this. I stand at the sink and look out the window that overlooks the backyard. The landscapers were here today, and the yard looks good. Aiden pops into my head. *Why the hell did he just pop into my head?* I think. I roll my eyes at myself and my silly thoughts and walk back upstairs. Dammit, I need to sleep. I lie back down.

October 2012

The kids are a mess. They sleep in my bed that night. I avoid phone calls, because I don't want to speak to anyone. I leave Kevin in charge of that. The kids eventually fall asleep, and I leave them in my bed and head downstairs. Kevin is on the couch with a bottle of scotch in his hand. I can tell by the way he is sitting that it's not helping.

"You OK?" I ask as he jumps up.

"I didn't hear you come down." He looks down and takes a deep breath. "I need to talk to you about something, Hannah." I sit down next to him on the couch, pulling my knees up to hug them.

"When I got to Chase, he was still alive. He was saying something to me." His eyes look haunted, and he can't find the words. Kevin pulls the bottle to his lips and takes a long swig. When he is done, he sits in silence for a few minutes.

"He told me to take care of you. He told me to tell you he loves you." The tears fall from my eyes and I can't move. I don't even want to imagine what he looked like, lying there dying, but I can't stop. I move toward the bottle and Kevin passes it off. I'm not a drinker, but I'm hoping it will take the edge off. I take a sip and it's warm as it goes down, then feels heavy in my stomach. Not caring, I take another sip, Kevin takes the bottle back and drinks again.

"He told me to take his place; he wants me to help you raise the kids."

"I can't do this right now." I get up and walk away. This is way too much.

"Han, I don't want to upset you, but I'm here. I'll always be here." He looks down again. I throw a pillow toward him.

"Go to sleep. We can talk about this another time when things are easier."

"Han, please get some sleep. Your mom called the doctor and got you a prescription for sleeping pills." I roll my eyes.

"I don't need drugs to sleep. I just need Chase back to sleep."

June 2013

I sit up. I should take the sleeping pills. I haven't thought of them since that night. When I look at the clock, it's a quarter to five. No sense in taking them now; I will never get up for work. I sit up and turn the TV on and watch the news for a mindless hour, then get out of bed to start my day. I get out of the shower and decide I should do my hair again. Aiden pops into my head again. Why does he keep popping up? Well, I might as well look good if I am going to be seeing the incredibly gorgeous Grace men today. I laugh inside. Wow, I actually felt the need to laugh! It feels good. I dry and straighten my hair, then decide on some makeup. I swirl and tap the powder and brush it lightly on my face, then apply mascara and some lip gloss. I look better but am still tired. I dress without much thought as I pull on a camisole and grab my scrubs. I prefer to bring my scrubs home and wash them myself, rather than wearing the hospital's clean-but-not-soft scrubs. When I walk toward the hallway, Ella is already up. I grab her hand, and we walk downstairs together. Hunter is sitting at the table eating Cheerios.

"When did you get up, baby?" He shrugs his shoulders.

"When you were doing your makeup, Mommy."

I pour Ella and myself a bowl of Cheerios, and we all begin to eat.

"Mommy, I like your hair that way," Ella says, running her little hands through my hair. It's been a long time since she has played with it.

"When I get home from work tonight, we can play beauty shop. You can do my hair, and I'll do your nails?" I say with an animated voice to ramp up her excitement.

"Oh yes, Mommy, I can't wait! Can I have the hot-pink color, and can you paint my toes too? Please!" Her pitch is high, and she smiles from ear to ear.

We need this light, happy conversation.

"Yes, of course. It's a date! Now go upstairs and get dressed for school." She runs to the sink and throws in her bowl so that it makes a loud crashing sound, then runs up the stairs. I love the sound of her feet running around. It makes me smile. Hunter is still sitting in his chair, quiet.

"How about I let you paint the airplane you and Uncle Kevin put together the other day?" He perks up, and the smile finally appears.

"Can I paint it any color I want?"

"Of course you can," I say, kissing him on his cheek. "Now go and get dressed." He clears his bowl. He looks at me and smiles, then runs up the stairs.

We run through the morning routine quickly today. I drop them off at school and head to work. One more day after today, and I will be off. I like working part-time. I get time away from the house to help me be a person again, and I get my time as a mother, but no longer a wife. I feel the hurt again and push it down. I need to get busy. I head straight into my office, where I check my messages before heading in to see Michele. She sits at her desk, talking on the phone, but she motions me to sit down as she hangs up.

"I've been calling you all morning." I pull out my cell and realize it was on silent. Opps.

"Sorry, Michele. Is everything all right?"

"It's Mrs. Grace. She was getting loud with the nurses, and they called me, but I couldn't calm her down. She was asking for you. She said you would understand." She looks at me, confused, and I am sure I look just as confused.

"I'll go and see her now." I walk straight to the elevator, get in, and press the doors shut. Why would I understand? Why would she want me? I only spoke to her briefly yesterday. This is weird. She definitely is a strange patient. When the doors open, I find Aiden there.

"Thank God you're finally here; she has been crazy all morning, and she won't listen to anyone. She keeps asking for you." He looks at me, trying to figure something out, but I don't give him the time. I can hear her shouting and throwing things.

"Get your filthy paws off of me, you tramp." I can hear the anger in her voice, and I see Jane leave the room, face reddened, with her head down. I slip in the door to see Shane and John trying to calm her down, but she won't look at them. When I walk in, they both stare at me.

"Mrs. Grace, I hear you were looking for me," I say sweetly as I walk over to touch her hand.

"Well, it's about time, Hannah. I've been waiting for you. I thought you were working last night, and I kept asking for you, but you never came back." Shit. I think back. When I did my last rounds, she was sleeping.

"Mrs. Grace," I begin and she stops me.

"Please, Hannah, call me Tori; I told you Mrs. Grace was my mother-in-law." She is still sharp, even though she looks tired and disheveled.

"Would you mind giving me a moment with your mother?" I ask as I look at Shane and John. They look at their mother, who nods. Aiden steps in to disagree, and she shoots him a glaring look. He turns and follows his brothers.

"Tori, are you OK? What can I do for you?" She sighs and looks down at her hands.

"I don't need anything. I just don't trust many people, and I like you. I feel like I can trust you. I don't like the nurses here; they are in here every moment to flirt with my sons. They don't leave us alone." I smile, taking her hand.

"Tori, I'm sure they aren't in here to flirt with your sons. They are here to care for you." She rolls her eyes at me. "Let me go and check your chart. I thought you were supposed to be moved out of here last night."

When I walk out, the three Grace men are outside the door. I walk right past them, and they follow me. I can feel Aiden's stare. He has a chip on his shoulder, for some reason. I stop and they stop. I turn and all three are looking at me.

"Gentlemen," I say, looking at all three. "Can I help you with anything?" Shane laughs.

"Can you come and live with us?" I look at them with a shocked face.

"Excuse me?"

John blushes and replies, "She doesn't listen to anyone, and you walk in, and she listens to you right away." I look at him, just as tangled in the thought.

"I'm just going to review her chart, and I have to go back to speak with her. Can you give her a few minutes to calm down?"

"Yes, of course. We will be in the waiting room," Aiden says with a snap, and he walks away with his two brothers following. I skim through her chart, and everything looks normal—great, even.

"Jane, can you call down and see why Mrs. Grace's room isn't ready yet?" Jane looks embarrassed and rushes over to me.

"Mrs. Grace's room isn't ready yet—" she starts, but I cut her off.

"I'm going to get on the phone and rip someone a new one." I walk toward the phone.

"Stop," Jane continues. "Her son called yesterday after surgery and insisted he have a room redone for his mother to stay in. It's been made into a suite. I saw them carrying in a huge TV and computer. A new state-of-the-art bed was delivered." She is excited by this gossip.

"Oh…I didn't know that." I sit and think about this new information. "Do you know which son made these arrangements?"

"Grant Grace." She blushes just saying his name. I still have no idea who he is.

"Jane, Mrs. Grace is my priority today, so if she needs anything, please page me, and I will take care of it."

She shrugs her shoulders.

"Fine with me, Hannah. She is a bitch. She threw her water at me this morning. I only volunteered to go in there to look at her sons." With that she turns and goes behind the desk.

When I walk back into Mrs. Grace's room, she is sitting up, taking a sip of water.

"Mrs. Grace—eh, Tori—your room should be ready shortly. You are doing very well. Would you like to get out of bed and take a stroll?" She looks tired, but agrees to the walk. I lift her up and wrap her robe around her shoulders. It is soft and feels heavenly in my fingers.

"I wish I had my own clothes. Grant sent for a shopper to buy clothes for me. It's never what I would pick out."

"Why? This is beautiful," I say kindly as I put my arm out and she takes it. Slow and steady, we head out the room, and I purposely walk down the opposite hallway of the waiting room. If they see us, they will want to join us, and I don't want her pissed off. Why do they drive her crazy?

"Grant, is he your son?" She looks up and smiles.

"Yes, Grant is my eldest son." Huh. I guess I had pegged Aiden wrong.

"He is a busy man; he is in London right now opening his latest hotel. He wishes he could be here, but I told him not to worry about me." She glows when she talks about him. With that we are back at the room. I help her back into bed. She's starting to look tired.

"Get some sleep. I'll make sure no one disturbs you. I will be here until five today, so if you need anything, call the nurses' station and they will page me. I'll make sure to be available when you move rooms. Is there anything else you need?"

"No, Hannah, you have been more than helpful." She reaches out her hand, and I take it. Her skin is thin and soft. She closes her eyes, and I place her hand gently on the bed. I think she is asleep. As I walk down the hallway, the three stooges are waiting for me again. I walk up to them, feeling small. They are all so tall, I feel like a child standing next to them.

"Your mother is doing very well. I took her for a walk and she's sleeping now. She would like to be left alone. She should be moving to her new room within the next few hours." Aiden rolls his eyes, and Shane gives him a sharp glance. You can feel the tension around them. "You guys might want to go and get some fresh air; she will probably be asleep for a while." They all look at each other, not knowing what to do.

"I'll be back shortly to check on her." I nod, smile, and can't help but notice their eyes. They all have breathtaking eyes, reminding me of a day at the beach when the sky is a perfect blue. I start to walk away, but I can feel Aiden on my heels. I stop at the elevator and press the Up button. He stops behind me.

"What did she say to you?" I can feel his breath against my ear.

"Nothing," I say as I turn around to face him. He glares at me, looking me dead in the eyes. This prick is not going to intimidate me. I step close to him.

"And even if she did, it's nothing I am willing to discuss with you." The doors open, and I slide in. I stare at him as the doors close. What the hell was that? Am I missing something? I have a patient who likes me, which makes me happy, but why me? I think of the eyes I saw when I first walked in. The hurt, the pain. I know those eyes all too well. It's like looking in the mirror.

Back at my desk, I sit down and start to eat some lunch. Doing rounds and showing extra attention to Mrs. Grace has left me famished. I get halfway into my sandwich when the phone rings.

"Hannah Redman," I say as I swallow my food.

"Hannah, it's Jane. I just got word that Mrs. Grace's room is ready." OK, no more lunch.

"I'll be down in five." I wrap up my lunch with hopes of eating it later.

When I arrive in her room, the three stooges are there, and they are fighting.

"Oh, fuck Grant, Mom; he is an arrogant asshole who couldn't even come here while you were half dead." Aiden sounds angry.

"Don't talk about your brother that way. If it weren't for him, you would have never gotten through college or where you are now," she snarls.

I walk in and all eyes turn to me. Aiden moves to look out the window. John stays by his mom.

"Are you ready to move?" I ask, trying to pretend I didn't hear anything.

She smiles at me. I help gather her belongings , and we are on our way. It's a short trip to her new room, only two floors up. I walk behind her bed as it's pushed into her room. The room is beautiful; it looks like a luxurious hotel room. There is a huge, new, state-of-the-art bed with a beautiful cream comforter, and instead of the normal uncomfortable chair next to the bed, there is an oversized cream chair with a light-pink cashmere blanket draped over the side arm. It looks like you would sink right into it. The windows are covered in the most beautiful draperies. The theme is creams and pinks. I love it, and so does Mrs. Grace. She looks happy and relieved. I bet she is going to sleep like a dream tonight.

Aiden gets one glimpse of the room and exclaims loudly, "You have got to be fucking kidding me."

"What?" Shane questions. "Are you jealous you didn't think of this first?"

Aiden's hands form into fists, and his eyes go dark. "Fuck you, Shane." His voice is loud and deep.

Shane keeps antagonizing him.

"That's your problem with Grant, isn't it? He keeps coming up with the ideas before you, and it's driving you crazy." Shane's ears are getting red, as well as his face.

Aiden's eyes are cold, and he takes one step toward Shane. I cringe because I hate confrontation, and I have a feeling I will have to end this. I wait, hoping it will die down, but the room gets more intense.

I grab Aiden's arm and drag him out of the room. I think everyone is shocked. When we are in the hallway, I get in his face.

"Listen, I don't know what is going on, and it is none of my business, but your mom is my business. If you're going to keep throwing temper tantrums in there like a child, I will kick you out of the hospital and not allow you back in. She just had open-heart surgery, and you are stressing her out. You need to stop, right now." I can feel his body tense. With that I turn and walk back into the room, leaving him staring at me.

"Gentleman, could you please excuse us for a moment?" I stare Shane down and he flinches apologetically for antagonizing Aiden.

Mrs. Grace looks amused, with a smirk on her face, as her sons file out quietly.

"I am going to make them all leave the hospital if they keep behaving this way ," I say, still very flustered.

"Well, Hannah, I have never seen anyone handle Aiden like that." She giggles like a schoolgirl. "He can be overbearing at times, but it comes from a place of love." She pauses and looks pale. I quickly walk over to check her monitors. All looks good except her heart rate. It has picked up speed. She looks up at me.

"Their father died when they were young, and they all grew up much faster than they had to. Grant held us all together, but he is hardly ever here. Aiden is just mad at him for not dropping what he is doing to be here." Her heart rate steadies, and I can breathe again.

"Hannah dear, do you have children?"

I smile, thinking of Hunter and Ella. "Yes, I do, two children—they are twins, Hunter and Ella." She can see the pride beaming out of me because she feels the same for her children.

"I don't mean to be rude, but are you married?" she asks. I look down at my hands. I'm wearing my wedding band and engagement ring. I haven't been able to take them off. I don't think I ever will. I feel uncomfortable, and I shift my weight from one foot to the other.

"I'm widowed," I whisper.

"Oh, I'm sorry." I shrug my shoulders and give her a forced half smile. We are in the same club.

"Hannah, honey, if I can give you a bit of advice…" I look up into her lost, lonely eyes.

"Sure." At this point I'm so lost, I don't know up from down.

"Move on, dear. I made the mistake…" She pauses, and I can't read her expression. Guilt, maybe? "I never moved on, and the boys suffered from it." I just stare at her. How could I move on? How can anyone compare to Chase?

"Don't try now if it's all still new, but think about it. I regret not having a man in the house to give the boys what they needed." She looks down at her hands. How did she know it's still new?

"Mrs. Grace, I think you did a fine job with your sons. They are wonderful men who love and care about you." I rub her arm. "You need to rest now. I will be back in a bit to check up on you before I leave."

I walk out of the room with so many thoughts filling my head. Lately I have been able to shut everything off as best I could, and now my mind is on overdrive. Why did she ask me if I was married? I have my rings on. Did she know? Why does she feel the need to tell me I have to move on? She never did, and she looks like she is doing just fine. I try to push all these thoughts out of my head as I go through the rest of my busy day.

Before leaving I make my last pit stop in her room, and the three stooges are nowhere to be found.

"Is everything all right?" I ask with a soft tone.

"Oh yes, dear, Grant just called, and he is coming back a few days earlier than planned. Shane and John went to the airport to pick him up. I think you will like him, dear. He is a wonderful man." Is she kidding me? Is she trying to set me up with her son? She is out of her goddamn mind. She must know I'm not ready, or am willing, for that matter.

"I'm happy for you, Mrs. Grace. I will be leaving for the night, and I will be back tomorrow. I put Sara in charge of you tonight, so I would consider it a personal favor if you were nice to her. I can assure you she will not flirt with your sons," I say, smiling, and she agrees by nodding her head.

I have to get home for my date tonight. Yes, a date with my wonderful, beautiful children. As I get into my car, I take a deep breath. I can do this; I can put the happy face back on and have a great night with the kids. I stop at a store on the way home to pick up a few new shades of nail polish; maybe I'll even do my nails. When I walk in the door, they both come running, excited to start the fun stuff. They have already finished eating, and Hunter has gotten my mom to cover the table with newspaper. We are all set and ready to go. My mom leaves smiling. She can tell I'm coming back. I'm finding my way back out of the deep, dark forest. I start painting Ella's nails when I hear the front door open.

"Uncle Kevin, come quick and help me paint my helicopter." Kevin comes in with a bouquet of roses. Beautiful pink roses with cream tips. He leans down and kisses my cheek. I look at him with frustration. I give him the not-here-not-now look. He bends down to Ella and hands her the flowers. *Good*, I think. Good diversion.

"Oh, Uncle Kevin, they are beautiful! I love them! Mommy, can I put them in my room?" Her look is so sweet, I can't say no.

"Of course, honey. After I have painted your nails, we can put them in a vase, and I'll carry them up to your room." I smile gently at her.

"Oh, Mommy, this is the best day ever!" I love the look in her eyes. It looks like she is getting her innocence back. It makes me feel a little better.

Once we are done with arts and crafts time, I take the kids upstairs to take a bath. Kevin stays as usual. He is here at least three nights a week. I have been trying to get him to come less. He has to get on with his life too. We tuck the kids into bed and head downstairs. I sit on the couch and flick on the TV.

"Can I get you a glass of wine?" he asks. I know where this is going, and I don't want to have the same argument over and over again, but if we are, I need a glass of wine.

"Sure," I say, not even glancing over at him.

With that he pours two glasses of wine and sits next to me.

"Hannah, we need to talk." He has aged immensely since Chase died. His face is gaunt, as he has lost weight.

"Why, Kevin? So we can have the same fight we have been having since Chase died? I don't see the point. You're not going to change my mind." I stand and walk into the kitchen.

I place my arms in front of the sink and bend my head down; I can feel the stretch down the back of my neck and into my shoulders. This cannot happen again. When Chase died Kevin wanted to step in. For a brief moment I considered it, I really did. I thought I could possibly love him one day. I knew the kids would be ok with him as their father, and then I realized I would be replacing him as Chase. I couldn't do it, I felt like on some level I was cheating on Chase. He could never replace Chase, and I would be using him. I can't do that to him, I love Kevin like a brother, but he wants to be more. He promised Chase on his death bed, that he would take care of me. The problem is, he doesn't know how to do that without being my partner, lover, or father to my children. I startle at Kevin's touch. He is standing behind me with his hands on my hips. I can feel him pressed against me and instantly I move away from him. I can't have this conversation again. I turn and look into his eyes. They are almost black they are so dark. I know he is scared of pushing me too far, but it doesn't stop him keeping his promise to Chase.

"Kevin…no. This is never going to happen. I care for you, but not in the way you want me to. You were Chase's best friend. How could I ever be with you?"

"Hannah." He leans his arms on either side of me, trapping me between the sink and him. When I look to the side, he grabs my face with just one hand to make me look at him. The other hand is still at my side.

"Hannah, I love you. I want to be with you. Can't you just try for the kids' sake?" He is pleading with me as he always does when we talk about this.

"Are you out of your fucking mind?" I'm angry. My reaction to his come ons are always the same. The thought of being with him makes the bile rise in the back of my throat. He is more like my best friend or brother.

"What do you want? For the kids to call you Uncle-Daddy Kevin?" My words are sharp, slicing through him like knives. "Or is it that you just want to fuck me in the bed where Chase used to fuck me? I have no need to do any of those things with you. How many times do I have to tell you that? I need you as a friend and nothing more. The kids need you as Uncle Kevin." I'm breathing fast, and he steps back in shock. Its then I see the hurt in his eyes. Seeing the pain in his face does not make me feel good, but I have to make it clear that I am not interested in him.

"Kevin, I think you need to get over this. It's not happening. If you keep doing this, I am going to tell you not to come over anymore. And I don't want that. The kids wouldn't want that, so please drop it." I'm shaking and the tears begin. I wish Chase were still here; then I would never have to deal with any of this.

"What happened to Vanessa?" I ask. Kevin just shakes his head and runs his finger along his jawline.

"I fucked it up. I fuck everything up. It's what I do best." He's looking down now. I feel bad but this is how I feel. I can't do it. I can't be with him in the way he wants. He starts to walk away, and I follow him. We stop at the door, and he cups my neck. I lean my head to the side and close my eyes. He slips one of his hands into my hair and pulls me close to his chest. I can feel his heartbeat against my ear. I haven't been this close to anyone since Chase has been gone. The pain surges deep in my chest, and the hurt creeps back. I take a deep breath, and he kisses my cheek.

"I love you, Hannah. I don't want to hurt you. I'll leave you alone; I will do anything you need me to." I kiss his cheek and he leaves. I lock the door and feel exhausted. I go into Chase's office and get on the treadmill. I need to run until it hurts. I want my body to hurt as bad as my heart.

I run for two hours, until I can barely make it up to my bed. I lie back, still all sweaty, and the memories come back, crashing down on me like giant waves.

CHAPTER SIX

October 2012

I sit all night staring up at the ceiling. Hunter is sideways in the bed, with his head on my stomach. He is restless. I gently slide his head down to rest on the bed before sliding out of bed and walking to the safe. I pull out an envelope. I remember the agent handing it to me when Chase and I did our life insurance policies.

"I hope you never have to open this," he had said as he handed it to me.

"I hope so too," I had said, taking it from him.

That day I had put it in the safe and never thought about it again, until now. I open it up, and start to read. It is the usual legal mumbo jumbo. I get a million. We chose a million for both of us. It will pay off the house and leave enough for me to open two trust funds for the kids. I sigh; I never thought I would have to do this. Before I know it, I have everything emptied out of the safe, going through all of Chase's business info. He owns fifty percent, and so does Kevin.

I have no idea what I am going to do with Chase's business. I'll probably just sign it all over to Kevin. The pain begins to consume me. It pulses through every cell in my body. The subtle ache in my chest begins to crest and swallow me whole. I weep hidden on the closet floor behind Chase's clothes. I pull down a shirt and bring it to my nose. It smells like him. If I close my eyes maybe I can pretend like he right next to me. I can pretend his arms are around me. This makes the tears come harder and faster. The kids wake up and start to cry for Daddy. I cry too, because I can't give them what they so desperately want. I can't bring Chase back, and just the thought of that breaks me down all over again. As a parent I'm supposed to protect my children, they were never supposed to feel pain of this magnitude. We are all lying on the floor when Kevin walks in. I go to sit up, but he stops me. He gets down on the floor with us, taking Ella out of my arms and bringing her to his chest. I watch as wraps and arm securely around her tiny frame while the other brushes through her hair. He cries softly into her blonde hair. I watch Ella cling to Kevin, like he will soon disappear. Glancing down at Hunter, I see Chase in all of his features. I run my hand slowly down his cheek catching the stream of tears. He looks so lost and fragile. I push my fears out of my head in hopes of becoming stronger for them. The room is filled with so much angst. I get the strength to get up.

"Come on, guys, let's go eat." We make our way down the stairs as my parents walk in the front door with food in tow. I begin to relax; I need my mom and dad so much. My dad pulls me in, and my mom gets the kids into the kitchen. I fall right into his arms.

"Honey, you are a strong woman. You can do this. All you have to do is keep it together and get through each day as it comes." His words are comforting, but I know this isn't possible; I can't do anything but sit and cry. While my father rubs my back, and comforts me. Then I hear the phone ring.

"Mom, can you please get that? I don't want to talk to anyone. I know nothing yet. I have to call and make the arrangements today." With that she answers the phone and starts protecting me. I want to turn the ringer off, because when she hangs up, it rings again. This happens all day. I grab my cell phone. I have thirty-one missed calls. I call Becca, because we have been friends since we were three, and even though we live on opposite sides of the continent, she will listen even if I don't talk.

"Hey, mama, how's it going?" She doesn't know, and for a second I want to keep it that way. I want to talk to someone who isn't going to have pity on me.

"Han, are you there?" I try to talk, but I'm so choked up.

"Oh, Becca." I start to sob into the phone.

"Han, what's going on? Are you all right?" She sounds serious now; the happy carefree Becca has left, much like me.

"Becca, it's Chase. He…he…died." I said it.

It hurts more than I thought it would, and my heart crumbles. The pain is back, and it's so bad, I can't breathe again.

"Hannah, I'll be there in a few hours." I hear her yelling at her assistant to call the pilot and get the plane ready.

"Becca, you don't have to—" I start to say, but she cuts me off.

"Hannah, are you kidding me? No way in hell you can keep me away. I'm leaving the office now; I'll have clothes sent to me or something… don't worry. I can cancel everything." She stops, and I think it has finally hit her too.

"Hannah, are you OK?" she asks in a whisper.

"No," I say, but I'm not sure she heard.

"I'm leaving now. I will be there as soon as I can. I love you." I can tell she's rushing around.

"Thanks, Bec, I'll see you soon." With that I hang up. I feel a bit relieved, knowing that she will be here. She can make it better; she always does.

I can't make another one of these calls. It takes too much out of me. I head into the kitchen, where Kevin is on the phone. I hear him talking about having Chase's body moved to the funeral home. I guess it's better that he does all of that, because I can't even think of where to begin.

"Hannah." I look up. Kevin is standing next to me. I'm in the living room, and I have no idea how I got in here.

"We have an appointment in an hour. Do you want to get ready?" I can't move. He helps me move and begins to walk me to the stairs.

I slowly walk up the stairs and go into the shower. The burning water doesn't feel like anything against my skin. My whole body is numb. I get out when the water turns cold. Teeth chattering, I throw my hair back wet and put on my yoga pants and Chase's favorite sweatshirt. I can smell him on it. The pain comes back again, overwhelming me as I fall to my knees. I cry so hard. I can't find my way out of the maze that has become my life. I remember the smell, when he would come behind me and wrap his arms around me. "Baby, I need you," I whisper.

It's Kevin who finds me on the floor of the closet.

"Hannah, come on. We have to go." He helps me up and we hug. It's not the same. I can feel his chin on top of my head. I push away and run away from him.

I try to dry my eyes the best I can before I kiss the kids good-bye. When I walk into the kitchen, Hunter is on the floor on his knees, praying, with tears running down his cheeks. I quickly go next to him.

"Honey, what are you doing?" I can tell he is angry.

"I'm fighting with God. I hate him. He is a bad man." He is so innocent.

"No, honey, don't be mad. Be proud that he chose Daddy for such a special job." I kiss his head and pull him close.

"Mommy, do you think Daddy wanted this job? Do you think he wanted to leave us? Why didn't he say good-bye to us?" So many questions, and I don't think I have the answer for any of them. I don't have the heart to say the words, because Daddy was murdered.

I let out a deep breathe. "I don't know, honey." He looks up at me.

"Mommy, he won't take you too, will he?" I feel the hot tears leaving my eyes.

"Oh no, honey, I am not going anywhere. I promise." I hold him close and rock him back and forth. The tears just keep coming.

June 2013

I sit up in bed and see that it's 3:30 on the dot. I get up and wash my face with warm water before I get back into bed. I started sleeping on Chase's side of the bed. I yearn to smell him again; I miss the way he smelled. The mixture between his natural earthy cinnamon smell, mixed with his cologne. I take a deep breathe through my nose in hopes I will smell him, but I don't. Turning on the TV, I watch infomercials for two mind numbing hours, before I finally decide to get out of bed. Somehow watching some guy sell sports memorabilia makes me feel better. It reminds me of Chase sitting on the couch watching ESPN. The sound used to bother me, but what I wouldn't give to watch him sitting there for hours again. I turn on the shower and stand for a while. I find that the shower soothes me, and gives me renewed strength. A motivation to fix myself up.

I proceed to do my new morning ritual of hair and makeup. Little by little, I can do this. It feels good to start doing these little things again. I look in the closet and realize I never did laundry, so I have no scrubs. Shit, now I have to get dressed. I take it as a sign to continue to do things to make me feel better about myself, if only physically. I find a pretty dress and grab my heels. Downstairs I put on the kettle. I'm in desperate need of caffeine. It's one of the few vices, I still enjoy. Ella and Hunter run down together laughing. Our morning goes by fast, and we are out the door again. As I pull up to the school, Ella reminds me that it's movie night and it's her turn to pick.

"OK, lovey, whatever you want." She looks happy and runs out the door. Hunter stops and kisses my cheek.

"I love you, Mommy," he says quickly before he follows behind his sister.

Driving through rush hour traffic, I head to the hospital, and as I walk in the door, I remember Mrs. Grace's son, Grant, has arrived. I bet he is just as gorgeous as his brothers. With that thought I smile and walk over to the elevators. When the doors open, I'm still smiling, and I see the most beautiful man. He looks at me with the most amazing eyes and smiles back. I quickly look down, because I know it has to be Grant. They all have the same beach-blue eyes. He is tall and has dark brown hair that looks as soft as silk. He is wearing black dress pants and a blue dress shirt that is tucked in; the top buttons are open, revealing the top of his tanned chest.

I step in and press the three and watch it light up. I can feel him behind me, and I can sense his eyes on me. It gives me the chills. I feel his magnetic pull, and my chest starts to pound loudly. I take a few deep breaths to quiet it down. Why am I reacting like this? He is a stranger. The doors open and I step out, making sure I don't look behind me. I feel myself blush. I have never been like this; now I'm blushing like a schoolgirl at the sight of a man. Shit…

Michele pops her head in my door a few minutes later.

"Mrs. Grace is waiting for you. She's had you paged five times already today. I don't know how you do it, Hannah. She's tough. She isn't even pleasant to me, and I saved her life!" she laughs.

"She's not as bad as you think; she is a sweet woman. I should get going; I bet she is yelling at someone right now." I stand up.

"Wow, you look pretty today." I look down and realize I should have changed when I got in.

"I have to go and get scrubs on."

"Why bother? Just put on your lab coat. I told you, you don't have to wear scrubs every day. You look pretty. Keep it on!" She is in a playful mood.

"Maybe I will." After she walks away, I take my white lab coat off the hanger on the back of the door, slide it on, and clip on my ID. This will have to do.

The elevator doors open, and there he is again. I feel a lump in my throat; he is a sight for sore eyes. He has his hands in his pockets, and he is leaning against the back wall. His jawline is sharp, and I can see him clenching his jaw. He looks at me again with those breathtaking eyes. I give a half smile and start to press the seven, but it's already lit up. I feel his eyes on me again. Then he takes a step closer, and I feel the pull again. Breathe Hannah. I can smell him; his smell reminds me of a memory, but I can't place it. The elevator comes to a stop and the doors open. I tell myself to walk, and I do. I head right to Mrs. Grace's room. I can feel him behind me.

"Oh, Hannah, you're finally here. You look nice today." She's polite but seems distracted.

"Come here, dear, come sit. I want to introduce you to Grant. He left about twenty minutes ago, so he should be back soon." With that said, I feel his eyes burning a hole through me, before I can see them. "Oh, Grant darling, this is Hannah. She is the one who has been taking great care of me." I turn and put my hand out. I look up, and I'm met with those eyes that make me breathe a little faster. My chest instantly starts to rise and fall at a fast speed. He takes my hand. It is a giant, strong, calloused hand. He has long fingers that wrap around my hand.

"Grant Grace. Pleasure to meet you. My mother speaks highly of you," he says with a smirk, looking at his mother.

"Hannah Redman. Nice to meet you, Mr. Grace. You mother is a wonderful patient." He gives me an exaggerated look of shock. His face is heavenly to look at, and his lips are…oh my!

"Are you talking about my mother? She has never made a good patient. I have had hospitals call me, begging me to come and pick her up." He laughs and winks at his mom. They are having a secret conversation with their eyes.

"Mr. Grace, I can assure you we will not do that here. She has been a perfect patient so far. Mrs. Grace, I'm going to review your chart and see how all your tests came back from yesterday. I will be back shortly." I make eye contact with Mrs. Grace, then Grant. He looks amused by something; then he nods and gives me a beautiful smile. He has perfect, straight teeth, but then again, all the Grace men have perfect teeth. I try to get out of there before he can see me blush. I have never been affected by a man this way before. Well, Chase, but no one else, and I can feel a pang in my heart. Am I betraying him?

In the nurses' station, I begin to read her chart. It all looks fine. I'll have to talk to Michele about when she wants to discharge Mrs. Grace, maybe Friday. It's Wednesday—thank God, my last day. Then I have off until Monday. I love these hours.

I head back to her room. Her IV needs to be changed, and she needs her meds. I have to hunt down pain management, and when I tell them I will give Mrs. Grace her meds, they practically throw them at me. I walk back in with a fresh pitcher of water and her meds. My feet are killing me, because I am so not used to wearing heels at work. I walk around way too much, but I will not be the woman who wears a pretty dress, then puts on sneakers. Becca always tells me beauty is pain.

"Mrs. Grace, it's time for your meds." I place the cup of meds on the table in front of her and fill her glass with water. She obeys and puts the pills in her mouth, then takes a sip of water and swallows. I start to walk around the bed to get to the IV when I spot Grant over by the window. He is looking out the window talking on the phone; he is speaking Italian, I think. The conversation sounds mysterious and sexy. Changing her IV I notice she looks tired.

"Mrs. Grace." She shoots a look at me. "Tori, are you OK? You look tired. Did you not sleep well last night?" She looks down.

"No, dear, I didn't. I stayed up watching Grant work. I have missed him so much." I smile at her and give her hand a squeeze. I can hear the three stooges entering the room. Shane smiles at me and walks over to Grant. They give a half shake and half hug. John follows after Shane, but Aiden stays in the doorway, leaning against it. He looks good today. He is wearing an orange short-sleeved shirt that shows off his tan and the tattoos on his arms. I never noticed the tattoos. I think back to yesterday and what he was wearing: a long sleeved-shirt, I think. His shirt is tucked into his jeans, showing off the perfect V his body forms. His belt is tan, and his jeans hang on his hips in a delicious way.

"Hey, little brother, are you too good to say hello? Come give your big brother a hug." I know he is teasing him by the tone of his voice, but Aiden looks irritated.

"Fuck off, Grant." Aiden sounds harsh. Mrs. Grace looks like they are ripping her newly fixed heart into pieces. Grant takes another step forward, and so does Aiden. Why are men like this? What is their problem? And why do they keep doing this in front of their sick mother? Both of their eyes narrow, and Aiden looks like he going to start swinging. It is a pissing war in here, and neither of them is backing down. Why do I have to keep playing peacemaker?

"Out, now. All of you." I can't believe my voice. It startles me as much as it startles them. I put one hand on my hip and point the other to the hallway. Shane and John are out the door in a blink, and Aiden slowly steps back. Grant stands and stares at me.

"Who the fuck are you to tell me what to do? I'll have your job if you ever talk to me like that again." He is in my face, and I get right back in his.

"Mr. Grace, I do not appreciate your choice of words. You mother is a sick woman, and I have been dealing with these outbursts for days. If you would like her to be able to go home, I suggest you and your brothers keep your issues outside of this hospital. I have no tolerance for this behavior. May I suggest you leave to cool off?" I raise my eyebrows at him to get the point across. He is infuriated, and I could care less. He looks at his mother, who is smiling like a child who was just given candy.

"Grant, please give me a moment with Hannah." He looks at her and his eyes soften. He turns to me and walks closer than needed. Was he was trying to make a point? What, to intimidate me? Now that's not going to work.

"Hannah, I think he likes you." She almost laughs this.

"Mrs. Grace, all of your sons are lovely, but I have no interest in any of them. It would not be professional of me."

I turn to walk out and I hear her say, "Give it time, honey. You'll come around." I roll my eyes and keep on walking.

The four of them are standing outside her room waiting for me. Grant immediately walks away when he sees me. *Good, piss off, asshole,* I think as I watch him retreat down the hallway. The other three smile. What the hell is going on here? Aiden looks amused.

"Thank you, Hannah. I don't think anyone has ever stood up to my brother like that before." He smiles, putting his fingers to his lips. Oh, his mouth, his perfect lips. I could just bite them. Where in the hell did that come from? They all look at me as if I had said that out loud. He licks, then bites his bottom lip, and I find this distracting. I finally speak.

"I don't see the big deal about your brother, Mr. Grace. He is human like the rest of us. He's allowed to have his moments, just not in front of your mother. My main concern is your mother and her health, and I will not tolerate this childish behavior." They smile in unison.

Aiden steps forward.

"Hannah, I apologize for any frustration I have caused you or my mother. I will personally make sure nothing happens again. Grant, on the other hand, will do everything in his power now to piss you off." He smiles, and they go back into his mother's room. I have never in my career met such a complicated family. The normal family would walk on eggshells around their sick parent, bending over backward to make her happy. These four grown men have issues. I hear my name being paged to the director's office. Today is going to be one of those days. I shake my head and make my way to the elevators.

As I step into the director's office, I see Annabelle, his assistant, looking worried and busy.

"Hey, Annabelle, is he ready for me?"

"Oh, Hannah, please go right in." What the hell could he want? I make my way into his office, and when I open the door, I see him. That fucking rat asshole Grant is sitting in front of the director's desk. They both rise as I enter. I walk right over to the director and shake his hand.

"Director Winterfield." I almost want to look at Grant and stick my tongue out at him.

"Hannah." We all sit down. "Mr. Grace has had some concerns about his mother's care. You have been treating her correct?" He nods at me knowingly, and I take over.

"Yes, Director, Dr. Mitchell did her triple bypass early Monday morning. I have looked after her since, per her request. She is doing very well, and we are expecting a full recovery." He begins to write something down. Grant is sitting back in his chair, looking happy.

Smug bastard. He is trying to get me fired. This asshole thinks he is so powerful. Two can play at this game.

"Director, may I suggest you go and speak with Mrs. Grace? She is a lovely woman. I am sure she will be able to fill in the blanks." I give Grant a cold look.

"I will consider that, Hannah. Mr. Grace, would you please excuse us? I would like to talk to Hannah for a moment." Grant stands up and shakes the director's hand, then gives me a sharp look. I want to laugh. *Sorry, buddy, this one isn't going to work; he's family, so back off.* I smile back sweetly, batting my eyelashes at him, and he pauses, his expression cold. Then he is out the door.

"Shit, Hannah, what is going on here?" My father-in-law Richard, takes off his glasses and rubs between his eyes as he leans back in his chair.

"Richard, I have no idea what is up his ass. Grant and his brothers were fighting in his mother's room, and I asked them to leave. I can assure you I was professional. He cursed me out. He is an arrogant little prick who always gets his way." I lean back into my seat, crossing my arms over my chest. I feel like an angry teenager.

"I had a feeling he was overreacting, but we need to tread lightly around him. He has made a substantial contribution to this hospital, and he is threatening to withdraw from a proposal he has made. He has offered to give us the funding to redo the emergency room."

I'm shocked! What the hell does he do that he has all this spare money lying around to spend on redoing hospitals?

"Hannah, I mean it. I have assured him this will be your first and final warning. He wants you fired. We need to get her better and out of this hospital before we lose the money." He looks tired. As do I.

"Richard, it's a good thing I only work part-time!" I smile at him. "I hope she is gone before I get back on Monday. Are you still coming over for dinner Friday?" Richard laughs as he gets up out of his chair. Chase looked so much like him. The hurt creeps up.

"I'll be there. I found some of Chase's old toy trucks. I want to bring them over for Hunter." He looks sad as he says this. I touch his arm.

"Hunter would love that." I give him a kiss on the cheek.

"I want to talk to Mrs. Grace," he says. "I want to hear what she has to say."

"You do that," I say, then I head straight to Michele's office. She is at her desk eating lunch. I plop myself down in front of her.

"These Grace men are killing me." She smiles at me; I have her full attention. "Grant fucking Grace is an absolute asshole. He went to Richard after I asked him to leave his mother's room because he and his brother still think they are five years old." I'm so angry. Michele begins to laugh.

"You mean he told on you?"

"That is exactly what I am telling you. He didn't like something, so he tried to get me fired. I almost died laughing when I was walking into Richard's office. I guess I'm lucky I kept my maiden name. He has no idea." I lean back and marvel in that fact.

I eat lunch and do some rounds, then catch up on some paperwork. In the two hours since the fight, I have steered clear of her room. In just a few more hours, I will never have to see the Grace family again. I remember how sorrowful her eyes looked, so much like mine. I shrug my shoulders at the thought and get lost in the pile of paperwork on my desk. When my phone rings, I jump.

"Hannah Redman." I lean the phone on my shoulder.

"Hannah, it's Sara. Director Winterfield just left, and Mrs. Grace has asked to see you." *Crap,* is the only thought echoing in my head.

"I'll be up in five." I slam the phone down harder than needed, but it feels good. I hope he's not there anymore. I can't deal with his pompous ass. Why does he think he is holier than God? I check my reflection in the elevator door as I wait for it to open. When it does, of course the stalker Grant Grace is standing there. I swear this man has been riding this elevator stalking me since he arrived. I glare at him as I walk in. I turn and see that the button for the seventh floor is already lit up. I face the door and up we go. I can feel him stepping closer to me. I can feel his warm body standing close to mine, almost like we are touching. I can feel his breath on the back of my neck. I feel the pull again. This man is an arrogant fuck who likes to intimidate me.

I see his long finger reach past me and press a button. With that the elevator comes to a halt. I almost lose my balance, then fall back into him. His hands are quick to wrap around my waist. I freeze. His hands on my body leave me jumbled inside. He slowly runs his hands down my sides, then down my thighs, pulling my dress up. His lips are on my neck. I can feel his lips glide down to my shoulder, as he pulls my jacket off. I'm starting to panic. Quickly I take a deep breath before I turn and slap him right across the face.

I rapidly press the button again, and we start to move. *Come on... come on!* I scream in my head. When I turn to look at him, he is smiling at me and rubbing his red face. I can feel my hand pulsing. I hit him hard. I have never hit anyone before. The doors open and I run out. I don't want to go into Mrs. Grace's room, so I head straight to the nurses' lounge.

I close the door quickly behind me and lean against it. My heart is pounding as if I just ran a marathon. That was the sexiest thing ever. His touch was controlled and he knew what he was doing. I can feel his fingers tracing my legs. I am so stupid. I wanted to be touched like that. I am a stupid woman, stupid, stupid woman . Then the thought hits me. That bastard. He was doing this to set me up, I bet. He wants to get me fired.

The anger is back. I feel used. I prefer the anger over the yearning for him. I need to hate him again. I get my breathing under control and squeeze my eyes shut tight. *Shake this off, Hannah, two can play at this game.* I head back into the hallway and go straight to Mrs. Grace's room. I glance at the clock when I walk in and see it's almost time to go. I feel relief come over me.

"Hannah, I've been waiting for you. I just had the most wonderful conversation with Director Winterfield. He speaks so highly of you." She sounds like she knows my secret. Of course she knows my secret; she can read me like a book. I hope Richard didn't tell her.

"Yes, Tori, Director Winterfield is a wonderful man. I admire him deeply." This is the truth; I admire him on so many levels.

"He was telling me you have off the next two days. It saddens me to think you won't be here tomorrow. I was told I can be discharged on Friday." I can see she is up to something, but what?

"We had a lovely talk, and he assured me you would be available to work tomorrow and Friday, just to finish up any loose ends." Are you kidding me? I laugh, and I realize it is out loud.

"This won't be a problem, will it, dear?" She is manipulating me, and for some reason I'm happy she is.

"I will have some things to figure out, but I'm sure it won't be a problem." I haven't worked full time since Chase died. The hurt creeps up again. She is reading my face and sees the pain wandering around in my soul.

"Hannah, if it's going to be a problem…I don't want to cause you any unnecessary frustration." *Too late for that, your son just did that in the elevator.* I suddenly realize he isn't in the room. Good. He probably has to wait for the redness to go away in his cheek before he can show his face to his mother. I notice Aiden sitting on the couch. He is very still, but his eyes are on me. I smile politely at him, and he smiles back. His lips are full. They look so appetizing. His face is beautiful. I can feel my blood start to rush at warped speed throughout my body. I shake myself out of the fantasy as I begin speaking again.

"Mrs. Grace, I can assure you it won't be a problem. I just need to make a few calls to get some help with my kids when they get out of school. Let me just get your meds. It seems like you might be overdue for them." As I take a step, she smiles.

"No need, Hannah, Richard gave me my meds." She is grinning ear to ear. Richard?

"OK, Mrs. Grace. Sara will be taking care of you again tonight. You seem to be getting along fine with her, no?" I give her my no-bullshit look. She smiles.

"Yes, she is OK, Hannah, but not like you." I grin at her. I like her.

"I have to get home. I have a date night with my kids."

"Enjoy them because they grow so fast." She looks at Aiden, showing the affection and love she has for all her sons. I feel the same about my babies.

"Have a good night." I smile and leave. I decide to take the stairs, because every time I take the elevator, Grant is there.

"Hannah." I look back. When I see it's Aiden, I breathe a little better. I'm relieved it's not Grant. "Mr. Grace, how can I help you?" I look up into his eyes, and they are captivating.

"Call me Aiden, please. I was wondering if I could ask you a few questions about my mother. I can walk with you, if you don't mind. I know you are trying to get home to be with your kids."

"Sure." I decide it should be safe to take the elevator, so we walk that direction, making small talk. I hold my breath when the elevator doors open. Oh thank God, he's not here. We enter, and as the doors are closing, I catch a glimpse of Grant. Aiden laughs.

"What's so funny?" I ask.

"Nothing," he says, shaking his head.

We head to my office, where I grab my things. I am impressed with Aiden's questions; he seems to have done his research. We head back to the elevator, and I pause. I walk past and Aiden follows, deep in his questioning.

"I hope you don't mind, but I would like to take the stairs to stretch my legs a bit," I lie. He strides ahead of me and opens the door.

"I'd follow you anywhere." His voice is sexy and seductive. I can feel myself blush, and he is blocking the door so that my body brushes against his to get through the door. I slowly make my way past him. My muscles deep inside me clench. I take other step, and I can feel his hand in mine. I turn and before I know it, he pushes me against the wall. In one fast motion, he picks me up by my legs, and I am wrapped around him. He is breathing hard as he starts to kiss my neck and nips at it. The feeling shoots through me like fireworks. His hands run down my back onto my bottom; he pulls me higher and kisses me. His tongue meets mine, and they begin to dance. He tastes like cherries.

I can feel my body start to pulse. His body is pressed against me, and I let out a soft moan. He is enticing and I want him inside of me in the worst way. His hands make their way down my neck, and he pulls the strap of my dress down. His fingers slip my breast out of my bra as he begins to play with my nipple, which responds immediately to his touch. His mouth makes its way off of mine and down my chin. His lips are like silk against my neck. I can feel how hard he is against me. Then I hear talking, and he shakes out of it faster than me. He pulls my strap back up and puts me down, taking my hand and leads me down the stairs. I'm still lost in the moment. I would follow this man anywhere right now.

When we get to the main floor, he opens the door for me. Still playing the same game, I brush my body past him. He follows me out with a sexy grin.

"Mr. Grace, I hope I have been able to answer all of your questions." I smile. I want to touch him, but we are surrounded by people.

"Yes, Hannah, you have, but I'm sure I will have more for you tomorrow." He brushes my hand with his.

"I look forward to it." I smile and turn. I feel sexy all of a sudden and I want to run and jump with excitement. I grin the whole way home.

I walk in the door, and the kids come running. Kevin is here already.

"Mommy, you got flowers," Ella is screaming as I take my shoes off. Flowers again? I have to tell Kevin it isn't necessary to buy me flowers all the time. I see Kevin make his way out of the kitchen.

"I signed for them. Some arrangement." He looks at me with suspicion. Who the hell sent me flowers? I'm smiling ear to ear, still basking in the sun over what just happened with Aiden. I never thought I would want another man after Chase. The hurt begins, but the excited feeling swirling inside me keeps it at bay.

"Here's the card, Mommy," Hunter says as he pulls it from the massive array of flowers. There are so many different colors of roses. There must be at least five dozen. They are beautiful. As I open the card, all eyes are on me.

To Hannah
Thanks for the slap.
GG

What is he thinking, and how did he get my home address? I tear the card up and throw it in the garbage. The kids can sense my anger, so they get off the table and head into the den to watch TV. Kevin leans against the counter, looking amused.

"Not a love letter?" He looks at me, trying to hold back his amusement.

"No." I walk out of the kitchen and head up to my room to change.

When I come back down, I see Kevin on the floor, wrestling with Ella and Hunter. The kids are laughing, and I smile instantly. He is so good with them. I watch them for a bit and Ella sees me.

"Mommy, I have the movie all picked out. Can we watch it now?" She is eager, and I get an idea.

"Yes, we can. I thought you guys might want some chocolate milkshakes while we watch the movie. What do you think of that?" They both stand up and start cheering.

"Get on the couch, and Uncle Kevin will start the movie. I'll be in, in a minute."

They make their way to the couch and start jumping. I get the blender out and start to make the shakes. I smile as I think about the time Chase made shakes, and forgot to put the lid on. I had chocolate ice cream and milk everywhere. I giggle at the happy time as I pour the kids' shakes into plastic cups with lids. I take a tray out and line it all up, grabbing the roll of paper towels, just in case, and tucking them under my arm. The kids are staring at the TV when I come back in, so I wave it in each of their faces. They smile from ear to ear when I hand them their shake.

"Thank you, Mommy," Hunter says before he starts to drink the shake down.

I hand Kevin his and sit down on the oversized chair next to the couch. I get cozy in it and start to think about my day. Two of the Grace brothers made passes at me today, and I could barely resist either of them. What the hell am I going to do? I guess it's a good thing that they hate each other, because they will never talk about me to each other. Oh God, what have I done? This is so unprofessional. I could lose my job over this. Richard would be furious with me. What would Chase think? I feel the shame loom over me like a dark cloud. What is Grant up to? He made such a scene in Richard's office, makes a move on me in the elevator, but then he sends me flowers. What the hell? Aiden was out of left field. I would have never expected this out of him, but his touch just hypnotized me. Even if I wanted him to stop, I don't think I could have.

I run over the whole thing in my mind. It was so sexy. I never thought I could bear the touch of another man. I just keep on surprising myself every day. I shut my eyes, trying to block all of it out. When I open them, the movie is over and the kids are sound asleep alongside Kevin. His eyes look heavy when they meet mine. I think he has been watching me battle myself internally.

"I'll help you get them to bed," he whispers. I take Ella and he takes Hunter. I tuck Ella in, then go into Hunter's room to kiss him good night. I stop at the door. Kevin tucked Hunter in and is sitting on the edge of his bed, staring at him. I used to love to watch Chase tuck the kids in. The hurt consumes me. I swallow hard as if I am going to push it down, but it starts to invade me. Tears begin to stab at my eyes. Kevin meets my eyes and stands up and walks over to me. He wraps his arms around me and gives me a squeeze. I pull away like I always do. When I walk out of Hunter's room, Kevin follows me.

"I have to work tomorrow and Friday. My mom said she can take care of the kids tomorrow. I was wondering if you could help me out Friday?" I stop halfway down the staircase and think of Aiden's touch on the stairs. My blood starts to rush.

"I don't think it will be a problem; maybe I'll take them out to dinner and a movie." He offers a half smile. I can tell he is exhausted, and

I feel bad asking him for help. He has a girlfriend that he never sees, and now I'm asking for a help on a Friday. No wonder she hates me.

"I think they would like that."

"Good night, Hannah." He leans over, kisses the top of my head, and walks out the door.

"Good night, Kevin," I say as I close the door and lock it. I stand there, leaning against it for a while. What have I done today? What was I thinking? Well, apparently I wasn't thinking. I want to kick myself. What came over me? I beat myself up for a few minutes, then head up to bed. I get into bed and pull the covers over my head, like it will protect me from my thoughts. I'm haunted, like I am each and every night. The memories come back. Crashing down over me, like giant waves.

CHAPTER SEVEN

October 2012

I go back to sitting in front of the funeral director. There are so many decisions to make, and I can't make a single one. I wish Richard would get here already so he can help me. As time passes, I just nod to everything that is being said to me. I take out my checkbook and write a few checks.

When I'm done, Kevin drives me home. I have a list of things I need to get together. I have to make a collage of Chase. I can bring in as many pictures as I please. They said they would put them out around the room. I sit in Kevin's car and stare into space until I hear my name and I look up. I see Kevin squatting next to me with my door open.

"Hannah, I have been saying your name for like five minutes. Where were you?" He takes my hand.

"I'm lost in my own head, I guess." My world has crashed down, leaving me lost, burning in the flames. I hear a car pulling into the driveway. It's Becca. I get out of the car and run into her arms. I didn't realize how much I needed her here until now. I collapse onto the driveway, and she is right there to catch me. We sit on the ground for what seems like forever. She lets me cry and just brushes my hair with her fingers. I can hear her making gentle *shh* sounds to me.

"Hannah, you have to get up; we should go inside." I become a robot and start to go through the motions of getting up and walking into the house. My mom is at the table, and I hand her all the information I have. It's a thick manila envelope filled with instructions.

"Kevin, can you drop Chase's suit off at the funeral home for me?" I say the words, but they barely make their way out of my mouth. I never thought I would ever speak these words. Kevin nods his head.

I go upstairs and stand in the closet, staring at his suit that I just picked up from the cleaners earlier this week. I pull up the plastic and run my fingers down the sleeve of the jacket. Last weekend we went to an event, and I was cold, so Chase took off his jacket and wrapped it around me. The tears are burning as they leave my eyes. I pull the plastic down and take the suit off the rod. I look for my favorite tie. I pick up his shoes, and head over to his drawers. *I can do this,* I repeat it in my head as I try to think of what I need next. I get out a white shirt, his favorite underwear, and dress socks. I walk over to my jewelry box and take out his cross.

I shut down when I feel the cold metal in my hand. I trace the cross with my thumb, and fall to my knees. I feel so broken. Chase is the only person who is able to put me back together and I no longer have him. "I miss you baby, I love you so much it hurts." I whimper. I pray that he can hear how much I love him. I think about the last time he told me he loved me. I play it over in my head. He came over to me before I went up to bed. He cupped my neck with his hands and ran his nose up the side of neck. My head fell to the side, and he feathered kisses up to my ear. His warm breathe caressed my ear. "Have I told you yet today how beautiful you are?" He whispered. I closed my eyes as he kissed down my neck and nipped at my collar bone. "I love you Hannah. You are my heart, my soul, my everything." The memory fades out. Taking a deep breath I get up on unsteady legs and force myself to finish gathering Chase's things. I head into the closet and put everything in a bag. Stopping at the door I turn around and look at our room. "You are my heart, my soul, my everything." I repeat his word back into the room knowing he is hearing me.

As I get to the bottom of the stairs, Kevin is waiting by the door. I hand him everything and begin to cry again. He holds me tight, and

I can feel his tears on me. He pulls away and walks out the door. I try to take a deep breath, but the lead feeling takes over again. I just stand and stare until I can get it together. After a few minutes, I go to find my mom.

"Mom, can you make a few calls for me?" I'm sure the phone chain will start, and all the information about the when and where will spread fast.

"Of course, honey, you go and spend time with the kids." I can see the kids out in the backyard. They are lying on the trampoline, side by side, just staring up at the clouds. Chase loved to do that with them. They would find all sorts of animals in the sky. Becca puts her hand in mine and leads me outside. We both walk over to the trampoline and neither of them notices us until we reach them.

"Aunt Becca," they both say in unison. They sound a little happy.

"Hey guys, come give me some love," she says as she holds out her hands. She takes both of them and hugs them tight. Ella looks up at her.

"How long are you staying with us, Aunt Becca?" Without missing a beat, Becca looks her deep in her eyes.

"As long as you need me to, sweetheart." Ella looks happy.

"Can you sleep in my bed with me tonight?" She looks excited.

"Of course. How about we have a big sleepover?" Becca always knows just the right things to say to them.

"OK, guys," I interrupt. "It's time for some dinner."

We all head back into the house. I'm still avoiding phone calls, so my mom has had the phone to her ear all day. I go through the motions of dinner and bath time. I tuck the kids into my bed again. Becca and I lie there, talking about when they were babies. They love to hear those stories.

Soon they fall asleep, and we go downstairs for some much-needed wine. I sit in the den while she gets the drinks. She is all caught up-to-date from Kevin. I remember hearing them talk earlier when I was getting the kids out of the tub. I am so thankful for Kevin. He has done all the dirty work for me so far.

"Becca, what the hell am I going to do? I can't do this alone." I lean forward and put my elbows on my knees. I rub my face and start to cry. I never thought it was possible to cry this much. Just when I think I am empty, more follows. We stay downstairs until about two, just talking about everything. After we crawl into bed and curl up with the kids. She holds my hand and falls asleep. I lie there until I see the sunrise. Today is the day I will see Chase in a casket. I have a shiver run down my spine. I am hollow, emotionally drained, and lost.

CHAPTER EIGHT

June 2013

I sit up in bed and look at the clock. It's 3:41 a.m. I put my legs out in front of me and stretch for a few minutes, feeling my muscles loosen. Aiden pops into my head. I lie back on the bed, reliving my escapade with him in the stairwell. I wanted him so badly. I'm surprised at myself for letting him touch me. His hands felt so good on me. I don't know why I gave in so easily. Then again, I gave in pretty easily to Grant. He was just, hypnotizing. Oh crap. I sit back up and stretch over my legs, till I touch my toes. Why am I so stupid? Grant is nothing like Aiden. He thinks he can get whatever he wants when he wants it. I'm so happy I slapped him. Oh, and the flowers. Why the hell would he send me flowers, and how did he get my home address?

I don't want to go to work today. Why did I say I would go in? Why did Tori say she thinks Grant likes me? Well, she can read her sons like books. I wonder if she will know what happened between me and Aiden. I bet when he went back into the room, she read him like a book. Oh God, I hope she can't read me like a book. I need to get my poker face on. I have to ignore the both of them.

Grant and Aiden both keep popping into my head as I shower. I can still feel their touch on my body, and I want that again. I get out and do my new morning rituals. Well, if I have to face them,

I want to look good, just in case Aiden feels the need to ask me more questions. I wonder if that was his intent the whole time. I walk into my closet and pace. What should I wear? Scrubs or regular clothes? Scrubs are more comfortable...I try on about ten things before I find the perfect combination. A gray fitted pencil skirt and a light-blue blouse. I put on my lacy underwear and matching bra and start to dress. I leave the shirt's top button open just for some sex appeal, then I think *no* and button it. I grab my highest heels. If I'm going up against Aiden, or Grant, for that matter, I need to be taller. They have almost a foot on me.

I hear the kids in the hallway and hurry to meet up with them. We all head to the kitchen together. We finish up our breakfast and the kids go up to get dressed. I stand and sip my tea as I look at the flowers. What was Grant thinking? Is this his way of making a peace offering? *Thanks for the slap.* He could have thought of something much better, like...*Sorry I tried to molest you in the elevator. It will never happen again.* No, Grant is cocky; he seems like the type of guy who would never say the words *I'm sorry.* I don't think those words are in his vocabulary. Clearly they aren't, or he would have put them on the card. I shake my head. I help the kids brush their teeth and wash their faces, and we are off.

When I get to the hospital, I park the truck and turn it off but I don't get out. I don't want to go in. I'm embarrassed, and a little ashamed of myself. I hear both my shoulder figures all the time. Today my angel is telling me I have been bad and should feel ashamed. Then the devil chimes in, saying, *let's do that again, it was fun.* I agree with both of them. Time to get out of the car. I head to the elevators. When the doors begin to open I hold my breath. *Please don't be in there.* The coast is clear. I head into my office and see a single pink Gerber daisy on my desk. What the hell is he doing coming into my office and leaving me a flower? I quickly pick it up and slide it into my drawer before anyone can see it. I don't need Michele prodding into my business. I'm closing my drawer when I see a note.

H,
I have more questions if you have more answers.
A

I lean back in my seat and smile. Michele pops her head in my office, interrupting my gleeful moment.

"What are you smiling about? Who is that from?" She is so nosy. I thank God that I put the daisy in my drawer.

"It's nothing. Hunter wrote me a note at school." I shove it into my purse before she can ask to see it.

"How is Mrs. Grace?" I try to distract her and it works. She comes in and goes over all the tests.

"She should be good to go home tomorrow. I spoke with Grant last night, and he is having her flown back to her house in Cape Cod. He has been interviewing nurses to come around the clock for the first few weeks she is home." I give her my 'that's no surprise' look. He seems like a control freak; he wants to call all the shots with her. She is going to be furious when she hears this news.

"Hannah, he is so good-looking. I don't know if it's me and the lack of you know what." She raises her eyebrows and makes a funny expression. "But I could just stare at him all day." Michele looks happy when she talks about Grant. I wish it was her in the elevator rather than me. She has been divorced for about a year, and much like me, has no desire to date.

"Michele, they are all good-looking," I say, smiling as I stand. "Let me go check on my favorite patient."

"I think I will join you," she says, following after me. When we get to the elevator, I feel better knowing I have someone with me. The doors open, and there is my stalker, waiting for me. He looks coolly at me, and I narrow my eyes at him. I turn and face the door.

"Dr. Mitchell, Hannah." His voice is deep and echoes inside of me. I think of yesterday, at the way his hands touched me, the magnetism we had.

"Mr. Grace, how are you?" Michele has her flirting face on, and I turn to look at Grant's reaction. He is nice, but shows no interest in her. I'm sure he gets this all the time.

"Dr. Mitchell, I am very well. How is my mother doing today?" They make small talk. The doors open, and Michele is out first. Shit, she is fast! I follow her, but he is right behind me. He walks next to me and places one hand on my lower back. I elbow him in an attempt to shake his hand off, but he remains, touching the small of my back. I follow Michele into Mrs. Grace's room. Shane is helping her get out of bed.

"Hannah, I'm glad to see you. Would you mind taking a stroll with me?"

"Sure. How do you feel today?" I ask as I help her put her arms into her robe.

"Good, Hannah. I slept well last night." She scrunches her nose and smiles. Michele looks a little lost.

"Mrs. Grace, I just wanted to let you know that your test from last night came back. You are recovering nicely. I can assure you that if you keep doing this well today, we will discharge you tomorrow."

"Thank you, Doctor. Could you please excuse me? I would like to walk now." She is practically dragging me out the door. Michele follows us. Grant is in the hallway on the phone. He hangs up when he sees us.

"Mother, do you need some help?" His voice is gentle and soothing.

"Yes, Grant, that would be wonderful. I feel better when I have two arms to hold." I know this look. She is up to no good. She is plotting.

"Hannah, don't forget we have a meeting at eleven." Michele looks disappointed that she isn't part of the walk.

"OK, Dr. Mitchell, I will be there."

We walk past a few rooms before any of us speaks. Mrs. Grace is the first to talk.

"Grant, how much time do you have until you have to leave?" Her words are soft.

"I have until you get better. I have been doing everything over the phone and computer. I had a meeting in the middle of the night last night. These time changes are a killer." He is smooth in every way. He has confidence like no one I have ever seen. Well, Aiden, but they are one in the same, I guess.

"Which hotel opened last week?" She seems annoyed with herself that she can't remember. I interrupt.

"London, right? You told me that the other day, remember?" I say, looking at her.

"That's right, London. How did the opening go?" He looks at me with gratefulness in his eyes for helping his mother, but it is brief.

"It went well. Better than we projected. We were supposed to open in Rome tomorrow, but we had to postpone it."

"Oh, Grant, I hope you didn't have to do that because of me," she replies sadly.

"No, Mother, it's not like that. We had a lot of unfinished business, and I used you as an excuse. You kind of saved me." He winks at her and smiles. They have so much love for each other. I think they have forgotten I was here. By now we have done a full loop of the floor.

"Are you up for another lap?" I think she can do it. She needs to start moving more. "Sure, Hannah. Why don't you tell me more about yourself." She looks at me, trying to read me. *Poker face,* I tell myself.

"What would you like to know?" I love to answer a question with a question.

"Grant was wondering if you were dating anyone."

"Jesus, Mother," Grant blurts out, annoyed. "I can ask my own questions if I have them." I laugh. It feels good to laugh. I like the banter they have between them . Maybe he isn't like I thought he was. Maybe I have him all wrong.

"Well, if you must know, Grant…" I look into his eyes that are a blue oasis. "I am married." I can tell he isn't buying it. I can feel Tori squeeze my hand, and it makes me think of what she said. Give it time; I will come around. Yes, I want to come around, but with which one of your sons? I lead her back into her room, take her soft robe off her shoulders, and help her into bed.

"Hannah, please sit with me for a moment." She pats her hand next to her on her bed. Grant stands at door, staring at us.

"I'm going to get some coffee. Hannah, would you like anything?" Wow, he's being nice today. I guess he just needed a good slap.

"No, thank you, Mr. Grace."

"Please call me Grant." He looks at me in such a way that I almost feel naked. He is so seductive. I shake off his look and turn back to Tori. She looks pleased.

"He likes you, Hannah." I try to stop her, but she waves her hands at me.

"Grant is a challenging man, Hannah. He is stubborn and arrogant, but yesterday he came in here and curled up next to me in bed, like he used to do after his father died. I was shocked, but then I looked at him and realized he was afraid that he could have lost me."

"Life is short, Hannah, don't miss out on anything. I made mistakes in my life. I dated only one man after my husband passed, and he couldn't handle four boys who weren't his. It didn't last long, and I gave up after that. I wish I had pushed myself to date more. I wouldn't have to put all my burdens on my sons." Her eyes have tears in them. I can feel the tears swell up in mine. I rub her arm, and we hug. She is still so fragile. I know what she is doing. She is trying to help me not make the mistakes she did.

"And I could have killed you when you said you were married." She lightly slaps my back.

I hear someone at the door and we both laugh, wiping the tears from our eyes.

It's Aiden. I perk up and smile. He has three cups in his hands. He walks over and hands one to his mother.

"I got you a tea, Mother—black, just the way you like it." She smiles and takes it.

"Hannah, I thought you might want one as well." He hands me a cup. "I hope you like it." I take a sip, and it's the perfect temperature—hot, but not too hot.

"Thank you, Aiden." I smile and he smiles back. Tori touches my hand and looks at me knowingly.

"Well, I should get going. Tori, you really should rest; you took a long walk. When I come back later, we should try to walk again." She smiles and takes a sip of her tea. I smile at Aiden as I walk past him. I'm on cloud nine as I walk over to the elevator. I look at my watch, and it's eleven on the nose. Shit, I'm late for the meeting. I rush into the elevator and head back down. I practically run into the meeting, trying not to spill my tea.

"Sorry I'm late. I was held up with a patient who had a million questions." I see one chair is still empty, and I quickly sit down. Michele rolls her eyes and begins. I can't seem to pay attention; my mind is on Aiden and Grant. I look up at the clock and only ten minutes have gone by when Richard walks in the door.

"Sorry I'm late; a small problem arose that I had to handle." He smiles at me and sits down. Over the next forty-five minutes, we discuss patients and procedures. Michele finishes up and looks over at Richard. He nods at her and stands up.

"Hannah, Dr. Mitchell, can I please have a word?"

"Sure, Director," Michele says cheerfully. He looks around and everyone makes their way out of the room. Richard looks flustered.

"Hannah, I just had another meeting with Grant Grace; he apologized for yesterday's stunt." I look down at my hands, thinking of the elevator. "He has made the hospital a very generous offer I don't think I can refuse." He looks down, trying to find his words.

"Richard, are you OK?" I lean over to him.

"Yes, I'm fine; Grant gave me a check for twenty million, so we can start the remodel." I lean back in my seat. Twenty million dollars. Where did he get all that money?

"There's more." He pauses to gather his thoughts.

"He has offered another twenty million, if you would be willing to accept his offer."

Offer? What fucking offer? Is Richard selling me to him? What the fuck is he up to now?

"Hannah…" I can hear the hesitation in Richard's voice, and it's making my head spin. All I can do is stare at him while he struggles to find his words. "Grant is asking that you accompany his mother home tomorrow. He would like for you to stay for a few days, to acquaint the home nurse with his mother's case." He pauses and stares back at me, trying to read my expression. He can tell I am furious.

"Hannah, I didn't give him an answer. I told him it would be entirely up to you." His eyes look shameful, and they should. He's trying to pimp me out for $20 million. This is ridiculous, I think , as I stand.

"I don't know what to make of this. I can't do this, Richard. I can't leave the kids." I shake my head, which is spinning.

"Hannah, please consider it. I already spoke with Mary, and she would love to have the kids to herself for a few days. Mrs. Grace is being discharged at noon tomorrow, and you won't have to come in till then."

"Richard, I can't do this. I have no time to get everything in order. I can't just blindside the kids and run off for days at a time. No. My answer is no." I make sure I say the second *no* louder to make my point clear. I glare at him and he looks down.

"Hannah, I think you should go." I turn and look at Michele whom I completely forgot was in the room.

"Director, can you please give us a moment?" I see the hope in his eyes as he gets up. She turns her chair and pushes a chair toward me, gesturing for me to sit down. I take a deep breath and sit.

"Hannah, this is a great opportunity. You should consider it." I shake my head. "You haven't even left the county since Chase died." The words pierce my heart. Chase…I miss him so much right now. The hurt creeps up once more.

"Well, Michele, I have no desire to leave my kids." I scowl at her.

"Think about it. You need a change of scenery; this sounds like the perfect chance to relax a bit." She's trying to sell me. Why? So she can get a piece of the twenty million? I'm getting angrier by the second, and my eyes stab into hers.

"Michele, are you freaking delusional? I will be taking care of a patient." She looks hurt by my words.

"I can't tell you what to do, but I think you should go. You're only going to be three hours away, and you could come home anytime." I lean back in my chair and rub my eyes.

"I'm not going." I get up and walk out of the room. Richard is still outside the door. "The answer is no," I say as I quickly walk away. I need to get out of here. I take the stairs and think about Aiden when I open the door. I push him out of my head and focus on getting away.

CHAPTER NINE

It's nice outside. The sun warms my skin. I never realized how cold the hospital is. I start to thaw out as I sit on the bench in front of the hospital. I feel someone behind me. When I see it's Aiden, I relax. He is leaning on the back of the bench with his hands on either side of my shoulders, his head directly above mine. I steal a glimpse of him. His lips glisten in the sun.

"So I hear you won't be accompanying my mother back home tomorrow." His voice is unreadable as he takes a deep breath.

"My mother is quite disappointed, as well as myself." I can only shrug my shoulders and look down at my hands.

"I wish I could help, but I just don't think I can." I suddenly feel the need to cry. I try to hold back. *Please don't cry, please don't cry,* I tell myself. I feel his hands slide onto my shoulders, and his fingers begin to trace my collarbone. My body instantly starts to pulse.

"I wish you would reconsider. Shane told me about the proposal, I think you should think this over." he whispers in my ear, then kisses below it gently. He gives my shoulders a squeeze before he walks away. I can't help but watch him walk away. He is beautiful. I would even go as far as saying, that he's breathtaking. I can see his muscles flex through his white shirt as he walks. He is wearing flip-flops and khaki-colored shorts that show off his thick calves. Why do I have such a weakness for this man? I can easily see myself falling for him. He is kind, loving and easy going. Unlike his brother, he isn't an ass. I sit for a few more minutes before I finally decide to go back inside. As the doors open, I walk in to hear my name being paged to Mrs. Grace's room. Oh God, not her too. I want to walk right out and go home, because I bet she will have a good guilt-trip to lay on me too.

I press the Up button and wait. I am lost in thought until I feel a nudge at my side. I look over, and it's Grant. Great. The doors open, and he gives me the "after you" gesture with his hands. I go in and press the seven. It's just us in the elevator. What is it with him and elevators? The door closes, and suddenly his body is wrapped around mine. I can feel his lips on my ear; they form a trail down my neck and over my chest. It all happens so fast. He pushes me against the wall, taking my hands in his. He pulls them over my head and kisses me. He tastes like oranges, and my tongue marvels in his taste. He is so aggressive as he bites and sucks on my bottom lip. When I feel the soft tip of his tongue glide against mine, I give in. His hands drop mine, and they wander down my arms, over my chest, and linger at my waist. My hands fall onto his shoulders. As the elevator comes to a stop, I pull away from him. My heart is racing, and I can feel how hot I am. My body is ready for him, but my mind stops it. I walk out and he grabs my hand.

"Hannah, please." I pull away and walk as fast as I can. What the hell am I doing? Three days ago I lived a fucked-up life, but I was used to it, now I live in a manipulated world, where I feel even less in control. I barge into the nurses' lounge and sit at the table. The room is empty, and I'm thankful for it. I bang my head on the table a few times, trying to knock some sense into myself. I hear my name being paged again. Shit…I sit up and remember where I was going. I get up and head straight to Tori's room. I can't take much more of this.

When I walk into her room, Grant is on the phone, looking out the window, and Aiden is on his computer, sitting in the cream, over-sized chair. He doesn't look like he's concentrating much. Our eyes meet, and I look away, meeting up with Tori's eyes. She has to know something is up.

"Hannah, I'm ready for my walk." She's smiling at me. I walk over, grab her robe, and ease her out of bed. Aiden gets up to offer a hand.

"No, Aiden, let Hannah." His eyebrows furrow, showing his disappointment.

"Up we go," I say, and she slowly creeps up. I can see the pain in her eyes. For the first time, I'm not sure if it's from her deep incision on her chest, or from the scars that had already laid on her heart before it was repaired. I gently lay the robe over her shoulders as Grant hangs up the phone. He walks over to take her other arm, but she protests.

"I think I can handle one arm this time." She smiles sweetly at him, and he nods with a fake smile, then looks at me. I give him a half smile as we walk out of the room. We set a slow pace as we head down the corridor.

"Hannah, Director Winterfield was here before." She pauses but doesn't look at me.

"I'm saddened that you aren't able to accompany me on my journey back to the Cape." She rubs her hand over my arm. I know what she is doing. It's guilt-trip time. "I understand, dear, that it will be hard for you to leave your children. I know this because I never wanted to leave mine. Sometimes I wish I had taken more time for myself." There it is. She is trying to get me to not make the same mistakes she did.

"Tori, it's still too soon. I just don't think the kids will be OK." It's the truth. I haven't left the kids for more than a few hours in months. It took me five months just to go back to work.

"Hannah." Her voice is motherly and loving. "You should reconsider. I would feel much safer on the plane and back at the house if you were there. Maybe you shouldn't stay the whole week. Maybe just till Sunday?" A week, a whole week; I never heard this. Richard never said anything about staying that long. I can't do a week. I can do a long weekend, but not a week. I shake my head. When was he going to tell me about the whole week? Then I realize what my other thought was. I could handle the weekend. I laugh because I just negotiated with myself. I look over at her, and she looks hopeful.

"OK, I will go, but I have to be home by dinnertime Sunday night." She smiles at me, enjoying her victory quietly. I can't believe I just agreed to this. We only do one lap and head back into the room. I get her back into bed. She takes my hand and squeezes it.

"I have to go speak with Director Winterfield. If you need anything, please have me paged."

"Thank you, Hannah." I smile at her and turn to leave. Aiden stands up and makes eye contact with me. I nod and walk out of the room. Oh God, what was I thinking? I can't do this. I can't be with the two of them all weekend.

I head up to Richard's office. Annabelle smiles as I walk in the door.

"Is he busy?"

"No, go right in. I think he has been expecting you." I take a deep breath and walk in his office; he is on the phone, but he waves me in to sit down.

"Mary, I'll see you in a little bit; Hannah just walked in." He pauses and smiles.

"OK, sweetheart, I will. Love you too." I remember those conversations with Chase. I miss them so much. My heart lunges into my throat, and I have to swallow hard to push it back down. I watch him hang up, and his eyes meet mine.

"I spoke to Mrs. Grace, and we were able to come to an agreement. I will fly with her tomorrow, and come home Sunday." He leans back and looks relieved. He takes off his glasses and rubs between his eyes.

"Well, Han, I don't know what to say." He looks like a million pounds have been lifted off his shoulders, or maybe twenty million pounds.

"Well, a thank you would be nice, or maybe a wing named after me?" I smile, and he walks around his desk to hug me.

"I hope you know I'm getting paid for every minute I'm there." I smirk at him.

"Double time, I promise," he replies, laughing.

"You just secured the hospital forty million dollars in funding." The number floats through my head. I can't grasp that amount of money. "I will pack everything for the kids, and I have to pack myself. I have to go finish up if I'm going to leave here by five." Richard takes my hands.

"Hannah, you saved my ass." I give him a smile and walk out.

I go back to my office to finish up the pile of charts on my desk. I see Michele walk by. "Michele," I yell so she can hear me. She walks into my office and sits down; she still looks upset.

"I decided to go." I stare at her. She looks up, smiling. "I leave tomorrow, and I will be back Sunday." She's still smiling.

"Hannah, I have to admit I'm jealous." I shake my head at her.

"Why would you be jealous? It's not like I'm going on vacation to Bora Bora." I've always wanted to go to Bora Bora. Maybe I'll take the kids with me, or Aiden. Oh shit, why does he keep popping up in my thoughts?

"Hello! Earth to Hannah," I finally hear Michele say. What has come over me? I switched my mind and all thoughts off a long time ago, but all of a sudden the last few days, I have been flooded with thoughts.

"Sorry, it's been a long day. I have a lot going on up there," I say, pointing to my head.

"I'll take care of all your paperwork and don't worry about coming in next week I'll get someone to cover your hours. Go and take care of Mrs. Grace. I expect a phone call when you come back about how it all was." She is grinning at me. She grabs the charts off my desk. "I want a postcard," she mumbles over her shoulder as she walks out.

It's ten to five as I lean back in my chair. I have to iron out all the plans for tomorrow.

I take the stairs up to Mrs. Grace's floor. I'm anxious and need to burn some energy to settle this feeling. Once I get up to the seventh floor, I pause and take a deep breath, partly to catch my breath and partly to pull it together. I head to the nurses' station, where I grab her chart and start to write notes.

"Sara, I'll be back tomorrow at eleven. Can you make sure Dr. Mitchell has signed off on Mrs. Grace's chart by then?"

"Yes, of course, Hannah." She smirks at me while she continues typing. I head back to Mrs. Grace's room. Grant and Shane are laughing at something John has just said, but they all look up as I enter the room.

"I was just wondering what is the game plan for tomorrow?" They all look excited. Grant stands up and pulls out his Blackberry.

"I have the plane on standby from eleven on. I was hoping to be at the airport by noon. It's a short flight, so we should be back at the Cape by one fifteen." He looks at me with the look he gave me earlier. *Please don't look at me like that*, I think. I don't think I could push him away from me again.

"I will be back here at eleven tomorrow. I already spoke with Dr. Mitchell and the staff, and they have assured me she will be ready to be discharged by then." I look over at Mrs. Grace, who looks delighted at the news.

"Good night." I make eye contact with all of them and realize that Aiden isn't in the room. Grant walks over to me.

"Good night, Hannah," Grant whispers in my ear as he touches my arm. His breath on my ear makes me warm in all the right places. I walk out of the room before anyone sees my reaction to Grant's touch.

I become lost in thought again as I head out of the hospital. I stop when I get outside. The sun feels good again, slowly melting my skin. I feel hands on my lower back, pushing me forward into a walk.

"So I hear you're coming with us tomorrow." With us? Why did I say yes? I didn't think Aiden was coming too, but then again, why wouldn't he?

"I wasn't aware you would be joining us," I say, still enjoying his hands on me. He laughs.

"Well, we are going home." Home? Oh, that's right, Mrs. Grace lives in Massachusetts. They must all live up there. *I'm so stupid*, I think for the millionth time today. While I navigate my way through the parking lot, neither one of us speaks. I click the Unlock button and turn to him once I've reached my bumper. He looks around and takes my hand, leading me to the side of my truck. His body moves against me, pinning me against my truck. He bends his head to my neck, and I lean to the side, giving him permission. His lips are softly grazing my neck, then across my throat. He kisses my jawline, then he is on my mouth.

I can't help myself. I can't resist any longer. I place my hands on his face. Our eyes meet. Our tongues thrash around each other like waves crashing. I bite his lower lip and hear a faint groan. His hands are all over me, like he can't touch me fast enough. His hands slide my skirt up, and he picks me up. I wrap myself around him. My body pulses. I want to take his clothes off so I can feel his warm skin against mine. My phone rings, and he stops and looks into my eyes. I grab his face and kiss him hard. His hands wander, and I let out a small whimper. He smiles.

"You like that?" He grins and I nod, wanting him to do so much more. He starts kissing me again, and it only intensifies. I can't get enough of him. My phone rings again. What the hell? Just leave a message. He stops, and gently puts me down, pulling my skirt back down. He places his thumb on my chin and kisses me, then playfully nips my bottom lip.

"I'll see you tomorrow." He leans against me once more, pushing his body into me. He rubs my sides and kisses my forehead. My phone rings again, as he walks away.

"What?" I yell into the phone, trying to catch my breath. I'm angry. What if my phone never rang? What would he have done?

"Hannah, have you left yet?" I realize it's Michele, and I blush. If she only knew what I was just doing.

"I'm in the car," I say as I get in.

"OK. I just wanted to let you know that Grant gave me the itinerary for tomorrow. He scheduled a car to pick you up at home. It will be at your house at ten thirty." I remember the flower delivery.

"Did you give him my info?" I snap back. I didn't mean it to come out that mean.

"No, he already had everything, probably from Richard." She pauses. Of course he does!

"Thanks, Michele. I'll see you tomorrow." I hang up before she responds. What have I gotten myself into this time? I lean against the steering wheel and bang my head once again. *You need to stop,* I tell myself. No more, no more anything with Aiden or Grant. The next time they get close, simply walk away. Yes, I can do that. I will just walk away. I make myself believe this. *I'm so fucked up,* I think as I pull out of the parking lot, but I can only smile and touch my swollen lips as I think about how Aiden's were just on them.

CHAPTER TEN

I begin a packing list in my head as I drive home. I take inventory and think about the laundry I have to do. I pull into the driveway and sit for a minute. Why do I feel like I'm doing something wrong? I shouldn't go…What am I going to tell the kids? What if they start crying and don't want me to go? I'd have to call the hospital and tell Mrs. Grace I can't go. Part of me is saddened by this and the other half is relieved. I'll let them make the decision. I see them at the door so I get out of the truck.

"Mommy," they both yell as the run toward me. I get my stance ready. They're not so little anymore, and with both of them running, I know they can knock me over. I grab them both tightly, and I feel an ache in my heart. Maybe I shouldn't go. I'll miss them too much. Hunter grabs my face to get my attention.

"Mommy, Grandma called and she says you're letting us spend the weekend at her house. She said we can go swimming and play with the dog and go to Chuck E. Cheese." He is so excited.

"Mommy, Grandma said I can play dress up, and she will take me to the hair salon." Ella is even more excited. I feel relieved. They are so happy to spend a weekend away from me. It shouldn't hurt my feelings, but it does.

"I'm happy that you're so excited." I have to push the words out.

"Mommy, can I go and pack?" Ella looks at me, beaming with excitement.

"Yes, take the clothes out and lay them on your bed." They both jump down and run back into the house. I follow behind them and watch as they run up the stairs. I walk into the kitchen, put my stuff down on the counter, and hear my mom sigh.

"So, Mary told me you are going away this weekend with a patient?" My mom doesn't know what to make of this, and she is eyeing me.

"It's not what you're thinking, Mom." I give her the teenage voice. "Mrs. Grace is a special patient. Her son has donated forty million dollars to the hospital; he is expecting the best patient care for his mother. I'm just going to make sure she remains stable on the trip, because she shouldn't be flying in this condition." I give her the 'that's it' look. It's nothing more than that. I am going to take care of a patient and nothing else. *Nothing*, I scream at myself. She looks satisfied with the answer. I must be getting better with my poker face.

"I told Mary to call me if she needed help. I would be more than happy to help." I realize she is disappointed she isn't watching the kids.

"I'm sure Mary would like that." I give her a hug and squeeze her tight.

"I would much rather you take the kids, Mom, but Richard jumped on the chance to have them." I feel bad.

"No, it's OK. Another time Hannah, another time." She swipes my hair behind my ear and kisses my check.

"I have to get home to feed your father." And with that she is gone.

I start to gather the laundry and put in the first load. I go into each of their closets and take out their overnight bags. Ella did a surprisingly good job picking out her clothes. She has all different piles. Socks, underwear—she is so organized, much like me. I laugh as I refold everything and pack it all away neatly. One down, one to go.

Hunter's room is a mess. He is much like his father. I see clothes everywhere. I start to refold them, making piles of what to pack and what to put away. When I finally finish, I head down into the living room, where the kids are picking out movies to take with them.

"Two each," I yell. This is a fight waiting to happen. They both choose two and shove them into a bag. The night goes fast; I never thought that they would be up for this. After their bath they get into their pajamas, and we snuggle for a while. I let them stay up a little later than usual. I do this more for me because I need to get my fill. I tuck them both into bed and go into my room. What the hell am I going to pack? I'm sure I won't have to wear business attire; I will be in their house. I start to gather things, laying them all out on my bed. *This will have to do*, I think as I get my suitcase out.

For the next few hours, I finish up with the odds and ends of packing and laundry. In the bathroom I get my makeup bag out and start to gather up my stuff. My phone rings. Who is calling me this late? I think as I walk over to get it.

"Hey, it's me," I hear after I say hello. It's Kevin. Shit. I have to cancel on him for tomorrow with the kids.

"I was just calling about tomorrow." He sounds so tired.

"Kev, I meant to call you before, but I got caught up with the kids. I have to go away tomorrow on a trip." I pause. *Let me rephrase this.* "I have to fly with a patient and get her settled. I'll be coming home on Sunday. Mary and Richard are taking the kids for the weekend."

"Oh, OK. I'll stop by their house this weekend." His voice is low. "You OK, Han?"

"Yeah, I'm fine. I'm just scrambling around to get everything in order before I leave." I sit down on my bed.

"Hannah, have a safe trip and call me when you land."

"I will, Kevin. I'll talk to you tomorrow." I hang up and stare out my window. All of a sudden, I'm there. My bubble has burst and Chase's death haunts me.

CHAPTER ELEVEN

October 2012

Hunter starts to stir and I rub his back. He rolls over and looks at me. I know what he is thinking. I don't want to say anything; the tears swell up in his eyes, and I pull him close. I rub his back for a while, and he just cries.

"I'm so sorry, honey. I miss him too." I kiss the top of his head, and we lie for a while.

Ella wakes up and climbs over Becca to be with us. All three of us just lie together and cry. I hold them tight so they can feel my love. *Am I going to be enough for them*? I push the thought away. "Let's go and eat some breakfast," I say, they haven't been eating much lately.

I know I'm not hungry, but they have to be, since they didn't eat dinner last night. As we head out of bed, Becca wakes up and joins us. Kevin is in the kitchen when we walk in, and he takes Ella in his lap and hugs her tight. She hugs him tighter.

"I stopped and got bagels on my way over, I got the French toast ones." he said.

I get a glimpse at myself in a mirror, and I don't recognize whom I see. I see a pale face with dark circle and a hollow soul; seeing this makes me sick. We get through the morning, and I realize that this is how I will have to start living my life. I have to get through one minute at a time. I head up to my room to get some time alone. After running a bath, I get in and go underwater. I like that I can't hear anything under the water. I tried to turn off all my thoughts after I saw Chase's body lying on that table.

I come up out of the water and catch my breath. I can see Chase in my mind, his sexy smile and the way he used to look at me. I will never feel his hands on me again. I push my big toe into the Roman faucet that is sticking out of the wall. I can still hear the sound of his voice in my head. I miss not only the sound of his voice, but his touch, his body. I don't even feel the tears leaving my eyes anymore. I stand up and walk over to the shower. I need white noise, and the running water satisfies that need. I stand there, not wanting to wash my hair. I'm procrastinating getting ready. I just want to stay in my house and never leave again. When I get out, I sit on my bed, just staring at nothing. Becca comes in.

"Hey you." I look over at her. I can't even stir up a fake smile. She walks over and runs her finger through my wet hair.

"It's going to be a long day." She sits down beside me.

"I hope you don't mind, but I got some new clothes for you to wear today and tomorrow." She smiles at me.

"No, it's fine. I don't want to think about things like that, so whatever. I trust you." She seems to be relieved, like she expected me to argue .

"Good, come try this on." I go in the closet and look at the two outfits. One is a pantsuit, and the other is a black dress. I go for the pantsuit. I pull my hair back into a bun, rub in some face lotion, and stare at myself in the mirror. I don't know why this has happened. Did I have such a good life that I have to be punished for being happy? I used to have it all. A wonderful, gorgeous husband who worshiped me and supported me in everything I did. Beautiful children and an amazing home. Chase was my home. The rug has been ripped from underneath my feet, and I can't get back up. What am I going to do? I feel Becca's hand on my shoulder. I look up at her, trying to find the answers.

"It's time to go."

June 2013

When I roll over, it's only 2:43 a.m. I've barely slept 3 hrs. I get up and wander around my room. I find myself thinking about the Grace men again. What I am allowing them to do to me. It's unprofessional, and I don't know what has come over me. It's not like me to act this way. I never thought I would be thinking about another man or men so soon. I can't believe I kissed two different men in random places around the hospital. I start to laugh mirthlessly. It felt so good, and I want to do it again, but no, I can't do it again, and I won't. I just need to keep focused and do my job. I think I'm almost convinced I can do this. I lie back down trying to distract myself with what tomorrow will be like, but it doesn't help. My mind goes right back to Chase.

October 2012

I find myself standing in front of Chase's casket. I lean over and touch his hand. He is cold and lifeless. This is not my Chase anymore; it's just his shell. I look around the room that is decorated with our life story. I see pictures from when we first met to the most recent pictures we took last weekend. I wish I could rewind time and get all those days back. We are smiling in the pictures; we were so happy. I wonder if I will ever smile like that again. Will the kids smile like that again? Over the next several hours, I stand in front of Chase while people hug and kiss me and tell me how sorry they are. I just nod and hug them back. I can hear people talking, but I have no idea what they are saying. I'm just so detached from everything and everyone.

The priest comes in and does a small service. The room is so crowded, and I don't think I know all the people, but they all knew Chase; they are all here for him. Kevin hasn't left my side since we arrived at the funeral home. I take his hand in mine during the service, and he gives me a half-forced smile. When it's over, we take our place and start shaking hands and hugging people again. I'm relieved when I realize it's time to go home. One day down and one more to go. Tomorrow will be my final good-bye. Tomorrow will be the day I have to stand up in front of everyone in the church and talk about my life with Chase. My heart hurts, and my soul is bare. Please don't make me say good-bye.

June 2013

When I look up, I realize it's already dawn. I turn on the TV and listen to the weather. I should look up the weather for the Cape. I grab my phone and look it up; it's the usual—partly cloudy, partly sunny. This always drove Chase crazy; he would talk about how many different ways the weatherman can tell you the same thing. Looks like rain late tonight, then nice the rest of the weekend.

I get out of bed and head into the shower. I take my time to deep condition, then shave and exfoliate. I decide to leave my hair wavy. It needs a trim; it has been way too long, but there is nothing I can do about that now. I take out gel and scrunch it a bit. Once I approve, I walk into the closet and get dressed. I want to be comfortable, but I want to look professional. Black pants should be good, and I grab a lacy tank and cardigan, then my flats. I put a little makeup on, and then pack up all my remaining things. I zip the suitcase closed and lug it down the stairs. Ella is the first one up.

"Do I have to go to school today?" she whines.

"Yes, lovey. Grandma will pick you and Hunter up after school, and then you can have your weekend of fun." She jumps down each step with excitement, as she follows me down the stairs.

"I want blueberry pancakes, Mommy." She is smiling ear to ear. How can I say no to that face?

"Well then, I better start making them if you are going to be on time for school today." We head into the kitchen. Hunter doesn't come down until the pancakes are on the table. He is fully dressed and ready to go. We all eat and then the kids head upstairs to finish getting ready. I pack up their toothbrushes and toothpaste. I should pack their Tylenol and thermometer too. I grab a bag and put it all in. We are all downstairs, and I leave all their stuff by the front door for Mary to get later.

When I get to their school, I get out of the truck to hug them.

"Mommy, you're so embarrassing," Ella yells at me. I hug and kiss her anyway. Hunter is standing there patiently waiting for his turn to be hugged and kissed.

"Mommy, I'm going to miss you so much," Hunter whispers in my ear. I can feel tears coming to my eyes, and I push them back the best I can.

"I'll miss you more, buddy."

I watch them run into the school. I can't believe I'm leaving them for the weekend, and I can't believe they are fine with it. I get back into the truck and head home. I have everything ready to go, so all I can do now is wait. I walk into the kitchen and finish cleaning up breakfast, when the phone rings, and I see Becca's name on my caller ID and smile.

"Hey, Bec, what's up?" I miss her.

"Nothing, just calling to catch up. What's new?" I pause; she is going to see right through me and know what I was up to these last few days.

"I am going away in a few hours." I pause just to see what her reaction will be.

"What…You're going away? Where are you going and with whom?" She is so overprotective of me.

"It's not like that. I have a patient—a top-priority case—who lives in Cape Cod, and I will be escorting her back home and staying with her until Sunday just to get her settled. Her son made a large donation to the hospital, so Richard wants to do everything in his power to make sure we secure the funding." There it is, the truth. This is what I will be doing this weekend. It's nothing more and nothing less than that. Who am I kidding?

"Oh, why did Richard pick you?" She is always filled with questions. I guess that's why she is a powerhouse lawyer who dominates the West Coast.

"I was on her case, and she took a liking to me. Her son made Richard the proposal, and I kind of agreed to it." *Don't ask me any more questions, please.*

FALLING INTO GRACE

"I guess I can't ask her name because of all the privacy laws, but what is her son's name?" Her and her damn questions.

"I'm not allowed to say. He wanted the donation to be anonymous." I am such a bad liar, and I am pretty sure she will see right through this.

"Well then, I guess you will have to tell me all about it when you get back. I was wondering what you were doing next Friday night?" I can't believe she bought it!

"Let me check my book. You know, I am such a busy woman, I have appointments lined up for days. Yeah, you lucked out. I'm free. What's up?" My sarcasm has come back as well this week.

"Aren't you just so funny? I have a gala to attend Friday night in the city. I was wondering if you wanted to be my plus one?" She pauses, waiting for my answer.

"I have to see if I can get a babysitter. I'm sure my mom would love to watch the kids, but I have to see how the kids take me going away this weekend. If it's good I'll be there. If they aren't good, I won't leave them again." I'm such a buzzkill sometimes.

"Han, I totally understand. I got two tickets, so if you bail, I'll make Kevin come with me, but I will be at your house Thursday afternoon. I hope you'll be up for some company for the weekend."

"I'm sure Kevin would like that, and of course I'm excited for you to come for the weekend," I tease. Poor Kevin; he is always our backup on everything. "All right, Bec, I have to get going. The car should be here soon to pick me up."

"Be safe, Hannah. I love you, and call me when you land." Overprotective as usual.

"Love you too, Becca." As I hang up the phone, I see a black Range Rover pull into my driveway. It's show time. I take a deep breath and walk to the front door. When I open the door, I see Grant about to ring my doorbell. Shit, why is he here?

"Hello, Mr. Grace," I say, trying not to seem surprised. Be cool Hannah.

"Hannah, you look lovely today." I remind myself that I need to stay focused on being professional and do my job.

"Thank you." I turn and start to gather my things. I catch a glimpse of him again and think he looks good today. He isn't in the normal business attire I'm used to seeing him in. Today he's in a T-shirt, jeans, and flip-flops. His aviators are hanging from his necklace.

"Hannah, don't worry about that. I'll have Sam get it." Before I know it, a man is taking my suitcase out of my hand and taking it to the open trunk.

"Thank you," I mutter as he walks away. I grab my purse and continue out the door. I run through a mental checklist as I lock my door to make sure I haven't forgotten anything. I think I'm good; I finish locking the door and follow Grant over to the SUV. Sam is waiting with the passenger back door open. Grant stands to the side and lets me in first. I slide to the other side. I need distance between us. This weekend nothing will happen. I will not let myself be put in that kind of position. He gets in, stretches his long legs, then sprawls his arms across the back of the seat.

Turning to me, he asks, "Do you want to stop for coffee?"

"No thank you, I'm fine, but go ahead if you would like to stop." He grins at me. This is going to be a long weekend.

"So, Hannah, tell me about yourself," he says as he leans into me. Why do we have to do this?

"Why don't you tell me about yourself?" I say, turning the tables.

"Answering a question with a question. I like your style, Hannah." I smile and roll my eyes at him. "What would you like to know?" He's playing my question-with-a-question game.

"What do you do for a living?" I do want to know this; it has been bothering me ever since he donated $40 million to the hospital. He looks me in the eye.

"I do a little bit of everything." What's that supposed to mean, a little bit of everything?

"You're being vague, Mr. Grace." I smile at him. He places his hand on his chin like he is thinking.

"I have my hand in many cookie jars. I own hotels, I own companies, I like to buy companies and sell them. I like to build things. I like variety."

"It seems you keep yourself busy with all your cookie jars. I just have one last question for you. You made a generous offer to the hospital. Why did you make another generous offer on the contingency that I would go home with your mother?" I feel the need to know the answer. He is looking out the window. I wait.

"Well, Hannah, first, please call me Grant, and second, I saw how you were with my mother. She is a hard woman to get along with and the two of you bonded immediately. I have never seen my mother so comfortable with someone who wasn't family. I knew it would make her happy to have you accompany her back to her home and to feel secure that someone was there whom she could trust." He looks at me tentatively, trying to see my reaction to his response.

It was exactly what I wanted to hear. All about his mother; she is the reason I'm going on this trip—to make her feel secure, not to fool around with her sons. I smile while leaning my head to the right. He smiles back and touches my hand. I let his hand sit over mine for a moment before I withdraw my hand from under his. *It was just a nice gesture*, I tell myself as I look out the window.

"Is there anything else you want to know about?" I hear him say. I look at him and shrug my shoulders.

"What do you want me to know?" I like playing this game; let's see what he thinks I want to hear. He smiles at me, wanting to play the game too.

"I really am a boring man, Hannah. I travel way too much, I'm never home, and my family is always annoyed with me." OK, he is telling me everything I already know.

"How about you, Hannah? You're still a mystery to me." I laugh. *Me, a mystery?*

"I'm a boring person much like you. I work, I go home and take care of the kids, and that's about it." He looks at me, puzzled. Then I see him looking at my hand.

"And what about your husband? What does he do?" Oh my God, he doesn't know. I never told him the truth. What does he think? That I like to cheat on my husband? I did tell him I was married. I slapped him once and pushed him away the other time. I get nervous and feel like I have to hide my hand to protect Chase. I never thought I would be saying these words to another man.

"Chase was into building; he was creative in that way." I stop. That's all I say.

"We are similar, I guess." He looks like he wants to ask me ask me a question, but isn't sure how to.

He pauses, before asking, "Has he changed jobs? You said he *was* into building." His eyes soften like he feels bad for asking the question. He can probably see the hurt in my eyes. I look down at my hands.

"He passed away last year," I say in a half whisper. I have to force the words out. I know he can relate with the death of his father at a young age, but I don't want his understanding, and I don't want his sympathy. He touches my hand again, and I feel relieved he's not going to say anything else. We ride the rest of the way to the hospital in silence, with his hand over mine. This time I don't bother to move my hand away. I like this side of Grant.

The driver pulls right up to the front doors. I can see another identical SUV already parked out front. The driver gets out and opens my door for me, and Grant walks around and offers his hand. I smile and take it as he helps me out. As we walk side by side into the hospital, I see a camera crew waiting at the door.

"Fuck," I hear Grant growl. He ushers me in, and we dart to the stairs.

"What was that about?" He is already on his phone.

"Derek, we have a situation at the hospital. I thought you told me you took care of this." He pauses. I can tell he doesn't like what he is hearing.

"Well, fucking take care of it!" He sounds so angry. He puts his phone away and takes my hand, and we run up seven flights of stairs. I can keep a steady pace, but he is taking two steps at a time and I'm exhausted. I stop when we get to the seventh floor to catch my breath. He laughs and kisses my cheek before he opens the door. I blush and don't care that he is seeing it. It's not like he can tell why my cheeks are flushed. I did just run up seven flights of stairs! Plus he now knows my secret, and he has been sweet to me since I told him. I head to the nurses' station, where Michele and Richard are waiting for me.

"Director Winterfield, we have an issue at the entrance. Can we use the ambulance exit?" Grant is standing next to me, and he wastes no time solving the problem downstairs. Richard nods and picks up the phone to make a call.

"I'll have the SUV's leave and come back through the emergency room entrance. I don't need this all over the news." He picks up his phone and makes a call as he heads into his mother's room. Why are photographers watching him? *I have to Google him*, I think. I've never heard of him, but why would I? I bet Becca knows about him. She knows about everyone.

"Hannah, we are all set." I hear Michele talking to me, so I look up.

"Are you ready for this?" she asks.

"As ready as I will ever be," I answer back, smiling. I get a wheelchair and head into Mrs. Grace's room. She looks good, wearing a matching velour jumpsuit, it's light blue and makes her eyes look even bluer.

"Oh, Hannah, it's good to see you." She walks over and hugs me. I lightly hug her back, not wanting to hurt her.

"Are you ready to blow this Popsicle stand?" I say, turning the wheelchair around for her to climb in.

"Am I ever," she is laughs as she climbs in. Aiden comes over and helps ease her into the chair.

Grant hangs up the phone. "We are all set to leave out the back entrance."

I scan the room to see if she forgot anything. Shane is holding her bags, and John is holding onto a cart that has a few floral arrangements.

"OK, let's go." We head down the hallway and into the elevator. It's crowded with all of us in there. I navigate my way through the hospital, looking around suspiciously to see if anyone is looking at us. I head to the ambulance entrance, and we are good. There is no one around. The drivers hop out of the SUV's and open our doors. Aiden, John, and Shane get into one. I help Mrs. Grace into the other. I help her get her seat belt on, and she smiles at me. It's a smile I hadn't seen on her before. She looks truly happy. Grant walks around to the other side of the car and opens the door for me. I give him a small smile as a thank you. He closes the door and walks around to get in the front. The driver has a heavy foot and drives like a bat out of hell, the other car keeps the same fast pace.

CHAPTER TWELVE

It's a short drive to the airport. We pass the departure terminals and drive into an entrance marked private. As the gates open, I see a plane in the distance. Of course we are flying private. What other way would Grant fly? It's probably the best way for Mrs. Grace to travel. Only the best for his mother. I guess I must look impressed, because Mrs. Grace grabs my hand.

"This is the best way to fly, my dear." She rubs my hand with hers. I give her hand a playful squeeze as we pull up right in front of the plane. The driver gets out and opens my door. I slide out and walk around to help Mrs. Grace. As I get around the SUV, I see all four of her sons at her door, easing her out of the car. John has one arm and Grant has the other. Shane leads the way up the stairs of the plane. Aiden spots behind her. I follow behind. Aiden turns around and offers his hand to help me up the stairs, and I graciously take it.

The plane is beautiful. It is decorated in all cream leather and teak wood. Mrs. Grace takes a window seat, while I sit across from her. Only a small table separates us. Grant quickly steps in front of Aiden and takes a seat next to me. Aiden smiles at me and sits next to his mother. He stretches his legs out, and Grant kicks him.

"Hannah dear, would you mind changing seats with Grant? They need more legroom than we do." I smile and get up. Grant looks at me and slides behind me, touching my sides and brushing his body against mine. I can feel the pull again. I look at Aiden to see if he notices, and he does. I settle into my new seat, and place my feet in between Aiden's under the table. I give him a little nudge for fun. He gives me one of his sexy smirks. The captain comes on to announce we are ready for takeoff. I'm a ball of nerves, and I don't know if it's because of the flight or this weekend. I fumble with the lap belt as I put it on.

"Are you nervous, Hannah?" Mrs. Grace asks, looking at me with concern.

"A little, I suppose," I say. For the first time, I feel shy around them. They are all family, and I am an outsider.

"I am too, dear. I don't like to fly. It helps if you hold someone's hand." She winks at me and takes Aiden's hand. Aiden holds his other hand out to me. I place my hand in his. It's warm and makes my hand look so small. Grant takes my other hand and places it in his lap before taking his mother's hand. We sit as if we are in prayer as the plane takes off. It's nice, and I feel almost part of the family.

Once we are up, I feel more relaxed. I let go of Aiden's hand and make eye contact with him. I could stare into his eyes for hours. Grant lets go of his mother's hand. Aiden looks at his mom and winks at her, not letting go of her hand. I try to release my hand out of Grant's, but he holds on. This is uncomfortable. I look at Aiden and he can sense my uneasiness. He opens his water bottle and takes a drink, then sets it on the table. When it falls over, we all jump up. The flight attendant quickly comes over and dries up the water. I sit back down and place my hands in my lap.

I mouth the words *thank you* to Aiden. He smiles at me.

"Aiden, would you please let me through? I have to go to the ladies' room." Mrs. Grace stands, and Aiden and Grant do the same. So do I.

"Tori, do you need help?"

"No, Hannah, I think I can get along on my own."

I watch her walk down the small aisle into the restroom.

I'm all by myself with them. Luckily, Shane leans over the aisle.

"So how old are your kids?"

I look at him and relax. "They are five."

"Oh, my wife is five months pregnant. What are their names?"

"Ella and Hunter. Congrats. Do you know what you're having?"

"Yes, we are having a girl. First girl for my family." He looks so proud. "So you have twins? Did you do in vitro?"

"No, it was luck of the draw. Twins run on my husband's side." This is weird to say.

"Is your husband a twin?" Shane is easy to talk to, and I'm happy he doesn't know my secret. I just go along and answer his questions.

"No, his mother and father are both from pairs of twins."

He looks at me, impressed. I see Mrs. Grace walking toward us. Aiden stands and helps his mother back in her seat.

"What did I miss?" Mrs. Grace asks as she settles down.

"Hannah was just telling us about her family," Shane says.

"Oh wonderful, fill me in." Of course she is interested as well.

Shane takes over. "Well, she has twins, Hunter and Ella. Twins run on her husband's side. Her in-laws are both twins," he announces as if he is still impressed with the information.

I try to read Mrs. Grace's expression. Only she and Grant know about Chase.

"That's wonderful. Did you tell her your good news?" she asks Shane.

"Yes, of course. I've been telling everyone I see," he laughs. "We have to start working on the baby shower. Annie wants to register this week."

The rest of the plane ride is filled with easy conversation. Shane tells me that he and his wife had to do in vitro to get pregnant. She has lazy ovaries and they were lucky to get pregnant the first time. He tells me the story of how they first met. He had asked her out for two months straight before she finally agreed. It took one date, and they have been together ever since. I wish it were that easy for me. I wish I could meet someone and be able to let go enough to trust someone and let him into my life.

The pilot comes on, announcing our arrival and we start our descent. I place my arms on the armrests and Grant takes my hand. He holds it like Chase used to, souls touching. I quickly change the position of my hand, and I see Grant look over at me. I stare straight ahead into my comfort zone, Aiden's eyes. He pushes his legs out, and with his feet, he pulls my legs straight. I follow his move and stretch my legs out. He places his legs on either side of mine, and gives my legs a squeeze with his. He can be so cute. We descend and land smoothly. I pull away from Grant's hand and he lets me go this time. I unbuckle my lap belt and feel relieved. I wasn't scared about flying, but I am sure as hell happy we are on the ground again.

CHAPTER THIRTEEN

We travel to their home in a black Escalade. Mrs. Grace and I are in the back, and once again, Grant is in the front with the driver. Cape Cod is beautiful. I just stare in awe out the window at all the sights. We drive down Main Street, which is filled with eclectic boutiques and trendy restaurants. I love it here already. Mrs. Grace's house, or should I say estate, is to die for. The long driveway leads up to the house, which is perfectly landscaped. The house is sided with cedar shakes, and the salty air has changed the once-golden color to a pale almost-gray. It is a wonder to look at, with all its peaks and balconies. Mrs. Grace leans over to me.

"Grant Senior had this house built for me as a wedding present. He wanted a house big enough to raise six kids in."

"It is beautiful."

I'm impressed. So she has the money?

"We got to four, and it was a joy to raise my children here. I can't wait to have grandbabies running all around here."

She looks happy at the thought.

We pull right up to the front door, and everyone gets out. The front door opens, and a woman who looks about the same age as Mrs. Grace walks out, heading straight to Mrs. Grace.

"Oh, Victoria! You had me so worried." She wraps her arms carefully around Mrs. Grace.

"Oh, Addy, there was no reason to worry about me." Mrs. Grace hugs her back.

After a few seconds, they separate from their embrace.

"I'm so happy my babies are home." Addy looks at the Grace men and opens her arms. They all walk over and hug and kiss her. I feel like an outsider again. Aiden introduces me.

"Addy, this is Hannah Redman. She came along to help take care of my mother." Without any notice I am in her arms.

"I'm a hugger, baby." I laugh and hug her back. "I have lunch all ready for everyone if you all are hungry. Victoria, the nurse arrived this morning. I put her in the guest quarters, so you'll have to decide where you want Hannah to be."

"I will have to think about it. Let's all go and eat. We can talk about it later." Mrs. Grace starts making her way into the house.

I follow behind everyone as we go in. Why is there a nurse here already? I thought she was coming Sunday. As I walk into the house, I am distracted from my thoughts by how amazing the house is. It's the kind of house you can walk into and feel comfortable right away. It is enormous, and the theme is nautical, with shades of blues, creams, and greens. The entire back wall is floor-to-ceiling windows at least eighteen feet tall. The view overlooks the water. I walk over to the windows and take it in. My eyes wander over the sparkling water, and in the distance I can see sail boats. I would love to look at this every day. The tranquility of being surrounded by water has always been a dream to me. Chase hated the water, so when we bought a house, he wouldn't consider looking at one on the bay. The kitchen is filled with chatter and teasing, and I can tell this house is filled with love. Grant stands next to me, and begins to tell me what I'm looking at.

"This is the Vineyard Sound. Beautiful, right?"

He seems like a different person, more at ease. I wonder how old he is.

"My dad built this place in seventy-five. He designed everything in here."

I start to look around and can't believe how much intricate detail is around the house. Exposed beams can be seen overhead; everything is rustic and beachy. I love it here.

"Grant, this is beautiful." He leans into me and nudges his shoulder with mine.

"Are you two lovebirds ready to eat?" I hear from the kitchen. It's Addy; she has the table filled with food, and she is directing everyone to sit down.

"Oh, Addy, I have missed you," Grant says as he hugs her again.

I feel like I have been caught doing something wrong. I walk over to the table, and Aiden pulls out the chair next to him. I'm amazed when I look at the spread on the table. Addy has gone all out, with homemade potato salads, macaroni salads, barbequed chicken, steak, and fish. Everyone starts digging in.

I glance over at Mrs. Grace and notice that she looks tired. I should go and get my equipment to check her blood pressure and her incision. It didn't look so good when we left the hospital. When I stand, everyone looks at me.

"I'm just going to get my bag," I tell Mrs. Grace. "I need to do a check on you."

"Hannah, eat something. Relax." She leans back in her chair, and everyone catches on to what I see.

"Mom, let her check you. That's why she is here, so we don't have to worry," Grant says as he sits next to her. I don't wait for her response. I go back to the front door, thinking my bag would be there, but it's not. I hear someone come up behind me. I turn to see it's Grant.

"I had your stuff brought up to your room. I'll show you where you will be staying."

I nod and follow Grant up the stairs. I look at the pictures on the walls, which tell the family's life story. I see a wedding picture, and I can tell it's Mr. and Mrs. Grace. She looks beautiful; they look so happy and in love. I feel the hurt creep up.

"Is this your father?" I know I shouldn't pry, but I opened up to him earlier today, so I feel we are on the same playing ground. He looks so much like his father.

"Yes." He stands next to me, looking at his parents. He slips his hand into mine, and we stand looking at his parents. I wonder if this is what Hunter will be like when he grows up. I wonder if he will remember his father, or if the memories he has of him will slip away as he gets older. The thought makes my heart sink. I wish my children never had to be dealt this shitty hand. Grant pulls my hand up to his chest and starts to walk. I quickly pull my hand away. We go down two more doors, and he grabs me by my hand and pulls me into a room.

His eyes are wild. He closes the door and starts to kiss me with such a passion. Where is this coming from? Surprised, I try to slow him down, but there is no stopping him. He kisses me and starts to walk me over to the bed. I try to stop him, but he pushes me down on the bed. I sink right in, his full weight on top of me. His hands start in my hair and then slide down my neck to my chest and down to my waist. I take his hands in mine and push him back, but he pins my hands on the bed next to my head.

"Stop, I can't." I speak the words softly. He stops and presses his forehead against mine. He hugs me and I feel so lost. What the hell am I doing? What the hell is he doing? I can't be doing this in his mother's house. I have to walk away. I told myself I would walk away. I lie beneath him for a moment, feeling anxious that we might get caught. He rolls over so he is lying next to me on the bed.

"This was my room." He moves onto his side and places his hand on his head.

I look around the room. French doors lead out to the second-story wraparound porch. The walls are a soft blue, and the furniture is all a deep cherry color. He takes my hand in his and kisses my fingertips. I get up, get my stuff out, and walk right out of the room, leaving him on the bed. *I have to walk away*, I repeat in my head.

Mrs. Grace's vitals are good, but she really needs to rest.

"Hannah, if it will make you feel better, I'll go and take a nap." She looks at me with tired eyes.

"Yes, that would make me very happy," I say in a matter-of-fact tone. When she stands, Addy is at her side, she tells me to sit and eat. I feel useless as I watch her help Mrs. Grace to her room. I sit at the table and just soak in the Grace men's conversation. I think they are talking business, but I'm not sure. Each of them has his Blackberry out, and they are discussing e-mails. I feel like the outsider again. I sit and eat, trying not to be noticed. I just sit and listen. They are going over schedules, meetings, and who is doing what in the office and with their mother. So I guess they all work together? I should Google them, or I could just open my mouth and ask, but I want to keep going unnoticed.

I hear a woman's voice coming from the front of the house. Shane stands up, and I see who I assume is his wife, Annie. She is petitie and cute, with short reddish-brown hair and a little baby belly. Shane walks over and kisses her belly first. She rolls her eyes, then he takes her in a romantic embrace and dips her while he kisses her. I can hear her giggle. The men don't even look over. I just smile at them, and my heart swells a bit. I miss that kind of greeting from Chase. I feel a hand on my knee, giving it a squeeze. I look over and it's Aiden's giant hand on me. I don't flinch and I don't look around to see if anyone else is looking at us. I just look into his consuming eyes. I feel relaxed around him. Shane and Annie make their way over to the table, and the men get up to give her hugs and rub her belly. Aiden talks to her belly. I think it's so sexy to see men this way. Aiden makes the introduction.

"Hannah, it's so nice to finally meet you. Shane told me so much about you already. Anyone who can handle Mrs. Grace and not rip out her own hair deserves a medal in my book." Annie has a face filled with freckles and a large toothy smile. She holds her hand out, and I take it, shaking her hand softly.

"Everyone says the same thing, but Tori has been nothing but a pleasure to be around." She looks at me, confused, but I have been getting that reaction a lot lately when it comes to Mrs. Grace.

"Tori?" Annie says, looking at me in shock.

"Yes, Tori." I repeat her words.

"I have been with Shane for eight years and not once has she asked me to call her Tori. You must have the special touch." She looks at Shane and he nods at her in a 'See, I told you' way.

I just smile, and Annie is quickly distracted by Shane. She sits in between Shane and me and begins telling Shane all the latest gossip that has happened since he left for the hospital. I finish up and bring my plate into the kitchen where I find Addy. I never saw her come back.

"I'll take care of that," she says as she takes my plate out of my hand.

"Why don't you go and get settled, then explore?" She raises an eyebrow, then smiles at me. I wonder what she knows. Did she see Grant taking me upstairs?

"Thank you, I think I will." I smile back at her and turn to leave the kitchen.

Grant is saying good-bye to everyone. I give him a small wave and head upstairs.

As I walk up the stairs again, I slow down. I love looking at pictures; they are wonderful little pieces of frozen time. I stop at the wedding picture again, then slowly step up each step, looking at the moments from the past. I can tell who is whom. By looking at the baby pictures, I can tell they are all about a year apart. I wander into Grant's old room and sit on the bed. What am I doing here? The nurse pops into my head. I wonder where she is and why I haven't seen her yet. Is she not on until Sunday? So many questions fill my head. I walk around the room, viewing Grant's past achievements and pictures from the past. I run my fingers over the beautiful, dark, cherry dresser and make my way over to the French doors. I open them, and my skin starts to rise in goose bumps as the breeze sends a chill down my body. The view is striking; I could stare all day long at the Vineyard Sound.

I hear my door close, and I cringe. I hope it's not Grant. Aiden appears in the door and leans against it. I turn and lean against the railing, folding my arms over my chest.

"We are all heading out, but we will be back for dinner. I thought I would let you know, so when you come down, you don't think we all ran off, leaving you with my mother." He smiles that beautiful smile at me, and I feel myself starting to melt.

"Thanks. Do you all live close by?"

He walks over to me and places his hands on my waist and turns me around so I'm facing the water. His hands feel good on me. He leans in close to my ear like he is going to tell me a secret.

"You see that blue house over there?" He points with his finger. "That's my house. That green house is Shane's, and the yellow one is John's." Then he points in the other direction.

"That white one is Grant's."

"So your family owns the whole coast?" My voice shows my shock. When I turn around, he places his hands on the railing, trapping me. We are face to face, and only inches separate our bodies. I want to be closer to him.

"My father bought all the land when he built this house. He always wanted family to be close." His look is sad, and I feel bad for asking him.

"That is a wonderful thing your father did, and it's even better that all of you stayed." He smiles at me and licks his bottom lip, leaving it glistening in the sun's rays.

"Yeah, I guess we are all close, and if anything happens to my mom, we can all be here in minutes." He tucks a piece of hair behind my ear and rubs my cheek with his thumb. A fire explodes inside me. Just his touch, and I want to jump on him right this moment, but I have to walk away. I just stand there in his trance. He leans down and kisses my cheek before he begins to walk away. He stops at the doors and turns around.

"I forgot to tell you it's game night tonight, and you're on my team." He gives me a sexy smile and walks out of sight.

I barely know this man, and I want him to touch me in the worst way. Grant pops into my mind, and I realize his presence does the same thing to me. It was hard to push him away, but I don't think I could push Aiden away as easily. I smile at the thought and start to relive what happened yesterday next to my car in my mind. I need to stop this.

I head downstairs to distract myself. I smell Addy's cooking, and it is heavenly. Something Italian maybe? As I walk into the kitchen, she greets me with a smile.

"Hannah, honey, can I get you anything?" She is busy chopping, but she pauses.

"No thank you, Addy. I was wondering if I could help you with anything?"

She just looks at me. I'm not sure if I upset her or overstepped my boundaries. I know this is her kitchen, but I thought I could help her cook to distract myself. She is still staring at me.

"Is it OK?" I wonder what the hell she is thinking, but she starts to laugh.

"Hannah, in thirty-three years, I never had someone walk into this kitchen and offer a hand." She shakes her head and walks around the island and hugs me.

"I would love to help. Can I be your sous chef?" I look at her and give her my best 'pretty, pretty please' look.

"I would like that." She walks back to her spot at the island.

"So what are we making?" I look over at all the pots on the stove.

"I have a sauce on with pork, sausage, and meatballs. I have the water on for the spaghetti, the bread is in the warmer, and I am just going to make an Alfredo sauce for anyone who doesn't like the meat sauce." She is a busy woman.

"Do you cook like this every night?"

"Only when the boys are home. Victoria is rather easy to please." Addy looks at me and smiles. "How about you make some desserts? What do you like to bake, honey?" She sizes me up.

"I have a few good cookie recipes, or I can make a cake. What does everyone like?"

"Honey, the boys will eat anything. How about some cookies? We can snack on them during game night. Everything you will need is right over there." She points to a door, and I walk over to it. This has to be the biggest pantry I have ever seen. Every shelf is lined with cans and glass canisters neatly labeled. I start pulling out flour, sugar, and all the odds and ends for chocolate-chip cookies. Maybe I'll make oatmeal peanut-butter chocolate-chip cookies. They are a hit in my house. I look around and find everything. When I make my way back to the island, Addy has placed bowls and cookie sheets out for me. *I wish I had some music to listen to,* I think as I start to mix everything together, but Addy soon starts chatting away, telling me her history with the Grace family.

"Grant is the oldest," she begins.

"How old is he?"

"Grant is thirty-three, Aiden is thirty-two, Shane is thirty-one, and John, my sweet baby John, is thirty." She looks around to see if anyone is near before she continues.

"Mr. Grace died when the boys were three, four, five and six. It took a toll on all of them. He was the center of their world. He was such a great father. He always included the boys in everything he did. Whether it was taking them to work or bringing them sailing, he was always doing something with them." She lowers her voice again.

"Victoria took it hard and stayed in bed for a few months, so I had to step in and become a stand-in mom. I love those boys like they are my own." She gets teary eyed and turns her back to me. I hear her sniffle.

"These onions are making me all teary eyed." She gives me a half smile.

"They are lucky to have you. Please, tell me more about them."

She walks over to the stove and starts cooking.

"Well, let's see, Shane is married and having a baby. John and Grant are dating and most likely getting married, even though Victoria hates Grant's girlfriend. I think everyone hates her, but he has been with her for two years, and Aiden is single." She looks over at me and raises an eyebrow.

"He was in a serious relationship for a while, but then she up and left him one day, and that was that. He hasn't been interested in dating since." My head is spinning. That fucking asshole. I can't believe he made moves on me when he has a girlfriend. What the hell was he thinking? What that hell was I thinking? I didn't know he had a girlfriend. I am so happy I slapped him across the face. I wish I had hit him harder. I can't believe this. I told him about Chase, and he didn't tell me about her. I realize Addy is still looking at me.

"So tell me about you, Hannah. I see you are married. What does your husband do?" Her question is innocent. I am wearing my wedding band, so why wouldn't she ask?

"Chase was into building; he was successful with it." I pause and figure, *why not*. "He passed away last year." She walks over to me and hugs me.

"I am so sorry, baby. I had no idea. Do you have any children?" She pulls away and walks back over to her spot at the island.

"Yes, twins. Hunter and Ella, they're five." I start to scoop the first batch of cookies onto a cookie sheet.

We spend the next hour talking about my family and hers and the Graces. She has so many funny stories about the 'boys' as she calls them. Soon after, Victoria comes out of her wing of the house and sits at the island and watches us.

"Hannah, I just spoke with the nurse, and she is available to work overnight. I figured it would be best for you." Mrs. Grace still looks tired.

"If that's what you would like. Why don't you sit in the recliner that was delivered? It will be more comfortable for you." I help her get settled in the chair and hand her the TV remote.

"You stay here," I tell her, and she gives me a shy smile. The timer goes off as I head back into the kitchen, so I take out the last batch of cookies. I am placing them on the cooling rack when John walks into the kitchen. He kisses Addy on the cheek, then smiles when he sees the cookies.

"Can I try one?" He looks at me for permission. I smile and nod. He takes the cookie and gives me a thumbs-up as he walks out of the kitchen over to his mother. Addy starts to take out serving platters and preparing the finishing touches on dinner. I fill up a large platter with cookies. Addy takes them and gives me a wink.

"We have to hide these if we want any for later." She opens a bottom cabinet and places them in. "Go. I have this all taken care of. Go check on Victoria."

"It has been a pleasure cooking with you," I say, before I head into the large, spacious living room on a mission to check on Mrs. Grace. When I take out my equipment, she rolls her eyes at me.

"This is why I'm here," I tell her cheerfully.

"If you must." She puts her arm out, and I take her blood pressure and check her pulse. She is doing well. She pulls the zipper down on her jumpsuit so I can see her incision. It looks much better than this morning.

"See, it didn't hurt," I tease her. I look up and I see Aiden, Shane, and Annie are back. Annie is looking at us with interest. She sits on the large couch to the right of Mrs. Grace.

"Mrs. Grace, how are you feeling?" Annie looks uncomfortable having to ask this question. Does Mrs. Grace make her feel this awkward?

"I'm fine, Annie." She makes quick eye contact with Annie and makes a dismissive hand motion. I just sit and observe the family dynamic. Shane sits next to Annie and gives her cheek a quick kiss. I think it's an apology kiss for the way his mother is acting. She places her hand on his leg, while giving him a loving glance, letting him know she appreciates his support. I feel the couch cushion I'm on sink in as Aiden sits next to me placing his arm over the back of the couch.

"Hey," he says. At the same time, John wanders out of the kitchen.

"You guys have to try Hannah's cookies. Addy hid them, but I know her hiding spot. It hasn't changed in the last twenty years." He smiles proudly as he places the last bite of the cookie in his mouth. I laugh, shaking my head at him.

"So we are just waiting on Grant and Carla?" Mrs. Grace looks at Shane for a response.

"They aren't going to be making it to dinner, Mom, but Grant said they would be coming for game night," Shane replies. He then leans into Annie's neck and playfully kisses her.

"Oh Shane, enough of that. Let's eat." Mrs. Grace seems annoyed. I'm not sure if it's over Shane's playfulness with Annie or because Grant won't be here for dinner. I get up and offer my hands to Mrs. Grace then I ease her out of her chair and walk her over to the large dining-room table. I didn't notice the table before, but it is made from long, old beams. The imperfections in the wood make it more beautiful.

I help Mrs. Grace into her chair, and she motions for me to sit next to her. Aiden is next to me and pulls my chair out. He is attentive and has great manners. All the Grace men have great manners; their mother has done a wonderful job raising them. I hope Hunter turns out this well. Addy and John start bringing all the serving platters and bowls out, and dinner is served. Everyone starts filling their plates, but Mrs. Grace just looks at the food.

"Do you want me to make you a plate?" I ask,

"I'll have Addy do it, dear, please go ahead and eat." With that Addy walks in with Mrs. Grace's plate already made. She made her something different. It looks like salmon and a small side salad. Shane clears his voice.

"I would like to say a blessing tonight." He takes Annie's hand and his mother's. Mrs. Grace takes mine, and Aiden takes my other hand. John is holding Aiden's other hand. I bow my head like everyone else, as Shane begins.

"Heavenly Father, I want to thank you for this wonderful feast you have set before us. I would like to thank you for my wonderful family and for keeping my mother in good health. She had us worried, but by your saving grace you guided and protected her. For that we thank you, in God's name, amen." We all repeat, "Amen." Aiden gives my hand a squeeze before he lets go.

I discreetly let my eyes wander around the table, watching the family's dynamic. Annie isn't much of an eater. When I was pregnant, I ate everything that wasn't nailed down. This seems to be annoying Shane.

"Annie, you have to eat more. Stop worrying about gaining weight. You're pregnant, it's natural you should be gaining weight." She just looks down.

"Addy, I would prefer a salad, please," Annie says. Addy goes right to the refrigerator to pull out the ingredients and starts to make her a salad.

"Hannah, could you please tell her she should eat more." I didn't want to be caught staring, so I had looked down, focusing on my food. I look up in shock. I don't want to get involved in a fight between them.

"Annie, I wouldn't worry about gaining weight. Think of it as a free pass to eat whatever you want." With that said I dunk my bread into the sauce that's on my plate and eat it. Maybe with my mouth being full, they will stop asking me questions.

"That's easy for you to say. You've never been pregnant," Annie snaps, while looking at me with some attitude.

"I have five-year-old twins. I know what it's like to be pregnant. You think you're gaining weight? I was a blimp when I had the twins." I smile at her, trying to get her off the defense.

"Oh. I didn't know that." I just smile at her and watch her lean over and grab a piece of bread and butter it. Shane looks over at me and smiles. John breaks the ice, and the boys start to talk about the hotel in Rome. I let out a small sigh of relief.

CHAPTER FOURTEEN

Dinner goes by fast. Everyone heads back into the living room. I clear my plate and offer to help Addy, but she pushes me into the living room with everyone else. Annie is setting up for game night on the big coffee table. We have Taboo, Apples to Apples, and Pictionary. My attention is caught when I hear a voice coming from the front door, and John jumps up. I see a petite woman with long, jet-black hair walk in. She looks very exotic.

"Hey, babe," John says as he wraps his giant arms around her. He has more than a foot on her. She stands on her toes, and they kiss.

"Autumn, come and meet Hannah." I stand and shake her hand.

"Nice to meet you, Hannah."

"Nice to meet you too, Autumn." She turns around and starts to say hello to everyone. Mrs. Grace stiffens up.

"Hello, Mrs. Grace." She walks over to her and they do a double-cheek air-kiss.

"So where are Grant and Carla? I thought they would beat me here." With that said we hear talking coming from the front door. I hear Carla's high heels click on the floor before I see her. Grant is walking in front of her, then she appears. She is beautiful. I hate her immediately. She is tall and all legs. Her hair is blonde and cut in a short bob. She is tan, with a perfectly small waist. I catch Grant's eyes and send him daggers. He is such an asshole for making moves on me.

Not even six hours ago, he was on top of me, kissing me while Carla was God knows where. I should have hit him again.

"Oh, Mrs. Grace, you hired new help?" She looks at me with a foul look, and I hate her even more.

"No, Carla, this is Hannah Redman," Grant says. "She is my mother's cardiovascular physician's assistant."

"Oh, so she is hired help," Carla repeats again, crossing her arms over her chest. I make no attempt to greet her. Two can play at this game. I walk over to Mrs. Grace.

"Tori, why don't we get up and go for a walk?" I hold out my hand, and she takes it. I help ease her out of her chair and lead her past the twit. I don't even bother to look at her. Mrs. Grace leads us outside. We walk along the huge patio that sits overlooking the beach. Mrs. Grace breaks the silence first.

"I can't stand that woman. She talks down to everyone. She feels since she came from a wealthy family, she deserves everything. She doesn't love Grant, you know." She looks over at me. "She just loves him for his money. She is a leech; she just wants everything his money can buy."

"Well, maybe he loves her." Why did I say that? He doesn't love her; if he did, he wouldn't have made moves on me. I try to stay positive for Mrs. Grace's sake.

"Hannah, I'm his mother. I know when my son is happy. When I met you, I thought maybe, just maybe, he would meet you and break up with her. I thought you had something that would make him take a second look and realize she is not for him. He needs a strong woman like you. Someone to stand up to him and give him a run for his money." She's still looking at me intensely, but I keep looking ahead. *Oh crap, why did she say that?*

"Tori, I am flattered, I really am, but it would be unethical for that to happen." I keep looking ahead, because I can't look her in the eye when I lie to her. What should I tell her, that I've been kissing both of her sons, and Grant is not the one I'm interested in, but Aiden is?

"Hannah, between you and me, I don't care about ethics. I want my sons to be happy, and you are the first girl I have met that I thought maybe, just maybe, this woman would make a great daughter in law." We stop and take in the view in silence for a few seconds. I just want the breeze to take me away.

"I don't need to be with one of your sons for that to happen." I take her hand in mine.

"Let's head in; it's getting chilly out here." She slips her hand onto my arm, and we head back into the house. "Do me a favor and kick her ass in game night." Mrs. Grace laughs after she says this.

"She doesn't stand a chance."

Everyone looks up when we walk into the house laughing. Mrs. Grace gets back into her chair, and Addy has pulled her chair to sit next to her. I see Aiden has left a spot for me next to him on the couch. I sit next to him, soaking up his beautiful body.

"OK, everyone, tonight we are playing Taboo," Addy tells everyone, then quickly gives us a rundown of the rules. Addy and Mrs. Grace go first. Addy reads the card and shows it to John. Mrs. Grace has to guess.

"OK, you did this once in Aruba and hated it." Addy looks at her.

"Oh! Scuba diving," Mrs. Grace yells.

"OK, next, when you drive, you touch your...when you change lanes." She looks at Mrs. Grace.

"Directional?" Addy shakes her head.

"What's another name?"

"Signal?" Mrs. Grace yells again, all excited.

"No, another name for it."

She sits and thinks. "Blinker?"

"Yes. OK, next one." Addy reads it, and her eyes strain as she thinks.

"All the king's horses and all the king's men couldn't put—"

Before Addy finishes, Mrs. Grace yells, "Humpty Dumpty."

"Time!" John yells.

"We got three," Mrs. Grace says, excited.

"Our turn." John looks over at Autumn. "I'll talk first," he says, then picks up a card, looks at it, and hands it to Aiden. He lets me sneak a peek as well.

"You drive over this on the highway all the time and scream." She looks at him, confused. "Someone runs over a squirrel, and leaves it, and it's called…"

"Oh. Roadkill," she smiles proudly.

"OK, you have this with breakfast every morning."

"Egg whites?"

"No, uh, it's round and small."

They go back and forth for a while, but the timer goes off. He is mad at her because she couldn't figure out the small and round thing was an *orange*. I start to get nervous; it's our turn.

"I think you should talk first and let me guess," Aiden says. I just nod and grab a card. I look at the card and then hand it to Shane.

"If it ain't…don't fix it." I look into his eyes.

"Broke." He is fast to say it. I grab another card. Shit! I'm going to have to sing this one.

"You're a mean one, Mr.…." Again I'm lost in his eyes.

"Grinch." He smiles at me. He is good at this. Two for two. I grab another card.

"When you drink a Slurpee really fast, you get this."

He cuts me off. "Brain freeze." We work well together. I grab another card and see we are almost out of time. I look at the card and smile at him.

"What's your last name?"

He looks at me confused, then says, "Grace." I smile. Four for four, we are winning, and I see the last bit of sand run through the hour-glass.

"You guys got easy ones," John says in protest.

"You're just jealous we kicked your butt," Aiden says to John. He squeezes my knee. It's Shane and Annie's turn. I tune everyone out and enjoy my small victory with Aiden. His large hand lingers on my knee, and I don't push him away. I can feel Grant's eyes on me, but

I make sure not to look in his direction. Shane's yelling pulls me out of my thoughts.

"How could you not have gotten that?" Shane shrills.

Annie rolls her eyes and shrugs her shoulders. It's Grant and Carla's turn. Carla is talking first. I feel my phone vibrating, and take it out of my back pocket.

It's Richard's house. I stand up.

"I'm sorry, I have to take this," I say, apologizing. Mrs. Grace nods and I walk into the kitchen.

"Hey," I answer the phone.

"Mommy, I miss you." It's Ella and I feel homesick. I miss them so much.

"Hey, lovey, I miss you too. Are you having fun with Nana and Grandpa?"

"Yes, Nana let me put on makeup, and we did our hair." She sounds like she is pumped with sugar.

"That sounds like so much fun." I smile. I can just imagine her angelic face.

"OK, Mommy, I'm going to put Hunter on. I love you." I can hear her kiss the phone. I can feel tears come to my eyes. I miss them so much.

"I love you too, baby." I don't think she heard me because I hear Hunter right away.

"Hey, Mommy, I miss you." My sweet Hunter.

"I miss you more, baby. Are you having fun?"

"Yeah, me and Grandpa just came back from the park. It was fun. When are you coming home?" Oh, the dreaded question. I knew I shouldn't have left. This makes my heart sink.

"Oh, sweetheart, I will be home on Sunday afternoon. I can't wait to come home and hug and kiss you." I try to cheer him up. I hear Richard tell him to say good-bye.

"I love you, Mommy."

"I love you more, baby. We can have a date in your dreams tonight, OK?"

"Me, you, and Daddy?"

"I wouldn't want it any other way. I love you, Hunter." The tears are in my eyes now. I take a deep breath and try to hold them back.

"Bye, Mommy." He sounds happier. Richard comes on the phone and assures me everything is fine. I let him know everything is going smoothly here as well. I hang up the phone and lean against the counter for a minute, just to get myself together. I hear cheering in the other room, as I head back in.

"Just in time. It's our turn. John and Autumn are ahead of us by three. We have to beat them," Aiden informs me. He has this great big grin on his face. He licks his bottom lip and pulls out a card.

"It's a Madonna song. Like a..." he starts to sing.

"Virgin." He grabs the next card.

"You probably feel this way being away from Ella and Hunter." I look at him, a little surprised he remembered my kids' names.

"Homesick?" I say with a sad face. He smiles and touches my hand. "Yes."

"OK, you sit on these. They are outside of the hospital, and people sit on them. I talked to you while you sat on one."

"Bench." He grabs the next card; if we can get this, we will beat John and Autumn.

"You are one hot..."

I give him a puzzled look.

"Your kids call you Mommy, or..."

"Oh, mama." I laugh. Does he think I am a hot mama? I see we still have a little time left. He grabs a card and laughs. He passes it to John, and John laughs. John grabs Aiden's shoulder.

"You have to act this one out." Aiden looks at the timer and then at me. I'm not sure what he is doing, but he is getting closer to me. He leans in and kisses my cheek. I feel myself get red, because his whole family is watching his every move.

"Kiss," I whisper, looking him straight in his blue-oasis eyes.

"Time," John yells. "I would have gone for the lips," he teases Aiden. I just roll my eyes and laugh. I would have died if he went for the lips.

I sit and study the family once again. Aiden shifts on the couch so our arms are touching. I half listen to Shane and Annie while thinking about Aiden's soft kiss. Shane and Annie got two, but we are still the winners.

It's asshole and bitch face's turn. Grant picks up the card and half laughs; he hands it to Shane, who laughs even harder. Annie takes the card and smiles. She hands the card to me, and I hold it out to Aiden. It says gold digger. I want to laugh, but I contain myself. Everyone laughs and passes it around. When Mrs. Grace gets it, she comments about how appropriate it is. Grant scowls at her.

"OK, Carla, the first word is a material a ring or necklace would be made of." He looks at her.

"Platinum?"

"No."

"White gold."

"Close, drop the white."

"Gold?"

"Yes. The second word is…OK, when you plant flowers you need to…a hole."

Any normal person would get that, but princess can't grasp the concept.

"Grant, you know I don't garden. We have people who do that." She smiles at him and pats his knee. She is so stupid. What the hell does he see in her?

"Sweetheart, think about it," he says callously; she rolls her eyes at him.

"Gold marigolds?" she says. We all look at her.

"I thought it was a flower. Isn't there a flower called marigolds?"

"No, the first word is gold. I'm trying to get you to guess the second word." His impatience is starting to show, and he looks over at the timer as the last few grains of sand pass through. John yells time.

Grant walks into the kitchen as Aiden jumps up and picks me up, throwing me over his shoulder.

"We won." I feel embarrassed, and as I look back, I notice Mrs. Grace and Addy are smiling in their chairs.

"Put me down. I'm not a toy," I tell him. He walks into the kitchen, slides me down his body, and sits me on the counter.

"It would be fun if you were my toy," he whispers in my ear. His breath warms my body. His hands are still on my thighs. I can feel myself turn crimson. I smile at him, but don't say a thing. I would love to be his toy. Grant is at the fridge, and he is looking right at me. I ignore him. I slide off the countertop, letting my body slide against Aiden's. He smiles at me, but I walk away. I hear Carla getting loud in the living room.

"What was the word? Why won't anyone tell me?" She is standing up, looking at Mrs. Grace, who seems to be flat-out ignoring her.

"Tori, you must be tired. Do you want help getting to bed?" I ask as I walk over to her.

"You, you saw the word. What was it?" The bitch is pointing her finger in my face.

"I have a name you can call me by," I say nicely.

"I'm not interested in getting to know the help. Answer my question." She takes a step closer to me. Are you fucking kidding me? Who the hell does she think she is? That's why Grant likes her. They are both arrogant assholes. *Birds of a feather stick together* pops into my head, and I almost laugh. I walk around to ease Mrs. Grace out of her chair. Carla keeps talking and annoying everyone. When I start to help Mrs. Grace up, Carla stands in front of me again.

"I'm talking to you. Don't ignore me," she says, waving her finger again.

"The word was *gold digger*, I believe," I say, and Mrs. Grace starts to laugh. Carla raises her hand at me, but Grant comes in fast and grabs her hand.

"What the hell are you doing?" he firmly asks her. She flinches like he is going to hit her.

"This bitch just called me a gold digger," she says, starting to cry. Oh, she is good at playing the victim.

"I did not call you a gold digger. I told you the word was gold digger." I roll my eyes and look at Grant. I'm not sure what he is thinking, but I shouldn't care. He looks at me, then at Carla.

"We are leaving. Get your things. Hannah, I want to speak with you in the other room."

"Grant, I'm getting your mother to bed. We can discuss this tomorrow," I say, looking at him with a dark expression. I'm not intimidated by him in the least. I turn around and put my hands out for Mrs. Grace to take.

"Addy, take Mother to bed." I have no time to protest, because he is dragging me out of the room by my arm.

I hear Carla yell, "Fire her!" as we walk away. I shake him off as he pulls me inside a door I never noticed before. He turns on the light, and I see it's an office. A huge sailboat sits on the mantle of the fireplace. By the fireplace are two brown leather chairs. The room is warm. I can imagine the boys as kids in here on a cold winter's night, all around the fire. I get shaken out of this thought when Grant slams the door behind us. I turn around, ready to battle him, but he grabs me, spinning me around and pushing me against the door. His body is against mine, and his breathing is fast.

"I have never met anyone who has made me feel this way. You are so fucking complicated and stubborn." He starts to smile. "And sexy and smart. You are a challenge, Hannah."

We are nose to nose. Shit, I can't do this. I shake my head.

"Carla looks like a lovely woman," I say sarcastically. I put my hands on his chest to get space between us, and try to give him the nastiest look I can muster.

"I'm not interested in talking about her, and you know this, Hannah." He allows me to have my space, but he keeps his hands on my hips. Control freak!

"You should be she is your girlfriend. I'm working, Grant. I have no desire to mix work and pleasure. I thought you would have gotten that hint already. I believe I slapped you once before, didn't I? Or do I have to do that again?" I have to stick to my game plan of walking away. I push his hands off me.

"This is what I mean. You're not afraid of me." He places his hands on me again, and I try to block out the connection I feel.

"Mr. Grace, I have no reason to fear you. You are my patient's son. Nothing more, nothing less." I push him away finally and start to open the door.

"Well, maybe something more." His hand touches my back and slides up to the back of my neck. He takes a step closer.

"Really? You're going to do this with your girlfriend in the next room? Do I need to slap you? Carla would really wonder now, wouldn't she?" I snap at him. He just smiles at me.

"Well, stop talking to me like that; it turns me on," he says, grinning at me. *He is so arrogant*, I think.

"Oh, get over yourself," I say as I open the door. Carla is hovering outside. When I walk out, she gets in my face.

"I hope you enjoyed your job while it lasted," she snarls at me.

"Good night, Hannah." Grant is leaning in the doorway with a smirk on his face. Carla turns around and glares at him, then me.

"Good night, Grant." I look over to bitch face. "Carla." I give her my sweetest smile and walk away. I hear her high heels clicking behind me, then her hand is on my arm. I shake my arm out of her hold and turn around.

"I don't know who you think you are, but—"she snaps, but suddenly Grant is between us.

"I'm sorry, Carla, I don't know what you are talking about," I say. "I don't think I'm the one with the problem." She starts to speak, but Grant shuts her down.

"Jesus, Carla, can you just shut the fuck up?" He is getting angry with her. I take that as my opportunity to leave, and walk away. God, this family is so fucked up. I can hear her high-pitched shrills as I walk away. Why did I come here again?

CHAPTER FIFTEEN

As I walk into the living room, I see Aiden. He is on the couch by himself. I look around and see no one else; everyone must have left.

"Hey, you," he says. I meet his eyes and instantly feel relaxed.

"Hey. I have to go and check on your mom," I say, standing in front of him.

"I'll go with you." I follow him through the house. Addy is walking out the door to Mrs. Grace's bedroom as we reach it.

"She just laid down. Rose will be watching over her tonight," Addy says as she closes the door.

"I thought I would just check on her," I say as I step closer to the door.

"Hannah, honey, you are off the clock," she says as she looks at her watch. I just stand there looking at her, confused.

"The nurse will be taking nights. Mrs. Grace said you should relax. It's been a long day for everyone." I shrug my shoulders, mutter "Ok", and head back to the living room. I glance at my watch and see it's almost eleven. Today has gone by so fast. It's never a dull moment when you are around the Graces.

"Come sit with me for a while," I hear Aiden say. I sit down and pull my legs close to my chest as I look over at Aiden. He looks tired, but still amazingly beautiful.

"So what are your plans for this weekend?" I ask as I turn to face him better.

"I'm staying here tonight and some of tomorrow, then Grant is taking over till Sunday night. Then John will do a night, then Shane. This way she isn't alone...even though she isn't alone." I like that they are all so good to their mother. I remember my mom telling me when I was younger that you can tell how good a man will treat a woman by how good he treats his mother. All of them treat their mother so well. I wonder how they treat their women. Is the saying true?

"It's nice that all of you are willing to help out." As I trace the seam on the couch cushion, his hand covers mine, which makes me look up into those eyes.

"She is our world. Without her we have nothing." His voice is a little sad. I wonder if this is how Hunter and Ella will feel when they get older. I look out the window at the rain starting to fall.

"You have each other," I say quietly.

"Hannah, can I ask you a personal question?"

"I guess." I don't know where this is going, but I just sit still as his thumb strokes my thumb.

"How did he die?" he asks. I look up at him and want to cry all of a sudden. I keep tracing the seam on the cushion as I take deep breaths. We sit in silence for a while, and he doesn't push me to talk. How the hell does he know?

"My father died in a boating accident. He left to go sailing and never came back." He looks down at his hands, which are now tangled together.

"I'll never forget the sound of my mother's voice when the coast guard called. It haunts me still to this day." His head is hung low. I wonder how painful this is for him to relive. Will Hunter think this way? Will the moment I told him about Chase's death replay in his head like it does mine? I slip my hand into his and shift closer to him on the couch. It starts to rain harder, and the sound soothes both of us.

"Chase was in a building doing a final inspection when he was shot." That's all I can get out. The tears swell in my eyes, and a large lump blocks my throat, making it hard to breathe or swallow. He looks over at me and takes my face in his hands. He kisses my hair, bringing me close to his chest.

"I never said good-bye to him that morning. The kids didn't see him the night before; they never got a good-night kiss." I start to choke up, and he pulls me tighter as if he is going to make it all better.

"They will remember him. I remember my father—every detail of his face and the sound of his voice. As a child, whenever I heard a car drive up in to the driveway, I would run to the window, thinking it was his car. They will never forget him, I promise you." He lays a gentle kiss on my forehead. The room lights up from the lightning outside.

"I hope not. I feel like he is slipping away from me. I think I can remember his voice, but I don't know anymore." I sit up and get distance from him and suddenly feel stupid for sharing too much. "I think I'll head up to bed," I say, looking at him through my cloudy, teary eyes.

"You know your eyes turn aqua when you cry? They look beautiful." He slides his knuckles over my cheeks, wiping the tears from my face. I take his hand in mine and open it so it cups my face. I lean into his hand, holding it close to my face. He gently strokes my cheek with his thumb. We stay in silence for a moment, before I take his hand in mine, give it a squeeze, and then walk away from him, heading to my room.

I go right into the shower and stand there, hoping all the emotions will get washed away by the water. I replay our conversation and how he touched me. Everything he did was to comfort me, not to hit on me, unlike Grant. As I step out of the shower, I get dressed in my pajamas without drying myself off. I brush my hair towel dry it fast and feel a magnetic pull to go outside and watch the storm.

The storm is in full force as I walk onto the porch. I stand at the railing, feeling the cool rain trickle onto my fingers. The feeling gives me chills deep in my soul, as if the rain is cleansing me. I pull my hand back and dry it on my pajama pants. The night sky is filled with shooting lines going in all different directions. The brightness of the lightning nearly blinds me, making me hold my hand up.

I settle down into a large Adirondack chair. I can feel the dampness of the chair under me, but I want to sit and watch Mother Nature's show. The rain pours down harder and its glorious sound fills my ears. I sit and stare, then I catch a shadow out of the corner of my eye. It's Aiden on the other side of the porch, and he has been watching me. I watch him slowly get up and walk over to me. Our eyes don't leave each other. I'm sitting with my knees to my chest, and he stops when he reaches me. He puts his hands out. His caring hands with much promise behind them. I feel my heart starting to pound. I take his hands and he stands me up, pulling me close to him. I'm automatically consumed by him. I don't think I could pull away even if I tried.

He takes my hand, places it over his heart. His hands slide around to my lower back, pulling me closer to him, as if we are melting into each other. I can feel his heartbeat under my hand. I rest my head on his chest and wrap my arms around him tight. We start to slow dance to the sound of the rain. He rests his chin on the top of my head. The lump is back in my throat.

"Let go," he whispers in my ear.

I have to let go. I know I do, but I'm afraid. I promised myself I would never fall in love again. I don't want to get hurt again, and I don't want the kids to get hurt again. I convinced myself months ago that I was the black widow, and that any man I fall in love with will die. I take a deep breath, push the thought out of my head, and urge myself to relax. We just stand and sway for what feels like hours. His hands start to wander, as do mine. He takes control, slowly kissing my bottom lip; my lips part, and he fills my mouth. He tastes like cherries again, and it makes me smile. His hands surround my face and make their way in my hair. I move mine to his face, and in one motion he picks me up. I wrap my legs around him. Our breathing is getting faster, and our hands are everywhere. I let out a small moan, and he pulls away, looking intensely at me.

"I like that sound." He looks sexy as hell. I nip his chin, and he kisses me deeper, invading every part of my mouth. He glides his teeth over my bottom lip and I can feel the energy whirling around us. I have no control, and I'm sure I would do just about anything with him right now. He pulls back and looks at me again.

"You are so beautiful." I'm lost in his words. I have never had any man say this to me except Chase.

"So are you," I say, but my voice cracks. I'm under his spell, and I don't think I want to get out. He sits me on the railing. I know I'm on the second story, but I have no fear being in his arms. I draw my legs tighter around him, forcing him closer to me. His hands slip down my shoulders, over my breasts, and linger at my sides. He tips my chin up so I'm looking at him. Then he parts from me, helping me off the railing. He backs up and sits in the chair. He lowers me onto his lap, and I sit, obeying his every move. I rest my head on his muscular chest. For the first time in a long time, I feel safe, protected. I let go…and relax. He leans his chin on my head, and runs his fingers up and down my thigh while he kisses my hair. The rain is still falling, and the sound is like a soft song, I just lie on him, letting go.

"Hey, sleepyhead," I hear in the distance. I'm still in my peaceful dream, and it is heavenly. I open my eyes and realize it isn't a dream. I'm really here with him. I snuggle into him. It's like he knows what I need, and is doing everything he can to give it to me. He kisses my lips softly and runs his fingertips along my jawline. I look over the railing and realize the rain has stopped and the sun is starting to rise. Orange and pink line the horizon. It is beautiful, and I'm happy to have this moment with him, here in his strong arms. I sit up and straddle him. A grin appears on his lips. I pull myself close so my warmth is on top of his hardness. He pulls me closer, pushing his hips up into me. We slowly get into a rhythm. Our mouths meet again, and it's filled with passion. I hear a growl from deep in his throat. I pull away from him and look into his eyes. The blue oasis that I could get lost in forever.

"You like that?" I steal the line that he used on me in the stairwell. He just nods, looking into my eyes. His hands rock my hips so we are grinding each other. I feel myself fill with pleasure. If I don't stop…I need to stop; this is wrong on so many levels. I'm caring for his mother. *This is so unprofessional*, the angel on my shoulder scolds me, but the devil me tells me…*Fuck it, go for it*! I deserve it, all of it. I shift back and he pulls me back in.

"Don't stop. Let go. I'll catch you." He stands me up, and slowly slides my pants down my legs, tapping each ankle for me to lift my foot. My hands find their way to his shoulders for support. His hands caress up my calves, then his fingers whisper up the inside of my thighs. My head falls back from the sheer pleasure. I feel his hands leave my skin, and a small whimper escapes my lips. I look down at him and the sexual tension builds. I watch as he unbuttons his jeans and takes his long, thick hardness into his hands. I stare in shock as I watch him pumping himself with his hand. I find this very erotic, it's unlike anything I have ever experienced before. We make eye contact and I swear I am going to come just by watching him pleasure himself. His other hand coaxes me to again straddle his lap.

"Come here, baby." When I feel his hot skin rub against mine, I have to close my eyes. I haven't been with anyone else since Chase and a part of me is scared. My body is humming with euphoric sensations, but it's my mind that's holding me back. I have to let go of the guilt I carry; I need to let go of Chase.

"Hannah, open your eyes." Opening my eyes, I focus on Aiden's. I look into his ocean blue eyes and let all of my insecurities slowly fall away. He licks across my bottom lip, before he sucks on it. "Mmm…" I moan. "I want you so much," he groans. The crinkle of the foil lets me know this is happening. His hands make quick work, then wrap around my waist to help guide me. My sensations are on over drive. Aiden set off every alarm in my body without me knowing. One minute we are gently rocking into each other, and the next, we are ripping each other's clothes off as if we aren't close enough. He pulls my shirt off, throwing it behind him, as he looks deep into my eyes, and my heart instantly begins to pound.

"You're like Christmas morning," he whispers. "I can't get you unwrapped fast enough." Our naked bodies are pressed against each other. Every time he enters me, I moan with need. I throw my head back and let his delicious rhythm keep pushing me towards the edge. He teases me with hot kisses on my breasts. His slow thrusts are my undoing. I begin to feel the first wave crash over me. It hits me hard, and I try not to scream out of pure pleasure. I pull myself to his neck and begin to bite it. First gently, then hard. It only makes the waves crash longer. I finally let go of everything, and find myself floating in pure bliss.

"God Hannah, you feel so good. I want to make this last." The sound of his voice only makes the waves crash again. This time I lean back and place my hands on his knees. I want him to take me hard. I look into his eyes and he reads my mind. In one second he lays me on the floor and starts to pound his long hardness into me, making my orgasm fly higher. My toes curl and my arms are wild. I wrap my legs around him and push him into me. His pace quickens, and we end at the same time. Our breathing is erratic, and I begin to giggle. If this is going to happen every time I let go, I will be falling into Grace often. He props himself up on his elbows, his hands in my hair. He laughs with me and lays his full weight on top of me. We melt into each other.

He is the first to move.

"Let's go for a walk on the beach." I nod as he eases out of me. I want him to stay inside of me, but the angel tells me to stop. *Fuck,* what have I done? Guilt makes its way back into my body, as well as shame. I lie there, rubbing my face, trying to avoid all the feelings. Aiden stands over me, staring at me.

"You're better than Christmas morning," he says. I look over his sexy, muscular body. His shoulders are broad, and his body forms the perfect *V*. His abs are deep and chiseled, and his hardness is still straight out. He puts his hands out, and I reach up; he makes everything so graceful. I stand up and he turns me around. I look over my shoulder at him.

"I'm just making sure you didn't get splinters." He runs his hand down my back and bottom, then kisses between my shoulder blades. This makes me pulse quicken again. He picks up my bra and starts to dress me. I do the same with his clothes. I wish I didn't have to get him dressed. I catch a glimpse of his watch, and it's 5:23 a.m.

"Let's catch the sunrise." He grabs my hand and leads me down a staircase near his room. I follow him, feeling like we are teenagers sneaking out of the house. We walk over the huge patio, and I see stairs leading down to the beach. He holds my hand down the steep stairs. Once we get on the beach, he stops and I almost bump into him.

"Get on," he says as he lowers himself so I can climb onto his back. I jump on and enjoy the scenery. I lay my head on his back and soak in his smell. I take advantage of touching the top of his chest. Once we get to the water, he swings me around him so we are face to face. He kisses me gently and puts me down. We walk in silence down the beach and back to the house. As we walk back up the stairs, he pulls me in for one last savage kiss. It gets me hot again, but he stops.

"I'm clean." It takes a minute for his words to register. I have never had this conversation, and it feels awkward already.

"I'm clean, and we also used a condom," I say. "I have an IUD in, so don't worry about getting me pregnant." I smirk at him and he kisses my forehead. I walk back to my room and head straight to the shower to go over the last few hours in my head.

Guilt is looming over me. I can't believe I was so reckless. *I am a stupid, stupid woman*, I tell myself. Were a few minutes of pleasure worth risking my job, and heart? The water feels good against my skin, and I just stand there. When I get out, I get ready as if I were going to work. I straighten my hair and put on some makeup.

CHAPTER SIXTEEN

When I get downstairs, Addy is in the kitchen cooking breakfast.

"What can I get for you, honey?" she asks sweetly. She looks at me for a second longer. "Looks like the Cape agrees with you, Hannah. You have a glow today." I think she knows something.

"I slept like a baby last night. I think I just needed that." I walk over to the stove and see the kettle is still hot. Addy hands me a mug with a tea bag in it.

"Thanks," I say, and fill it up. I perch on a stool at the island and begin to make small talk with Addy.

"Is Mrs. Grace up yet?" I ask her.

"No, dear, she is a late sleeper. It's only seven fifteen. You have at least another two hours. I just got up to make the boys breakfast. They are early risers. You just missed Aiden; he just went for a run. I bet he will run to his house and shower, get ready, and come back." I nod and just sit there.

"What would you like to eat? An omelet, pancakes, waffles... whatever you want." She smiles.

"I'll have whatever you were making for the boys," I say. I'm easy to please. Before I know it, I have an omelet in front of me with a fresh glass of orange juice.

I enjoy my breakfast, and then head outside. I sit on a big out-door couch and look out onto Vineyard Sound. Small waves crash along the water's edge, and I lean back and smell the salty air. I decide to call Richard's house to check on the kids, but there is no answer; they probably went out to breakfast. I contemplate calling his cell, but decide not to.

"Hey you," I hear, and I don't have to turn around to know it's Aiden. *His voice is one I will never forget*, I think. Then I feel stupid for thinking it, because I don't need to remember his voice like I need to remember Chase's.

"Hey," I say once he reaches me. He is dressed in a three piece suit, all ready for a business meeting. *He looks good in a suit*, I think, and I start to grin.

"If things were different, I would take you on that couch right now, not caring if Addy is watching." He sits down next to me. I want to snuggle up to him, but I bet Addy is watching. He rests his hand on my leg, and I let him, because I'm sure she can't see it. He begins to slide his hand up until he reaches the top of my thigh.

"Oh, what I want to do to you, Hannah." I roll my eyes at him and swat him away.

"Aiden, I can't repeat last night. It was wrong, and I should not have acted like that. It was unprofessional..."

"Don't do this. We are two adults, and we can't help how we felt last night. It was right what happened, and I would like to repeat it tomorrow on the plane ride home." He smiles at me and I turn red.

"So you are accompanying me home tomorrow?"

"Yes, I have business there. I will be in the city till Saturday. I just have to tie up a few loose ends today so I can leave tomorrow with you." He leans forward, getting ready to get up. "I'd like to repeat last night." He raises his eyebrow, then stands.

"Keep dreaming." I smile at him sweetly.

"A boy can always dream," he says, putting his hands up in defense. "I will see you tomorrow. Grant will be here later to spend time with Mother. Don't let him piss her off, please."

"You have nothing to worry about. I can handle my own." I smile at him and watch him walk back into the house. I feel a little sad he won't be here tonight. Then I realize what he said. *Oh shit*, I have to deal with Grant. I sit for a few minutes, then head back into the house. Mrs. Grace is at the table eating her breakfast, and Aiden is across from her, reading the paper while he eats.

"Good morning," I say as I sit next to her.

"Oh, good morning, Hannah. I take it you slept well last night," Mrs. Grace says, smiling at me. I guess I do have a glow. I'll let them think I slept well, but only Aiden and I know it's the 'I just had amazing sex' glow.

"Like a baby," I say to her. Aiden walks over to his mother and kisses her cheek.

"I have to go. I have a nine-thirty meeting." Addy walks in, and he kisses her cheek, then kisses mine in front of them. I try my hardest to brush it off.

"Have a good day, ladies." He smiles and winks, then walks out of sight. Mrs. Grace and Addy look at each other and I try to ignore it.

"He has it bad for you, Hannah," Addy says, then walks into the kitchen. I ignore her comment and look over at Mrs. Grace, who looks confused.

"She is right, Hannah. I know Aiden, and he is up to something. You better be careful with him; he sucks girls in and spits them out when he gets bored. Don't fall into his trap; he is a playful one. I see girls come and go, and I know he will never settle down. He's not the type to settle down; he doesn't like anyone getting too close to him." She seems sad as she says this.

"Tori, I don't know what you see, but I don't see the same thing. We played a game last night and talked for a bit, that's it. I told you I wasn't interested in your sons." I smile at her, trying to believe the lie I just said.

"Hannah dear, I told you I thought you would be good for Grant. He is the one you should spend time with. He is hard to warm up to, but once you do, he is a wonderful man who could give you another chance at love." She looks at me while I let out a little laugh.

"Mrs. Grace, I came here to care for you, not for you to play match-maker with me. Please. My friends are bad enough, and now I have you pushing Grant on me. I believe he is in love with Carla," I say matter-of-factly. She just shakes her head.

"He doesn't love her, and last night when Carla raised her hand at you, he flew across the room to come to your rescue. I bet he didn't even yell at you when he took you into the other room. Grant is a yeller when he is mad, and I didn't even hear him raise his voice. You have a calming effect on him."

"Oh, I do? Is that why he tried to get me fired when I told him to leave the room?" I'm getting aggravated talking to her about this.

"Grant doesn't like being told what to do, but he did listen to you. That speaks volumes to a mother. You are the first woman he has ever backed down to. And I would put money on it that Carla saw this as well last night. He took your side and not hers." She is looking at me like some lightbulb is about to go off above my head. But it doesn't. I need to change the subject, and quick.

"What would you like to do today?" This should distract her.

"How about we go for a walk outside? Then I'll take out some old photo albums I have been meaning to go through." When she gets up, I can see the pain rise in her eyes. She is still sore, and I feel bad.

"OK." I walk over to her, and she takes my arm. We do just what she wants to do, and the next few hours fly by.

We are buried in photo albums. I see her wedding album, and she lets me look at it. The first picture looks familiar, and I realize it's the one I saw hanging yesterday. They looked so happy and in love. I bet if I looked at my wedding album, I would unravel. In time I will be able to look at it and not cry. I need to start letting go and moving on. She talks about him, and this shocks me a bit. She tells me how they first met and how she couldn't stand him because he was extremely arrogant. I guess that's where Grant gets it. He chased her and finally she realized she loved him. They married fast and had kids right away.

They were together for seven years before he died. The same amount of time Chase and I had together.

I feel the tears stab at my eyes, but I fight them back. I wonder if she is doing the same or if it gets easier thinking and talking about them. We have a quick lunch, then go back to the albums. She has each one of her son's lives recorded through pictures. I love the bath-tub ones. All four of them in the tub filled with bubbles, smiling. I have the same shots of Hunter and Ella. We laugh and she tells me the stories behind the pictures. She has a great memory. I always get nervous that I will forget some things, but I guess as a mother you never forget the moments, not the important ones. We are giggling on the couch when Grant walks in. Neither of us notices him at first, but he stands and watches us. Mrs. Grace starts to tell me a story about him and Aiden.

"You have it all wrong, Mom," he interrupts. He settles on the arm of the couch and tells us the story.

"We stole a pair of scissors and thought it would be a good idea to cut each other's hair. When we chopped each other's hair off, we real-ized it looked horrible, so we thought it would be a believable story to tell you a bird attacked us and ripped our hair out." He smiles. "We were four and five; we didn't know how to create a good lie." I look over at the picture and laugh. Their hair was a mess. Some spots are long, while other spots are missing.

"You boys drove me up the walls," Mrs. Grace says, looking at Grant with such love.

"Oh, Mom, we weren't that bad."

"Oh no? So when you thought it was a good idea to jump off the pool-house roof into the pool, you thought I wouldn't have a heart attack?" She gives him the evil eye, but his charm wins her over.

"We didn't get hurt, did we? We never did anything too crazy that would put us at risk." He gives her a warm and loving smile, and she melts.

"I would like to take a nap now. I'm very tired from looking at all of this. Grant, would you mind going and getting some gelato?" She looks at him, showing how tired she is.

"Of course, Mom. I'll help you into bed."

"No, Addy can help me. Why don't you take Hannah with you? Show her around. I feel bad having her cooped up in this house."

"Tori, I don't mind staying here," I say, but I know what she is up to.

"What did you drive here in?" she asks him.

"Dad's Porsche." He directs his attention back to me. "I would love it if you joined me, Hannah. I would like some company." I see tears swell up in Mrs. Grace's eyes. I feel like I am missing something. Addy comes in to tell Grant to get her some too, then takes Mrs. Grace into her room.

"Let me just go and get my bag," I say to him.

I head into my room—well, his old room. I spray some perfume on and grab my bag. He is waiting for me at the bottom of the stairs. He looks relaxed again today, wearing jeans that hang nicely on him. They sit right on his hips; he looks good. He has aviator sunglasses hanging from his necklace again. When I get to the bottom step, he steps back and opens the door for me.

"After you," he says, and I walk out of the house. I see his father's Porsche and my jaw drops. *My father would be in heaven*, I think to myself.

"Is this a Fifty-Five Speedster?" I ask him. He is so James Dean.

His head jerks back to look at me.

"How do you know that?" he asks, in shock.

"Mr. Grace, I know things." I smile at him, as he opens the car door for me.

"Do you want me to put the top up?" he asks when he gets in.

"No, leave it down. I like the wind." I settle in my seat and put my seat belt on. The car is a classic and is kept in pristine condition. He starts the car and we begin to drive.

"So how do you know so much about cars?" he questions me.

"My father is a car lover, so I've picked up things from him."

"I'm impressed, but I would be even more impressed if you knew the exact model." He is challenging me, and I think I'm up for it.

"It's a 1953 -356 -A Speedster," I say.

"OK, when can we get married?" he jokes. I roll my eyes and look over at the coastline. "I have never met a girl who knew about cars."

"You never told Carla about the car when you two were driving around?" I ask, giving him a jab.

"You are the first girl besides my mother, of course, to step foot in this car," he says without looking at me. He is smooth as he shifts gears. The car roars down the road, pushing us back in our seats. The wind is loud, so we don't talk. I look at all the sights and think, *I'm the first girl to be in this car besides his mother?* What does that mean? When we get to Main Street, Grant breaks the silence.

"I would go there for gelato, but my mother hates it, so we have to go a few towns over. We have to go on the highway; you might want to put your hair back. She hasn't stretched her legs in a while, so I thought I would work her out." I smile and take the hair tie from around my wrist and pull my hair back. He places his hand on my leg and gives it a quick squeeze.

"I'm happy you came with me." He smiles. I wish I could see his eyes.

"I'm happy to be the second girl to ever ride in this beautiful machine." I smile at him and a grin comes over his face. He licks his bottom lip, then bites it. I stare at him. It is so freaking sexy. Traffic starts to move, and I watch him shift. In a few minutes, we are on an open highway, and he goes to work, getting her up to ninety-five. I look over at him, not worried in the least, but I get nervous we might get pulled over. I bet if he did, he wouldn't get a ticket. We get off a few exits later, and Grant navigates to the little ice cream parlor. He pulls around the building and parks.

"That was amazing. I bet my father will be jealous when I tell him!"

"If you would like, I can teach you how to drive her." He looks at me in a way he never has before. Maybe Mrs. Grace is right about him. Once you get past all the bullshit, he is a loving man.

"I wouldn't want to step on any toes," I say, smiling.

"Stay, I'll open the door." He gets out and walks around. It's a nice gesture, but I don't think I have ever had a man do this.

"My lady." He laughs as he says it and makes an 'after you' gesture with his hand.

"I don't think that suits you much," I tease him. I stand up and walk around the car. He is behind me and stops me. I turn around, and he starts kissing me. I can't stop it. Yesterday I was able to push him off, but today he is even more aggressive. His hands are holding my face. My hands go up to his arms and rest there. I don't even try to push him off. His hands slip in my hair, and I bring mine up to his face. I am wearing flip-flops, so I am much shorter than he is. He is leaning down, so I go on my tiptoes to get some height. He is passionately kissing me as he nips at my lips and his hands slip to the small of my back. He stops, leaving me spinning.

"I needed to get that out of the way."

I just stare at him and begin to laugh mirthlessly. He takes my hand and we begin to walk. I pull my hand away.

"What?" he snaps at me.

"You are so fucking complicated, do you know that?" I snap back at him. "You have a girlfriend, and you have been making moves on me all week. For some stupid reason, you put me into a tailspin and I give in to you. I can't do it anymore. Where is Carla? Why isn't she here with you?" I'm getting heated. He looks around and no one is around.

"Will you please keep your voice down," he says quietly.

"Are you kidding me? I'm not yelling and no one is around. You didn't answer my question. I will start screaming if you don't talk." I feel like a little kid threatening to scream in the grocery store if her mother doesn't get her candy. He just stares at me.

"You wouldn't."

"Oh, I would. Do you want to test me?"

I open my mouth, getting ready to scream, but he steps forward and kisses me again. I sink into his arms and kiss him back. I run my hands through his hair and down his neck onto his shoulders, making my way down to his rock-hard abs. He groans a little as I touch him. I pull away this time.

"I know what you are doing. Stop changing the subject." I glare at him in delight, trying to hide my smile.

He takes my hand again, and I give in and follow him.

He lets go of my hand when we reach the door and lets me go ahead of him as we enter the shop. He places his hand on my back and leads me through the ice-cream parlor. Its old school and I love it. I look around at all the ice-cream flavors.

"What do you like?" he asks me. My face beams.

"All of it," I joke. "I'll have whatever you're having. I'm not picky." I walk over to the wall and look at all the pictures, while Grant places the order. I feel him behind me, then his hands slip around my waist, and he starts telling me what I am looking at. We both hear his name and turn around. It's an older man. Grant shakes his hand.

"Mr. Peters, this is my friend, Hannah Redman," he says, introducing us. I put my hand out and we shake hands.

"Grant, I'm excited about Friday," Mr. Peters says. "We are flying to Manhattan Wednesday to catch a few plays before the gala."

"I look forward to seeing you there," Grant says, then they shake again and Mr. Peters gives me a nod.

Our order is up, and it is a huge bag. What did he get?

"You said you liked everything, so I got us a sample of the top fifteen best sellers." I just laugh at him.

"Maybe I'll share with you," I say as we're walking out. He opens the door to the car. I pause and look at him.

"What?" he asks.

"You know my last name is Winterfield, right?" He looks at me, confused.

"I thought you told me it was Redman when you introduced yourself." He looks like he is thinking back.

"I did. I use my maiden name at work, but my last name is Winterfield," I say again, waiting for him to catch on. I get into my seat and take the bag from him. I place it on the floor and balance it between my legs.

"OK, so you know the director?" He is starting to catch on.

"Yes, he is my father-in-law," I laugh.

"So when I went in there and threw a fit, he was never going to fire you, and you knew this?"

"Yes, and it gave me great pleasure watching you think you had the upper hand. But no, I was never worried about losing my job." He leans over and kisses me.

"You never cease to amaze me," he says as he starts the car. We ride in silence until we reach a light.

"When we get closer to home, I'm going to let you drive," he says. I perk up in my seat.

"Have you ever driven a stick before?" he questions me. I decide to play with him.

"No, but I'm a fast learner. Aren't you afraid I will strip your gears or something?" I say, trying to dumb the statement down. My father taught me how to drive a stick shift when I was fifteen. He told me I had to learn, so when he bought my first car, of course it was stick.

He starts to say something, then stops.

"What is it now, Grant?"

"I broke up with Carla last night. I just thought you should know." I watch his face as he says this, and he gives nothing away.

"I hope not on my behalf," I say softly. He gets serious.

"Hannah, you opened my eyes. She isn't anything I wanted. She was just something to pass time with. You, on the other hand, have an opinion and you speak it, whether I want to hear it or not. You're not afraid of me or my moods." He looks over at me, and I am smiling a big smile.

"I think it's funny that you think people are afraid of you. You're a person, Grant, not some king of the world. Well, at least not that I know of. I still don't know what you do." We stop talking because we are heading onto the highway. The wind whips around us, and I look over at the speedometer. He gets her up to one hundred. The speed is powerful and exciting. We head off the highway, and shortly after that Grant pulls over. He looks at me.

"Don't make me regret this," he says as he steps out.

"Well, if you think you will regret this, then don't bother." I sit and cross my arms. He is such an asshole sometimes.

"Oh, stop," he says as he opens my door. "Don't make me pick you up," he teases me.

"You wouldn't," I reply, testing him.

"I guess you don't know me that well. I will never back down." He leans over and tosses me over his shoulder. I slap his wonderful backside and laugh. He places me down in the driver's seat, then slides the seat closer and begins to show me where everything is. I nod at everything he tells me, even though I already know it.

"Just get in the car before I leave you here," I say to him.

"You can't. You don't know how to drive a stick." I smile at him. I start the car, push it into gear, and start creeping forward.

"I guess you don't know me that well. Oh, and I never back down," I say, smiling at him. Each time he reaches for the door handle, I creep forward a little. I see the wildness in his expression. I can't help but laugh.

"OK, I'll stop," I say, placing my hands in the air. He jumps over the door and lands perfectly in the seat. Once he is in, I look over my shoulder, signal, and roar out onto the road. He gives me directions, and I follow them. This car is a work of art. It is smooth and I love it. He leans forward and turns on the music. 'Life Is a Highway' comes on, and I smile as I stop at a red light and he looks over at me.

"I could get used to this, you know," he says.

"Anytime you want me to drive this around, I will jump at the chance," I say, looking ahead. I head down his mother's block and pull into the driveway. John is about to get into his car and his jaw drops. I wave at him, and Grant starts to grin. I park in the same spot Grant was in earlier, and turn off the car. He looks over at me and gives me a sweet grin.

"I'm happy you came with me." I nudge his arm and get out. John walks over to us.

"What the hell was that?" he questions us.

"Oh, Grant lost a bet, so I got to drive the car," I say nonchalantly.

"What was the bet?" he asks seriously. I look at him and smile.

"Ever play the back-down game?" He looks at me, confused.

"Yeah, when I was a horny teenager."

"Well, your brother was bragging to me about how he was the king, so he bet me if he backed down, I could drive the car." I love making up fun stories. John is wide-eyed. Grant is trying to control his laughter.

"What did you do?" he asks me, very interested.

"I will never reveal my secrets, Mr. Grace." I smile and grab the bag of ice cream and gelato and walk into the house. I'll let Grant take over. I'm just stirring the pot. I figured John would be the best to do it to, since he was encouraging Aiden to kiss me on the lips. I think about Aiden and last night and push it out of my head. I can only deal with one Grace at a time. I head to kitchen to put away the goods.

CHAPTER SEVENTEEN

Addy is in her usual position by the stove, cooking up another meal for the family. She stops when she sees me and starts to take the bag.

"I can do it. Finish cooking," I say, smiling at her. She shrugs and goes back to making dinner, while I put everything away. Grant definitely wasn't kidding when he said he got fifteen different flavors.

"What did he buy, the store?" Addy asks as she sees all the containers. She gives me an amused smile.

"Pretty much!" I say to her, grinning back at her.

"Oh, Hannah, you had a good time, didn't you?" she says, turning to look at me.

"I did. Grant let me drive the Porsche." She nearly chokes on her drink when I say this.

"What? He has strict rules! No one but Victoria is allowed in that car. I have known him his whole life, and he has never taken me out. I think his brothers have gone for a ride with him, but I don't even think they have driven it." Her voice is almost shrieking. "Hannah, Victoria is right. He has it bad for you." I roll my eyes.

"Addy, the Grace's are wonderful people. They have been nothing but kind, and they have welcomed me like family. Maybe they think of me like a sister or something." I almost laugh when I say this, but I hold it back. If only they knew what was going on. Oh God, what would they think? I cringe at the thought and push it out of my head.

Grant walks in and walks over to the stove to taste what Addy is cooking. She swats his hand and he laughs.

"I'm going to check on Mother," Grant says, leaving the kitchen. I sit and watch Addy cook. Then I hear Grant yelling my name and go into a panic. I run through the house and into her room. She is lying in bed, looking very pale.

"She said she was having trouble breathing." I can sense Grant is scared.

"We have to get her to the hospital. Do you want an ambulance, or do you want us to drive you?" I ask her. She nods at me. It takes Grant and me to help her up. Addy comes into the room with a wheelchair. We help her into it, and Grant pushes the chair to the front door. Addy is running behind us with a set of keys. Grant brings her over to the Escalade we arrived in on my first day here .

"Grant, she can't climb into an SUV. It would be easier if she was in a car." I look over; his Porsche is the only car here.

"Take her, and I will follow you." He changes direction, and we get her into the car. He puts the top on, and we speed away. The adrenaline is pumping as I follow close to him. I would be screwed if I lost him, because I have no idea where we are going, and I don't have Grant's number. I blow a light and cringe, hoping I won't get pulled over. As I panic I start to see the signs for the hospital. I decide to call Richard. I reach him on the first ring and tell him what is going on. He tells me he will call the hospital and have her chart faxed over ASAP. I know all her details, but that means nothing. They will want her chart.

I tell him the hospital's name as I pull in and see the welcome sign. He gets right on it. I have pulled up front, right behind Grant. I run in and grab a wheelchair and I see a crowd of people coming out. By the time we get her in the wheelchair, five doctors are at her side, asking questions. I feel a little better that we are here. Grant and I follow behind the staff as they wheel Mrs. Grace inside. I take his hand and give it a squeeze. When he looks over at me, I can see the fear all over his face. They take her straight into testing.

Grant and I stay in the emergency room's waiting area. I sit next to him and feel bad, that somehow this is my fault. If I hadn't been running around with her son, I would have caught this sooner. I hope everything will be OK. I feel Grant slip his hand into mine and watch as he brings it to his lips, giving me a gentle kiss. I look over at him.

"This isn't your fault," he says softly, as if he is reading my mind.

"Yes, it is. I should have stayed home with her," I snap back. The guilt weighs heavy on me. It's like an elephant sitting on my chest.

"Don't think like that, Hannah." He takes a deep breath and releases my hand to run his hands through his hair.

"Even if you were home, she wouldn't have said anything." He is trying to convince me it's not my fault, but I think he is making me feel worse. I can feel tears leave my eyes.

"Did you call your brothers?" I ask.

"No, not yet." He lets out a long sigh. "I figured I would wait for some tests to come back before I worry them again." I let my mind think about all the things it could be. I'm going to drive myself crazy. I get up and pace the floor. Grant watches me. After a few minutes he gets up and stops me.

"Hannah, stop, you're making me crazy." He wraps his arms around me and I let him hug me. I nestle into his chest and breathe in his scent. He smells so good, like fresh air mixed with his own earthy scent. I get lost in his smell and his body. He kisses the top of my head and rubs slow circles across my back. I should be comforting him. I look up at him, and he leans down and kisses me. I let him in, and let go. His hands cup my face and it is an open-hearted kiss on both our parts. Our kiss lets out all of our worries and passion for each other. I feel more tears fall down my face; the kiss is so good, it makes me cry. I think I am falling for him. I want to run from it, but in his arms, I don't want to leave. I don't think I want to be anywhere but here.

We stop when we hear the door open, but we don't move. We just stand there in each other's arms staring into each other's eyes. He needs me right now. I have to be strong; this isn't about me and my baggage. This is about him and his fear of losing his mother. I realize that no one walked into the room. I look up at him, and his eyes are wild with fear and something else. I wonder what it is.

"She is going to be fine. I know she is," I tell him, trying to believe it myself. We sit back down, and Grant leans his elbows on his knees and puts his hands on his face. I rub his back, trying to soothe him. I feel his back muscles relax a bit. He sits back and places his arm around my shoulders, and his thumb moves back and forth in a rhythmic motion on my shoulder. We wait for what seems like forever.

When the doctor walks in, we both jump up.

"She is doing fine. We are waiting on one more test to come back, but I believe she pulled a muscle in her chest. This is fairly common. I gave her some pain medication, and she is resting. I want to keep her overnight to observe her, but I believe we will release her in the morning."

"I want to see her," Grant says.

"That's fine, but only family can go in," the doctor says, looking at me. My heart sinks, but I understand. I have said the same thing to too many people in my day.

"This is my wife. She is family," Grant replies without missing a beat, and he slips his hand into mine.

"I'm sorry, Mr. Grace, I didn't realize. You both can go up." He smiles at us and walks out. Grant follows him, practically dragging me. The doctor tells us where to go, and we head to the elevators. The doors open and we step in. I look at Grant and shake my head.

"Mr. Grace, it's not nice to lie," I tease him.

"Mrs. Grace, I don't know what you are talking about. I do believe you are wearing a wedding band." He steps closer and kisses me. I start to melt.

"Mrs. Grace, I like the sound of that," he whispers close to my lips. I roll my eyes and give him a playful slap on the chest. Once the doors open, we head into her room. Mrs. Grace is sitting up in bed and she looks much better. The pain medicine must be working.

"Mom, you had us worried. You have to stop doing this," Grant says as he gently hugs her. I walk over to her and take her hand, but she reaches out for a hug as well. I bend down and hug her and whisper in her ear.

"You had me so scared," I say. She releases me.

"Hannah, I should have told you before, but I thought it was nothing. They think it's just a pulled muscle. I should have taken it easy."

"It's all my fault," I say. I feel the tears in the back of my eyes.

"No, it's not your fault. I think it was the fault of Rose, the night nurse. When I got out of bed last night, she almost dropped me. I think that did me in."

"I thought I was on twenty-four hours a day when I took this job. I would have stayed with you." If I was with her, maybe I wouldn't have been making mistakes with Aiden last night. "Hannah, you are human. You need sleep too. I am grateful for you even being here." She rubs my hand with hers.

"Mom, is there anything you need or want?" Grant asks, looking somewhat relieved that she will be fine.

"I would like some sleep. It's almost nine. Take Hannah back to the house. I will be fine. I need to rest. They will release me first thing in the morning." She looks at him with a face that tells him not to argue with her.

"I'll stay with you, Tori," I say.

"Hannah, that is nice of you, but they won't let you take me out of bed or help me. You don't work here." The pain medicine is starting to kick in, because her eyes are getting heavy and her speech is becoming slurred.

"Go, leave me alone, please. I just want to sleep." Just as the last word slips off her tongue, she falls asleep.

"What do you want to do?" I ask Grant.

"I think we should go home. She never wants us to stay over. She let me stay once last week, only because I fought her on it." He holds out his hand for me to take, and we walk out. The doctor is in the hallway.

"She is fast asleep," Grant says.

"Mr. Grace," he says, then looks at me.

"Mrs. Grace." I smile and look at Grant, who winks at me while squeezing my hand.

"Your mother is fine. Everything came back perfect. Her heart is healing wonderfully, and we think she pulled a muscle."

"That is great to hear, Doctor. What time can we expect her to be released in the morning?" Grant is all business now.

"By ten, I would say." The doctor looks down at the chart.

"I will be back here at eight tomorrow morning. Please let the staff know I will be here so I don't have to fight them in the morning." He gives the doctor a stern look, and the doctor nods at him.

"Of course, Mr. Grace. Have a good evening." Grant leads me back to the elevators.

Once we are in, I can feel Grant staring at me.

"What is it with you and elevators? Every time you're in one, you misbehave," I scold playfully as I look over at him, and he slams me into the wall. It takes me by surprise and almost knocks the wind out of me, but that feeling is quickly distracted by his kiss. He is like fire all around me. His hands can't move fast enough, and he picks me up and wraps my legs around him. I follow his every move. We are getting into it when the elevator comes to a stop. He puts me down before the doors open, but we stand there, eyes still locked, when the doors open. An older man is waiting to get in. I am the first to move out of the way. Grant takes my hand and follows me.

"To be in love again," the older man says, smiling at us.

"I'm a lucky man," Grant tells the man. I turn the brightest shade of red. As we walk outside, I take my ticket out and notice Grant's car is still parked out front. I look over at him.

"What, do you own the hospital?"

"I told you, Hannah, no one drives this car but me, and apparently you," he says, taking my hand and kissing it.

"Leave the SUV here. We can get it tomorrow when we come back. I don't want you to have to drive around at night."

"What, are you afraid the boogie man might get me?" I tease him.

"Sarcasm isn't sexy, Hannah." He shoots me a serious look, and I roll my eyes at him. "You don't know your way around here, and I want you to come with me."

"That's all you had to say." I roll my eyes again at him.

"Come here," he says, opening up his arms, but I don't move. "Suit yourself," he says, then picks me up and tells the valet he will be back tomorrow for the SUV. I just balance over his shoulder, not making a sound, but my hands start exploring. I slip my hands into his jeans and skim over his very firm, very perfect butt, and he almost drops me.

"Shit, Hannah," he says.

"I guess I can beat you at the back-down game," I say as he sets me into the car.

"No, you took me by surprise. I wasn't expecting you to fondle me in front of the valet attendant."

"I wasn't expecting you to carry me over your shoulder." I put my seat belt on and lean back in the seat with my arms crossed.

"Oh, Mrs. Grace, you are a difficult one." He starts the car. We drive for a while before he talks again.

"What's your favorite song?" he asks.

"Depends on my mood."

"Well, if you had to pick a theme song for yourself, what would it be?"

"Right now I would have to say..." I pause and think, biting my lip.

"Far Away," I say. I can feel his eyes on me.

"Hannah, you always seem to surprise me."

"You know the song?"

"I can play it for you when we get back to the house, if you would like," he says gently and reaches for my hand. I wonder how he knows the song and how he can play it. The more time I spend with him, the more confused I get. I wish it could be like this afternoon again, fun and carefree. The scare with Mrs. Grace has drained me, and I'm starting to get really tired. I think I will sleep tonight.

"You never told me yours."

"What I Got," he says, not talking his eyes off the road. Sublime? *He is full of surprises too*, I think. I lean back in the seat and close my eyes.

When I open them, I see Grant at my door, which is open.

"I thought you were asleep." He is taking my hands, helping me out of the car.

"The sound of the engine was putting me to sleep," I say, yawning. I walk into the house with his arm around my waist.

"I'm starving. Do you want something to eat?"

"No, I think I'll just go up to my room." I don't look up at him. I just head up the stairs.

CHAPTER EIGHTEEN

O nce I get into my room, I peel my clothes off and put my pajamas on. They feel soft against my skin, and I climb into bed and turn on the TV. I flip through the channels before I find the Weather Channel. Tomorrow is going to be another nice day, and I get to go home. I realize I never talked to the kids today. I get out of bed and grab my phone. I have one missed call from Richard. It was from ten minutes ago, so I quickly call him back.

"Hey, how did it go?" I assure him everything is fine and update him.

"Are the kids still awake?" I miss them so much, my heart hurts.

"Yeah, we are just finishing a movie." I hear him tell them I'm on the phone, and then I hear their angelic voices shouting my name. Tears prick at my eyes again.

"Mommy, I thought I was never going to talk to you again," Ella says, all dramatic.

"I know, baby, I was so busy today taking care of my patient. I tried calling earlier, but there was no answer. Did you go out to breakfast?"

"Yes, we did. I had waffles. Grandma took me shopping today, and I got a new bathing suit and a new dress. It's so pretty. I'm going to wear it tomorrow."

"I can't wait to see you in it, lovey. I miss you so much." The tears are running down my face now.

"I can't wait to hug you, Mommy. Grandma told me you will be home tomorrow. So all I have to do is go to sleep, and when I wake up, I will get to see you." She sounds so happy.

"Yes, sweet pea, I will be home tomorrow. I can't wait."

"I love you, Mommy."

"I love you more, baby." I hear the phone being shuffled around before Hunter gets on the phone.

"Mommy, when are you coming home?" He sounds sad, and my heart breaks a bit. I wipe the tears from my cheeks.

"Oh, buddy, I come home tomorrow. I miss you." I hear a knock at my door, and Grant walks in with a tray. I motion him to come in. He puts the tray on the nightstand and sits on the bed.

"Promise, Mommy? I want you to tuck me in. Grandma and Grandpa don't know how to tuck me in."

"Oh, honey, don't say that. Grandma and Grandpa do know how to tuck you in. They tucked Daddy in when he was your age, so they have more experience than I do."

"Really, they used to tuck Daddy into bed?"

"Of course, baby."

"Mommy, can we have a date in my dreams again tonight? We had so much fun last night. Me, you, and Daddy were jumping on the trampoline. He was being so silly; he kept tickling us." The words send my tears into overdrive. Grant looks at me and I put my hand up.

"I'm happy we had so much fun. I'll meet you in your dreams in a little bit. Go and brush your teeth and go to bed. We will be waiting for you."

"I love you, Mommy," Hunter says, excited.

"I love you more," I whisper as I wipe the tears off my face. I can taste them in my mouth. Hunter hangs up the phone. Grant shifts closer to me.

"Is everything all right? Do you need to get home?" He picks up his cell in anticipation of me saying yes. I shake my head no.

"What is it?" he asks as he scoots next to me in bed and takes me in his arms.

"Nothing, just something Hunter said set me off. I'm sorry. I'm just a hot mess sometimes." He wipes the tears from my cheeks. I don't feel embarrassed in the least for showing my emotions around him.

"Shhh, don't apologize to me. What did he say?"

I take a deep breath and try not to cry again. He senses this and pulls me closer. I let him.

"He said he dreamed of me, him, and Chase, and we were having fun jumping on the trampoline. He said Daddy was being silly tickling us. It sounded so real when he said it. He wants to have another dream date tonight with the three of us." I feel the hot tears again.

"I wish I was able to do that after I lost my dad. I would give anything to have my father in my dreams, just to see him and talk to him." Grant shifts and kisses a tear from my cheek, then licks his lips.

"I have the perfect cure for you," he says, looking over at the tray. It has fifteen cups on it and two spoons.

"Ice cream makes everything better," he whispers in my ear, and I start to smile.

"See? It's starting to work already." He leans over and grabs the tray, placing it on my lap. He starts telling me what each one is. I take the cookies and cream first. It is heaven in my mouth. I leave half and move on to the next, leaving each cup half full. When I make it to the seventh one, I stop for a drink. He also brought up bottled water. I try to open it, but I'm so tired, I can't get it open. He opens it, then takes a sip and hands it to me with a grin on his face.

"I like that you're not afraid to eat." I look at him, confused.

"Normally girls don't eat around men, or at least not the ones I have dated." I laugh at him.

"I like to eat, and I don't care who is around. I could finish all of these on my own. I'm just being nice and sharing it with you." When I nudge him, his hand fumbles, and his spoon drips ice cream on my shoulder. His pupils dilate, and he leans over and licks it off. I get chills. He kisses his way up my neck and kisses my jawline. He trails around my face and leaves the last kiss on my lips. He grabs the tray off my lap, placing it back on the nightstand. His weight pushes me flat on the bed. His hands hold mine on either side of my head. Our hands are tangled and our souls are touching.

I don't push him away this time. I just let him in. I let him in everywhere. His breathing is getting faster as he nibbles on my lips. His stubble tickles, but I like it. He makes his way down my throat to my chest. He peels off my shirt and bra with ease. I lift myself up a bit to make it easier, and once everything is off, I run my hands down his chest and take his shirt off. I look at his body, and he looks at mine. He gently leans back down and kisses my lips softly.

"You are so beautiful, Hannah." His eyes are wild with desire and something else. I can't place it still. He starts to make his way down my body, stopping at one of my breasts, circling my nipple with his tongue before he takes it in his mouth. My back arches, and I let out a moan. His hands go down my sides and stop on my hips. I can feel his hands wrap around my hip bones as he moves to the next nipple, and it makes me arch my back more. After he sucks on it, he blows gently, making it harder. The feeling echoes throughout my body. I grab his face and pull him to my mouth. I kiss him with everything I have. I feel vulnerable and nervous. I start to feel things I haven't felt in a long time.

His hands run down my body, and he finds his way down to my wet heat. He circles my clit before plunging into me with his finger. I moan louder into his mouth. He circles his finger inside me, and then adds a second finger. I feel like I'm close, so I roll him over and get on top of him. He doesn't take his fingers out of me. I leave his mouth and start to kiss down his chest. I feel his chest rise as he takes deep breaths. I can feel his hardness, and I want to get it in me. He has to pull his fingers out as I get lower, and when he does, he brings them to his lips and slips them into his mouth. I can hear him moan in appreciation as he savors my taste.

I kiss his happy trail and unbutton his jeans. He bursts out of his jeans, and I take him in my mouth. I can taste him, and it turns me on even more. I plunge him deep in my mouth, and he lets out a groan. His hands make their way into my hair. I wrap my hand around the base of his length and ease my hand up and down as I suck on it. My other hand cups his balls, and I gently play with them. He starts to move his hips with my rhythm. I take him out of my mouth and lick from the base to the tip and gently suck on the tip. I can taste him more.

"Fuck, Hannah," he says, almost pleading with me to keep going, and I do. I suck harder and deeper. His hands start to push my head so I can go deeper. I take a good portion of his length into my mouth. I swirl my tongue around it as I come back up. This makes him crazy. His hips are moving faster, and I can tell he's about to come.

"Hannah, I'm going to," he breathes, and I let him, sucking harder, taking him deeper. He comes, and I drink him up. I suck a little more after he does. Then he flips me over and gets on top of me.

"Fuck, Hannah. You taste so good, I want more." He pulls my pants down and spreads my legs. He looks at me, completely exposed, before meeting my eyes. He kisses me hard, then trails down my body. He goes down on me. He sticks a finger in again and swirls it around. I can feel how wet I am. He starts to lick me. I moan again and pull on the sheets. My hips start to sway. I feel the buildup. He leaves my clit, removes his finger, and plunges his tongue in me. When he hits the spot, I come fast and hard. He sits up and puts a hand over my mouth, then quickly plunges two fingers inside me, his thumb on my clitoris. I come again, pushing my hips up to his fingers, and he goes deeper in me, swirling them around. When I finally finish, he lies next to me, slowly sliding out his fingers. He looks at me and licks them.

"You taste better than the ice cream," he says, grinning at me.

"So do you," I reply as I kiss him.

"You are always surprising me, Hannah," he says as he runs his finger over my collarbone.

"I have to tell you, that was the best head I have ever gotten. Do you not have a gag reflex?" he asks as he rolls over and stretches with a sly smile on his face. I lie on my side and enjoy the view of his body.

"Not that I know of," I say, raising my eyebrows and biting my lip so I don't start laughing.

"I feel like I'm a teenager again. I haven't fooled around in so long, especially in this bed. I forgot how good foreplay really is." He slides his hand down the side of my body and stops on my hip. I smile at him and think how different he is like this. The man I met earlier this week has disappeared. I like this one much better. I grin at the thought as I look over his body.

"Let's finish the ice cream," I say.

"Yes, you need it," he says as he squeezes my hip bone.

I roll over and grab the tray and put it between us. He feeds me and I feel pampered. We lie naked in bed, eating ice cream and talking about anything and everything. I find out they all went to Harvard. He graduated with a 4.0. I wouldn't expect anything less from him. He talks about his father, and I talk about Chase. When I look over at the TV, the Weather Channel is still on. It's three o'clock in the morning, and we are still talking. Grant sees the time and orders us to sleep. I roll over and he pulls me into him. I fit perfectly in his arms. It's like two puzzle pieces fitting together perfectly. He kisses my neck.

"Good night, Mrs. Grace," he whispers.

"Good night, Mr. Grace." I smile as I float away. Chase's death won't haunt me tonight.

When I wake up, the Weather Channel is still on. Grant is still wrapped around me; I haven't moved. I stretch a bit, arching my back, and my butt rubs right into him. His body responds to mine, and his hand glides down to my hip, but stops there. I realize he is still sleeping. I just lie there and see that it's a quarter after six. I should get up and start to get ready so we can make it back to the hospital before eight. I gently slide out of his arms and sneak into the shower. I stand under the water and let it hit my face.

I struggle in my mind with everything that has happened this weekend. It's not like me to act like this. I don't know who I have become. I think about Aiden, and how we had such an animal attraction. He makes my body swell up just being around me. Then I think about Grant. I have sexual desires for him, but there is something else I just can't place a finger on. I finish washing, and I am standing under the water when I hear the door open. Grant gets in the shower, slipping his body behind me, hugging me while kissing my neck.

"I didn't hear you get out of bed," he whispers in my ear.

"I didn't want to wake you," I whisper back and start to get out.

"Hey," he says, grabbing my hand.

"Hey, yourself," I say, smiling back at him. When he lets go, I walk back into my room and get dressed before he gets out. I don't need any temptation from either him or his brother. I have to stop this.

I battle with myself once again and suddenly realize I will never see them again. A part of me is relieved. I can just say good-bye, because we have no attachments to each other. They live in another state, and when they are in New York, they are in the city. I will never have to deal with this again. I can breathe a little better as I think about this. I will be just a memory to them soon enough. Maybe in the future one of them will say something about me, and they might even realize what I did. I will never have to face them about it, because at that point, I will be a thing of the past. I smile as I make this scenario in my fucked-up mind.

Grant comes out of the bathroom with a towel wrapped around his waist. He pulls his jeans on from yesterday, and I see he is going commando. I try not to look at him, but every now and then our eyes meet. He gets his shirt on and picks up his underwear.

"We don't want Addy finding this today," he says as he picks them up. "We have to stop off at my house so I can change quickly. Can you throw these in your bag?" I nod and he shoves them in.

"I'm all set," I say as I get up. I didn't do my hair, just scrunched it quickly, and it looks like shit. I will pull it back once we get back in the car anyway. He walks over to me and hugs me.

"I slept good last night. How about you?" He starts to tickle me. Playful Grant is fun to be around.

"I think it was what we did before we went to sleep that made me sleep so well," I say, running my hands over his chest.

"Yes, it was…" He stops and starts to kiss me. It's slow and sexy. His hands run down my backside, and he gives me a squeeze.

"Let's get out of here. Addy is probably waiting outside this room for us." I freeze a bit. Shit, I hope she isn't. He looks out, then grabs my hand and pulls me out. I shake his hand off mine when we reach the stairs. We are out the door free and clear of Addy. He opens the door for me and takes the top down. It is still cool outside. *I should have brought a sweater,* I think, but I'm sure I'll be fine. He hops into the car without opening the door. I laugh. I wonder if he has ever missed and fallen out when he jumps in that way. He looks over at me and smiles. "What's so funny?" It just makes me laugh harder. I think I have lost my mind.

"Nothing," I say.

"You have to tell me now. We aren't going anywhere till you tell me." He sits in protest.

"Well, looks like we will be here all day."

"Don't make me honk the horn," he threatens. "It will get Addy's attention, and I bet she will be right out here."

"Go for it," I threaten right back. "I would love to see her expression when I tell her what we did last night." He just looks at me and smiles, then starts the car. His house is less than a five-minute trip down the block. We pull into a street marked Private Lane. I soon realize it's not a street; it's his driveway. It curves around the property line, then plunges back, bringing his house into view. It reminds me very much of his mother's, but touches of him are all over it.

We pull up to a huge garage, and the doors open. He parks the car in the only open spot. He has all sorts of cars, it looks like every guys wet dream. Grant takes my hand and pulls me into the house. The kitchen is huge. Everything is top of the line. I walk around and see that the island has a built-in grill. I'm immediately jealous.

"Do you like to cook?" I ask him.

"No, I'm not really home enough to cook." He turns on his answering machine to listen to his phone messages. I hear Carla's voice over the machine, pleading with him to take her back. He deletes the message. The next message is from her too. He just stands and deletes all fifteen of them before checking his mail that is piled up on the counter.

"How long were you together?" I ask.

"It doesn't matter, does it?" He slips his hand into the front of my pants and pulls me close to him. I just stand there in his arms.

"Go get your underwear on. We have to go," I tell him. He starts to laugh.

"I don't think anyone has ever said that to me before." I smile back at him and he leans down and plants a kiss on my lips. He picks me up and puts me on the counter he was just leaning against, spreading my legs so he can stand between them. I wrap my arms around his neck and enjoy his kiss. His hands are on my back and make their way down to my bottom. He picks me up.

"Let me show you something." He looks like he is up to no good. *It better not be his bedroom*, I think, *because I have no self-control.* We walk into an adjoining room, where a baby grand piano sits in the corner. He seats me on top, sits down, and starts playing my song. I cross my legs and get lost in his playing. He doesn't take his eyes off of me. He stops after a few minutes, and we are still staring at each other.

"What song are you today?" he asks me. I look up at the ceiling, debating.

"A mixture of *Blister in the Sun* and *Say Goodbye*." He laughs.

"That's a mix, but why do we have to say good-bye? I want more of last night." He walks around the piano, and stands in front of me.

"Grant, you know that's not going to happen. We live in different states and you travel. This is not going to happen, and I'm OK with that. We had fun while it lasted." I grab both of his hands in mine to pull him into me. He steps forward, but doesn't give in. I have to be the rational one. I know this will never go anywhere.

"What if I want to make it last?" he questions me.

"How? You told me yourself your family is always annoyed with you because you are never home. Do you think I will feel any different? And even if I didn't mind it, I don't think I want a relationship right now. We don't even know each other. We just…" My voice trails off.

"I guess you're right," he finally says.

"But what's the point of thinking about that now? I still have you for a few more hours." He brings his hands to my face and kisses me. I instantly pull away from him.

"Go get dressed." He helps me down, and he walks away. I follow him to the other side of the house. His room is vast. He has a California king-sized bed that is positioned in the middle of the room so you can watch the sun rise and set from bed. I walk over to the window and gaze at Vineyard Sound from his view. It is beautiful from both of the houses. I see a sailboat and think about his father. Once Grant is dressed, he walks up behind me and wraps his arms around me. I can smell his cologne and his scent mixed together. He tugs me out of the room. We walk back through the house hand in hand. He leads me back into the garage, this time toward a Mercedes. He opens my door and kisses me, then he holds my hand the whole way to the hospital.

CHAPTER NINETEEN

Whance we pull up to the hospital, Grant kisses my hand and gets out, so I get out too. When he makes his way to my side, he sees I didn't wait for him and makes a face at me. "What?" I look at him, smiling. He walks over to me while looking around, then kisses me. I roll my eyes at him when he releases me. I'm starting to get used to his sweet kisses, and for a second I think I might even miss them.

When we step into the elevator, he turns to me.

"What are you doing Friday night?"

"My best friend is flying in from California. I'm spending the weekend with her." He looks disappointed, but I choose to stay quiet. We head into his mother's room, where the doctor is talking to her.

"Mr. and Mrs. Grace, good timing. I was just getting ready to release your mother." I can feel Mrs. Grace's eyes on me.

"Thank you," Grant says, shaking his hand, and the doctor leaves.

"Mrs. Grace?" Mrs. Grace says with a smile on her face. "It suits you," she teases.

"Well, call me Hannah; Mrs. Grace is my mother-in-law," I say back to her. We both begin to laugh. Grant doesn't say anything, and I notice Aiden in the corner of the room.

"Are you all signed out now?" Aiden asks, sounding annoyed. "Can we leave?" She nods at him. I wonder when Grant called them last night. A nurse comes in with a wheelchair, and we get Mrs. Grace settled.

When we get out front, I realize I have to get out the slip for the SUV. When I look in my bag, Grant's underwear is still in there. I laugh out loud and Grant walks over.

"I still have your underwear," I whisper, and he starts to laugh.

"I'll get them when we get back to the house." I get the slip and hand it to the valet attendant, who is back in under a minute.

Mrs. Grace and Grant are already in the car waiting for me. When the SUV pulls around, I hop in and begin to follow them home. I look in the rearview mirror and see Aiden is behind me. I follow along, until Grant speeds up to miss a red light. I slam on my brakes so I don't run the red light. Aiden slams on his and almost slams into me. *Shit*, I think, *I have no idea where I am going, and Grant is out of sight.* The light turns green and I go; Aiden changes lanes and speeds up. I slow down for him to get in front of me. I see up ahead that Grant has pulled over, and we pass him. I wave, and so does he. I look at Grant's driveway as I drive past it. I push the feelings that start to stir inside of me. *I can't do this*, I tell myself. I have to leave it all here.

We all line the driveway, one car after another. I get out to help Mrs. Grace, but Addy and Aiden are all over her. I start to walk in behind them, but remember I have to return Grant's underwear. I head back to his car, open the door fast, and shove them under his seat. I quickly close the door and catch up to everyone else. I think Grant sees me, but if he did, he doesn't say anything.

We are all in the foyer when Addy tells us she has brunch ready. It's then I realize how hungry I am. We all make our way to the table. Grant takes my chair out and I sit down. Aiden sits on the other side of me. *Fuck* echoes in my head, but I busy myself with filling up my plate. I feel like I haven't eaten in days, so I dig in. Grant nudges my arm and I ignore it. Under the table Aiden's hand begins to wander on my leg and then it rests there. If I make any sudden movements, I feel like it will be obvious, so I ignore him too.

We get halfway through brunch when Grant's hand slips on to my other leg. *Shit, shit, shit,* I think. I remain still, hoping neither one of them moves his hand and feels the other's hand under the table. I begin to choke on my quiche and stand up. They both jump up, trying to give me a glass of water, and Grant asks me if I am choking. I grab the glass of water and feel better. I sit back down, but have lost my appetite. This is harder than I thought it was going to be. I can't handle two men, especially brothers. What did I get myself into? I look at my watch and realize I will be leaving in two hours. I excuse myself from the table, using the lame excuse of needing to finish packing. Mrs. Grace nods her approval, and I head upstairs.

In my room I throw myself on the bed. It hasn't been made yet, and I can still smell Grant on the sheets. I lie there for a few minutes, soaking in his smell. I make the bed and put my suitcase on it. I have everything packed already, so I just reorganize it and add a few items I had left in the bathroom. I zip it up and sit next to it. When I look over at the door, Grant is in the doorway. I don't know how long he has been there, and I don't want to ask. I have to make a clean break from them. I don't need to go home with feelings for them, and I don't need to see them again. I am done with the Grace family the second I leave this house—well, the second I get off their plane. I have to get through this. Grant walks in and closes the door behind him. He takes my suitcase off the bed and sits next to me. I bring my knees to my chest as if they will protect me from him.

"I have to leave. I thought I would say good-bye." He bumps his shoulder into mine.

"I..." My voice trails off. I don't know what to say to him. I ease myself off the bed and stand in front of him, placing my hands on his knees. I push them open and he pulls me into him. I stand there in his arms, thinking, *I thought this would be easier.*

"It was fun while it lasted," I muster up.

"It can last longer if you want it to," he replies. If only I was ready for this, he would be the perfect man for me. But I'm not ready.

I have kids and a home and a job. He lives, breathes, and is consumed by his company. *He doesn't have time for me*, I tell myself. I pull away.

"Maybe another time or place." I smile, and he kisses me softly. It's the kind of kiss that takes my breath away and sends my heart plunging. I feel my insides dancing with excitement. When we part, he puts his forehead against mine.

"I look forward to another time and place." He breathes these words into my soul.

"Let's leave it to fate, 1 don't believe in that stuff, but with you, I know anything is possible." he whispers.

"To fate," I say and we kiss on it. He grabs my bag. I follow him down the stairs. We stop at the bottom, and he gives me a hug and a quick kiss on the cheek. I watch him walk out the door and feel a little plunge in my heart. I try to breathe it out. One down, one to go. I hope saying good-bye to Aiden won't be like this. In the living room, I see Mrs. Grace and Aiden playing chess. I sit across from them and watch. They are into their game, because neither looks at me. I never got into chess, but they look intense.

"Checkmate," Mrs. Grace grins. Aiden leans back in his chair and smiles at her. They notice me after having a moment together.

"Hannah, just the person I was thinking about. Could you help me in for my nap?" Aiden stands and answers his phone. I help her up, and we walk into her room. She points to her private patio, and I help her out the large French doors. We settle into seats and enjoy the view and the salty breeze. We sit in silence, just listening to the waves crashing. Mrs. Grace is the first to break the silence.

"John told me he saw you driving Grant's car yesterday." She is looking at me, amused.

"How did that happen?"

"I was impressed with the car, and I think he was impressed that I knew about the car, so he asked if I wanted to drive it, and I jumped at the chance."

"You have made quite an impact on him in the short amount of time you have been with us." What the hell do I say to that?

"He has never had anyone else in that car before, so I was kind of surprised he was willing to take you. I knew you would be great for him. Just give it time and you will see it as well, Hannah." I lean back in my chair and close my eyes for a bit.

"Tori, Grant is wonderful, and I see it, I do. It's just I don't want that right now. I need to find myself first. I'll leave it to fate." Mrs. Grace smiles at me.

"Fate has brought you together. If I hadn't had my heart attack in New York, we would have never met you, and you would have never met Grant. This is fate telling you to be with him." I laugh and roll my eyes at her. She is so pushy sometimes.

"Well, fate will have to work her magic again."

"What are you doing this weekend?" she asks.

"My best friend is flying in from California, and we are spending the whole weekend with the kids." I see she is frustrated with me.

"Tori, it has been a pleasure to work for you, and getting to know you, and your wonderful family. You have made me feel part of this family." I reach out for her hand.

"I feel like you are the daughter I never had. I want you to be part of this family. Please promise me you will stay in contact and that maybe you will come back and visit with the kids. There is so much to do here, I bet they would love it. I would like to hear kids running around again. Please think about it." I smile and nod, but I know it probably won't happen. I don't want my kids to come here and fall in love with them like I did and not see them ever again. I can handle it, but I don't think they could. I break out of my thoughts when I hear Aiden walk in.

"It's time to go, Hannah."

I get up, and Mrs. Grace does as well. We hug and she whispers in my ear, "Don't wait too long. You can take fate into your own hands, Hannah."

I feel tears leaving my eyes for the second time today. I pull away and see the tears in hers as well. I hug her one last time, then leave her in her room and walk out. When I reach the living room, I see everyone has come over. *Maybe for a Sunday dinner*, I think. Shane and Annie walk over to me.

"We wanted to come and say good-bye to you before you left," Annie says, giving me a hug. Shane hugs me after her.

"Thank you," he says. "I mean it from the bottom of my heart. You have brought a part of my mom back that we haven't seen in so long."

"It wasn't me," I laugh at him. "It was her heart attack that was the wake-up call."

"No, Hannah, it was you," John says, walking over to me.

"She has never liked a single woman who came near her, or us, for that matter. You walked into the room and something changed. She came back to us that day." Autumn steps over next.

"It was you, because she has never reached out to Annie or me, and yesterday she called us to go out to lunch next week," Autumn says with a smile. She hugs me.

"Thank you."

I shake my head at all of them. They are all crazy. Shane wraps his arms around Annie.

"And the best part of the whole weekend was that Grant finally got rid of that bitch Carla." Everyone cheers, and I look down, hiding my smile, because I might have had something to do with that.

"You ready?" Aiden asks, and I am so distracted in thought about Grant that he puts his hand on my shoulder to shake me out of it.

"Yes, sorry. I'm ready when you are," I say shyly back to him. I watch Aiden hug his family good-bye. They start talking about their upcoming plans for Friday. I hear Annie say my name.

"Are you coming Friday?" she asks me. I have no idea what they are doing, but I shake my head no.

"Why? You have to come," she pleads.

"I am sorry. I have plans with my friend who is flying in from California."

"Well, bring her. I'll make the arrangements," she says, brushing me off.

"Really, I would love to do whatever you guys are doing, but we have plans. I already promised her." I feel bad because she looks disappointed.

"I will put you down with a plus one. It is the biggest night of the year for the Grace family. Think about it. I'll e-mail you all the info and have the invite overnighted to your house," she says to me with a genuine smile.

"Thank you, Annie. That's very nice of you." I still have no idea what they are talking about because everything in this house is so cryptic. I could ask, but I don't. The less I know, the better.

Aiden starts to guide me away from the group, and we are outside climbing into his Range Rover before I know it. As we head out the gates, we are stopped by a man who flashes a badge. Aiden rolls down his window.

"Aiden, I hate to disturb you on a Sunday, but we were exercising a new dog, and he went crazy when we got to the woods down the block. I was wondering if it was OK if we let him search. I bet it's nothing more than a group of kids who were smoking pot and left some behind." He looks hopefully at Aiden.

"Sure, Harry, I'll let the groundskeeper know. Let me know if you find anything good."

"Thank you." He tips his hat and Aiden rolls up the window and speeds away.

When we get into town Aiden's hand finds its way onto my leg. He rubs down to my knee, and I cave in and smile.

"I missed you last night." His voice is coarse and sexy as hell. I take his hand in mine and try to hold it, but he doesn't let me. His hand makes its way in between my legs. My reaction is to spread them apart and let him explore.

"I can't wait to fuck you on the plane," he says, not looking over at me.

"Are you a member of the mile-high club, Mr. Grace?" I tease him.

"Yes, and in about forty-five minutes, you will be screaming my name as you become a member too." He is raw and to the point.

I would normally be repulsed by a comment like that, but coming out of Aiden's mouth, it makes me hot.

"We will have to see about that," I say, playing it cool by looking out the window.

"No, Hannah, I can guarantee it." He unbuttons my pants and finds my spot, causing my eyes instantly to shut in pleasure.

"I'll start to warm you up, this way you can beg me later." He plunges into me, and I spread my legs wider, pulling my hands over the top of the headrest. I let out soft moans as he does circles in me. Fuck, he is talented. He gets me off while he is driving us to the airport.

We pull right up to the plane, and I get out, feeling the wetness between my legs. Aiden walks around the car and takes my hand and kisses it.

"Ready to beg?" he asks.

"I think you will be the one begging," I respond.

"I hope so." He picks me up and throws me over his shoulder before I can protest and carries me onto the plane. Then he gently sets me down in a seat and straps me in.

"Don't move," he says, pointing a finger at me. I nod and he disappears to the front of the plane. A few minutes later, he comes out and settles next to me.

"We will be taking off in a few minutes." He looks at his watch. "Then in about fifteen minutes after takeoff, I'm going to take great pleasure in fucking you in the room, back there." He points behind us, and I look over. Excitement comes over me and I can't wait to take off.

When we reach altitude, the captain comes over the system and lets us know we are free to roam the cabin. Aiden unbuckles me from the seat, and like a caveman, he drags me into the back room. He picks me up and throws me on the bed, then pounces on me like an animal. He is a savage, ripping my clothes off, and I am right there, tearing him out of his jeans. I unleash his thick, long hardness from his zipper and take him in my mouth like I did last night to his brother. Grant fills my mind as I pull Aiden deeper into my mouth. I am turned on even more, thinking about it.

Aiden pulls me off him, slides a condom on, and pushes me down on the bed. He plunges right into me, making me cry out in pleasure and pain as my body adjusts to his size. I grab at his back and begin to claw down it. I come immediately undone as he pounds into me with heavy thrusts, filling me. We are both panting for each other.

"You are so tight when you come, Hannah," he hisses through his teeth. "I want to make this last." I wrap my legs around his waist, pulling him to me at a faster pace. He comes hard in me, screaming my name. Then he settles on top of me, bearing down with all his weight. I feel the air leave my lungs, and I gasp for air. He shifts his weight to his forearms.

"I thought I was supposed to be the one screaming names," I tease. I can feel his hardness still in me, and he starts to move again, taking me by surprise.

"Oh, you will scream my name." He pulls out of me and trails down my body. He finds my sweet spot and directs all his attention there. I'm swollen and sensitive, but he works his magical tongue in waves over me. I start to feel the rhythm of my hips pick up pace. I grab at his hair and spread my legs farther apart. I start to cry out his name, louder and louder, until I come again. He quickly pulls himself back into me and ravishes me yet again. I come one more time before he flips me over and takes me from behind, placing his hands on my hips to steady me. I arch my back and feel him deeper in me. He lets out a cry.

"Fuck, I didn't think you could get any tighter." He grabs my hair and pulls it hard. I am surprised by this, but it turns me on even more.

"Fuck, Hannah, your pussy is so wet for me," he groans.

"You make my pussy wet," I purr back to him. He slams into me a few more times and comes again, slapping my ass hard. I can feel it stinging, but I don't care. I can close my eyes right now and sleep for a week. At that moment the captain comes over, saying we need to get seated for our descent. I rush to the bathroom, where I clean up and get dressed before heading back to my seat. Aiden is already seated.

I slide past him as I get into my seat. He straps me in again then holds my hand.

"I'll be in Manhattan all week for business. I would like to see you again." He looks over at me. I debate if I should or not. I told myself I would be done with them when I got off the plane. I need to shake them and get away from them, but I can't stop myself from saying,

"Yes, we need to do this again this week."

He looks at me with a wicked grin.

"I will check with my assistant and see when I have time to see you." I can see the darkness in his eyes. "I have plans for you, Hannah. I hope you can handle what I have in store for you."

I look at him with wide eyes. Whatever he wants to do to me, I am more than ready and willing. My ears pop, and I can feel the plane descending. We land hard, and I squeeze Aiden's hand.

We taxi around, and I follow Aiden's lead. When he unbuckles his belt, he turns to me and starts to help by moving my hands away. Just this act alone, and I am ready for him again.

"Do you want to get something to eat before you go home?" he asks, looking at me. I feel like he can look right into me.

"No, I want to go straight home. I miss my babies." I make a sad face, and he wraps his hands around my face and kisses me softly. My lips are sore and swollen from before, but I don't care. I have no control when he is around. He kisses the center of my palm, sending little shivers through me.

"Let's get you home." His words are music to my ears.

When we exit the plane, a Range Rover is waiting for us. The same man who picked me up on Friday is opening the door for me.

"Mrs. Redman," he says as I get in.

"Sam, nice to see you again," I say to him, thinking *it's Mrs. Winterfield,* but I don't correct him.

CHAPTER TWENTY

It seems to take forever to get home, but I know it's the anticipation of seeing the kids. When we finally pull up to my house, I see the kids waiting for me at the front door. I jump out of the car, and they fly out the door. We meet in the middle of the lawn with our arms open wide. I grab them both in one swoop. I swear they each grew a few inches. I hug them for a while before I let go and plant kisses on them.

"Just look at both of you! I think you grew a foot since I left." They start to laugh at my exaggeration.

"No, Mommy, I didn't grow a foot," Hunter giggles.

"Mommy, who is that?" Ella asks as she glances behind me. I look over and see Sam bringing my bags to the front door and Aiden walking toward us.

"Hunter and Ella, this is Aiden. I was taking care of his mommy. She had to have surgery on her heart." Ella steps forward.

"Is your mommy better now?" she asks him with her gentle voice.

I watch Aiden squat down to get to her eye level.

"Yes, every day she is getting better, thanks to your mommy." He smiles at her and she takes my hand. Hunter steps forward next.

"Where is your daddy? Is he taking care of your mommy now?" His question is innocent but hits home hard. I see Aiden shift a bit before answering Hunter.

"My daddy is in heaven. He went there when I was about your age." His eyes show sadness I never noticed before. Ella walks over to Aiden and places her little hand on a necklace that rests on top of his shirt.

"Is this your daddy?" Ella asks, holding the charm in her fingers.

"No, this is St. Michael. My daddy gave me this when I was a baby. St. Michael is the saint that gives me strength and courage. I needed that after he went to heaven." Both Ella and Hunter are nodding their heads at Aiden. Hunter takes a step closer to Aiden.

"What do you do for Father's Day?" Hunter questions. "I have a party at school, but I don't have a daddy. My teacher said I could bring a grandpa." *Shit*, I yell in my head. I totally forgot about Father's Day coming up.

"Honey, we can figure it out. I bet Grandpa would love to go with you, or even Uncle Kevin." I try to give Aiden an out on this question.

"Hunter, my grandpa used to come to school with me on Father's Day, and my uncle came with me to other things as well. If someone asks you why your daddy isn't there, you can tell them he is an angel in heaven, and they work a lot." He winks at Hunter, and I can see Hunter starting to relax a bit.

"Thanks," he says. He gives Aiden a high five before Ella walks over to get her high five. They start to run all over the front lawn.

"I better be going."

"Thank you, Aiden, for everything." I touch his arm, and he can tell I'm too nervous to want anything else as a good-bye in front of my family.

"I'll talk to you later," he says, then walks over to the SUV.

I head into the house, and the kids follow. Richard is by the front door. I'm greeted with a big hug from him; I can feel a little of Chase inside him.

"I didn't want to walk out. I thought it would be better if they didn't know about our relation." He seems a little uneasy.

"I doubt they would even care, Richard." I remember that Grant knows the secret.

"So tell me all about it. How was it?" I ponder the question for a moment and quickly relive the weekend in my head. I keep the private moments to myself, but tell him all about the house and the family dynamic. We discuss the hospital visit, and he tells me it wasn't my fault. It feels good to be home. Richard and Mary don't stay long, and I'm thankful for that, because I want time alone with the kids. We head outside to play on the trampoline, and they fill me in on everything.

"Uncle Kevin spent the day with us on Saturday," Hunter tells me as he jumps.

"He took us to the movies to see *Brave*," Ella screams as Hunter bounces close to her.

"Vanessa came with us, and we got popcorn, soda, and candy." They don't tell me any more about the movies, but I'm happy to hear Vanessa is back in the picture. I take my phone out and order us a pizza. We bounce a little longer, then head inside to wait for the pizza. Hunter and Ella stay at the door waiting. They love it when we get pizza delivered. I let them pay and take the pizza into the kitchen. As we start eating, I notice Hunter is getting uneasy.

"What's wrong, Hunter?"

"Nothing, I was just thinking about that man who was here. I don't know anyone who doesn't have a daddy, except me and him."

My heart starts to ache like it used to.

"Can we get a necklace like him?" Ella asks.

"If that's what you want, I can go and look for one tomorrow."

"I think I need one. He said it was for strength and courage. What's courage mean?" Hunter asks as he puts his pizza down, and they both look at me. Oh shit…I have to think fast.

"Remember the movie *The Wizard of Oz*?" They nod. "The cowardly lion was looking for courage. Remember how he was scared of everything? Well, courage helps you face things when you are scared of them."

"Is it like being brave?" Ella asks.

"Yes, it is." I see that they get it. They are both filled with courage and strength. They've been through so much this last year, and have experienced so much sadness and hurt. Life is so unfair sometimes. I look into my children's eyes and see life coming back every day; they are going to make it through. I just hope Chase will remain in their hearts. I feel the weight on my chest again.

We finish dinner on a lighter note and make our way upstairs for bath time. I go through the evening routines, all the while thinking about Chase and the kids, adjusting back to my world after leaving it for a few days. The night goes by fast, and I find myself on the couch after I put the kids to bed. I sit and stare at nothing. I feel tears on my cheeks. My heart begins to break all over again, and for the first time I'm not sure if it's over Chase, the kids, or because of the little piece of my heart that I left in the Cape. I see it's only ten o'clock. I walk into the kitchen and open the cabinet where my sleeping pills are kept. I take two to ensure I don't dream tonight. I shower and by the time I get out, I feel drowsy and ready to succumb to sleep.

CHAPTER TWENTY-ONE

When I wake the next morning, I see the sun shining in through my window. I still feel relaxed and want to remain sleeping. I look over at the clock and fly up like a rocket. The kids need to be at school in twenty minutes. I run to their rooms, get them up, and throw clothes at them. I quickly get dressed, then check on them again. They dress quickly, and we run downstairs for breakfast. I grab granola bars and move them into the bathroom to brush their teeth. I fight with Ella about eating in the car on the way to school. I explain we don't have time today to sit and eat. She is in a mood, and I ignore it. Truthfully, I'm still very relaxed from the sleeping pills and really don't care.

I finally get them out the door and to school with no time to spare. Ella didn't eat breakfast to spite me, and I tell her she has to starve until lunchtime. As I watch them walk in, I take out my cell to e-mail Ella's teacher to make her aware of the mood and lack of breakfast. After I press Send, I see I have a text.

"Aiden" reads across the top of the screen. How the hell did he get my phone and put his number in it?

I look at the text.

Tuesday and Thursday I have lunch open at twelve. Let me know beautiful.

My stomach flips and I feel excited. He checked his schedule and fit me in this week. Then reality hits me and I tell myself, *no more.*

I hear out the angel and devil sitting on my shoulders. I agree with both, but go with the devil. She knows what she is talking about, so I text him back.

Hello, stalker. Where do you want to meet?

I press Send and start driving home. I feel my phone vibrate in less than a minute.

How am I a stalker? Can you come to me? ☺

I look at the smiley face and laugh. I wait until I get in the driveway before I text him back.

You took my phone and put in your number...that is stalkerish to me! I can come to you as long as I leave by 1.

I send the message and head into the house. By the time I open my door, I feel my phone vibrate.

I wanted to make sure I could see you again. I thought that was smart, not stalkerish, if that is even a word. I will take any amount of time you can give me.

I sit at the kitchen table and giggle to myself. I feel like a teenager again, thinking about what I should say back to him. I want to keep it cool and easy.

Send me the details of what you have in mind.

I press Send. I pace, waiting to hear the vibration of my phone, but give up after five minutes. I start to clean to help with my anxiety and hear it vibrate after I fill the dishwasher.

I'll have my driver pick you up at 10:30 tomorrow. Then he will pick me up and take us to my favorite spot. Thursday I'll have you picked up again, but we will have to eat at my office. I look forward to seeing you tomorrow.

I get the chills reading it. I'm getting more excited for tomorrow. I start to text him back, but decide I should make him wait a bit. I put my phone down and finish cleaning. The next few hours pass right on by as I daydream about tomorrow. Before I pick the kids up, I grab my phone and see a text from Aiden again.

You're making me wait...I don't like waiting...

I laugh out loud and text him back.

Mr. Grace, I am a busy woman. I like the plans for tomorrow. Look forward to seeing you.

I press Send, and then head out the door to get the kids. When they get in the car, they tell me they want to play with the boy that lives next door to us. I agree to it. As I pull in the driveway, I see a package at the door. We hop out and I see Tyler from next door running over. I motion to the backyard, and they all go running. I pick up the package and head into the house. As I pull open the top, I realize it's from Annie. I pull the folder out and open it as I make my way through the house and out to the patio. I sit at the table and start to read.

Hannah,
I hope you and your friend can make it. Please let me know this week either way. I really hope to see you there!
Annie

I lean back in my seat and start to look through the package she sent me. Mending Broken Hearts is the name of the charity Mrs. Grace created. I wonder what it's about, so I open up the pamphlet and start to read. I feel the tears prick my eyes as I read about Victoria Grace's trials and tribulations as a widow. She started the charity two years after losing the love of her life, Grant Grace. I read on to see that this charity was her way of moving on and helping women just like her to move on as well. The last page of the pamphlet features pictures of Tori with different women. These must be pictures of women she has helped.

I put everything back in the package and think about calling Becca to see what her event is Friday night. I look at my watch; with the time change, she is probably busy. I will call after I get the kids to bed. I watch the kids play for a couple hours, then send Tyler home for dinner. When we go inside, I see Kevin pull in the driveway. The kids go running to the front door, and I watch him hug them. He is, in theory, my second husband, and I think the kids consider him the closest thing to a father. When he sets them down, he walks over to me and hugs me.

"Hey, you," he whispers in my ear.

"Hey," I whisper back. He pulls away and looks at me.

"The Cape seems to agree with you. You look great, Hannah." I turn away to hide my red cheeks. *If only he knew how well the Cape agreed with m*e, I think.

"Oh, stop," I say as I walk away from them and into the kitchen.

"What's for dinner?" he asks as he follows me.

"Whatever you want. You want to go out or order in?" I ask him.

"Let's go out." He turns toward the kids and lets them choose. I grab my bag and we head out. Kevin takes my keys after I lock the front door and drives to the restaurant. As we walk in, I wonder if people think we are a family. From the looks of it, we appear to be a husband and wife out to dinner with our kids. I yearn for the normalcy we used to have when Chase was alive. I realize this is normal now for the kids and me. We have Kevin, and he fills the void left by Chase's death. We sit down at the table and have a normal family dinner. The kids dominate the conversation, and Kevin and I laugh when they say something funny. When the check comes, Kevin grabs it. He ignores me and slips his card in, then hands it back to the waitress. He is such a pain in the ass sometimes.

On the way home, Hunter brings up the Father's Day event at his school.

"That sounds like fun, Hunter. Can I come with you?" Kevin asks him. I feel my stomach flip as I wait for Hunter's answer.

"All right, Uncle Kevin," is all he says. I feel sad over this, but what should I expect? This is our first Father's Day without Chase. I have no reference to compare it to.

Kevin stays to help give the kids their baths and tuck them into bed. I hear Kevin and Hunter talking about the Father's Day party when I'm tucking Ella in. Her teacher doesn't do Mother's Day or Father's Day parties, and I am thankful for that. I kiss and hug her tight before closing her door. I stand in the hallway listening to

Kevin talk to Hunter. I try not to cry when I hear Kevin tell Hunter he loves him like a son, and he is so happy to be going with him. When I walk in the room, they both get quiet, like it's some kind of secret they were talking about. Kevin rubs the top of Hunter's head, then walks out of the room. I sit on Hunter's bed and start tucking him in.

"Mommy."

"Yes, baby?"

"Are you going to marry Uncle Kevin?"

I feel like I'm going to fall off the bed.

"Why do you say that?"

"Well, he is like a daddy, and he is always here, so I thought you might make him our daddy."

I bet his words would make Kevin smile, but it will never happen.

"No, honey, I'm not going to marry Uncle Kevin. He was daddy's best friend. I bet Daddy is happy to see him doing all these nice things with us. Uncle Kevin has Vanessa, and I think they will start a family of their own one day."

"Will we ever have a daddy again?" These words stab at my heart, and I feel tears coming to my eyes.

"I don't know, honey."

"Aiden said he didn't have a daddy. Maybe he could be my daddy?" This puts a smile on my face.

"Go to sleep, Hunter. We can talk about this another time." I kiss his forehead, and then leave his room.

Aiden as his father? That would be interesting. I think about our lunch date tomorrow and start to smile. I shake out of it when Kevin asks me what I'm smiling about.

"Nothing," I say, but it makes me smile more.

"Hunter was talking about a man named Aiden and a necklace?" He leans against the countertop as I sit at the table.

"Yes, my patient's son drove me home yesterday, and the kids met him. He lost his father when he was young, so he kind of related to the kids." I start to stretch as I speak. "Ella noticed his necklace. It was a St. Michael charm, and he was telling the kids about it. They asked for one."

"What's his name?"

"Aiden Grace."

He looks at me wide-eyed.

"*The* Aiden Grace, as in Grace Industries?"

"I think so. He has three other brothers who run the company too."

"Yes, Grant, John, and Shane. Holy shit, Hannah. Is that who you were taking care of this weekend?"

I simply nod to him as I eat a piece of chocolate.

"They bought one of our buildings last year, and they are looking into buying another. I have a meeting with Shane on Wednesday." I want to laugh. I bet if I told them I owned half the company, they would be more likely to buy it.

"If you need help with anything…" I shrug my shoulders and stuff another piece of chocolate in my mouth.

"Hannah, that would be great! If Shane is down, then I get a meeting with Grant. I heard he is a real asshole, but I guess that's how he made his billions." I look at Kevin. Billions?

"Grant is the difficult one, but you're great at what you do. There is no reason you should be worried." I can see why he would dread meeting with Grant. He does come off as an intimidating asshole, but when he lets you in, he is a totally different person.

"Thanks, Hannah." He gets up and kisses my check. "I have to go. I told Vanessa I would be home soon."

"I'm happy you're working it out with her."

"Me too." I watch him leave and feel happy. I call Becca and she picks up on the second ring.

"Hey, mama, what's up?" I hear her shuffling through papers.

"Oh, nothing. I was just calling you to see what the plans are for this week."

"I fly in Thursday, but I have a meeting, so I won't come over till four or five. Then Friday I have dresses coming for us to try on. Then we will leave your house by six thirty, because it starts at eight." I hear typing now. She is always multitasking.

"What is this dinner?"

"Something about hearts. I thought you would be interested in it. An associate of mine invited me as a bribe, I think."

"Is it called Mending Hearts?"

"I think so. How do you know?" I smile and come up with a plan.

"Becca, it's a charity dinner for widows. Of course I know about it." I enjoy the lie a bit.

"Oh shit, Hannah, I'm sorry. I thought it was about hearts, and surgery. You don't have to come if you don't want to."

"No, Bec, I told you I would. Don't worry about it."

"Thanks, Han. I have to run but will call you tomorrow. Love you." Before I respond, she hangs up. I smile as I think about what I am going to do. I grab the package I got and find Annie's e-mail address.

Annie,
I would love to attend the charity dinner. It just so happens that my best friend had already been invited. I look forward to seeing you Friday.
Hannah

I press Send. I wonder if I should tell Aiden I will be attending, or should I leave it a surprise? I decide on surprise and head to the cabinet for my magical sleeping pills. I take one and a half this time, hoping I don't oversleep again tomorrow. I need to sleep and not think about anything tonight. I set my cell phone alarm and the alarm on the clock next to my bed. *This should do it*, I think to myself. Then I crawl into bed and turn on the TV. I watch a little, then feel myself let go, and drift off.

CHAPTER TWENTY-TWO

The next morning I wake up to the sounds of a rooster and music. I roll over and turn off both alarms. I look at my phone and see a text from Aiden. I sit straight up and read it.

I can't wait to see you today.

It says it was sent at five thirty this morning. This makes me think of what Addy said about them being early risers. I sit for a few minutes to daydream about Aiden before I get into the shower and then head into my closet. *Shit,* I really need to go shopping. I make a mental note to make an appointment for a haircut as well. Then I will go shopping for something really cute to wear on our rendezvous on Thursday. I settle on a cute aqua-colored maxi dress before I straighten my hair. I look at the clock and decide to do my makeup after I drop off the kids.

Ella isn't as cranky this morning, and Hunter is happy as a clam as they eat breakfast. I decide I should talk to them about Friday night.

"How would you guys like to sleep over at Grandma and Pop's house Friday night?"

I try to read their expressions.

"Are you going away again?" Ella asks.

"No, lovey, Aunt Becca is coming here this weekend and asked if I could go to a big charity ball with her. I can't take you guys with me, so Grandma said you could sleep over at her house."

"Are you going to get dressed up like a princess?" Ella asks with big eyes.

"Yes, Aunt Becca and I have to wear big, fancy dresses," I say, watching the excitement come over her face.

"Can I stay and watch you leave?" Hunter asks me.

"Of course, Grandma and Pop can come over here, and you guys can watch us get our hair and makeup done."

"OK," they both say. Why do I always expect the worst?

"OK, let's get going, or we are going to be late." With that they both jump up and head into the bathroom. We are out the door and in the car less than five minutes later. I kiss them good-bye and watch them run into the school. I rush home to finish getting ready for my big lunch with Aiden.

Later I stand in front of my full-length mirror judging myself. The dress seems all wrong, so I change into another dress with thinner straps. I stand in front of the mirror again and settle on the cute, shorter floral dress. I walk downstairs and wait for the driver to pick me up. I should have just driven in myself. I'll talk to Aiden about that over lunch today. I wonder if we will eat lunch. I get the mail and flip through it, then spot the car out of the corner of my eye. I take a deep breath and grab my clutch. I answer the door and see it's Sam.

"Mrs. Redman," he says.

"Sam, please call me Hannah." I follow him, and he opens the door to the Range Rover. I enjoy the ride to the city. I hear Sam talking on his earpiece.

"Hannah, we made good timing. Mr. Grace will not be ready yet, so he said I should bring you to his jeweler. He wants you to pick up something he ordered." I nod at Sam, confused. What the hell did he get me? I don't know him well enough for him to be buying me jewelry. I look out the window as we drive down Fifth Avenue. I love the hustle of the city. Sam pulls in front of Tiffany's, and my heart drops. I feel shaky as I ease myself out of the car. I need to pull it together. Sam rushes in front of me to open the door to Tiffany's. As I walk in, my eyes wander in every direction. I walk around, looking in the cases, until someone comes up to me.

"Can I help you?" a woman asks. She is older than me and looks refined.

"Yes. I am here to pick up a package for Aiden Grace." She looks at me, almost impressed.

"You must be Hannah." I just nod at her.

"Please follow me, Hannah." I follow her toward the back of the store, where she stops near a diamond case. I start to get nervous.

"Mr. Grace is an important client of ours. We were happy to work with him." She takes out two boxes. She starts to open them, but they are facing her. My heart starts to beat faster. What the hell is he up to? Then she turns them around and I look at them. I feel the tears come to my eyes.

One box has a St. Michael charm in yellow gold, and the other in white gold. He thought of them. I wasn't coming here for me; I was coming here for them. I feel the smile reach my lips.

"Do you like them?" she asks me.

"Yes, very much. They are beautiful." She wraps them back up, and I watch her place them in a Tiffany's bag. I take the bag from her and thank her again. As I walk out, I see Sam is still parked out front. I walk over to the car and get back in.

"I'm so sorry, Mrs. Redman, I didn't see you come out." He has a bit of fear on his face.

I laugh. "No worries, Sam. I know how to open a door." He looks a bit relieved and starts to drive again. It's only a few short blocks before we stop again. We are still on Fifth Avenue. I look out the window and see a sign for Grace Industries. We must be at Aiden's office.

"Mr. Grace is on his way down." He gets out and stands next to the car, waiting for Aiden.

I spot Aiden when he walks out. He looks like a dream. He is wearing a three piece suit that is black with thin, white pinstripes. I see a few women slow down to look at him, and it makes me smile. As he gets closer, I see him getting off his cell and place it in the inside pocket of his jacket. He stops and speaks with Sam for a moment.

Sam nods, then opens the door for Aiden. I watch him get into the car. Everything this man does is with ease and grace. He sits and looks over at me.

"Hey," he says, then he leans in and kisses me. I feel his lips against mine and I start to purr. His hand wanders on my leg, but stops just above my knee. I feel a little disappointed.

"Hello," I finally manage to say back to Aiden.

"Did you like the trip to Tiffany's?"

"I was quite surprised, to say the least. Thank you so much. The kids are going to love them." I lean forward and kiss him lightly, then pull away.

"Where are we going for lunch?"

"My apartment." He places his hand in mine and leans back into the seat. I look out the window and wonder where he lives when he is in the city.

It's no surprise that we drive for only a few short minutes before we stop again. Aiden steps out and takes my hand to help me out. The doorman opens the door and tips his hat to Aiden.

"Mr. Grace." Aiden gives him a nod and continues into the building. The lobby is like a museum, with a huge statue in the center and pictures lining the walls. The security desk looks out of place to the left. I follow Aiden to the elevators, and they open immediately. Aiden motions me in first, not letting go of my hand, then steps in and swipes a card. He turns around and directs his attention on me. I take a step back and feel the wall. Aiden presses against me and kisses me hard. I place my hands on his belt line. I feel the elevator start to slow down, and Aiden pulls away.

"I have lunch ready if you are hungry." I grin at him. I'm hungry but not for lunch.

"I know that look," he whispers to me as the doors open.

"Do you?"

"Yes, it's your 'fuck me' face. Let's work up an appetite." He drags me down the hallway and into his apartment. It is masculine and much larger than I thought it would be. It has an amazing view. I walk over to the floor-to-ceiling windows and look around. I can feel him standing behind me, taking off his jacket. I turn around as he throws it on the couch. He picks me up and presses me against the window. I wrap myself around him, kissing him hard. Slowly he takes me away from the window and leads me to the couch. He drops me and I bounce on the couch, then he jumps on top of me. I can't help but laugh as he starts to take off his dress shirt. I work on his pants. Once he is unbuckled and unzipped, I push him to stand up. I slide his briefs and pants down his long legs, releasing my favorite part of him. He takes off his shirt, and then his undershirt. He slides my arms up over my head and takes my dress off. I lie back and he stands looking at me.

"I like this," he says as he brushes his hands over my sexy, matching lace set. "But not that much." He pulls the panties down, and then unhooks my bra with ease. I lie there, baring myself, and he starts to kiss me. He works his way down my neck and kisses over my collarbone to each shoulder, where he gives a little bite. I spread my legs so I can feel him against me. He starts to kiss my neck again, then makes his way down between my breasts. His hands take each breast, and his fingers start to play with my nipples. I let out a breath as he goes lower.

"I missed you," he mumbles between kisses and nips. I don't say anything, because I am on cloud nine as his tongue finds my sweet spot. I just moan as I grab his hair in my hands.

"Slow down," I murmur in my euphoric state. He slides on a condom. Then in one swift motion, he plunges his hardness into me. I groan as he pushes it all into me in the first pound. He quickens his pace, slamming into me over and over. I let out moans and yells as I come. He takes my legs and places them on his shoulders and takes me faster. I can feel him deeper inside of me, and it hurts so good. He slaps my ass and calls me a fucking whore, but I'm starting to come again, so I could care less what he calls me or how many times he spanks me. Once I come, I can tell he is about to come too. He gets faster, gripping my thighs closer to him, before I feel him collapse on top of me.

"Fuck," is all he can say when he is done. I lie there under him for a few minutes before he gets up. "Bathroom is down the hall, second door on the right." *So romantic*, I think as I get up.

I grab my clothes before going into the bathroom. Once safely inside I lock the door behind me. I look in the mirror at my backside and see a few handprints. I clean up and get dressed. My cheeks are red and my hair is wild. I splash some cold water on my face to cool down, and then put some lip gloss on and go back into the living room.

"Are you still hungry?" he calls from the kitchen.

"Sure, what's for lunch?" I sit at the breakfast bar as he serves me sushi.

"You like?" He looks at me.

"It's my favorite." We sit side by side and eat our lunch. Aiden's phone rings a few times, and he looks at it each time, but doesn't answer it. I look at my watch and see it's ten to one.

"I think we should get going," I say, turning to him.

"Yeah, we should. I have a meeting at one thirty that I need to do some work on." I get up with my plate to clean it off, but he grabs it and places it back on the breakfast bar.

"I have people to do that," he says as walks over to his jacket. He puts it on and watches me pick up my clutch.

"Ready?" I nod and follow him down to the elevators.

"Was your maid home just now?" I ask.

"Yes."

I feel embarrassed thinking about it. I hope she didn't see anything, or hear anything, for that matter. He takes my hand and I let him.

"How does your ass feel?" he asks as his hand begins to rub it.

"It's still stinging." I half smile. "So you think I'm a whore?" He smiles at me.

"Yes, you're my fucking whore, and I will do as I please with you." He looks at me with darkness in his eyes. I feel dirty all of a sudden and look away to break eye contact. As we get out of the elevator, I let go of his hand and open my clutch as a distraction. The doorman opens the door, and Sam is waiting for us at the SUV. When he opens the door, I get right in and move over. I need distance from Aiden.

"Did I say something wrong?" Aiden says after he slides in.

"Do you feel like you said something wrong?"

"Nope." He sits back and places his hand on my leg. I feel anger brewing inside. I sit and hope we can get to his building fast. I start to think of things to say to him, but speak none of them. He is calling me exactly what I have been acting like, a whore. The words hurt more than I thought they would. I want to give back the necklaces. I don't want the kids wearing them. We stop in front of his building, and he kisses me before he gets out. I give him my cheek. Am I overreacting? No, I was getting attached to him. I have to rip him off like I would a Band-Aid.

"Hannah, don't be like this."

"Like what?" I snap at him.

"Pissy towards me because of something I said."

"No, the heat of the moment is one thing. It was after, when I asked you how you felt about saying it and you repeated it proudly." I watch as he grows frustrated. Sam is out of the car now, and Aiden rolls down the window and tells him to wait. I watch as the window goes back up and Aiden turns toward me.

"If you didn't want to know the answer, you shouldn't have asked the question. I don't do the whole dating thing." I cut him off.

"Aiden, we aren't dating. I'm just a whore you fucked a few times." I give him a hateful glare.

"Don't be like this."

"You're going to be late to work, Aiden. I have to get back home to pick my kids up." I look away from him. He touches my hands but I pull away.

"Hannah, look at me." I can hear the urgency in his voice, but I keep looking out the window. I hear him take a deep breath. "Hannah, I said look at me." His voice is getting louder, and I don't care.

"I said fucking look at me," he screams in my ear, and then he kicks the seat in front of him. "Now you're acting like a fucking whore.

I know you fucked my brother. How do you think that makes me feel? I'm fucking the same woman as him *again*." I hear the emphasis on *again*.

Fuck. Why does he think I fucked Grant? I fooled around with him, but never... I finally look over at Aiden.

"I never fucked your brother. Get your facts straight." My voice is unraveling, and I hope he leaves. Why did he say *again*?

"Don't lie to me, Hannah." His eyes look like the sky right before a storm.

"I'm not," I snap back. "I never slept with Grant."

When he finally gets out, I let out a deep, shaky breath. Never in my life have I felt so ashamed of myself. I just want to go home and shower to get him off me. The whole car ride home, I fight with myself. The angel wins and the devil walks away with her tail between her legs.

When Sam pulls in front of my house, I hop out and head straight into the house. I run upstairs and get right into the shower. I feel the tears running down my face before the water hits my face. I stand under the hot water, scrubbing my body to get his scent off of me. I never thought a man could make me feel this way. Chase would have never said anything like that to me. The heat of the moment is one thing, but when I asked him if he thought he said anything wrong, he said no. Why did he think I slept with Grant?

My skin hurts as I get out of the shower. I quickly get dressed and leave to get the kids. *I need to clear my mind*, I think as I step outside, but I stop when I see the Range Rover still parked out front. I head to my truck and Sam steps out.

"Hannah, you forgot your Tiffany's bag." He walks toward me, but I put my hands up.

"No, Sam, I didn't. Could you please let Aiden know I don't need them?" I turn to get in my truck. Sam looks uncomfortable.

"Please, Hannah, take it. Mr. Grace is going to be angry if you don't."

"Aiden can go fuck himself and you can tell him I said that." I slam my door and roll down the driveway. I speed away to the kids' school. On the way there, I decide to go to my parents' house after I pick them up. I don't need to go home, and find Sam still there.

CHAPTER TWENTY-THREE

I get out of the truck when I get to the school and wait for the kids. I fidget with my phone and decide to make a hair appointment for tomorrow. When I get off, I feel a bit better. I made an appointment for a haircut, massage, manicure, and pedicure. I will spend the day relaxing. When I see the kids walking out, I start to walk toward them. I feel my phone vibrate and see a text from Aiden.

The gift was for the kids. Take it.

I delete it and bend down to hug the kids.

"Do you guys want to go over to Grandma and Pop's house?" I ask.

"Yes," they both yell. We drive straight to my parents' house. I don't bother calling because I know they are home and they will be happy to see us. My dad is mowing the lawn when I pull up. He stops the lawnmower and walks over to the truck.

"Hey, guys," he says when he opens the back door. The kids jump right into his arms. I walk around the truck, and he puts the kids down and hugs me.

"Hey, Han, you OK?" I hug him back and nod yes, but I try my hardest to hold the tears back. I pull away and head into the house. When I walk in, I feel the calm come over me, and I settle on a stool at the kitchen island.

"Hello," I yell as I sit down. I lean back and look out the front door at the kids. They are running around the front lawn as my dad finishes mowing. I don't hear my mom.

"Marco," I yell.

"Polo," I hear as my mom comes upstairs with a basket of laundry on her hip.

"Hey, sweetheart, what are you doing here?" She is studying me right away, and I don't blame her. I've come over here many times unannounced, just to hide from the kids and cry.

"I'm fine, Mom. I just wanted to come by with the kids to hang out and have some dinner. We didn't see you this weekend. I missed you guys." I get off the stool and hug her.

"What's on your mind, Hannah? I know something is going on." She knows me way too well.

"Nothing, Mom, really. Well, there is one thing." I stop and she looks over at me while she starts to fold towels. I grab a towel and start to fold it, contemplating what I'm about to say.

"Would you and Dad mind watching the kids Friday night? Becca is flying in Thursday, and she wants me to go to a charity dinner with her Friday night." I see the smile beam across her face.

"We would love to." I feel good that the kids will be with her, but I want to throw up at the thought of having to face Aiden again. I can't go back on my word now because I already told Annie and Becca I was going.

"What are you going to wear?" she asks me as we fold the towels.

"I have no idea. Becca is having dresses delivered for us to try on. I told the kids they could stay home and watch us get ready. I hope you don't mind."

"No, not at all. It will be like prom all over again." I can tell she is excited. I hear the kids running around in the backyard, and I turn to look out of the back sliding-glass doors. They are running from my dad, who is chasing them all around the backyard.

"Maybe you will meet someone at the charity event." Mom looks at me with hopeful eyes, but as usual I shoot her down.

"Not likely, Mom," I say, and she knows not to keep pushing. I go around the island into the kitchen and look for something to make for dinner. I find chicken defrosting in the sink.

"What do you want to make for dinner?"

"Whatever you feel like. I can make chicken cutlets or whatever," I hear her say as she walks into the bathroom and puts the towels away.

"I'll make dinner tonight. Do you want gyros?" I know she loves them.

"I don't have everything you need."

"I'll run to the store now and get everything." I wait patiently as my mom writes out a list of the missing items I need to purchase.

"That should do it." She hands me money with the list, but I leave the money on the counter. She always does this, and I always ignore her, but I bet one of the kids will come home with it in their pockets.

"I'll be right back." I head to my truck and see my phone is lit up from a new message. It's another message from Aiden.

Don't ignore me. It pisses me off, and you don't want to piss me off.

I delete it. He can go fuck himself.

In the grocery store, I grab a small basket and make my way through the store. I grab all the odds and ends I need for dinner and decide to pick up ice cream for dessert. I pay and head back to my parents. When I see another text, I start to ignore it, until I see Becca's name.

Change of plans. Dresses are being sent to your house tomorrow at 4.

Maybe getting dressed up will make me feel better. I will get all dressed up and look sexy, and he will be begging for me, and I will ignore him. I will get back at him.

When I get back to my parents, I start cooking. I always feel more relaxed when I am cooking, especially in my mom's kitchen. I hear them all out on the deck laughing and teasing one another, and it puts a smile on my face. I make the tzatziki sauce and pour some over the chicken. I start to cut up onions, tomatoes, and lettuce. I place each in its own bowl, then place the chicken in the fridge for a few more minutes. I walk onto the deck and see them all having fun. I sit down in one of the wooden Adirondack chairs next to my mom.

"How's dinner going?" my dad asks.

"Good. Everything is all prepped. I'm just waiting on the chicken to marinate a bit longer." I smile and enjoy the easy conversation. The kids start to tell my parents about what they did at recess, and I take the opportunity to slip back into the house and finish cooking dinner.

The night goes by so fast. After dinner we have ice cream, and it's after seven before I realize it. We all say our good-byes and head back home. When I pull in the driveway, I see the Tiffany's bag between my storm door and front door. I want to kill Aiden, and I want to kill Sam even more for leaving it there. I get out of the car faster than the kids and grab it before they can ask me about it. I shove it in the coat closet. *Asshole*, I think to myself. I begin to busy myself with the nightly routine of bath time and bedtime.

I take my sleeping pill right after I tuck the kids in. *I can't keep taking them*, I tell myself, but it doesn't stop me from popping one and a half pills into my mouth. I swallow them down with a glass of water and head right to bed. I turn the TV on to drown my thoughts. I feel the sensation of sleep creeping over me and give into it.

The next morning I again wake up to a rooster and music. I roll over and turn them both off. I notice a new text from Aiden, and it makes me want to throw my phone.

I will come to your house if you don't respond back to me.

I roll my eyes at the phone. I know I will need to deal with him eventually.

What do you want?

That should do it. I put on the Weather Channel and I feel my phone vibrate.

You.

He is such an asshole. I start texting him back.

Well, that's not going to happen, so get over it and move on. Forget my name and delete my number.

I feel better after I write this, but begin to wonder how I got here. How did I get caught up between two brothers? I vow to never see either of them ever again, then realize I still have to see them on Friday. Shit… I get up, shower, and start my day. I head down early and make the kids a big breakfast. When they come down and see it, they get all excited, like it's their birthday. I feel good today; I'm going to have a great day at the spa. The morning flies by, and I drop the kids off at school. Instead of going home, I stop and grab a cappuccino then head down near the water to clear my mind. I wander around the marina and look at the boats. I reach the end of the dock and stand there, looking out over the water. The view is beautiful, and it makes me miss the view of Vineyard Sound. I begin to think about Grant. I definitely was stupid for fooling around with Aiden, but Grant was different. I miss him. I miss the day we had together. The easy conversations and the easy silence we had. I dull ache starts to spread in my heart. I stretch to see if it goes away and it doesn't so I head back to the truck.

CHAPTER TWENTY-FOUR

I drive to the spa to start my relaxing day. I check my phone, and I am happy to see Aiden hasn't texted me back. As soon as I walk in the spa, the relaxing aromas start to calm me. I'm escorted to a room where I can store my things and get undressed and slip into a lush robe. I enter the room where my massage is; the next few hours are tranquil. I walk out feeling like a million bucks. My nails and toes match, with a French manicure, and my hair looks healthy again. I love the way they blow out my hair. It's shiny and feels silky. If only I could make it look this good on my own.

I do a good job of distracting myself in the hours between the spa and picking up the kids; I go to the mall and go on a mini-shopping spree. I think for a moment that I might be having a mental break-down, but I push it out of my head each time I swipe my card. I go home to drop off all my bags, and when I pull in the driveway, I see flowers lining my walkway. *What the fuck is he up to now?* I get my bags out of the truck and walk past all the flowers. I put the bags in my room and go back outside to survey the flowers. I jump as my phone starts to vibrate; I look at the number and don't recognize it.

"Hello."

"Hannah Winterfield."

"Yes." I start to pace the walkway.

"Is this Hannah Redman Winterfield?"

"Yes, it is."

"Hannah, it's Shane Grace." I hear him start laughing a bit, and I realize I do know the voice.

"Shane, is everything OK with your mom?" I start to panic.

"Mom is doing fine. I was calling because I just met with Kevin Waters, and he name-dropped your name. I was confused at first when he used the name Winterfield, but then he let me know Redman is your maiden name."

"Yes, it is. I use it at work, and I'm sure you already figured out why." Shit, I should have been more honest with them.

"Yes, because of the director. Kevin gave me all the gossip about you." He is laughing now.

"I hope it wasn't all bad." I cringe.

"Oh no, Hannah, I didn't mean it like that. I was just surprised that our paths are crossing. I am interested in one of the buildings you have. I spoke with Kevin, and I need you to come in to sign off on all the paperwork tomorrow, if that's possible."

"Yes, of course. Anything that Kevin needs me to do, I will."

"Hannah, I'm sorry to hear about your husband. I had no idea. I know this has to be hard for you, coming in to sign as his power of attorney."

I stare down at the flowers and feel the hurt in my heart.

"Thank you, Shane. It hasn't been easy, but I own half of the company, so I pretty much do what Kevin needs me to do."

"Great. What time works for you tomorrow? I know you have the kids, so if we need to meet on your schedule, I have no problem moving meetings around."

Shane is such a nice guy. I wish Aiden were more like him.

"Does eleven thirty work?"

"Perfect. I can make that happen. Annie tells me you are going to come on Friday."

"Yes, it happens that a friend of mine was invited last week, and I will be her plus one. Small world, isn't it, Shane?" I smile thinking about it.

"Yes, it is. OK, well, if you have any questions, call this number I just called you from, it's my line at the office. I look forward to seeing you tomorrow."

"Me too. Bye, Shane."

"Bye, Hannah."

I hang up and wonder when Kevin will call me about this. Just then I see his number on my phone.

"Hey, Kevin, I heard we have a meeting at eleven thirty tomorrow?"

"How the hell did you know so quickly? I just got out of there."

"The Grace men work quickly." I laugh as I say this.

"It's at eleven thirty?"

"Yes. I just talked to Shane, and he wanted to make sure I was able to juggle the kids and the meeting."

"Well, that was nice of him, and I'm sorry. I had no idea they didn't know about Chase or the director. I spilled the beans on that one."

"No, it's OK. Mrs. Grace knew, and I believe Grant knows. I didn't really want to make it known to them, but it's no big deal now." I pick up one of the vases, bring it around to the garbage can, and slam it down.

"What the hell was that?" Kevin asks.

"I was just taking out the garbage." I grab the trashcan, drag it over to the walkway, and throw away all the flowers.

"Kevin, I have to get the kids. I will see you tomorrow at their office."

"I'll pick you up."

"No, don't worry. After the meeting I have to leave to pick up the kids. What happens if you get caught up or have to stay?"

"All right, I will see you tomorrow. Bye."

"Bye." I hang up the phone, slip it into my pocket, and throw away the last vase of flowers. Twelve in total, and they filled up the can. I place it back behind my fence and give it the finger as if it were Aiden.

The rest of the day goes by at warp speed after I get the kids, and before I know it, the house is quiet and I find myself taking the sleeping pills again. I feel like a junkie, but it doesn't stop me. I need to sleep and not think of Chase, Aiden, or my meeting tomorrow. I pray when I get into bed that I won't see Aiden, and that it will go smoothly tomorrow. I hope someone hears me. I just hope Chase doesn't, because he would be disappointed in how I have been acting these last few days. I let go and fall asleep, thanks to the sleeping pills.

CHAPTER TWENTY-FIVE

The next morning I wake up before the alarm goes off. The house is quiet. I run through my routine feeling relaxed. When I look in the bathroom mirror after I turn the shower on, I notice my hair still looks kick-ass, so I tie it back and get in. I think about all the new clothes I bought yesterday, and I know exactly what I will be wearing. I got a new, black, pencil skirt that flares out at my knees and a new green blouse. I want to look my best in case I bump in to Aiden, and the green will defiantly bring out my eyes. I grab the new heels I got and do my makeup. I study my face. The dark circles aren't as bad as usual, and I guess it's from the sleeping pills. They are making me better. *I should keep taking them*, I tell myself, even though *junkie* pops into my head when I think this. I apply my usual makeup and wake up the kids.

While we are eating breakfast, Ella stares at me.

"Mommy, why do you look so pretty today?" Her question makes me smile.

"I have a meeting with Uncle Kevin today for Daddy's company."

She just smiles at me and finishes her breakfast. We get out the door in record time. I drop them off, then head back to the house to get out all of the paperwork. I go into the safe and pull out the envelope that I haven't looked inside of since the last time I had to sign for Chase a few months ago. It holds his death certificate and the paperwork for me as the power of attorney. I flip through it all and head into the kitchen, where I hear the phone ringing.

"Hello," I say as I lean it against my shoulder.

"Han, what's up? Did the dresses come yesterday?"

"Bec, what are you doing up already?" I look at my watch and see it's before six there.

"I'm on the plane getting ready for takeoff. I have a meeting as soon as I land."

"Oh, the dresses are here. I didn't look yet. I was going to wait for you."

"Try them on. Have fun today."

"I wish. I have a meeting today with Kevin for the company, but I will be home before you get here."

"Have fun. I'll see you tonight."

I hear the dial tone before I can respond. She always does that. I clean up the kitchen, then move to the living room and pick up the toys on the floor. Once I'm finished, I see it's a quarter after ten. I put on my heels and head out.

I arrive at the Grace Industries building with fifteen minutes to spare. I find a parking space down the block and walk into the giant building. I head through the massive lobby and hear my name. I turn and see Annie.

"Hannah, I was hoping I would catch you." She walks right up to me and kisses my cheek, then hugs me.

"Annie, it's so nice to see you."

"Shane told me you would be here today for a meeting." I can tell by her look that's not all he told her. "Hannah, I'm so sorry to hear about your loss."

"Annie, please, you don't have to," I say, putting up my hands. I don't want to feel like this before my meeting. I know the meeting will be hard enough on me.

"Let me take you up."

"That would be great, thank you." I follow her to the elevators, and she presses the top floor. Of course they are the top floor; nothing but the best for the Graces.

It seems to take forever, and my feet are throbbing already. When the doors finally open, I see *Grace* etched into the frosted glass. Annie slides her card to grant us entry. The office has a modern, open floor plan. I can see people staring in our direction. A woman walks over to us.

"Mrs. Grace, did you forget something?" she asks. She is pretty and well dressed.

"No, Lauren, I was just catching up with an old friend who has an appointment with Shane. Could you show her to his office?"

"Of course." She turns and stops as I say good-bye.

"Thank you, Annie. I will see you tomorrow night."

"Bye, Hannah. I can't wait." Her big smile is contagious.

"Right this way, Mrs. Winterfield." I guess he is waiting for me. I follow her to the back of the office, where I see a large office with *SG* etched into the frosted glass. She stops and knocks on the door and waits. In seconds she opens it, and I see Shane getting up. He greets me with a big hug.

"That will be all, Lauren," he says. I look around, and I am very impressed. The Grace men have done very well for themselves.

"Hey, I have to push you back fifteen minutes, if that is OK."

"No problem. Where do you want me to wait?" As I finish my sentence, John walks in.

"Hey, Hannah, what are you doing here?" He walks right up to me and hugs me.

"She is part owner of Winter and Waters. She is the Winter portion of the company," Shane says. I just smile at John not knowing what to say.

"Well…well…well…" John looks at me with a huge grin.

"John, can you show Hannah around? I have to get an update on Hong Kong. It should only take fifteen minutes." Shane smiles at John as he sits back down at his desk.

"Of course, anything for Hannah." John places his hand on the small of my back and leads me out of the room.

"Have you seen Grant yet?" he half whispers to me.

I look over at him, surprised.

"No, was I supposed to?" I feel stupid. I wasn't coming here to see him.

"Yes, let's piss him off a bit." I see a devilish look in his eyes and laugh. What is he going to get me into? I follow him down a long hallway and see Grant's office. It has *GG* etched in the frosted glass. By the looks of it, it is much larger then Shane's.

"Knock on the door, and don't answer him or go in when he tells you. He hates this." John starts laughing.

"Is he going to want to kill me?"

"You? No way, it will make his day seeing you." I walk over to Grant's door and see John sit down at an open cubicle nearby. I knock three times and cringe. I hear Grant yell, "What!" I just stand there and knock again. He yells, "Come in!" and I start to laugh quietly. I see John laughing like a little boy. All of the sudden, I feel a woman tap my shoulder.

"Excuse me, what are you doing?" I feel like I'm getting in trouble, but John motions over to her, and she steps back.

"You are going to get fired if you work here," she says sharply as she walks away.

I knock again and hear Grant cursing. I see the frosted glass go clear, and jump in front of the door so he can't see me. I hear him getting closer, because I can hear him call me an asshole. It makes me laugh harder. He really hates to be bothered. I put my arm up against the doorjamb and place my other hand on my hip as he swings the door open in a rage. I smile at him and see that I caught him off guard.

"Jesus, Hannah, I was about to kill you." I can see him relax as he slips his hands in his pockets to look me over. Then a sexy grin appears on his face.

"Mr. Grace, is that how you greet all your business associates?" I feel the pull between us. He steps forward, pulls me into him by my hips, and picks me up in a big hug. I wrap my arms around his neck, and he pulls me into his office and closes the door behind us with his foot. I look out the glass windows; a few people have stopped working and are staring in at us. Grant puts me down, brings his hand to my neck, and kisses my cheek. I realized how much I miss him as I follow him over to his desk. He presses a button, and the glass goes frosted again. He kisses me lightly on my lips and sits down at his desk. I smile at him as I sit on his desk in front of him.

"This is a first," he says, looking me over as I cross my legs and sit up straight.

"No one has ever sat on your desk?" He shakes his head no. "I'm happy I am your first," I tease him. I look down on his desk and see the Winter and Waters logo. I run my finger along it, remembering when they came up with it.

"You like the logo?" Grant asks me, and I nod as I look up into his baby blues.

"I have a meeting with them in thirty; poor bastards don't have a clue. They are selling a property to me for far less than I can sell it for, and their financials are a mess." My mind starts reeling at the words he just said. What does he mean by my financials are a mess?

"So what brings you here, Hannah?"

"I have a meeting here today, and John was just showing me around. He said it would make your day if I came in to say hello."

"Of course you would make my day. I missed you." He slides his chair in and places his hand on my legs. I hear a chime and look over at his monitor. He has his texts coming over his monitor, and I die reading the message. It's from Aiden.

Just fucked Shultz. She signed on to our team.

I freeze as Grant deletes it.

"Sorry," he says, rubbing my leg again.

"Please tell me Shultz isn't Rebecca Shultz." He looks at me.

"Yes, her name is Rebecca, but I doubt you know her. She is a law-yer in San Francisco."

"Shultz and Barker Firm?" I see the shock come over his face.

"How the hell do you know her?" He looks at me wide-eyed.

"She is my best friend since kindergarten, who was flying in this weekend." I uncross my arms and let him hold my hands. I hear another chime and look over, not being able to help it.

We are going to double. She said her friend was hot. No backing out. I said you would.

I turn and smile at him.

"Mr. Grace, it seems you have a blind date for the charity dinner." I smile as he pulls me close to kiss me. It feels so right to be with him. I look into his eyes and feel my heart sing.

"Grant, I need Hannah back." I hear Shane's voice over the intercom. I slide off his desk, and he pulls me in tight. I missed his body against mine. We fit together so well. His hands run up from my hips to my neck, and he kisses me with urgency. It's so sensual and sexy. I run my hands to his chest, and he kisses me softly one last time.

"Come back here when you are done," he whispers against my lips.

I like the promise in his words as they float into my mouth and throughout my body. He holds my hand as he walks me to the door, then opens it for me. John is talking to the girl who told me I would get fired. They both look at us in surprise when they see Grant lean down and kiss me. I'm just as surprised; I nearly fall, but Grant holds me steady and makes a spectacle of us by spinning me around in a circle. When he pulls away and sets me down, I slap his chest playfully.

"Behave, will you? I'm conducting business here today, and I don't want anyone to know I have an in with the owner."

He just smiles at me and slaps my bottom as I walk away. I turn and give him a warning look again. He gives me his sexy grin, and I realize I missed him more than I thought I did.

John is right beside me to bring me to the conference room.

"He has it bad for you, Hannah. I think his assistant had a heart attack back there when he kissed you."

"Please, John, I think he did that to get a rise out of you." I roll my eyes at him, trying to hide the fact that I hope he does have it bad for me.

I'm so fucked up, I think as John leads me down an adjoining hall. How could he want me? I think of how he would react if he ever found out about Aiden. I need to keep my distance and not get myself in any deeper than I already am. I see Kevin seated at a large conference table through the glass wall, as John opens the door for me to walk in.

"Come say good-bye before you leave."

"I will, John." I sit next to Kevin and watch John walk away. I lean over and look at the paperwork.

"I heard that you are selling the property for less than it is worth?" I question Kevin.

"Who told you that?"

"I have connections." I look up and see Shane walking into the room, so we stop talking.

"Sorry, I got caught up on the phone. I told John to walk you around, not leave you with Grant. Is he in a mood today?" He settles a pile of papers on the table.

"He didn't ditch me. We played a weird version of ding dong ditch. I guess he likes to piss him off?" I smile, thinking about the way he kissed me.

"Oh, and how did that go?" He leans back in his chair, bringing his fingers to his mouth and fixing his eyes on me.

"Fine. He's in a good mood today." I feel a grin on my lips, so I bite my bottom lip.

"And I bet it had nothing to do with you," he says. I can feel my face start to blush, and I try to stop it because I can feel Kevin's stare on me.

"No, it doesn't, Shane. How about we start?" I say, redirecting the attention off of me.

Shane pulls out contracts, and they start to go over everything. I watch the long, tedious process as they go back and forth. But then I hear the property address and I perk up in my seat.

"Excuse me. What was the address again?" Shane repeats it and Kevin cringes in his seat. I stand up, reacting to what Shane just repeated.

"Shane, can you excuse us for one moment?" I can hear the irritation in my voice. Shane leaves. I wish I could frost the windows. I walk over to the window and stand there, almost shaking.

"When the fuck were you going to tell me?" My voice is cold.

"Hannah, I have to."

"What the hell is going on, Kevin? I told you when I'm ready to sell it, I will."

"Hannah, Chase is gone; holding onto the place where he died isn't going to help."

"I don't give a fuck what you think. I will hold onto it as long as I damn well please." I see Shane outside looking in. I wave at him and he walks in slowly.

"I'm sorry to waste your time, Shane, but we aren't selling." He looks shocked.

"We can talk about this. Is it the price? I can go talk to Grant. We can give you more."

"No, it's not that." I see Grant walking in and my stomach drops.

"Hannah, what are you doing here?" Grant looks confused.

"She is part owner in Winter and Waters," Shane says.

Grant starts to smile as he walks over to me and whispers, "I guess I underestimated you. I guess I'm not going to get it for what I thought."

"You're not getting the building at all. I'm not selling it."

"Hannah, there has to be a price that will make you interested." Shane and Grant are standing opposite of me at the table. We are all standing except Kevin. I place my hands on the table.

"No, there isn't. I'm sorry for wasting your time. I really am." I shoot Kevin a look, and he starts gathering up his paperwork.

"Can I ask why?" Grant asks. I feel like his eyes can see right through me. I hold back the tears and take a deep breath and stand up straight.

"It's the building Chase was murdered in, and I'm not ready to let it go." We stand there staring at each other, and I can tell this bothers Kevin, who keeps shifting in his chair.

"Hannah, do you know the financial situation your company is in?" Grant says. I remember what he said before.

"I didn't know there was a situation." I look over at Kevin, but he is looking down.

"You have to sell, or you will be going under." I can tell he isn't enjoying saying these words like he normally would, because his voice has gotten softer.

"Kevin, start talking." Shane and Grant decide to give us a moment.

"Talk this one over," Grant says, and I nod at him.

"Kevin, I swear to God, I will kill you with my own two hands if you keep hiding shit from me. Tell me the truth. Are we going under?" I'm trying my hardest not to yell, but my voice is definitely louder than it should be.

"Yes." He doesn't even look up at me. I sit next to him and swivel the chair to face him.

"When were you going to tell me?"

"I wasn't planning on it. As long as we can sell this property, we will be fine." His eyes finally reach mine.

"Why are you still paying me if you don't have the money?" He just shrugs his shoulders.

"You have the kids. You need it more than I do."

"Kevin, I have a job too. The house is paid off, and I have money in the bank. If you were hurting, you could have told me. Take me off the payroll. I'm signing it all over to you."

"Hannah, stop. I don't want the company. I just want to make sure you will be OK."

"I'll be fine, Kevin," I snap at him. "I will handle them; don't say a word." I turn around and motion them in. They walk in and stand across from me again.

"Asking price has changed. I want five million." I look right into Grant's eyes.

"I'll give you ten." I feel like he is mocking me.

"Grant, don't be stupid." The words fly out of my mouth before I can stop them.

"I'm not, it's worth ten, and that's what I will buy it for." Shane nods his head in agreement.

"You're not paying double the asking price," I yell at him.

"Don't tell me how to spend my money."

"I just have to go and change some of the paperwork, and I will be right back," Shane says as he walks out. I catch a glimpse of Aiden and turn around. I guess I look like I'd seen a ghost, because I hear Kevin ask if I'm OK, but that is all disrupted when Aiden walks in.

"Hannah, can I have a moment with you?"

He leans in the door, and waits. I look at Grant.

"No, Aiden, I don't have time." Grant looks amused by this. I can see a smile on his full lips, but he is hiding it with his fingers.

"Hannah, please don't make me cause a scene." These words make Grant's eyebrows raise. I walk out of the conference room. He places his hand on my back and guides me into the next conference room, which is connected by a single wall of glass. I turn to him after he closes the door.

"What is there to say?" Anger builds inside me. I can feel Kevin and Grant's eyes on me. I don't look over at them.

"Stop." I place my hands up so he doesn't step closer, but he takes a step closer. "I don't know what your problem is, but stop acting like a fucking cunt." I slap him hard. I see Kevin standing up, alarmed. Aiden walks over to the bar and frosts the windows.

"I was going to let them watch me fuck you, but now I want to do something else to you." I see the darkness in his eyes, and it makes my heart beat faster and my stomach flips. I pray this is his sick way of making a joke.

"Oh, like you fucked my best friend this afternoon? Rebecca Shultz." I'm getting louder and angrier by the minute.

"So are we even? I fucked your best friend, and you fucked my brother." His words are sharp.

"I never fucked your brother, asshole. I told you to get your facts straight. Who told youthat?" My anger is soaring. I try to open the door, but it's locked and won't budge. I shake it again.

"Aiden, let me out." He grabs me by my arms, picks me up, and throws me down on the table. My elbows break my landing, and I feel pain shoot up my arms. I kick him when he gets closer.

"Get the fuck away from me!" I scream. I watch him unzip his pants and step closer to the table. It's fight or flight time. I feel my breathing change. Blood rushes through my veins; every hair on my body is standing on end, but I don't move.

"John said Grant told him."

"John and Grant are fucking liars," I yell at him.

He stops and stands in front of me, just far enough away that I can't kick him again. I watch him zip his pants back up, and he sits down.

Good, he is finally thinking rationally. What the fuck is going through his head?

"I don't like sharing, Hannah."

"Well, neither do I, Aiden, but you had no problem having sex with a business partner this afternoon." I'm sitting on the table still, and I decide to get off and sit opposite him at the table.

"That was just business." Does he believe the shit coming out of his mouth?

"It's over, Aiden, and I never fucked your brother."

"No, you didn't, you just sucked his dick, like you did mine." I look at him and feel horrified again.

"Yes, I did," I say through clinched teeth. The words are forced out. I never wanted him to know, but I'm not a liar.

"It's over, Aiden. We both fucked it up before it even began. You are going to the dinner with Becca, and I'm going with Grant, apparently."

"If I had known she was your best friend, Hannah, I never would have…" His look softens as he stops talking.

"Save the lies, Aiden. I'm sure there will always be another woman you will have to close a deal with." I walk over to the door again and he follows, grabbing me and turning me around. He tries to kiss me and I slap him hard again.

"What the fuck was that?" He spats, looking at me, pissed.

"What the fuck was what? I told you it's over. No, more. Do I need to spell it out for you?" I speak the words slow and bitterly. He grabs me again and pins me against the wall. I start swinging my arms and legs, but there is no hope, he is too strong. I get very still; I can feel my body react to the situation.

I wait until he is about to kiss me, and then I knee him right in between the legs. I almost twist my ankle as I run to the door. I pull on it again, and it doesn't open. I pull repeatedly. I can hear Kevin on the other side of the door. I run over to where Aiden was standing before and I look for a button. I see a picture of a door and press it. Before I reach the door, Grant opens it. I run out past him and Kevin. I hear yelling and a loud crash. I turn around halfway down the hallway and see that Grant threw Aiden right through the glass wall. Aiden is on the ground, and Grant is on top of him, screaming. I start to go back and Kevin is right beside me. Grant looks up at me.

"Tell me what that was about, Hannah," he demands, and I freeze.

Aiden is the first to speak. "I called her a fucking whore."

Grant kicks him in the ribs. I see Shane and John running down the hallway. John grabs Grant off of Aiden, and Shane helps Aiden up. My first instinct is to look Aiden over to see how badly he's hurt, but I refrain from going near him. I am shaking.

"Why did he call you that?" Grant pleads, placing his hands on my arms. I can't talk. I can only stare at him in shock.

"Yeah, Hannah, tell him why I called you that," Aiden says. I watch as Kevin punches him in the stomach. Shane and John let him have the cheap shot, then back him away.

I start to walk away from them, then find myself running to Grant's office. I walk straight to his desk and frost the windows. I curl up in his chair and cry. I try to hold back the sobs, but they get louder. It takes a while to steady my breathing. I wipe the tears from my face and look around for a tissue. I see them on a table next to the couch, so I walk over and sit on the couch. I wipe under my eyes, trying to clean up my mess of a face. I feel my feet pulse and lean down to take my shoes off. I lean back onto the couch and internally berate myself. Why am I here? How the hell did I let this happen? I remember my weak words to myself about walking away. I'm stuck in a place I never thought I would be in, between two brothers. How did I go from wanting no one to wanting two men at the same time? Grant walks in the door at what feels like hours later, and it startles me. Really it's only been a few minutes.

"I thought you left. Wendy told me you ran in here." He sounds worried. I see Kevin behind him and feel so embarrassed. I lean into the couch and cover my face with my hands. I need to make a break for it. I need to walk out of here and never come back.

"I have to go." I stand up and grab my shoes.

"Hannah, I'll get the kids. You stay here and calm down," Kevin whispers as he hugs me.

"We will talk tonight," he says after he kisses my cheek. I just nod and sit back down. *Shit*. I can't even make myself leave, because I want to be here with Grant. Just the sight of him makes me want to stay. I feel exhausted all of a sudden. My body is tired, and I want to lie down and sleep. I watch Kevin and Grant shake hands, and Kevin leaves. I don't want to talk to Grant; I don't want him to know what I did with Aiden. It will ruin everything. *I have ruined everything*, I tell myself.

The thought makes tears leave my eyes again. I place my hands over my face. I feel Grant's arms wrap around me, and I stiffen at his touch.

"It's just me," he whispers. I know it's him, but he is going to hate me forever. I dread the look of betrayal and sadness when he finds out what I did. I feel sick. I know I created this mess, but I don't have it in me to handle the shit storm I started when I allowed myself to get involved with both of them. I should just get up and leave and never see them again. I don't have to sell the building to them. The company can go under. I don't care. I just want to run from him. I want to run from the first man whom I think I could love and who could have loved me back.

"What did he do to you in there?" I wipe under my eyes.

"Nothing, Grant." I take a deep breath.

"Hannah." His voice sounds angry.

"He tried to make a move on me, so I kneed him in the balls." I take a deep breath to push back the tears. My elbows are still throbbing, and I begin to rub them. Grant just sits and looks at me.

"I am going to fucking kill him."

"Grant, I handled it. It's over." I stand and pace in front of him.

"Why did he call you that?" I'm ashamed of the words I have to say, even before they leave my mouth. I never thought I would have to explain anything to him. Why did I have to be so stupid and see Aiden this week? I look at Grant and feel things I haven't felt since Chase. I want to curl up in his lap and have him make it all better, but I know after I tell him what I did with Aiden, he will kick me out, and I will never see him again.

The little bit of my heart that I have been able to put back together starts to shatter all over again. I feel like I'm about to lose something, but I realize I never had him, and it hurts.

"He called me that because he thought I slept with you." I stop there. I'm terrified of saying any more.

"That's all he said?" He looks me deep in my eyes, searching for something.

"You don't want to know, Grant." I try to get out of the conversation. I pace more and stop, leaving my back to him.

"Yes, I do, Hannah." He stands up and wraps his arms around me.

"Kiss me one last time." I turn and look into his eyes, and they look cloudy.

"Why do you think it will be the last time?" I feel my heart breaking more.

"Please," I whisper.

He takes his hands and gently places them on my neck while lightly rubbing my jawline with his thumbs. He looks at me and places his lips on mine, kissing me so softly. He parts my lips slightly, kissing my bottom lip with his full lips. I stand there praying he can feel what I feel and that this all won't matter. I want him to kiss life back into me. I start to kiss him back desperately; I feel this will be our last kiss.

I place my hands on his chest and feel his heart beat under the palm of my hand. He pulls back and looks at me again.

"There is nothing you can say that will change the way I feel about you." I feel my stomach plummet down to the ground.

"Don't say that."

"Why? Its how I feel." He pulls me into his chest and wraps his arms around me. I hear his heart beat under my ear.

"Because things change and so do feelings."

"What happened, Hannah? Tell me...I want to make it better." He kisses the top of my head, trying to soothe me. I don't want to speak the words, but I know I have to be truthful with him. He is the first man I want to be with, and I fucked it up before it even started. Now I have to tell him how I fucked it up and face the consequences. My heart plunges deep in my chest.

"I slept with Aiden." The words taste like curdled milk coming out of my mouth. Grant pulls away a bit. His arms are still around me, but I'm not in his nook anymore. I think about how he will slowly push me away until I can't feel him at all. I stand and wait for him to react, but he doesn't. He just stands there, holding me.

"Hannah, breathe," I hear him say and I realize I'm not breathing. I gasp for air, and he pulls me back into his nook against his body.

"I'm so sorry, Grant. It was the biggest mistake of my life. I would take it back if I could. I wasn't thinking." I start to choke up again, and he just holds me, trying to make me feel better. I want him to make me better, but I fear when he pulls away, I will never get him back, so I stay still and pray he will forgive me.

"I have one question."

"Yes," I say into his chest.

"Why didn't you sleep with me?" I look into his eyes and know the answer immediately.

"I wanted to wait with you because I knew I could fall in love with you." I press myself to him and hope he can feel what my heart feels for him.

"You think you could fall in love with me?" he whispers, and I nod my head. He kisses the top of my head and hugs me tight.

"I'm falling in love with you too, Hannah." His voice is so soft and calm.

"You don't hate me?" I ask as I look into his eyes again. They look clearer.

"I hate what you did, Hannah, but no, I don't hate you." He pulls away from me and walks over to the couch. I feel like I'm going to lose him, so I follow. I settle next to him on the couch and curl my feet under me. Why is this going over so easy? I thought he would be furious with me.

"I deserve this," he says.

"No, you don't," I say, surprised.

"Hannah, you don't know what Aiden and I have been through." I watch him as he runs his hands through his hair and then he leans back into the couch. We both look up when we hear a knock at the door. Wendy, his assistant, walks in with a bag and places it on the bar near the door.

"Thank you, Wendy, that will be all." She turns and walks out without saying a word.

"You should eat something, Hannah. I ordered us lunch." He brings the bag over and places it on the table. I slip down to the floor and sit in front of the sandwich he placed in front of me. He sits next to me on the floor. I open the white paper and smell the Reuben. It's my favorite and somehow he knew this. I smile over at him.

"I asked Kevin what you would want." I have to give him credit; he thought to ask what I would want. It says a lot about him and how much he cares for me. I lean over, and he meets me halfway for a kiss. *How the hell did I get off so easy?* I wonder. Chase must have heard my pleas and granted me the wish of keeping Grant. I begin to eat and Grant starts talking again.

"Aiden is a spiteful bastard, and he has been waiting to pay me back, Hannah. I really can't blame you for what happened, or at least I don't want to. I slept with his girlfriend a few years ago. We got into a big fight and didn't talk to each other for a year. She was bad news, and I thought I was doing him a favor. He has seduced each girlfriend I have had since. He fucked Carla, I know he did. I never cared because I didn't love her and I wasn't home enough to care." I watch him take another bite and chew.

"I knew he was up to something. He overheard me talking to John about you. From then on I noticed him pulling you in. I know how he can be, Hannah. I send him out to our female clientele for a reason; he can be quite convincing when he needs to be."

I think about what he is saying. Did Aiden use me to get back at Grant? I feel like a dirty whore again and lose my appetite. I look at the sandwich with disgust and wrap it back up. I watch Grant finish his and crumple the paper up and throw it back in the bag.

"I don't care what you did in the past. It's from today forward that I care about. I want to be with you, Hannah. I want to make this work." I melt with his words, and they make me feel hopeful. I climb into his lap and lightly touch his face.

"I want to make this work more than I have ever wanted anything, Grant." I cup his face, and he pulls me in for a kiss. I wish I could sleep next to him tonight; I need him to hold me to make me feel better. For some reason he calms me. I can feel the pieces of my heart lift off the floor and find their way back to their home in my chest.

"Promise me, Hannah, that it will never happen again, because I can promise you I won't be acting like this if you do." His words make my chest tighten. I feel the guilt wash over me again. Why did I hurt this man? I am so stupid.

"Grant, if I am going to be with you, I would never be with anyone else."

"Hannah, you were never mine to begin with, so I can't get mad at you. You didn't cheat on me, but now you are mine, and I don't want to share you with anyone."

I take his face in my hands again and straddle myself over him.

"I am all yours, Grant. Only you." Our kisses start as soft and playful, then become frantic. Grant pulls me closer, and my body molds around his. He slows the pace, and my eyes open to find his looking right into mine.

"Only you," he whispers to me.

"Only you." I repeat back.

When we pull away from each other, I catch a look at the clock and see it's after four. He sees my expression and helps me up.

"I'm sorry this happened today," I say. "I hate myself for ruining your day." He helps me buckle my shoes, then runs his hands up my leg. I look at him apologetically.

"You didn't ruin my day. You made it better by being honest. Tomorrow night will be our first official date and I couldn't be happier." He is grinning at me, and I smile back at him. He knows just what to say.

"I'm happy fate brought us back together, Hannah." These words whirl around in my head as he grabs my waist and presses his body against mine.

"I hate to ruin the moment, but I have to go. I'm sure Kevin, the kids, and Becca are all wondering where I've been." I kiss him again, and we walk out hand in hand, with everyone looking at us.

CHAPTER TWENTY-SIX

We see Shane walking down the hallway toward us.
"Hey, I was just going to see if you were still here. Hannah, I am so sorry for what happened earlier. Aiden told me you got him good; you better not piss her off, Grant. She can kick your ass." They smile at each other, and I cringe, thinking about Aiden. "I was just seeing if you wanted to sign everything before you left, or we can reschedule."

"No, it's fine." I just want this to be over with. We turn around and walk back into Grant's office.

"I'll take care of it, Shane. Go home to Annie." Shane and Grant both look tired. I watch Shane go over something with Grant in a whisper, and he kisses my cheek before he leaves.

"I hope you're still coming tomorrow," Shane says.

"I wouldn't miss it for the world." Shane leaves and Grant takes out all the paperwork. I see that Kevin signed it already.

"Just go skim through it and sign under Kevin." I nod and read through anyway. He really gave us ten million for the building. I have to talk to Kevin when I get home about the business. We have to figure it all out. I sign my name about a million times, then flip to the last page. It's a deed, and I see it lists my name as the deed holder. I look up at Grant.

"You have this wrong. It's supposed to have your company's name here, not mine."

"No, it's right."

I look at the deed again. They are taking Chase and Kevin off and adding me on. It has to be wrong.

"Grant, it is wrong. Why would I be added to the deed?"

"Because it's your building. You're not ready to give it up." He places his hand on my shoulder. "I want you to have it, Hannah." I feel the tears in my eyes again.

"Grant, I can't accept this." I put the pen down.

"Yes, you can. You already did. Kevin signed for the wire transfer." Why is he doing this? "I want you to have it," he answers, as if he can read my mind.

"Grant you just sold me this building for double what it is worth, and now you are giving it back to me. It doesn't make sense."

"I saw how attached you are to it, and I figured when you are ready, you can sell it to me again, for a better price." He picks up the pen and puts it in my hand. I just look at him, bewildered.

"No, you bought it. It is your building." I push the papers away.

"I want you to have it. Just sign it." He pushes the pen and deed back in front of me.

"I can't take this Grant. Kevin accepted the wire transfer not the deed. I don't want it." I'm being stubborn, but I know I'm about to crack.

"Sign it, Hannah." I look down and shake my head as I sign it. How did I get so lucky? I get the man and get to keep the building.

"Let's get you home." He takes my hand in his.

"Thank you, Grant. You have no idea what this means to me." He kisses the top of my head as we hug.

"I think I do, Hannah." I smile. I love the way he always says my name with care. "I'm going to drive you home. I'll have my driver follow me and bring me back."

"No, you are too busy for that. I can get home fine." He gives me a pout. His lips look so good when he pouts, so I give in. I really do want more time with him. We walk out of his office again, hand in hand, and Wendy stands up.

"Mr. Grace, you have twenty messages. Would you like me to get the first one on the line?"

"No, Wendy, I won't be returning messages tonight. Call Derek and tell him to pick me up at Hannah's house." He kisses my hand in front of her, and her face rages with jealousy.

"Yes, Mr. Grace. Does he know the address?"

"Tell him to call Sam. He has picked her up before." He kisses me on the lips. I can tell everyone is looking at us, but Grant makes me feel like we are all alone.

When we finally pull away, we walk to the elevators. I start to press a button, but Grant pulls me over to another one. He slides his card and it opens right up.

"Is this your private elevator, Mr. Grace?" I ask him, teasing. He nods, giving me his sexy grin.

He holds my hand all the way to the bottom floor, behaving himself the entire time. We make the short walk to my truck.

"You drive this big thing?" he teases.

"It's no Porsche," I agree as he opens my door and I climb in. I watch as he walks over and gets in. I laugh at him because he has to adjust the seat all the way back. I realize that I feel relaxed for the first time today.

We aren't even out of the city when I feel my cell phone vibrate.

"Hey, Kevin. I'm on my way home now."

"Are you OK to be driving, Hannah?"

"No, Grant is driving me home." I don't hear Kevin again.

"Hello?"

"Sorry, Ella was talking to me." I know this is an excuse because I didn't hear her talking. I think he is surprised by the news.

"I should be home in an hour, depending on traffic. Is Becca there yet?"

"Yeah, she got here about an hour ago. I haven't told her anything yet."

"Please don't, Kevin. I mean it, don't say anything. I will talk to her tonight after the kids go to bed. Can you order dinner for them?"

"I already did; it should be here soon. They are worried about you, and so am I. Are you OK?" I look at Grant and smile.

"Yes, I'm OK." He places his hand on my leg.

"I'll see you soon." I hang up and see I have lots of missed calls from Becca. I have a lot of explaining to do later. I put my phone back in my bag, then lean down to take off my shoes. I take Grant's hand from my leg and place both my hands around it.

"What are you going to wear tomorrow?" I look over at him, surprised by his question.

"No idea. Becca had dresses delivered, but I never had a chance to look at them."

"I'm sure whatever you wear, I will love." He squeezes my hand. I sit and think about it. He will love...

"What time should I pick you up?" I begin to laugh at him.

"Why would you come all the way out to me, to come all the way back?"

"Because I am old-fashioned, and I want to pick you up. It's our first date. Shouldn't I come to the door, meet your parents, and wait in the living room with your dad, while you finish getting ready?" This makes me laugh more, because he is teasing me now. I missed playful Grant.

"You realize instead of meeting my parents, you will be meeting my children, and they will give you a run for your money."

"I can't wait to meet your kids." He gets serious as he looks at me. He pulls my hand to his lips and kisses the back of it. I am falling for him so hard, and I can't stop myself even if I tried.

We talk the whole way home about everything from music to religion. We are compatible. I would have never guessed. He seemed so out of my league when we first met, and now I know he is just as normal as any other guy, except he is rich as hell. He pulls into my driveway, and I see my in-laws are over. I feel a nervous wave come over me.

"What? Is Kevin having a party?"

"No, Chase's parents are here."

"I don't have to come in, Hannah, if you think it will be weird, I can wait outside for Derek, and no one has to know I'm even here." As the words come out of his mouth, they sound all wrong. I want him to come in.

"Don't be silly. Come in. Stay awhile; we could use a drink." I lean over to kiss him before we get out.

"What was that for?" he asks as his lips are still on mine.

"In case I can't do it later." He just smiles at me as he gets out. He walks around the truck and opens the door for me. I get out with my shoes in my hands, and he takes them from me and slips his hand into mine.

As I open the door, I can hear everyone in the kitchen laughing. I squeeze Grant's hand and lead him into the kitchen. Everyone looks at us when we walk in.

"Hello," I say, smiling at everyone. Richard looks thrown off a bit. He kisses my cheek, then puts out his hand.

"Mr. Grace, this is a surprise." They shake hands.

"Richard, please call me Grant."

Grant and Kevin shake, then I look over at Becca.

"Becca, this is Grant Grace," I say.

"We've met before," she says to him as their hands meet.

"I believe we have, in San Francisco, right?" She nods back at him. I introduce him to Mary, and she blushes as they shake.

"Mommy." I hear Ella and Hunter run in. They stop and look at Grant, then hug me, not taking their eyes off of him.

"Ella, Hunter, this is Grant. Remember when you met Aiden on Sunday?" They nod at me; his name still leaves a bitter taste in my mouth.

"This is his brother." Grant puts out his hand, and they slap him five. Grant makes an "ouch" sound when Hunter slaps his hand, and he shakes his hand like he is in pain.

"You are strong, little man. My hand hurts." Hunter laughs, and Grant puts out his hand again for him to slap it. He makes the sound again, and Hunter laughs harder. I watch them and think how he fits in already. Ella gets closer to him, and Grant kneels down. She looks at his shirt and he watches her.

"Do you have a necklace?" she asks. Grant loosens his tie, reaches into his shirt, and takes out his St. Michael charm. Ella smiles.

"Your daddy gave that to you, right?" Grant nods at her. She takes it in her tiny hand and looks at it. Hunter walks over.

"We don't have a daddy either," he says. We all get quiet, but Grant smiles at him.

"Yes, you do, he is in heaven with my daddy." I am impressed with his response.

"Do you think they are friends?" Hunter asks.

"Of course they are. They are looking down at us right now, and I bet they are happy we got to be friends too." I fall in love right then and there. He looks up at me and smiles.

"I want to show you my toys. Mommy, can I show Grant my toys?"

"No, honey, give Grant a minute. We had a long drive home."

"Is he staying here?" Hunter looks at me curiously.

"No, buddy, he is getting picked up in a little while." Hunter looks disappointed, but Grant gives in and lets Hunter drag him into the living room to show him his toys. I watch him take off his jacket and get on the floor to play with them. Becca stands next to me. She bumps into me to get my attention.

"Not too shabby, Han." I roll my eyes at her, walk over to the wine that is open on the counter, pour myself a glass, and take a big gulp of it.

"Well, we are going to get going," Richard announces. He walks in and says good-bye to the kids and shakes Grant's hand again. I kiss him on the cheek, then say good-bye to Mary. I feel better now that they have left. I never thought I would feel guilty, but I don't want Richard or Mary to think I am disrespecting them.

"Grant, do you want some wine?" Hunter is showing him how his remote-control car works.

"Sure."

"Do you like red or white?"

"Whatever is open. I like it all." His reply melts me a little more. He isn't the arrogant, high-maintenance asshole I first thought he was.

I pour him a glass. I notice it's seven thirty. Becca notices the time as well.

"I'll do bath time tonight." She smiles at me. She knows the routine so well. She did stay with me for three weeks after Chase died.

"Thanks."

"OK, guys, bath time, come on."

I hear Hunter complain, "Oh man." Grant follows them out of the living room, and I point at the glass on the counter.

"Mommy, is Grant going to be here when I get out of the tub?" Hunter asks.

"I don't know, buddy. Go on; hurry up and listen to Aunt Becca." He runs upstairs behind Ella.

Grant and Kevin begin to talk business and I shoot Kevin a look.

"I'm going to help Becca with the kids," he says, leaving us alone.

"The kids really like the St. Michael shield. I should get them one." I like the way he thinks, and at the same time I feel sick. I watch him drink his wine and place the glass back down on the counter.

"Don't bother, Aiden already did." I turn around when I say his name. I still feel guilt-ridden.

"He's not always horrible, Hannah. I hate him the majority of the time, but he is my blood." He turns me around so I have to look at him. I look up and he kisses me. It's my first kiss in my house. I feel like he is patching my heart back together. When we part, I smile at him.

"I know, but I'm telling the kids it's from you." I smile at him.

"Good. I need all the brownie points I can get." He reaches into his pocket and takes out his cell. "Grant." I watch him talk on the phone.

"I will be out in fifteen." Then he hangs up.

"Derek is here?"

"Yeah, I figured I'll wait to say good-bye to the kids, then leave."

"So do I have you all to myself tomorrow night, or are you going home after the gala?" Grant asks.

"No, I'm staying in the city; we have a room booked already," I answer.

"You can stay with me instead." He links his fingers into mine, and our souls are touching. When he kisses me, I enjoy the feeling of love again. He pulls away when we hear the kids running down the stairs.

"Mommy, someone is here."

We head to the front door, where Hunter is standing.

"No, honey, that's Grant's driver waiting to take him home."

Hunter looks at Grant. "Are you rich?" Grant laughs at him.

"Something like that buddy." He puts his hand out and Hunter slaps it. Grant makes the sound again, and it makes Hunter laugh.

"I have to go back to work. I will see you guys tomorrow." Hunter jumps up and down.

"Are you going to the ball with Mommy tomorrow?"

"Yes, I am. My family is throwing the ball."

"Mommy, is he a prince?" Ella asks. I smile at her and think, *yes, he is.*

"Say good night to Grant, everyone."

They say good night in unison, then run into the living room. I walk out the front door with Grant.

"You are my Prince Charming, you know that?" I whisper to him. He looks down at me as a huge grin forms on his lips.

"I like the sound of that." I reach into his pocket and take his phone out. I dial my number and press Send so I have his number too. Then I realize after I pressed Send, my name came up. I look at him, surprised.

"What?"

"You had my number already."

"Yes, because I needed it last weekend for my mother. I didn't want to abuse it. I was waiting for you to give it to me." He thinks he is so suave. "Good night, Hannah." He gives me a quick kiss, and I watch him get into the back of the SUV. I stand on the porch until I see the taillights fade into the night.

CHAPTER TWENTY-SEVEN

When I walk back into the house, I see Becca and Kevin at the top of the stairs. They quickly head down. I know they were spying on us, because from where they were standing , they could see us out of the window above the front door. I shake my head at them and settle on the couch between Ella and Hunter. I snuggle with them and feel a few new pieces of my heart find their way back into my chest.

"Mommy, is Grant's mommy a good queen or a bad queen?" Ella asks. I look down at her.

"Honey, she isn't a queen, but if she were to be one, she would be a good queen." Ella smiles at my answer and looks back at the TV.

"Mommy?" Hunter asks, "Is Grant rich?"

"Why would you ask that?"

"Because he said his family is having a ball. Only kings and queens have balls, Mommy, and they live in castles."

Kevin butts in. "Hunter, he has lots of money. Don't let Mommy fool you; he can buy anything and everything he wants."

"Stop," I say, as I shoot Kevin a narrowed look in warning.

"His ball is to raise money for people who need help. The people who are going to the ball are paying to go." Hunter doesn't like the answer or is bored by it, so he looks back at the TV. I let them finish the show before the three of us tuck them into bed. After I close Hunter's door, Becca drags me into the kitchen.

"I have been waiting all night to find out how and why Grant Grace drove you home. Kevin said you had a meeting with them today?" I look at her as she asks the questions.

"Kevin needed me to sign for Chase and it spiraled from there." I take a sip of my wine and look at Kevin. "I'm still pissed at you for hiding this from me."

"I'm sorry. I thought I could fix it without you knowing." Kevin looks upset.

"What am I missing?" Becca butts in.

"Kevin was selling the building Chase died in to Grace Industries. I had no idea till we were at the table with Shane Grace and he said the address."

"So did you sell it?" She is very interested.

"Yes, I had no choice. Grant made me aware of the fact that the company was going under, and I had to sell the building or we would be done." Becca places her hand on my arm.

"I'm sorry, Hannah. It must have been hard for you today. Did you get a good price at least?"

"Did we," Kevin laughs. "I asked for three million for it initially. Hannah stood in front of them and said five million, and Grant paid ten million for it." He takes the wire transfer out of his wallet and waves it around. I shoot him a look and slide my bag over to me. I open it up and take out a copy of the deed.

"Yeah, well, we got ten million, and I got to keep the building in the end." They both look at the deed.

"What?" Becca shouts.

"Grant gave it to me." I look at them in just as much shock.

"Why did he do that?" Kevin asks.

"He said he knew how much it meant to me." I run my finger along the edge of the table, feeling their eyes on me.

"He likes you, Hannah." Becca smiles at me with an eyebrow raised. I look up at her.

"When I'm ready, I will sign it over to him. I just need some more time, and he understands that." I look over at Kevin, who seems in another world.

"He would probably buy it from you again." I laugh at her.

"I know. He said he would."

"He is one of the richest bachelors in the world, and he is eating out of the palm of your hand. How did that happen?" I just shrug my shoulders at her.

"Luck…fate…I have no idea, but for the first time since Chase, I want to see where this goes. I think I like him."

"You should; he is the whole package. Rich, good-looking, power-ful, and sexy as hell. He and AJ have the same eyes."

"AJ?"

"Yes, his brother, AJ. Aiden James. I call him AJ. I think a lot of people do." His name still makes my skin crawl.

"How did your meeting go with him?" I ask her.

"I hope it was better than the one Hannah had." I shoot Kevin a shut-the-fuck-up look, and he freezes.

"How did you know I had a meeting with him?"

"Grant told me." I remember the text I read. I feel bad, like I'm invading her privacy.

"The meeting went great; I signed on to their team for a merger. What was your meeting with him about?"

"Nothing, we just caught up. So does this mean you are going to be here more?"

"Yes, it does. I was thinking about getting a place in the city. What do you mean, catch up?"

"It was their mother I was taking care of last weekend."

"You never told me that. So you really know them outside of the business world?" She is staring at me with interest.

"I guess. Why don't you stay here? I have the room for you." I'm trying to change the topic.

"No, I don't want to wear out my welcome. I figured with my hours and schedule, I would stay there during the week and come here on the weekends." She smiles at me, and I know I will have to tell her I slept with Aiden. I just don't want to, because Kevin doesn't even know.

"So what do you think of Aiden?" She leans back in her chair and waits for my response.

"Why do you want to know? Do you like him and are hoping I can set you up with him?" I tease her because I need to make light of this conversation.

"No, I don't need to be set up with him. I already have a date with him tomorrow night, and if I recall, Aiden was setting you up with Grant, because I told him I wouldn't go without you." She smiles, and I can tell she is thinking about him. She has that dazed look in her eyes.

"You should be careful with him, Bec," Kevin says.

"Why? He is great; he's the best guy I have found in a long time." I look over at Kevin, and he shuts up again.

"Ladies, I have to get home to Vanessa before she breaks up with me again. It's been a rough day, kid, get some rest tonight." He hugs me and kisses my hair.

"Good night, and don't think you are getting off so easy. We have a date with the books on Sunday. We are going to figure it all out." I think he gets my point.

"Later, Bec." She blows him a kiss and he catches it and places it on his cheek. I realize how lucky I am to have both of them.

Today has been a roller coaster, and I just want to sleep. I realize I have had a few glasses of wine. *Shit.* I can't take the sleeping pills if I've been drinking.

"Are you OK?" Becca asks.

"No, I wanted to take my sleeping pills, but I'm afraid to because I have been drinking."

"I wouldn't if I were you. When did you start taking them?" I hear the concern in her voice.

"This week. I just need some sleep."

"I will lie with you, like old times." She takes my hand and we walk up to my room.

She fills me in on the latest gossip going on with her sister while we get changed. I listen to her talking so happily. I have to talk to her about this. I feel like I have betrayed her.

"Bec, what's the deal with you and Aiden?" I need to tread lightly. I crawl into bed and look over at her.

"What do you mean?"

"I mean, what's the deal? How long have you known him, and what's going on between the two of you?" Her lips curve up, and I can tell she has it bad for him. Fuck. I know Grant was understanding, but I have no idea how Becca will react.

"We met about two years ago after his girlfriend cheated on him. He was pretty beat up about it, and we started talking then. Nothing crazy, but we had a fling one night last year." She rummages around in her suitcase. Crap, they had already slept together?

"When he called me a few weeks ago to join his team, I jumped at the chance. I was hoping we could start something, you know?" I nod my head and start dreading this. Maybe I shouldn't tell her. I think Aiden would agree to keep this a secret. I am so selfish; if she ever found out, I would lose her as a friend. I can't handle that and the kids would be devastated.

"Bec, I need to tell you something. I'm not proud to be telling you this."

"Han, what's wrong?"

"I just want to let you know something. I never knew that you knew Aiden." She is perked up and paying attention.

"I slept with Aiden." The words taste like vinegar coming out of my mouth. Becca's jaw drops. "It happened when I was in the Cape taking care of his mom. I was stupid and he was trying to get back at Grant. He was using me to get back at him. If I knew you had feelings for him, I would have never done it, I swear, Bec. I'm so sorry." She is just staring at me. "Say something."

I watch her brain digest what I just told her.

"OK," is all she can say. I wait for her to go on, but it takes her awhile.

"I get that you didn't know our connection, and I don't get your connection." I realize she has no idea I know they slept together today. "How did Grant react to this?"

"I told him about it. He wants a relationship, so I laid all my cards on the table. He knew Aiden was up to something because Grant was the man Aiden's girlfriend cheated on him with. This family war has been going on for a while. Bec, he has a dark side. I got to see it today, and it was bad. I think you should take this slow, if it's what you really want."

"What do you mean by dark side? He is the definition of charming and fun and..." She stops and looks at me. "What happened?"

I try to find the right words, then feel my cell vibrate and hope it's a text from Grant. I see Aiden's name on the screen.

A million times I'm sorry. I would have never hurt you. I talked to Grant, and I will never bother you again. I wish the best for you and your family.

I lock the screen and look at Becca again.

"It was just the way he said something to me that creeped me out. Just be careful with him." I believe everyone deserves a second chance, and this is my way of giving Aiden one. I open my phone again and text him back.

If you hurt a single strand of hair on Becca's head, I will hunt you down and make you wish you were never born. I can forgive, but not forget. She is my family. Don't fuck this one up.

I press Send and look at Becca, who is checking e-mails. I feel it vibrate again and look down. I start smiling because it's from Grant.

Missing you already.

These three words fill my heart, and I can feel a few more pieces come back to me. Becca's phone starts to ring.

"It's Aiden." She freezes.

"Answer it." I wave my hand at her. She gets up and walks out of the room. I decide I will call Grant.

"Hey, you," he answers, all sexy.

"Hey...are you still at the office?" I look at the clock, and it's 11:39 p.m.

"Yes, I have a long night ahead of me. I have a call in an hour." I can tell he is smiling.

"What's so funny?" My voice cracks, and I know it's because I'm so tired.

"How did you know I was smiling?"

"I can hear it in your voice." I lie down and wish he were here with me.

"Nothing, I was just thinking..."

"What were you thinking?" I tease him and I know he likes it.

"Promise you won't laugh at me."

"I promise."

"I was just thinking about how I can't wait to get these calls from you in the future, you being all concerned for me that I'm still at the office." He sounds so sexy over the phone.

"No, I will be calling you, asking when you will be coming home from the office." These words make my mouth spread into a huge grin from ear to ear. I can tell they do the same to Grant.

"I like your train of thought better."

"Do you?"

"Yes. I like the thought of you and home being one and the same. You sound tired, Hannah. Go to sleep. We have a busy night tomorrow." I pout at his words. "Don't pout, Hannah."

"How do you know I'm pouting?" I say, trying not to sound pouty.

"Because I do. Go to sleep, Hannah, and dream of me." His words hold so much promise.

"I will, and you do the same."

"I have since the first day I laid my eyes on you. Good night, Hannah."

"Good night, Grant." I hang up first and lie on my pillow, waiting for Becca to come back in.

CHAPTER TWENTY-EIGHT

I lie in bed wondering what Aiden is saying to Becca, and before I know it, I have fallen asleep and am saying my final good-bye to Chase.

October 2012

Everyone has left the room at the funeral home to give me time. I kneel down in front of him and hold his hand. I start to think about what I could have done differently that day. I wish I had the flu, so he would have stayed home with me. I play all the different scenarios in my head, but none of them can change anything.

"I love you, baby. I always have and I always will."

"Promise me you will always be around. I want to be able to feel you around me and the kids. We are going to need the little signs that you are still with us." After I say the words, I feel warmth come over me. I know this is Chase and his way of telling me he is here with me right know.

"Oh, Chase, how am I going to do this? How am I going to live without you?" I sit and ask questions that I know will never be answered. I continue to talk to him anyway. "I need you still. Why did you have to leave me? You make me whole, Chase. Without you, I can't do this. Please come back to me, please make me whole again." The tears are leaving my eyes fast. I can feel the hot streams fall down my face.

"Baby, I need you." I stand up and lean over his casket. I kiss him on the lips, but his lips feel different on mine.

"Stay with me, please." I see a teardrop fall on his face and I wipe it off. I look around and see the pictures of the kids, and the pictures Hunter and Ella drew him. My heart is pounding, and I feel like I have no control. I have felt this way since Kevin told me he was gone. I have been ripped in half, and I will never be whole again. I feel the anger in me and remember the five stages of grieving. I feel the first four of them at once. I know I will never get to the fifth stage. I know I will never accept his death and move on. I cry on his chest and hug him. I restrain from crawling in with him.

"I love you, Chase," I say to him. I give him my best smile and walk away.

It hits me hard when I walk out of the room. I walk past everyone who tries to touch me. I run out the doors and into the crisp air. I look around and realize the leaves have started to change colors. I walk over to the limo, and Kevin gets out and grabs me. I lose it. Everything I have been holding back comes out in the parking lot of the funeral home. I sob in his arms, and violently hit him. He just stands there letting me get it out, and holding me together. I go to a dark place that day. A place I never thought I would be able to get out of.

I hear a commotion and see men carrying Chase's casket to the hearse. My husband is in there, and I realize he really is gone. It hurts my body so badly thinking this. Everything in me aches. Kevin leads me into the limo, and we follow the hearse to the church. As we pull up, I think about our wedding day. We stood at the doors of this church posing for pictures, smiling at each other, madly in love. I get angry again, and the tears leave my eyes at a faster pace. Kevin wipes the tears off my face.

"Hannah, are you sure you are up for this?" he asks me softly.

I just nod at him. I look in my bag and find the tearstained papers I tucked in earlier that morning.

We pull next to the hearse. When I get out, my dad takes my hand and escorts me inside. We walk to the front of the church, and he sets me down in the first row. My anger subsides, but the hurt is still lingering in my soul. The church is filled with family, friends, and business associates. I never knew we knew this many people. I hear music start to play, and we all stand. I look down the aisle and see Richard, my Dad, Kevin, and Logan, Chase's brother, carry Chase down the aisle. Tears start to leave my eyes again, but a calm washes over me. I feel settled all of a sudden. I know it's Chase helping me through this. When they reach the front, they all look at me and I sit down. They move the casket on top of a table and come to sit next to me.

The priest holding the service is the one who married us. He gives me his condolences. I sit and listen to him talk, but absorb none of it. Then I hear my name. Kevin stands up to help me to the podium. I take a deep breath and feel the calm again. I take out my paper and begin to read from it. I stop midsentence and look up. I can feel Chase standing behind me, hugging me, and I breathe the first real breath since he left me. Tears fill my eyes, and I start talking from the heart.

"Chase is the love of my life. We stood on this altar seven years ago and exchanged vows to each other. I thought it would be appropriate to read a poem we had read at our wedding. It's a poem dear to my heart called *How do I love thee?*" I begin to speak the beautiful words of Elizabeth Barrett Browning from memory. I make sure to take deep breaths so I won't cry, but when I reach the last sentence, I crack and feel the tears on my cheeks.

"*If God choose, I shall love thee better after death.*" I stop and begin to weep. Then I have a moment of clarity. I feel Chase wrap his arms around me and whisper in my ear. "*Don't worry, baby. I'm OK, and you will be too. I will help you find your way.*" I look behind me to see if he is there, but the feeling is lost as fast as I feel it. I take one last deep breath and speak from the heart again.

"When Chase and I found out we were having twins, he said something to me that stuck in my head. He said God had bigger plans for us, and that God would only give us what we could handle. I think about his words now and wish I could see the bigger picture. Chase was an amazing man who let nothing bother him. He always made time for his family and friends. We were the most important thing to him. He would say a job is just a job; they can come and go, but a family is forever. Without love and nurturing, it can never grow. He devoted his life to loving and nurturing our children, and I hope they will always remember that."

I pause to hold the tears back. "I know he is here with us today and he is probably thinking we should celebrate his life, not mourn it." I look out to everyone in the church. "May the memories of Chase never fade, may we always remember his laughter, and may he always bring a smile to your face when you think of him."

CHAPTER TWENTY-NINE

June 2013

I wake up in a cold sweat. I sit straight up in bed; my breathing is erratic. Becca is at my side, wide-eyed.

"Hannah, you're still having the dreams?" Her voice is concerned.

I just nod my head and feel how dry my mouth is. I sit for a while trying to regulate my body, and it takes longer than normal. Becca hands me a cup of water, and I take it, drinking the entire cup. I look over at the clock, and it's 2:38 a.m. I can feel the tears on my cheeks, and I begin to wipe them off. I feel stupid that Becca had to see this, but I'm happy it's only her. She tries to calm me by rubbing my back, but I get out of bed and walk downstairs. Becca starts to follow me, but I shake my head at her. I walk straight to the cabinet and take two pills, washing them down with orange juice. I pace the kitchen and look at my cell, which I placed in my pocket before I slipped back in time. I see Grant has texted me.

Sweet dreams.

I see he sent it about twenty minutes ago. Before I think about what I am doing, I call his number and hear his voice.

"Hannah, what are you still doing up?" His voice is tired, and I think for a moment he might be sleeping.

"I'm sorry. Did I wake you?" I feel stupid for calling, but I needed to hear his voice.

"No, I'm just walking in the door from work. Is everything all right?"

"Yeah, I'm fine. I was just having trouble sleeping." I feel myself start to relax, and I'm not sure if it's because of the pills or because of Grant.

"Did you have a bad dream again?" I hear him say this and I freeze. How does he know about my dreams?

"Hannah, are you there?" I hear the concern in his voice.

"Yes," is all I can whisper.

"Tell me about it." I feel anxious and know I will never tell him what it was about.

"How do you know I have dreams?" I feel my words slow down; the pills are taking effect.

"When we were at the Cape, you were talking in your sleep. I comforted you, but I could tell it was some pretty heavy stuff because you were crying in your sleep."

I want to crawl under a rock. I don't remember dreaming that night when I was with him. I thought when I was with him, I was safe from the past.

"Hannah, it's OK. It's just me." His words make tears leave my eyes.

"I'm so sorry, Grant, I didn't realize I did that." I feel mortification swell inside of me.

"Don't apologize. You have a lot going on, babe. I was more than happy to hold you while you got through it. It didn't last long, I swear."

The tears are running down my cheeks. He held me through the dream and made sure I was OK.

"Drink some tea or warm milk and go back to bed. I promise you will sleep good tomorrow night." I can hear him grinning. I suddenly don't want to spend the night with him. What would happen if I wake up like this again? He doesn't need to see all my baggage. I don't need to put him through this.

"Sorry I called, Grant. I'll see you tomorrow."

"I'm happy you called me. I was missing your voice." His words are always what I need to hear.

"Good night."

"Sweet dreams, Hannah. I hope you can get some sleep. Call me if you can't, and I will stay up with you." His voice is more urgent now. Like he wants to fix me.

"Don't worry, Grant, I'll sleep."

"I can't wait to see you tomorrow." His voice is soft and deep as the words roll off his tongue.

"Me too. Good night."

"Good night, Hannah." I press End and feel my eyelids getting heavy. I make my way up the stairs. I get halfway up when my phone vibrates. Grant's name flashes over the top.

If there is anything I can do or anything you need, please call me. I mean it, Hannah.

I half smile at his message and reply back.

You already did. Thank you.

I walk back into my room. Becca is lying there, still awake.

"You OK?"

"Yeah. I took the pills, so I should be fine for the rest of the night." I roll over so my back is towards her.

"OK," is all she can muster up, and I let go and fall asleep.

CHAPTER THIRTY

When I wake up, my room is bright. I still feel like I could sleep longer. I look over at the clock and it's past ten. I fly out of bed and into the kids' rooms. Their beds are made, and they are nowhere in sight. I run down into the kitchen in a panic and see Becca at the kitchen table on her laptop. She looks up at me and smiles.

"I didn't want to wake you. I got the kids to school. Do you want a cup of tea?"

I nod and walk over to the kettle. I'm happy to see it's still hot. I grab a mug and tea bag and make myself a cup, then settle next to Becca at the table.

"So do you want to talk about it?" I can tell by her tone she is treading lightly.

I shake my head no.

"Well, your phone was going off, so I brought it down here. I think you have a few messages." I look at her and grab my phone off the table. I see Grant's name and open the messages. He sent three, at 7:15, at 8:37, and at 9:45 a.m.

I hope you slept well.

Are you alive?

Please call me when you get this. I'm getting worried.

I feel embarrassed and happy at the same time. He is concerned for me, and it makes me feel cherished, but I should have never called him last night. I look up at Becca; she is trying to read me.

"So what are we doing today?"

"She finally speaks." A huge smile comes across her face.

"Ha-ha. What are the plans?"

"We need to try on the dresses, and then we have hair and makeup coming at four."

"OK, I need to shower." I look at her, but she doesn't ask me anything else.

"Go take a bath and relax."

I run the bath and add lavender oil to the water. I tie my hair back and slide in. I lie there for a while and decide to call Grant. On the second ring, a woman answers his phone, which surprises me.

"Grant Grace, how can I help you?" She sounds a bit short, and I know she knows who this is because of the caller ID. It must be his assistant, Wendy.

"Hello, is Grant available?" I ask nicely. I think about how she looked at us when we kissed and the jealousy that was in her eyes.

"Who is this speaking?" I roll my eyes.

"Hannah Winterfield." I'm getting annoyed; she knows who this is.

"Mrs. Winterfield, I'm sorry. Grant is in a meeting and asked not to be disturbed. I can leave him a message."

"That will be fine. And whom am I speaking with?" I ask her with an attitude.

"This is Wendy, his personal assistant. I will personally make sure he gets the message, Mrs. Winterfield." She emphasizes the *Mrs.*

"Thank you, Wendy." And I hang up. I feel pissy all of a sudden. Good thing I didn't text him, because she would have read it. I turn on my iPod. I crave music to drown out everything in my head. I turn on my favorite mix and lie back in the tub, turn the jets on, and close my eyes.

I jump up when I hear my phone ring and realize I fell asleep.

"Hello," I say, trying to hide the sleep in my voice.

"Hey, you, you had me worried." His words make me feel bad.

"Grant, I'm sorry. I should have never called you last night; I never wanted you to worry about me."

"Hannah, I'm happy you called me, and I worry about you because I care. And another thing; Wendy told me you made a big deal about having her interrupt my meeting. I gave her orders to get me when you called."

"I have no idea what you are talking about. When I called you before, she answered and asked who it was. I told her it was me, and she said you were in a meeting and asked not to be disturbed. So I left a message." *She is no good,* I think to myself.

"I heard a totally different story." His voice is distant.

"Believe what you want, Grant." I hang up the phone. I hold my breath and go under. I enjoy the calming effect of being underwater. I stay there as long as I can, then come up for air. I see my phone lit up and look at the missed call from Grant. I probably overreacted, but I don't care. I hear my phone ring and see an unfamiliar number.

"Hello," I say with no effort.

"Hannah, what is wrong with you? I wasn't choosing sides; I was just thrown off by what you said."

"OK." I can hear the attitude in my voice.

"Hannah," but that's all he says. I sit in silence and listen to him breathing. "Just listen." "Wendy, I need to speak with you," I hear him page her on the intercom, and within seconds she is in his office.

"Please sit, Wendy."

"Now what did Hannah say?" He is speaking nice and slow, and I think this is one of his tactics.

"Mrs. Winterfield called, asking to speak with you, and when I said hold on, let me get him out of his meeting, she got annoyed with me and told me no, don't do that, just tell him to call me back when he gets out." She emphasizes the *Mrs.* again, and I can't help myself.

"*Bullshit,*" I yell into the phone. "Wendy, I called and you asked who I was. I told you my name, and then you proceeded to tell me Grant was not to be disturbed, which I had no problem with. I have just one question. Why the elaborate story? Why lie about something this insignificant?"

I wish I could see her face when I ask her this question. Then I hear Grant.

"Wendy, answer the question." He sounds intimidating.

"Grant, I think there is just a mix-up in wording." She is caught and doesn't know how to get out of it.

"OK, elaborate. How was there a mix-up?" She still doesn't have an answer.

"Aiden told me on Tuesday that if Hannah were to call you, not to give you the message, or he'd fire me. I felt bad about it when you came to me this morning and told me to interrupt you when she did call. I figured if I gave you the message, Aiden wouldn't find out about the call." My jaw drops into the water, and I hear Grant's anger.

"You fucking work for me. You answer to me and no one else. Do you understand?" His voice is loud, and I get scared for Wendy.

"Drop it, Grant," I hear myself say before I can stop myself.

Grant takes me off speaker and lowers his voice.

"Hannah, don't tell me how to deal with issues in my company." The words are harsh, but his tone isn't.

"Grant, things have changed since Tuesday. Think about it; she was in between a rock and a hard place."

"Wendy, next time Aiden talks to you, you come to me. Go order my lunch." He still sounds mad at her.

"Yes sir," I hear her say.

"I miss you," I say to him before he can say anything. I hear him take a deep breath.

"I miss you too, Hannah." I smile at his words.

"I have to go because I'm in the bath and I have to get into the shower, but I look forward to tonight."

"So you're telling me you're talking to me while naked?" I hear the amusement in his voice, and I blush. How can he make me blush over the phone?

"Yes, I am," I say, trying to hide my amusement as well.

"When you tell me something like that, my mind starts to think about the night in my old bed." I can tell he is enjoying himself.

"Have a good day at work, Mr. Grace," I say, laughing.

"Oh, I will. I will have a wonderful image in my head for the rest of the day."

"Good-bye."

"Good-bye, Hannah."

I hang up and marvel at the fact that he will be thinking of me all day.

I find Becca in my room with all the dresses. I start to look at them lined up on my bed.

"I think you should try this one on." She hands me a red dress, and I shake my head.

"You look better in red," I say, and pick up a black one. I hold it up; the silk feels luxurious.

"You have to try that one on." I take it into the closet, pull off my bra, and pull it over my head. The silk feels cool as it runs down my body. I feel sexy in it, but I can see my panty line. I slide them off and walk out of the closet.

Becca's face lights up when she sees me, and I look in the full-length mirror. The dress is beautiful. It comes to a V in the front, showing the perfect amount of cleavage. I turn around, and that's where it gets sexy. The straps cross across my shoulders, and the back plummets down to my lower back. It bunches there and flares out to a train. I turn back around and look at the front. From the front of the dress, you would never guess what was going on back there. This makes me smile. Grant will be surprised at this.

"Hannah, this is the one." I watch Becca go over to her suitcase and take some stuff out.

"I'll tape you up later," she says, holding up breast tape. I just nod at her.

"What are you going to wear under this?" she says as she feels the dress.

"Nothing," I say and she smiles. "What can I wear? It's silk. Everything will show."

"OK, if you say so." She walks into the closet with the red dress, and when she walks out, I know it is what she should wear.

"Oh, Becca, look at you, you look beautiful."

"You think? Do you think Aiden will like it?" I smile and nod at her.

"He would be stupid if he didn't."

She smiles at me and we both change back into our clothes. We lounge for a large part of the day, and then pick the kids up together.

When we get back to the house, we snack and get ready for the makeup artist and hairstylist. I have no idea what I should do with my hair. Up or down? My parents arrive as the two girls arrive to make us beautiful. We sit in my room and get done up. The girl doing my hair thinks I should wear it up to complement my dress. She comes up with a sexy Roaring Twenties look, with my hair swept back and wavy. I'm not sure I will like it, but when she is done working her magic, I am surprised my hair could ever look this good.

I move on to makeup and notice the time. Grant will be here in less than an hour. I start to get nervous. My mom was excited to hear that a man was coming to get us, and I told her it was nothing, but Becca gave her a look and she could tell it was something. When the makeup artist finishes with me, I watch her touch up Becca's makeup. Becca looks breathtaking. She has beautiful curls floating down her face, and her eyes are smoky like mine.

"Let's get dressed," Becca says. I glance at her, feeling more nervous. The girls leave us to dress. I unbutton my shirt, and Becca hands me the breast-cup tape things. I look at them, confused, and Becca grabs them and puts them on me. I laugh as she does this. I slip into the dress, making sure it doesn't mess with my hair. Once it's on, I look at myself in the mirror and smile. He will love this dress.

"Hey, I'm going to head downstairs," I say.

I walk down the stairs and place my shoes on the last step, then hear the kids running towards me.

"Mommy, you look like a princess," Ella says, making some kind of motion with her hand. It makes me laugh.

"Thank you, lovey." I bend down and kiss her and walk into the kitchen. I watch as my mom's jaw drops.

"Hannah, you look stunning." I smile at her and do a spin to show her the back. I can see she loves it by the look on her face.

"Where's the rest of the dress?" Dad asks, making me laugh.

"So when is your ride coming to get you?" Mom asks.

"I believe Grant said he would be here at six thirty." I look over at her to see her reaction.

"Oh really…so you're going with Grant?"

"Yes, and Becca is going with Aiden. She just signed a merger with them, and they decided we would all go together." The kids start yelling about a car being in front of the house. I glance out and see a limo. I take a deep breath and start to get anxious. I wait until I hear a knock at the door, then head to it. When Hunter opens it, Grant and Aiden are standing there. I smile to try to hide my surprise. Grant puts out his hand, and Hunter slaps it. Grant makes a sound, and Hunter slaps Aiden's hand.

"Hunter, let them in the door." I move him to the side.

Grant kisses my cheek, and then Aiden does the same, not looking me in the eyes.

"Becca should be right down. Do you want a drink?" Grant looks breathtaking in his tux. Ella grabs my hand.

"Do a turn, Mommy, show everyone your dress," Ella yells. She takes my hand and I turn around, revealing my bare back. I meet Grant's eyes again and smile.

"You look beautiful." He steps toward me, but we get distracted by Becca coming down the stairs. Aiden walks over to the bottom step of the staircase and takes her hand. She greets him with a quick kiss on the lips and a devilish look. I hear them whisper and look at Grant. I take his hand and lead him into the kitchen.

"Ready to meet the parents?" I ask, looking him over.

"I was born ready; parents love me." He shoots me his million-dollar smile, and I melt. I lead him into the kitchen for the dreaded introduction.

"Mom, I would like you to meet Grant Grace." She turns around and puts out her hand.

"Oh, Grant, it's a pleasure to meet you." He takes it in his giant hand.

"The pleasure is all mine, Mrs. Redman." I see her blush. "Dad, this is Grant." He puts out his hand.

"You have the Porsche, right?" My dad is all about the cars.

"Yes, I just got a 1966 Shelby Cobra. You should see that one. She is beautiful." My dad looks at him in shock.

"That's a rare one."

"Yes, it is. I stumbled across it. A car collector's family reached out to me, and I jumped at the chance."

"You're lucky. Must have cost you a pretty penny."

"You should see my collection. I think you would like it." They start to talk cars, and I walk away to get a drink. I start to pour a glass of water, when my mom walks over to me.

"Hannah, he is handsome."

"Yes, Mother, he is, and he is also richer than God." She laughs at me.

"Have fun tonight, that's all I'm saying. Enjoy yourself, let loose." She kisses my cheek and walks over to Becca. I see Aiden talking to Ella.

"Aiden, do you want something to drink?"

"No, thank you, we should be leaving soon." I nod and walk back over to Grant and my dad. They are in deep conversation about an engine, and I wonder if I can pull them out of it.

"Hey." I place my hand on Grant's arm. "We should get going soon, if you don't want to be late." He looks at his watch and nods at me.

"Mr. Redman, it's been a pleasure speaking with you." He puts his hand out to shake my father's hand.

"Grant, call me Gary." They shake and my dad smiles at me. I can tell he likes him too.

"Becca, are you ready?" I look over at her, and she is staring into Aiden's eyes. I can't blame her. I've been there, and I know how charming he can be.

Grant's eyes are all over me as he is talking to my mom. I can tell she likes this, because she keeps looking from me to him. I call Hunter and Ella over and hug and kiss them good-bye.

"Have fun at the ball, Mommy. Don't lose a shoe." She is serious as she says this, and I laugh.

"I won't, sweetheart. You be good for Grandma and Pop, OK?"

I feel Grant's hand on my bare back and it gives me chills.

"Cold?" he whispers in my ear.

"No." The sexy grin appears on his face. He puts his hand out to Hunter, and they slap hands. This time Hunter makes the sound, and Grant laughs. I kiss my parents good-bye and grab my shoes.

I feel the excitement as I notice two limos parked out front. I give Becca a look, and she smiles and shrugs her shoulders at me. Grant leads me down the driveway, helping me hold up the train of my dress. The driver opens the door and I get in carefully. I slide over and watch Grant slip in next to me. I place my clutch down between us and start to put my shoes on. Grant grabs my legs and swings them onto his lap. I watch him put my shoes on and strap them into place. When I look up, he meets my lips with his. His lips feel warm, and he parts my lips with his. The way his bottom lip pushes down on mine drives me crazy; he bites my bottom lip and grazes it with his teeth. I smile at him when he pulls back.

"I've been waiting to do that all day."

"Have you?" I say.

"After you told me you were in the bath, I wanted to leave work and join you." He gives me his perfect smile, and I lean in and steal another kiss.

"You look handsome tonight, Mr. Grace."

"You look absolutely stunning tonight, Hannah. This dress is…" He slides his fingers down my back, losing his words.

"I have a feeling you are going to be the talk of the gala. I have something for you." I watch as he leans over the seat to grab a bag. I perk up and look at it as he places it on my lap.

"When I saw it, I knew it would be perfect for you." I look at him with curiosity as I reach into the bag. I pull out a large velvet box. I move the bag to the side, and place the box on my lap and begin to open it. I become speechless when I see what's inside. It's a diamond bracelet. It is remarkable. I look over at Grant.

"Grant, this is too much. You shouldn't have." I feel like I don't deserve this.

"No, it's not. You deserve much more, but I didn't want to scare you off." He smiles at me, and I lean in and give him a soft kiss, then look into his eyes. Oh, those eyes.

"Thank you. I love it." He takes it out of the box and puts it on my wrist. It is heavy, and every way I turn my wrist, it glistens. I stare and wonder how many carats it is and how much it cost. Why is he spending so much money on me?

"It's a Harry Winston. When I saw it, I knew it was you. It has round and baguettes stones." I look at him in shock and grip it tight around my wrist. I never would want to lose this.

"Should I insure this?" I look at him, feeling stupid.

"I already did. I opened a policy for you, and we can just add other stuff on as you get it." He smiles, and I look at him, dumbfounded. Other stuff? I'm not used to lavish gifts like this.

"Grant, are you sure? This looks expensive; I don't want you wasting your money on me." I give him an uneasy look.

"Hannah, I want to give you the world." He leans over and wraps his arms around me. I snuggle into his nook and enjoy his scent.

"Do you want to know about it?" I look at him.

"Like what?"

"Well, it's forty-one carats." As he says this, I choke.

"Grant, are you out of your mind?"

"No, are you?"

"I don't need a forty-one-carat bracelet. I would be happy with a silly band from you. I'm not into the money and presents, Grant." I look into his blue-oasis eyes and try to figure him out.

"I told you money is not an issue. I want to give you everything you could ever want." I realize he means this.

"I feel inferior because I can't match these presents in return."

"Hannah, being with you is better than anything you could ever buy me. I wanted to buy you the matching necklace and earrings, but I thought it would be too much, too fast. I want you to have nice things, so let me do this." He picks up my hand and kisses it.

"I love it…" I want to tell him I love him, but I can't. I shift closer and take his hand in mine. "Thank you, Grant, it's the nicest thing I have ever gotten." I lean my head on his shoulder, and he wraps his arms around, pulling me in tighter. He takes my left hand and kisses where my rings used to be.

"You took your rings off." I don't look at him. I just stare at my hand. I have marks where the rings were and probably will for a while.

"I thought I would see how it felt not wearing them. Plus, I didn't want people thinking you were with a married woman." I try to smile at him but fail. He kisses me and we sit like this the whole way into the city. No words are spoken; we just enjoy being next to each other.

As we get onto Park Avenue, Grant sits up.

"Are you ready for this?"

"Ready for what?"

"The press line. I want you to walk it with me."

"What does that mean?" I sit up, alarmed.

"We stand and take pictures and answer questions about the charity and all that stuff." I freeze.

"Grant, I have never done this before. Are you sure you want me to go with you?"

"Of course. I want to show you off to the world." The grin comes back on his face, and I agree. I get butterflies in my stomach thinking about it. He wants me to do this for him, so I will. It's the least I can do, since he just gave me a forty-one-carat bracelet.

I begin to fidget as we pull up to the sea of people. I can see Becca and Aiden getting out of their limo, and I wish I could be like her. She is tall, beautiful, and confident. I watch as they begin to walk and see the flickering of all the flashes from the cameras. Our limo creeps up and I look at Grant.

"You OK?" His voice is gentle. I nod my head and he takes my hand while we wait for the driver to open the door. I watch as he steps out in one graceful movement and buttons his tux jacket. I slide over and see his hand out for me to take. I smile at him and take his hand. Slowly I step out of the limo and onto the sidewalk. Grant helps me straighten out the train of my dress, and I blush as his hand sweeps my bottom. He is what I have always wanted, but it wasn't until now that I realize this. He places his hand in mine so our souls are touching, and we begin to walk.

I see Becca and Aiden posing together farther down, and pray that I don't fall flat on my face. I can hear people asking Grant questions, and he shoots one-word answers back at them. As we approach Becca and Aiden, Grant stops me. He slips his hand out of mine and brings it to my back. His fingers are creeping into the side of my dress, and I shoot him a look. He gives me a sly smile and kisses me. I can feel him trying to relax and distract me at the same time, and he succeeds. He starts to lead me forward; the flashes of light are coming from every direction. I'm pretty sure I'm going to look like a deer in headlights in all the pictures. When we stop, he takes his hand from my back and wraps it around my waist to pull me closer to him. I steal a quick glance at his beautiful face and begin to smile.

People are shouting his name from every direction so they can get a photo, but he looks at me and whispers in my ear, "In case I forget to tell you later, I'm falling in love with you." He's falling in love with me, and I'm falling in love with him. It's now or never Hannah. Tell him how you feel. I let my hand wander down to his perfect butt and I squeeze it.

"Right back at you," I say, beaming with excitement. Then I hear my name. I turn and see Mrs. Grace.

"Hannah, I'm so happy you are here." I look at her in shock as she leans in to hug me.

"Tori, what are you doing here? You should be home resting." I pull away and take her hands in mine while getting a good look at her. Her tall, slender body looks amazing in a navy-blue gown. I see the high neckline, and I know she chose it to hide her incision line.

"Oh, Hannah, stop worrying about me. If anything happens, you're here." She gives me a wicked smile and winks at me.

"Mother, we have to keep moving," Grant says, interrupting us.

"Take some pictures with me." She gives him a loving smile, and he steps closer to her. I start to step back to get out of the way, but Grant grabs me.

"Oh no you don't, she wants us together." I smile at his words and think *yes, she does.*

He pulls me back in, with Mrs. Grace on the other side. With both of his arms around us, we pose for a few more pictures. I hear them yelling, "Who is your date, Mr. Grace?" Mrs. Grace steps away.

"This is Hannah, Grant's girlfriend," she announces.

We look at each other and laugh. We haven't even talked about it yet, and here she is telling the world we are together. I don't think he minds because he did just tell me he is falling in love with me.

After what seems like hours of posing and smiling, we walk into the hotel lobby. I feel like an arm ornament, and I want to find Becca. I glance over at Grant, who is in deep discussion about a hotel he is building on a private island and think he won't notice if I slip away. I slip my hand out of his, but he grabs it back. He stops talking and directs all his attention to me. The men surrounding him stare at me as well. I feel shy all of a sudden.

"I'm just going to talk to Becca," I whisper in his ear, trying not to draw any more attention to myself.

"I hate to see you go." He gives me the million-dollar smile and I walk away. I get a few steps away when I hear him say, "But I love to watch you leave." I turn around, blushing.

"Behave, will you." He takes the few steps that separate us and kisses me. I place my hands on his lapels and gently push him away.

"Come find me when you are done talking business."

"Do I bore you, my love?" I love the sound of those words as they slide off his tongue.

"Terribly," I tease. I kiss him again and walk away, smiling, because I can still feel his eyes on me.

CHAPTER THIRTY-ONE

I see Becca talking to a man, and as I approach her, I feel a hand on my elbow directing me away. When I turn, I'm face to face with Aiden.

"I need a moment with you." His voice is serious, and I follow him a few feet away to a small alcove in the lobby. When we stop, he faces me. "I don't want this to be weird." I sense his uneasiness.

"Aiden, don't." I make sure not to show any expression. We are surrounded by hundreds of people, and I don't want to draw any more attention. "It is what it is. I wish you the best with Becca." I smile at him and in a friendly gesture, I touch his arm.

"Hannah, I don't want Becca. I want you." His look gets intense.

I try to remain calm and collected, but his words hit me deep in my soul. I feel like the wind has been knocked out of me. I want to cry at his words, because they are what I wanted to hear days ago, before falling for Grant.

"Well, you fucked it up." My voice gets lower, and he steps closer to me. "I would be here with you if you didn't fuck my best friend and call me a fucking whore. You did this, not me." I step back and see Grant's eyes glued to me. The look in his eyes changes in an instant, and he walks away from the group of men he was in deep discussion with. I have to get away from Aiden.

"It's done, don't do this again." My tone is harsh, and I walk toward Becca, who seems to have been watching us as well. When I reach her, she smiles at me.

"Are you going to tell me what that was about?" Her tone is non-chalant, and I watch her take a sip of champagne.

"It was nothing." I brush it off.

I feel Grant's presence before he slips his arms around my waist. I enjoy the feeling of his hands as they glide around my waist on the silk.

"I'm not letting you out of my sight again," he breathes into my ear, and kisses it gently. Becca gives us a weak smile, then walks away to Aiden. "What did he have to say?"

"Nothing of any importance." I look into his eyes and watch as they adjust deeper and darker like a stormy night. It's amazing how he and Aiden have the same angry eyes.

"I don't want you talking to him, or anywhere near him. Do you understand?" I see a flash of lightning through his eyes, and I can tell he is pissed. I shift a little, feeling uneasy of his mood.

"I wasn't the one talking; he was just apologizing to me, Grant. I'm here with you, only you." I see the darkness fade from his eyes and the blue oasis is back. I take a deep breath and realize I diffused the situation fast.

When we start to mingle, I see John and Autumn. I begin to won-der if Grant really told him about us and if Aiden did the same. I feel my stomach turn at the thought and try to push it out of my mind. As always Autumn looks amazing. She is wearing a strapless fitted gown that hugs her curvy body perfectly. I can see a sexy slit that runs up her thigh, and her leg peeks out with every step she takes.

"Hannah, it's good to see you."

I lean in to kiss John on the cheek and feel awkward all of a sud-den, like he does know.

"Good to see you again, John," I say. Autumn pulls me in for a double-cheek kiss.

"Hannah, I love the dress."

"I love yours."

"You haven't seen Shane and Annie yet, have you?" I ask her.

"Grant didn't tell you? She was having some trouble with the baby." She looks around. "They haven't released it to the press yet, so don't say anything, but they put her on bed rest in the hospital. They are hoping to get her a few more weeks along so the baby can develop a little more."

"Grant never told me. I hope everything will be OK." I see Grant hugging Shane. I catch his eye, and he smiles at me as he walks over.

"Hannah, you look beautiful." He hugs me. When he feels my bare back, he pulls back, taking my hand so I can spin around.

"Lucky bastard," he says to Grant. I laugh at him.

"You look dapper yourself, Shane." I look his tux over and smile.

"Oh, this old thing?" He pulls at his bow tie and his perfect teeth peek through his lips. I wonder if I should bring Annie up or leave it alone.

"Annie wishes she could be here tonight, but you know, with the whole baby thing right now, I had to lock her up in the hospital room." He still has his sense of humor with all that is going on.

"Shane, everything will work out. It's best that she stays there. They can monitor the baby and her."

"She wanted to call you yesterday, but felt stupid."

"I wish she would have; tell her to call me whenever she wants. I would love to go see her. I can take the day shift, if that helps."

"Hannah, you don't have to worry about our problems."

"I wouldn't offer if I didn't care." I give him a reassuring look, and he returns it with a thankful one.

"Grant, you have a good one here; don't fuck it up." Shane slaps Grant's back and Grant takes my hand in his.

The giant ballroom looks exquisite. I look around at all the delicate details and feel the excitement in the air. Grant leads me through the room to our table. Of course it is the biggest and most extravagant table, in the center of the room facing the dance floor. Mrs. Grace is already seated, so I walk around the table.

"How are you feeling?"

"Hannah, stop worrying about me, you're not at work. I'm fine." I can tell she doesn't want to discuss her health. "You can sit next to me." She pats the seat next to her, and Grant pulls it out for me.

"Now, Mother, please don't scare her off."

I bat my lashes at Grant. "Your mother would never do such a thing." She nudges my arm and Grant laughs at us.

"You have no idea what she has done in the past." He gives his mother a stern look.

"It was never me." She looks offended, but a smile appears on her lips.

I love the family teasing and banter, and for the first time, I feel part of it. Shane, John, and Grant begin to talk about business, so I direct all my attention to Mrs. Grace.

"How have your follow-ups gone?"

"Hannah, relax, we are at a gala. I don't want to discuss my health."

"I'm not going to relax till you tell me." I cross my arms and lean back in the chair. Autumn and Becca are talking, and I can see Autumn looking over at us now and again.

"Fine," she finally says. "Dr. Mitchell cleared me, and my cardiologist at home said everything is going great." I see her tense up a bit.

"Are you lying to me? I can call Dr. Mitchell now, if you would like." I call her out. She sighs heavily.

"Fine, you got me. I'm going back in on Monday for some more testing. Something's up."

"See, that wasn't hard, was it?" I take her hand. "Now can you please relax?" She motions and a server comes over with champagne.

"I see my son has forgotten his manners, and hasn't gotten you a drink." She makes sure to say it loudly enough so her sons turn around.

"I'm sorry, Hannah, I'll get you a drink."

"No thank you, Grant. Your mother was thoughtful enough to get me one." I take a sip of the cold, crisp champagne, then wink at him. His sexy grin appears, and he takes the glass out of my hand and places it down on the table.

"I will return her shortly, Mother. I need to show her off a bit." I look at him, horrified.

"I'm not an accessory, you know." I try for insulted and fail.

"No, I thought you were more like a trophy or badge of honor I want to flaunt." I playfully slap his chest, and he takes me in his arms in front of his mother.

"You are out of control today; your mother is watching us," I whisper lightly in his neck.

"Let's give her a show then." With that he kisses me and picks me up. I surprise him by kissing him a little deeper and harder. He stops and places me down. "Will you behave? My mom is staring at us now." I love the amusement all over his face. I look over at Mrs. Grace, who is smiling from ear to ear.

"Please don't stop on my account. I don't think I have ever seen Grant this happy or affectionate before." Grant pulls me back into his body. People are watching us with interest.

"Mr. Grace, you seem to draw a crowd wherever you go."

"I think it's you and the dress."

"I'm going to mingle with the girls." I let my hand slide down his chest to the top of his pants, then walk over to Becca and Autumn, who are watching us.

"You definitely have a way with the most difficult Graces." Autumn nods toward Mrs. Grace and Grant. "I was just telling Becca that I have never seen Grant be so affectionate."

"Really?" I can't hide my shock.

"Never," she repeats again.

"Mrs. Grace was never nice to us till you came around. I think you should introduce Becca, or we can make it a test. We should have Aiden introduce her and see how rude she will be, then have you go over and tell her she's your best friend, and see if she changes." Becca agrees, so I nod. Becca gets Aiden's attention.

"Hey, are you going to introduce me to your mom?" I can see Aiden get uneasy at the thought as he shifts from one foot to the other. They don't see it, but I pick up on it. I'm somehow still in tune with his body.

He nods at Becca, but looks at me as he takes her hand. We watch as Mrs. Grace stares her down and doesn't shake her hand. I feel horrible that she is treating Becca this way.

"Go save the day," Autumn whispers in my ear. I can see Mrs. Grace roll her eyes at them, and it pisses me off. Why is she such a bitch to everyone?

"Hello," I say sweetly as I approach her. "Tori, I see you have met my oldest, and most cherished friend in the whole world." I smile at Becca and look over at Mrs. Grace.

"Yes, we just met; Aiden was telling me she just signed a large merger with the company. It's not the best idea to mix work and pleasure." I shoot her a look.

"Really, that's not what you were telling me when I was at your house." My loyalty is to Becca, and I'm going to make that clear. Mrs. Grace looks at me, shocked.

"Well, Hannah, that was different."

"Why? Love is love. Let Aiden find it where he wants." I'm not backing down to her. She doesn't intimidate me like she does the others.

"He doesn't like you, Becca. I hate to be the bearer of bad news, but I know Aiden." Aiden just stands there frozen and doesn't say a word. I can see Becca's expression fall.

"You are mean. That was uncalled for," I snap at her and take Becca's hand and walk away.

I lead her through the crowd of people and into the ladies room. She heads into the stall. I go into a vacant stall and hear women enter and start talking.

"Can you believe who Grant brought? I heard she was hired help at the estate in the Cape. He has a thing for charity cases."

"I heard all the Grace men have gotten a ride from her." I feel the blood leave my face, and I freeze. Where the hell are they hearing this?

"Well, she was hired help. I know she slept with Aiden." I know the bitch voice, and I fly out of the stall.

"Hello, Carla." I step in her face and she freezes. "Talking shit as usual, I see." I look over at the other two twits. "Ladies, you will have to excuse Carla. She is still bitter from her breakup. Keep it up, Carla, and I swear I will have Grant blacklist you from every event from here to Timbuktu." I get closer to her before I step away; I learned this move from Grant. I can see Becca coming out of the stall with her glass still in her hand. I step away and watch as she throws her drink on Carla.

"Looks like you will have to leave now. Take your flying monkeys with you." Becca is a pit bull. We walk out of the bathroom with our heads held high.

"Let's get the fuck out of here," I say to Becca.

"No not yet. I want to make him suffer a bit. The dick didn't even stick up for me," she says.

"Well then, let's make him suffer." I give her an evil laugh. "Thank you for sticking up for me with the old hag." I take her hand in mine.

"My loyalty is to you. These people are strangers to me."

"Hannah, would it be bad if I slept with him one more time?" I start laughing at her.

"No...Not. At. All." We hear that dinner will be served, so we head back to the table to take our seats. I make sure to leave the seat open between Mrs. Grace and me for Grant to sit in. Becca sits on the other side of me, and we chat with Autumn, who is a few seats away. None of the Grace's are in sight.

"Where is everyone?" I ask Autumn.

"It's speech time," she answers, and I hear the emcee come over on a microphone. He introduces the Grace's, who all walk out on stage. I avoid eye contact with Mrs. Grace. We all applaud them, then the room goes silent. Mrs. Grace steps up to the podium, her sons are on either side of her. I lean back and take a big sip of champagne.

"I would like to start tonight by telling everyone a personal story. A few weeks ago, I came down from the Cape to tie up some loose ends for this event, and in the process, I had a heart attack, which resulted in triple-bypass surgery. I was quite scared, and I'm sure I scared my sons as well." She looks over at them, and they all show her love and support.

"Before surgery I prayed." She pauses. "When I woke up, I met an angel." I finally look at her. "I met an angel, who cared for me and changed me forever." She looks at Grant, and he smiles at her.

"As I healed, I got to know her and her story. It is a sad one, much like mine and many of yours. Her husband was murdered last year." I feel the tears running down my cheeks. I was not ready for this. Why didn't she tell me? Fuck, I don't want everyone knowing my business or sob story. Becca's hand makes its way into mine, and I squeeze it. The hurt is heavy in my chest.

"I admire my angel in many ways. She is confident, loving, and stronger than I could ever be." Grant is staring at me. The tears keep running down my face. I see Aiden shift out of the corner of my eye and hand something to the emcee, who walks over to me and hands me a handkerchief. I thank him, then look over at Aiden and mouth *thank you.* I feel Grant's stare deepen.

"She is what my family has been waiting for. She came into our lives and showed us how to love again, and how to be loved. My courageous angel is a mother of two beautiful children who are so filled with life and love. She has experienced such hurt and sorrow in her life, and yet when you meet her, you see nothing but hope and love in her. I have to say I was lost when my beloved Grant died, and I think I still might be. My angel has picked herself up and has showed me there is still light at the end of the tunnel. I just need to keep walking to get to it."

I lose her there. I think about how I could possibly give off that I have it together. I have been lost every single day since Chase has been gone. My head is spinning with her words. I hear applause and watch as everyone stands up and Becca pulls me up. I wipe the tears away once more, and push my feelings down deep. They all leave the stage and come to the table. Mrs. Grace walks up to me and hugs me.

"You are my angel." She pulls me in, but I can't get over how she acted toward Becca.

"I'm still upset with you. Actions speak louder than words." I pull away and look at her. She steps to the side and takes Becca's hand.

"I'm sorry, Becca. I wish you and Aiden the best." Becca smiles.

"Thank you, Mrs. Grace."

"Aiden loves you, not her," Mrs. Grace whispers in my ear, and my heart drops to the floor. I must be white as a ghost because Grant steps in.

"Hannah, are you OK?" I nod my head at him and sit down. *No, I'm not OK,* I want to tell him, but I don't. I see Aiden sit next to Becca. How does Mrs. Grace know Aiden is in love with me? Does she know what happened between us? I want to run, but I'm frozen in my seat. I pick at the food on my plate and listen to all the conversations going on at the table.

"Hannah, you have to eat something; you look pale." I glance over at Grant and put a bite of potato in my mouth to shut him up. I shift the food around, but I can't get Mrs. Grace's words out of my head. He is in love with me? He told me he wanted me, but I never thought he was in love with me. Grant slides his hand down my back. I see my plate has been cleared, and I hear the band start playing a slow song.

"Would you like to dance?" He stands and holds out his hand. When I take it, he leads me to the dance floor. I can see others making their way on the floor. A woman begins singing '*At Last.*' Grant takes me in his arms and starts sweeping me across the floor. His legs are much longer than mine, and I struggle to keep up with him. It takes us a few seconds to get in tune with each other on the dance floor, but when we do, we own it. He spins me and dips me at the end of the song, and I hear people clapping. He lifts me up and kisses me. I stand in his arms for a moment, then break away when I feel a tap on my shoulder.

"May I cut in?" Shane is smiling, and Grant steps aside. '*What a Wonderful World*' begins to play and Shane takes me away.

"You two look happy," he says, looking everywhere but at me.

"I suppose," I say.

"You and Aiden looked the same way earlier." I catch his eye.

"If people looked at us right now, what would they think?"

"Good point, but I'm not in love with you like they are."

"This word keeps getting thrown around like it's nothing."

"What word?"

"*Love*. It's not a word that should be thrown around. It's a deep emotion for someone to feel. How do you know they are both in love with me?"

"Brothers talk, Hannah. I would never repeat what they tell me to anyone."

"That makes one of you." I look away and feel his stare.

"What the hell is that supposed to mean?" His voice is getting loud.

"I heard John was the culprit for the fight in the office. He told Aiden something that should have never been shared."

"I can't speak for my brother, but I was worried too, when I heard you fooled around with both of them." His words shoot into my like bullets.

"That's not fair, Shane. You have no idea what I got caught up in. I'm here with Grant, and Aiden is here with my best friend. Everything is clear now."

"Is it? Then why was Aiden the one to see you crying and sent you his handkerchief? He might be with Becca, but his eyes are always on you. You are setting up World War Three. I hope you realize this."

"Shane, how is this your business? I told you I'm here with Grant, and only Grant."

"I was just making sure." I roll my eyes. "Hannah, I'm passing no judgment on you. I have never seen either of them so happy. I just don't want to see either one of them hurt, and I don't want to see you get hurt." I feel another tap on my shoulder. I dread turning around.

"May I cut in?" Aiden's eyes are blazing, and Shane steps to the side.

He slips his arms around me as another song starts.

"Are you OK?"

"Fine."

"Hannah." He breathes my name into my ear, and I feel lost.

"Aiden, I'm here with Grant. He is going to get pissed off if he sees us dancing. He doesn't want me near you."

"Why?"

"Do I have to state the obvious?"

"I just have one question, and I swear I will leave you alone for the rest of your life." I finally look up into his eyes. "Did it mean anything to you?"

I see Grant staring at us. I struggle as I look at the man I'm falling in love with, and the man holding me.

"Did it mean anything to you?" I ask. I can feel my heart pick up its pace.

"It meant everything." I think he might kiss me, so I pull away and walk off the dance floor, leaving him standing alone. I see Grant heading toward me, so I make a beeline for the bar.

"I need two shots of Patron, please." The bartender nods and pours me two shots. I take them back to back and feel the warmth as they go down. I need more.

"Can I please have a bourbon?" I take the drink and turn around to find Grant standing behind me.

"I told you, no more Aiden. What the fuck was that?" He makes sure to keep his voice low and his face shows no emotion.

"What the fuck was what? We danced, and if you noticed I walked away."

"Hannah, I told you I didn't want you talking to him or being around him."

"Are you jealous of him?" If Grant and I are going to make this work, we need to get this out in the open.

"Well, you already fucked him, Hannah." I want to slap him but refrain from making a scene.

"That's all I needed to hear, Grant." I walk away, but he grabs my arm. I keep walking and he doesn't let go. I try to shake him off, but his grip tightens.

When I finally reach the table, I grab my clutch. "Let's go," I say to Becca. That's all I say, and she is up, and following me.

"Grant, let go of me." I try to pull my arm away.

"No, we need to talk." He picks up his pace so he is next to me. He follows me all the way outside. I keep walking, even though I have no idea where I'm headed.

"Hannah." I turn around and slap him right across his face. He stands there, shocked, and Becca steps back.

"I'm not doing this, Grant." He grabs me around the waist.

"Hannah, I didn't mean it."

"Yes, you did. You are going to throw it in my face whenever you feel insecure, and by the looks of it, I'll be hearing often about how I fucked Aiden." I turn and face him.

"I fucked your brother, Grant. I can't change it, but I choose you, not him." I point my finger into his chest.

"I still don't like it." His eyes are still dark, showing the storm within him hasn't subsided.

"I can't change the past. Never once have I said, Grant, you cheated on Carla with me, so that makes me think you will cheat on me." I get angrier and sarcastic.

"I never cheated on you. I was never with you. What I did in the past is in the past. I can't change it," I yell.

"It's my brother, Hannah."

"Well, side with him, Grant. I'm done with all of this." I wave my hand in the air and see my bracelet. I start to take it off.

"Hannah, don't be stupid. It's yours." I throw it at him.

"And I was yours." Becca has stopped a cab, and I walk away and climb in. I watch Grant run his fingers over the bracelet. He doesn't even try to stop me, and this breaks my heart. It breaks my heart because I am the one to blame for all of this. This is all my fault, and I have no idea how to fix it. I am weak, and because of my weakness I am walking away from the best thing that has ever happened to me. I feel the pieces of my heart fall to the ground, and I leave them all around Manhattan as we drive.

"Where to?" I hear the driver say, and Becca gives him an address. I look out the window, holding Becca's hand, while the tears leave my eyes. She doesn't push me to talk, because she heard the whole thing.

CHAPTER THIRTY-TWO

When we pull up to Aiden's high-rise, I look over at Becca. "Are you kidding me?"

"No, it's where our clothes are. We can get them and hightail it out of here."

The doorman opens my door, and I step out, not caring if I ruin my dress. When we enter the lobby, I remember how I felt when I was here last. I see Sam, and he walks over to me.

"Mrs. Winterfield, I was expecting to pick you up. Is everything OK?"

"Yes, Sam. I have a little problem. I need to get my suitcase. Is that possible?" He checks his phone.

"Yes. I brought it up to Grant's apartment and Ms. Shultz's to Aiden's."

"Could I go up and change?"

"Yes, I will take you up." He takes us to Aiden's first. Becca is in and out in under a minute. When she gets back into the elevator, we head to the top floor.

"I was thinking about kicking it old school tonight. I have clothes. You wanna go out clubbing?" Becca asks. I feel a little drunk from the two shots and bourbon, and I smile at Becca.

"Sam, would you be able to drive us somewhere?" He looks at me and nods.

When the doors open, I walk right in and look around. The view from the top is amazing. The sky is dark, but everything down below is lit up. I run my finger down the window and think of how I wanted to be with Grant tonight. I head down a long hallway and open up a door. It looks like Grant's master bedroom, and it smells like him, and that stops me dead in my tracks. I want to run back to him and tell him how sorry I am, but I'm a coward. I fear his rejection. Becca throws her suitcase on the bed and opens it. I take my dress off. She throws a new, shorter dress at me, and I put it right on.

"Bec, I have no underwear. This dress is way too short." We start laughing.

"When was the last time you let loose?" I watch as she puts on hot shorts and a tank top. She looks good in anything. I look in her suitcase and steal a pair of underwear. I slip them on, and we stuff our dresses in the suitcase.

"You ready?" I ask.

"No." Becca stops and takes out my perfume and walk over to his bed. She lifts his comforter and sprays it on his pillow.

"What was that?" I ask.

"Payback." Becca takes out another bottle and sprays me with it.

"Bec."

"It doesn't smell. It's pheromones. It drives guys crazy."

"Let's party then." I feel a drunken grin appear on my face.

Sam takes our bags as we go back down. As we leave the building, I see the other driver out front. Sam opens the door.

"Derek, please take the ladies anywhere they want to go." He nods and we get in.

"Where to?"

"A good club, please," Becca says.

"Any specific one?" We both shake our heads.

"Surprise us," Becca says, flirting.

I lean back in the seat and leave it all behind. I'm finally leaving them behind. From here forward, I will never see or speak with a Grace again.

I make the vow to myself and watch as we pull up to a club. The line is around the building, but the driver pulls up to the front door.

"Ladies, I had Sam call ahead, you will be seated as VIP." He walks around to open the door for us.

"Thank you, Derek," I say. Becca walks ahead of me right to the front of the line.

"Becca Shultz and Hannah Winterfield." He looks over the list and looks at Becca.

"I have a Hannah Redman with your name."

"That's me, that's my maiden name," I say. He lifts the velvet rope and we are in.

I can feel the bass of the music ring throughout my body. It has been forever since Becca and I went out clubbing. A woman wearing a leather jumpsuit greets us.

"Ladies, please follow me." We look at each other, impressed, and follow her to a table that is roped off.

"Can I get you ladies a drink?"

"We need four shots of Patron and two martinis, please." I'm ordering as much liquor as I can handle because I need to drink my sorrows away.

"I will have a cosmo," Becca adds.

"So I'm guessing this is one of Grant's clubs," Becca yells over at me. Fuck. Is that why Derek brought us here?

"You think?"

"Hannah, he owns everything."

The waitress comes back with our drinks. We each take a shot. I hold up mine.

"To the Grace brothers, the biggest fucking assholes I have ever met." We cheer and take the shots. She hands me the second shot and makes a toast.

"To Aiden, the best fuck either one of us has had in a long time." I clink her shot glass with mine and take the shot. I feel the effects of it fast. We drink at a steady pace, and the waitress keeps them flowing.

The music is getting better, and then we hear it. Becca's jam comes on, and she jumps up.

"This is my favorite song, let's go." I jump up and follow her to the dance floor. I let go and dance the day off. Becca and I have no shame. We are all over each other. A guy comes behind me, and Becca pushes him away, claiming me. I laugh as she acts out the unspoken girl rule: If an ugly guy comes along, it's your best friend's duty to act as your lesbian lover. She whips me around and grinds me from behind. We dance for a few more songs, then go back to the table to get some much-needed drinks. I feel tipsy and need more alcohol. I see a new round at the table, and we each take our shots and start laughing over the guy. I think I spot Aiden, and my stomach drops.

"Bec, let's go dance." As I say the words, another great song comes on.

"Hell yeah! Let's do it." She takes my hand and we get on the dance floor. I keep looking around, but by the end of the song, I'm drunk and don't care anymore. Usher comes on, and I can feel my body let go. I am carefree and loving it. Then I see Becca freeze. Grant is behind me. I look at him and keep dancing. I make sure to move closer to Becca, and we dance around each other. I see Aiden over Becca's shoulder. It's like they are surrounding us.

"Fuck, they're both here." Becca grabs me tighter. We dance with each other, ignoring both of them.

"Ready?" Becca asks. I smile then turn around, and we move like we used to. I can see Aiden moving around until he is standing next to Grant. Their eyes are glued on us. We separate and start singing to each other. She starts to sing, and I laugh at her and stumble at bit. I feel hands on me, and Grant pulls the guy from before off of me and throws him. I look at Grant as the next song comes on, but get quickly distracted. I'm so drunk right now that I can't stay concentrated on anything for long. Oh shit, they're playing LL Cool J's *'Doin' It.'* Bec and I sing to each other and totally forget they are here. Oh, it feels good to let go. She pulls my hair and slaps my ass to the words, and I let her. We go all out, acting the song out together. When I look over, they aren't around anymore. Bec shrugs her shoulders.

"Fuck 'em," she yells.

"We did." I'm beyond drunk and it feels good, like I've been liberated. Some Flo Rida comes on next and we go crazy. We start jumping to the beat and I feel his hands. Not Grant's, Aiden's. I know the difference immediately, but I don't care. I rub my ass into him, and he takes my hips in his giant hands. I turn around and sing to him. I sing how if I took him home, it would be a home run, and watch as his grin appears. I walk away and Becca gets on him. I take him from behind and show no dignity. It's dancing, not sex, but it still feels good with him. We sing about wild ones and saddling me up. It makes me think about when he told me he had plans for me.

I back off and dance around when I feel Grant's hands on me. I turn and sing the words to him as I rub against his body. I run my hands all over him and grind into him. He sings the man's part back to me, and I laugh. I would have never guessed in a million years he would do something like that. He sings that he will show me another side of him, a side I never thought I would see. We start to dance and he can move. I think about how good he would be in bed. His hips move in such a way that I can't help but think about him inside of me.

Rihanna comes on next and I think *how appropriate. 'Where have you been.'* Becca comes over to me and I leave Grant. We sing to each other and she is all I need; she has always been there. We dance with each other and I see Aiden looking at me. How fucked up is this? Two gorgeous men and they both want me. How the hell did this happen? Becca goes for Grant, so I go for Aiden. I slowly creep up to him like I'm stalking him. He stands there while I glide around him. I grab his ass when I'm behind him, then walk in front of him, and he grabs me. He takes my hands and brings them in the air and spins me.

I laugh at him and leave him to get Becca. Grant is dancing with her and I feel envious. I watch them and his eyes meet mine. They are dark, but I don't give a fuck. I want another drink. I head off the floor and back to the table, where I finish my drink in one gulp. I look over at the waitress and order another and a water. I watch Becca and Grant; Aiden sits down at the table. He must have changed after the gala, because he is no longer in his black tux. He looks more relaxed in jeans and a polo.

"How did you find us?" I sit on his lap, and his hand finds its home on my waist.

"Not hard when you used our driver. Hannah, Grant really loves you."

"Oh, fuck Grant, and fuck you too." I give him my best smile and laugh. I'm happy drunk, and they aren't going to ruin my night.

"Don't give me that face."

"What face?" I look at him.

"You know the face you're giving me; it's going to get us in trouble." His hand squeezes my side.

"He doesn't know my faces." Grant and Becca are making their way over to us.

"You still got it, mama," Becca says, sitting on Aiden's other leg.

"I try." I kiss her cheek and she takes her drink. I see the waitress bring over drinks.

"Mr. Grace." She smiles and blushes at both of them, and I roll my eyes.

"Oh please." It flies out of my mouth, and Grant looks at me. I raise my eyebrows and Aiden pokes me.

"See, he has no idea," I say. I take a shot and grab Becca's hand.

"You ready?" She finishes her drink and slaps my ass.

"Thank you, sir, may I have another?" I bend over a little, and she slaps my ass again. I can see Grant getting irritated by the way I'm acting, but I could give a fuck. When we get on the dance floor, I see Carla. You have got to be kidding me. I look over at Becca and she laughs.

"Let's hope she doesn't get in my way." I face Becca, who gives her a dirty look, and we dance.

It's awhile before Grant appears, but when he does, it's with Carla. Becca spots it first and turns me around. I see him behind her, his hands on her lower stomach. She has no game. She looks awkward; her hips show no rhythm. I laugh mirthlessly.

"Let me show her how it's done." I reel in Aiden. I take his front, and Becca is behind him. Usher comes back on, and this one is one of my favorites—'Scream.' I face Aiden and sing to him and he bites his lip. Oh, I miss that. I tell him I want to go all night and I know he can. I turn around and rub into him. He takes my ass and pulls me in. I can see Grant watching me. I start to sing to him and flick my pointer finger at him to come over. I shrug my shoulders and grab a guy who is more than willing to dance with me. His hands are a little too touchy-feely for me, so I back up off of him. He pulls me back in, and I back off again.

"Fuck off, asshole," I hear Grant say over my shoulder. The guy walks away.

"Go back to Carla. You look like you were having fun." I walk away and find another guy, who looks scared because Grant is still on my ass. He backs off and I turn around again.

"What the fuck do you want?" I stop moving as Usher is singing about being magnetic. This is what he is to me. Magnetic. I follow my instincts and walk up to him and kiss him. I jump up and wrap my legs around him and he takes me, all of me. I feel his hands on my ass, and I want to fuck him on the dance floor right now. My hands are on his face, and he brings one hand off my ass up to my hair. I pull away.

"Can you stop being a fucking douche?" He puts me down and smiles at me. I look over at Carla and smile. She's walking over like a rocket is up her ass.

"You fucking whore!" she yells at me.

"You just couldn't keep your man in line," I say. "That wasn't my fault, and didn't you fuck Aiden?" I have balls when I drink. She starts to slap me, but Becca slaps her first. I start laughing and feel Aiden's arm wrap around me to carry me away. I see Becca in his other arm. We are laughing hysterically. Grant walks Carla off the floor. I don't care what he does, and I'm not going to care. I just gave him the chance again, and he is walking away with her. What the fuck is wrong with him? He has no idea what he wants, and if he keeps doing this, I'll go home with Aiden and let off my steam. When we get to the table, I start to take a drink, but Aiden takes it away.

"No. Water." He places it in front of me and I pout.

"I guess Grant chose Carla, folks. Aiden, didn't you fuck her too?" I have no filter now. He looks at me and laughs. Becca perks up.

"Actually, Aiden, you have fucked all of us. Who would you say is best and worst?" He grins, pretending he didn't hear her.

"Come on, Aiden, you can tell us." I egg him on and give him my best 'fuck me' face.

"Carla was the worst, I'll give you that."

"And between us?" Becca asks.

"A gentleman never kisses and tells."

"You mean fucks and tells!" I yell.

"Who is a better fuck, me or Grant?" I lean across the table to look him right in the eyes, leaving our lips inches apart.

"I never slept with Grant." I see the surprise in his face. Did he really think we slept together? The music gets louder. I like this song.

"Let's go, Bec." I stand up and feel the room move. She hops up and we dance some more. I don't see Grant anywhere. *Maybe he left with his dead fish*, I think, and start to laugh. What a waste of time. I start to get belligerent.

"Fuck him!" I yell to Becca. She smiles at me and gives me the finger. We are laughing so hard, I need to pee. I lead her off the dance floor and see Grant walking out of the men's room. He tries to stop me, but I grab his hand and drag him into the ladies room.

"Jesus, Hannah," he says as he pulls me out.

"What? I have to use the powder room, Grant." I try to act sober but fail.

"I'll wait."

"Will you? Where did your girlfriend go?" I smile at him and bat my lashes.

"Hannah, cut the shit."

"I'm over it, Grant, you can do whatever you want. I don't care anymore." I turn around and walk into the ladies room. I pee for what feels like an eternity, and my thighs burn from squatting. I make my way to the mirror and decide I'm impressed. My makeup still looks good. I push a few bobby pins back into place and smile at my reflection as I wash my hands.

"Asshole alert," Becca yells as we walk out the door. I look at Grant and keep walking, but he grabs me and carries me through a doorway. He slams the door shut and pins me against it. He kisses me hard, and I let him. We are like two snake-eye magnets that finally snap together. We have been circling each other way too long.

The passion and anger all comes out. His hands are rough and mine are all over him. I bite his chin, and he moans deep in his throat. I kiss down to his Adam's apple and suck on it. His hands work my dress up, and his finger plunges into me. I shoot up from the pleasure and find his mouth again. His tongue flicks throughout my mouth, and our breathing is hard. He turns and throws me on a desk. I bring him down on top of me, but he hesitates.

"What the hell are you doing to me?" I ask. I lean up on my elbows and see his eyes darken. I sober up from this.

"I was thinking the same thing. You are the most complicated person I have ever met," He growls, before I pull him down and kiss him. His finger is still inside me, and I push into it. He pulls away again and pulls out his finger. I sit up on the desk.

"You know what, Grant, call me when you know what you want." I hop off the desk, but he blocks the door.

"I want you," he says. I see the storm still in his eyes.

"I think you did." I lean against the wall, feeling defeated. "But I don't think you do anymore. I think everything you said to me the other day in your office was bullshit. You told me the past was the past, then you threw it in my face." He steps in front of me, puts his hands to my hips, and kisses my forehead. I look up at him.

"No, it wasn't. I'm just struggling with it still. I thought dancing with Carla would make you jealous, but you didn't even care." I shake my head at him.

"I didn't care, Grant. It's just dancing. You were dancing with her but looking at me. I'm not a jealous girl. If I'm going to be with you, I trust you, till you give me a reason not to. I have never given you a reason not to trust me." I see the storm fade, and my blue oasis is back. I have him back. He leans down and picks me up, and I kiss him with all I have.

"I love you, Hannah." He breathes the words into my mouth.

"I love you, Grant."

"I love you." The words mean more to me now that he is looking me in the eyes.

"Take me home," I whisper as I kiss him.

"You want to go home?" He looks at me, hurt.

"Your house." I watch as a smile runs along his full lips, and I nip at them.

"I'll take you home." I can hear the promise in his voice. He puts me down and takes my hand, and we walk back to the table. Becca is on Aiden's lap, and they are having a great make out session.

"Yeah, Becca! You hit that shit," I yell. I'm still drunk and I like it. I want to go home and do the same to Grant. I want to do so much more.

"I'm going home," I say. She pulls away from Aiden and looks at me.

"With Grant. I'll see you in the morning," I smile and wink at them as we leave.

CHAPTER THIRTY-THREE

I wake up and the room is bright. Ugh. I place my arm over my eyes and feel like death. I roll over and look at the clock. It's 9:37 a.m. I see a card that says, 'Take me,' with an arrow pointing down, leaning against a glass of water. Grant isn't in bed with me. I have no idea what time we got home or how I even got here. I take the two pills he laid out for me and wash them down with water. Sitting up, I realize how hung over I really am. My head pounds and my body aches. I lie back down and will myself to get out of bed; I finally do because my bladder is about to explode.

When I get in the bathroom, I look in the mirror and scare myself. I start pulling bobby pins out and turn on the shower. I open a few cabinets and find towels. I step into the open shower and feel the hangover drip off of me. I lather his body wash all over myself. I stay in for a long time after I finish washing, just to relax under the water. When I step out, I walk back into his room and find my bag. I take out my toothbrush and makeup bag, then make myself look human again. I stand there naked in his bathroom, wondering where he is. I grab one of his T-shirts, smiling as I slip it over my naked body. It comes down to my knees and makes me happy.

I walk down the hallway and smell breakfast. Grant is standing across the room, looking out the window. When I get closer, I see he is on his cell. I tiptoe up behind him and wrap my arms around him, grabbing his chest. He doesn't jump; he just leans the phone against his shoulder and slides me to the front of him, pinning me against the window. I sneak a kiss on his beautiful full lips, and he kisses me back. Then he pulls away.

"I want an update in two hours." He hangs up, throws the phone on the couch, and picks me up.

"Good morning, sleeping beauty." His voice is raspy and sexy.

"How bad was I last night?" I place my hands around his neck and kiss his forehead.

"Let's just say pretty bad. You passed out in the car, and I carried you up." I take my legs from around his waist and slide down.

"I'm sorry, I really don't remember a lot." I rub my aching head and sit down. "Did I throw up?" I look at him with worry.

"No, you're a champ; you were quite amusing, I have to give you that. I believe alcohol is your truth serum." He sits next to me and pulls me into his lap. I lie there in his arms and listen to his heartbeat. What did I say to him? If only I could remember.

"So what did I say?" I look into the blue oasis and feel calm. It couldn't have been that bad; he seems relaxed today.

"Well, you told me you loved me." I look at him, giving him my full attention as I straddle him.

"OK, that's the truth. What else?"

"I don't think I should repeat what you said. You can be perverted, Hannah. I would have never guessed." I see the amusement reach his eyes, and he kisses me.

"That was the alcohol, not me."

"Are you sure? You had some pretty good ideas last night." I push back.

"Really? Did I try to act them out?" I ask, not really wanting to know the answer.

"Yes, but as a gentleman, I would not have hot, crazy sex with you in the back of the Rover with Derek watching." I roll off of him and bury my face into the couch. Oh my good God. Did I really do that? The last thing I remember is the dance floor, and he was with Carla. I think hard and an office pops into my head. I try to connect the dots and come up blank. I guess we made up, or I wouldn't be here. He starts to rub my legs.

"Trying to remember last night?"

"Yes, I'm so embarrassed." I bury my face deeper and he pulls me back onto him.

"Don't be. I liked taking care of you." He runs his knuckles down my cheek.

"So where does this leave us?" I straddle him again.

"What do you mean?"

"You watched me leave the gala last night and didn't seem to care. Then you showed up at the club, and you were all over Carla."

"And now we are here again." I shift on his lap and he grabs me, thinking I'm trying to get off.

"Relax. I'm not going anywhere."

"Well, you have a tendency of running."

"And you never follow me." I shoot him a look and he kisses me. He gets up with me in his arms and walks to his bedroom.

I feel all his weight on me as he lies us down on the bed. His kiss gets more urgent, and so do I. We need this; we need to get lost in each other, and it will fix everything. I pull his shirt up, and he pulls away so I can take it off him. I throw it across the room and he takes his T-shirt off me, realizing I'm naked under it.

"I like this look." He tosses the shirt. I pull him down to my mouth, and he invades every part of it. His skin feels so good against mine. He lifts me up and pushes me farther onto the bed. I grab his back and leave his mouth to kiss down his neck. He overpowers me and pushes me back down. I lie back as he kisses down my neck. My nipples harden as his skin brushes them. I arch my back when he starts sucking. I lie there under him as he teases me. I use my feet to try to push down his pajama pants. He slides back up, and I release him. I watch as he slides them off and climbs on top of me.

"You told me last night you don't want to use a condom." I nod and pull him closer to me so his head grazes my warmth. It feels so good right there. I wrap my legs around him and push him into me. As each inch pushes inside me, I feel myself pulse. He stretches me, and I start to move, my hips easing him deeper. I smile as he collapses onto me and starts to ease out of me and back in. It feels so good; every fiber of my body needs him.

"Hannah," is all he can breathe. He finds my mouth and kisses me again. I pull away when he starts to move deeper. I wrap my arms around his back and dig in with my nails. He takes me at a quicker pace, and I can't help biting his shoulder. I feel him enjoy the pain. I trail kisses up his neck. I nibble on his chin and then bite his lip. He rolls over, and I'm on top. I can feel his full length this way, and it hurts so good inside of me. I pull him almost out of me and push him back in. Hard.

He sits up at lightening speed and moves down to the edge of the bed while I ride him. I lean back and place my hands on his knees and he grabs my hips. When we start to move, I can't hold back anymore. He starts to rub my clit and I let go. I can hear myself screaming from the pleasure, and he lets me. He quickly rolls me over and gets back on top. I lie there out of breath; his breathing matching mine. I watch him pound into me over and over again. He is biting his bottom lip, and I want to suck on it. I grab his neck and pull him back down. I start kissing him and suck on his bottom lip. I feel his stubble rubbing against my face, but I don't care.

I begin to build again, and he can feel it. He slows and I look at him through hooded eyes. He watches me come undone again; I love that he is watching every move I make. I keep eye contact with him as I come again and watch him as he comes inside me. Then his body collapses on top of mine, and I respond by wrapping myself around him. My legs are wrapped around him as well as my arms. I pull him more into me, so he goes deeper, and he moans. We lie there for a while before he moves.

"I could stay inside of you all day," he says, propping himself up on his elbows.

"Then stay, you're more than welcome." I nip at his bottom lip.

"You're tempting me." I pull him back down and start to grind my hips. I can feel he is still hard, and I take advantage of it. Slowly I move again, and he matches my rhythm.

"I'm going to do exactly what you asked me to do last night." I look into his eyes and get excited. He starts to kiss all my favorite spots. I melt under him as he makes love to me.

When we finish again, I look at the clock and see it's after noon. I lie under him, running my fingers lightly over his back. I feel him react with goose bumps all over, and I hug him tight.

"So, is that what I was telling you last night?" My voice is hoarse.

"Yes, you pointed out all your favorite spots, and how you liked it, so I took notes." I kiss him. He is…I can't even find a word to describe him.

"You told me a few other things, but we have time to do everything else." He has a wicked grin, and I wonder what the hell I told him.

I let out a yelp when he picks me up and carries me into the shower. I feel the hot water run over my body and feel his emissions run down my legs. I want to stay here with him forever. I watch him shower and enjoy the view of his perfectly chiseled body. I kiss between his shoulder blades, and he turns around and starts washing me. He runs the soap all over my body, not missing an inch. I stand there, letting him do whatever he wants. When he finishes, I wet my palms with body wash and take him in my hands. Slowly I glide my hands back and forth along his length and feel him harden at my touch.

"I need to eat something if you want that again." I realize how hungry I am for food and him again. So I behave. I soap him up, and we rinse off.

I put the T-shirt back on and he puts his pants back on, not wearing anything under them. I smile at this as we leave his room hand in hand.

We sit at a table and eat a breakfast that has gotten cold, but neither of us cares. I jump when I hear his phone ring.

"What," he answers, then smiles at me. He likes to be intimidating. "Are you sure?" I watch as his expression changes from soft and sexy to hard and businesslike. "Do what you need to do. Search all the lots. Let me know when you get an ID." He hangs up and starts to dial on his phone.

"I just spoke with Harry; you gave him permission to search the woods?" He doesn't sound mad, but this is a tone I have never heard. "They found a body, Aid." I freeze. "Yeah, I told him to search all the lots. I know. I have to fly home tonight, then I will be gone for two weeks in Rome. Deal with it." He hangs up and looks at me. I don't want to piss him off.

"Are you OK?"

"I'm fine, but the press is going to have a field day with this." He runs his hand through his hair and dials his phone again. "Go to the Cape and watch over the investigation." He listens, and I remain still. "I need you there for the next two weeks while I'm gone. No bullshit. I want this quiet. Who the fuck knows what's going to come up? Take care of it. This leaks, and it's your ass." He hangs up.

"Fuck!" he yells. I watch as he walks to the window. I wait a minute before I walk over to him. I wrap my arms around him. His head hangs low, and he turns and rests his chin on my head. I stay there in his arms until we hear a knock. I startle when a man comes out of a room and opens it. I get behind Grant and hide.

"Who is that?" I whisper.

"It's Derek," he laughs.

"I thought he was your driver?"

"He does driving, security, everything."

I turn red as I see Shane walk in. Fuck. We are standing here practically naked, and here comes his brother. Since I'm hiding behind Grant, he doesn't see me.

"Hey, you hit that shit?" My jaw drops, and Grant steps to the side, leaving me exposed. I could kill him.

"Is that any of your business, Shane?" I ask. He walks over to kiss my cheek.

"Yeah, you hit that shit." He half hugs, half shakes hands with Grant. I just stare at them.

"I got a call from Harry." Grant gets serious. Shane walks into the kitchen and goes to the fridge.

"I just talked to Aid; he told me. I called John, and he is already home." Shane looks at Grant with an intense stare. They are talking their secret brother language that I don't understand.

"I'm going to get dressed." I head down the hallway and into his room. I find my cell and call Becca.

"Hey," she says.

"You OK?"

"I'm fine, walking into Grant's now."

I hear them in the living room.

"Come into his room." I hang up and wait for her on the bed. She comes right in and climbs on the bed next to me.

"So…" She looks at me with a smile.

"I passed out in the car last night. Apparently I tried to have sex with him in the car and embarrassed myself beyond belief." I look down, but can't help smiling. "But he made up for it a few times this morning."

"So how was he?"

"Delicious, couldn't get enough." I start to get dressed.

"We have to get going," Becca says as she answers her phone. "No comment," she yells, and then hangs up.

"What was that about?" I stop and look at her.

"Apparently some pictures got taken last night at the club, and I keep getting calls to confirm if I'm with AJ." I smile at her.

"So how was he?" She just looks down.

"We'll talk later." I cringe as I zip up my suitcase and lug it out of Grant's room.

The brothers are all standing together; they get quiet as we enter the room. Grant is still wearing his pajama bottoms, and they sit right on his hips, showing off his deep *V*. My hand wanders onto his butt as I walk by. He grabs me and wraps his long arms around me, pulling me into him so I'm facing Aiden and Shane. I try not to look at Aiden. Shane shows full amusement.

"I never thought I would see this day, Grant," Shane says. Aiden isn't showing any emotion.

"What day?" Grant asks as he kisses my ear.

"This," Shane waves his hand at me. "You, actually showing genuine affection to a woman." I roll my eyes. He had to have shown some kind of love to another woman before. Or is it true? I think back to game night and don't remember him touching Carla, or showing any affection toward her. I thought that was because I was there and we had kissed.

"Is this true, Mr. Grace?"

"Absolutely." I find this sad. He has lived his whole life without ever loving another person?

"I told you, Hannah, you changed our family. I heard my mother apologized to Becca last night." Becca smiles a forced smile. I remember Mrs. Grace's words: *Aiden loves you.* I look over at Aiden, but he's looking out the window. I slowly ease out of Grant's hold.

"Where are you going?" He pulls me back in.

"I have to go home. I have two little people there who need me, remember?"

"Give me a minute?" His brothers turn to leave. Aiden takes Becca, and in under a minute, we are alone.

"Do they always listen to you?" I lean my head to the side.

"Everyone always listens to me." I bite the inside of my cheek as I take in his words. "I love when you do that." His voice is still raspy.

"What?"

"Whatever you're doing, your lips look…" He stops and kisses me. I stand on my tiptoes to gain height.

"I will be in Rome the next two weeks." I see a pout come across his lips, so I pout too as I go back down on flat feet.

"I guess I will see you in two weeks." I kiss his chest and hug him.

"I'll call you." He leans down and kisses me again.

"Go put a shirt on," I say when I get to the door.

"Why?"

"Because you are walking me out to the car." He disappears to his room and reappears wearing jeans and a T-shirt. Oh, how I'm going to miss him and his perfect, sexy body. He takes my suitcase in one hand and my hand in the other.

We take full advantage of the elevator ride and fool around the whole way down. When the door opens, I can tell they know what we were doing. Aiden looks surprised that Grant came down.

"And you walk her down? You must have it bad." Shane teases. Grant doesn't tell them it was my idea, and I don't say anything either. I kiss him one last time and get into the SUV Becca has been waiting in. When I start to close the door, he stops it to steal one last kiss.

"Have a safe flight," I say.

"I will." Then he whispers in my ear, "I love you."

I look up at him and mouth the words back to him.

CHAPTER THIRTY-FOUR

The ride home starts off quiet. I can tell something is bothering Becca. I don't want to push her to talk, but that's never stopped her, so why should I let it stop me?

"So what happened last night?" I watch her tangle her fingers together.

"Nothing, we just talked."

"Talked?"

"Yup, apparently we have a lot in common." She forces a smile.

"Like what?" I look out the window and watch everyone in a hurry.

"We are both crazy about you."

Her voice is off. I look over to make sure she isn't crying.

"What?" I search her face.

"He was subtle, but he kept bringing you up and asking questions about me that would always lead to you. I asked him flat out after a while, and he said he wishes he never screwed it up."

"Well, you can't change the past." I feel irritated by this.

"Hannah, you realize it was my fault you're not together." I whip around and look at her.

"Not in any way, shape, or form is this your fault. He wanted you, and that's why he slept with you." I see her shift in the seat, and I can tell there is more to this story.

"Not exactly. I hit on him and told him he could close the deal if he closed the deal with me." Her voice is small.

"Bec, it would have ended up the same, no matter how you spin it. We got into a fight before you slept with him. I want to be with Grant." She takes my hand. We sit like this for a while.

"He wants to have lunch with you, Hannah. Would you consider it?"

"No."

"Why? Close the chapter and let him move on. You deserted him on the dance floor after he admitted he loved you."

"It would piss Grant off. I told him I would stay away from Aiden."

"And you all of a sudden answer to Grant?"

"No, I don't, but I want to be with him and not fuck it up. I don't want to be near Aiden, Bec. I can't."

"Why is it such a big deal, Han?"

I take a deep breath. Why is it so difficult? I want to be near Aiden, but when I am, things change; maybe I'm afraid my feelings will too. I don't want to hurt Grant, but I can't stand the fact that I left Aiden hanging. Why did I do this? I'm in so deep now, and I can't get it together.

"I just can't, Bec. Please stop."

"I stayed up most of the night with him talking about you, and..." She stops.

"What?" I can tell she wants to tell me something, but she hesitates. "What, Bec?"

"It was like hanging out with Chase." She cringes, and I feel the tears pierce my eyes.

"Don't even think about comparing." I look out the window, ending the discussion. How dare she even think about comparing Aiden to Chase?

CHAPTER THIRTY-FIVE

It's Monday morning, and I wake up to my two alarm clocks. I still feel tired; I don't know if it's from the emotional roller coaster I have been on or the sleeping pills. I get ready for work and get the kids ready for school. Today is the Father's Day party at school. Hunter already called Kevin to make sure he is still going. I get them out the door and to school on time, then dread heading to work. I know Michele will have a million questions, and I'm not up for it. Since Becca told me about Aiden, I have been lost. I never thought I would feel this way toward him, but I do, and I feel horrible about it.

I hear my phone and see it's Grant. I hesitate to pick it up, because when we talked yesterday, I was short and used the kids as an excuse. I do the calculation and it's the afternoon in Rome. I grab my phone.

"Hey." I try to sound happy but fail.

"Hey, are you at work yet?"

"Almost, just driving there now. How is Rome?" I meant to ask him yesterday, but I was so lost I forgot.

"Beautiful. I want to bring you here sometime." He is so confident. I cringe at his words. He loves me, and I'm second-guessing everything because of Aiden. The one man he knows can take me away from him.

"That would be nice, but it wouldn't be just me." Let's test the waters. See how he reacts when I throw the kids in.

"Do the kids have their passports yet?"

"No, we have never left the country."

"Maybe you should do that this week. It takes a few weeks to get them back now." I can hear people around him and wonder what he is doing.

"I'll think about it."

"It can't hurt to get them; it's a photo ID for them." It's a good point, but I don't see me taking the kids away with him. I barely know him; it was a big step to let him pick me up from the house and see them again.

"So how is work going?" I change the subject.

"Busy. We just took a break and are about to start up again. I miss you." I hear the words but struggle with them. He misses me, and I don't know if I miss him. I wish he were here. If he were here, I would never be tempted to see Aiden. I should tell him about Aiden wanting to have lunch with me. I don't want to lie to him, but I think I need to hear Aiden out and get closure. I want to be with Grant.

"Hannah." I shake out of it and realize I shouldn't do this now.

"I miss you too." My voice is low. I do miss him.

"You still love me?" I can hear the pout in his voice, and it makes me smile.

"You still love me? Or have you met a beautiful Italian woman?"

"Never. I have you, no one could compare. I love you, no one else." The words hurt. I do love him, but do I love Aiden too?

"I love you too, Grant, but I have to go into the hospital now. I'll call you when I get out if it's not too late." I park and wait for him to reply.

"Call me whenever. You OK?" He can tell even over the phone.

"I'm just tired." It's true; I'm tired from all the thinking.

"Dreams again?" My heart sinks because he knows about the dreams.

"Something like that." I use them as my excuse.

"I wish I could stop them." His voice is sincere and loving, and I start to cry. Why am I so emotional?

"Me too. I love you." I want to hang up, but I listen for his voice again.

"Love you too, babe." I smile at the way he is introducing this new pet name for me. *Babe.* I wish I could see him as he says it.

"Bye." I hang up and get out of the car.

I know today is going to be busy. I have been gone for a week, and I'm sure there is a ton of paperwork waiting for me. I have to get Grant and Aiden out of my head. I settle at my desk and play catch-up, until I see Michele staring at me from the door.

"Have fun?" I nod at her, not looking up.

"That's it? That's all? You're not going to give me any details?" She walks in and drops a paper on my desk. I see it's a picture of Grant and me at the gala. I look at it and see my smile. It must have been taken after he told me he was falling in love with me. We look so happy together, in love even. I start to read the article out loud: "Grant Grace with girlfriend, Hannah Winterfield. The new happy couple has been spotted multiple times around his estate in the Cape."

"I guess we are a happy couple."

"Is it true?"

"I guess, it's in print." I smile at the lame joke I made.

"Hannah." Her voice is growing frustrated.

"Yes, we went to the gala together, and yes, I believe we might be dating each other."

"So how is that going to work?" What does she mean how is it going to work? "Is he moving here?"

"He has a place in the city, but he's never there. He's in Rome for a couple weeks, and then I will see him when he comes back. Then I'm sure he will be off to another place."

"And you're OK with this?" I think about her words and my original concern for his workaholic tendencies.

"It's his life, Michele. I can't change him now. I never said it would work, but we are going to see where it leads us." I look down at the paper again. We look good together. I realize I do miss him.

"Can I keep this?" She smiles at me, then leaves. As soon as the door shuts behind her, I call him.

"Is everything OK?" His voice is low, and I realize I probably interrupted his meeting.

"Yes, sorry, did I interrupt you?"

"No, it's fine. What's up?" His voice is still low.

"I just saw a picture of us, and it made me miss you. That's all. Go back to work."

"I miss you too, Han. I'll call you later."

"OK."

"Love you." I smile at his words.

"Ditto, baby." I test the waters and hear him smile.

"Good-bye," he laughs into the phone.

"Bye." I hang up and feel a little better. I have a wonderful boyfriend who loves me. That's all I need. I don't need to see Aiden. I tell myself that a few times and begin to believe it.

The next few days pass fast, and I find myself home alone after I drop the kids off at school. I walk around the house and clean, but it doesn't settle the feeling inside me. I pick up my phone and battle for a while as I scroll through my phone and find Aiden's number. I put down my phone, grab my keys, and leave.

I drive down to the water and sit on the beach for a while, just listening to the waves crash along the shore. I clear my mind and enjoy the silence of the beach. I can see a few people starting to make their way down the sand to settle for the day. I people watch under my dark sunglasses. I watch a young couple throwing a Frisbee and laughing together. It makes me nostalgic, and I begin to think of Chase. I throw a pity party and begin to think about what my life would be like if he were still here. I wouldn't have the Grace problem. I bet I wouldn't have even thought about them if Chase were still here.

Chase was always like thirst; I could never drink enough of him. I feel the tears run down my face. I walk down to the water, where it rushes past my feet and splashes against my legs. It feels cold, and I back away, like I do with everything. I walk back to my truck and see the couple from earlier. They look so happy, and it makes my heart swell.

When I get home, I check my phone and see a few missed calls. I have a message from Shane, wondering if I would be able to visit Annie this week. I call him back at work; his assistant answers and transfers my call.

"Hey, Hannah, you get my message?"

"Yes, I was seeing if tomorrow would be good. I'm off." I hear him typing something and wait for his response.

"Yeah, that's fine. I figured maybe you could stop by and we could have lunch?"

Why does he want to have lunch with me? I think I'm overthinking the Grace men.

"That sounds great. What time?"

"You tell me. I don't have any meeting tomorrow, so I can go whenever. Just come over after you see Annie."

"OK. I'll see you tomorrow."

I hang up and feel like this is going to end up in some kind of talk. He is going to try to play peacemaker and attempt to fix me. I shake my head at the thought and leave to pick up the kids.

I go in a time warp, and before I know it, I'm taking my pills and going to bed. I see I don't have many left; I'm going to have to talk to my doctor about getting more. I dread the conversation. I get into bed, stare at the ceiling, and call Grant. On the second ring, I realize it's four thirty in the morning there.

"Hello." His voice is sleepy.

"Sorry, I forgot the time change."

"No, it's OK." I hear something in the background. TV, maybe?

"Go back to sleep. I will call you tomorrow."

"OK. I love you." He hangs up and I think about what I heard. It must have been the TV. I lie down and fall asleep from the magical pills.

CHAPTER THIRTY-SIX

I get to Annie's a little after ten. She looks great. I brought her a present, and she sets the bag down beside her bed to open later.

"So tell me all about the gala. I saw pictures of you and Grant, and I have to say you two look perfect together."

"It was OK." I'm too tired to relive that night.

"I heard some gossip. Tell me the story."

"It's the same merry-go-round, Annie. Grant is jealous of Aiden. Grant saw us dancing and got mad, blah, blah, blah." I see her give me a weird look.

"Hannah, I'm telling you this in strict confidence, so it never leaves this room." She looks at the door as if it's going to open up any second. "It's normal for a woman who comes into the Grace family to sleep with more than one brother." She cringes. I can't believe what she just said.

"What?"

She starts to laugh. "I slept with John before I was with Shane."

"What?"

"Yup, a few months before I met Shane, I slept with John. Autumn slept with Grant before getting with John." I just stare at her, because it's so fucked up. I can see how easy it is to get tangled up in the Graces' web.

"Hannah, Grant is controlling and can't stand the fact that you slept with Aiden, but he will get over it. They all got over it. It may take some time and a lot of convincing on our end, but he will be fine." I still can't believe she slept with John. Autumn slept with Grant. Wow, this is so fucked up. I start laughing.

"Wow," is all I can say.

"I know. Swear you won't say anything, because Autumn still denies it to this day."

"I swear. It makes me feel a little better that I'm not the first one to get tangled in this web."

"Well, you got tangled in the hardest one. Grant and Aiden. It's a tough decision."

"Annie, I'm with Grant." She looks surprised.

"Shane told me about Sunday morning, but he thinks...Well, I can't speak for him." I know exactly what our lunch is going to be like. Maybe I should ditch him—tell him I forgot and went home. "Hannah, follow your heart, and you will find the right person. You never know; it might not be either of them." She's right. I might jump ship and find love somewhere else.

"Thanks, Annie."

The next hour is spent talking about the baby and how she is going to get everything done at home in the Cape. I assure her everyone will help, and I would even go up to help myself. When I leave, I feel like I have found a great friend who really understands me and the Grace family.

I dreadfully drive over to Grace Industries and get stopped by the security guard when I walk in. I explain I'm having lunch with Shane, and he calls up to confirm. Once he talks to the office, I get a visitor's pass and head up. When I walk into the office, I want to walk right out. I see Aiden and feel the mixed emotions. He is talking to someone, but looks up and meets my eyes. I mouth "hi" to him, and he mouths it back. Aiden heads over as I tell the woman at the reception desk that I'm here to see Shane.

"Hey, you." He kisses my cheek and pulls me into a hug. I hug him back and melt in his arms. I'm the first to pull away, but he knows I felt it too.

"What are you doing here?"

"I'm here to have lunch with Shane. He called yesterday and asked if I could visit Annie, then come for lunch." A grin comes over his face. He brings his fingers to his chin and rubs it.

"Interesting," he says.

"What's so interesting?"

"Shane is in the San Francisco office. He left Tuesday and is coming back tomorrow." What the hell is going on? Annie knew I was having lunch with him. Why didn't she say anything?

"Oh." I stand there, confused.

"I'll have lunch with you."

"I have a feeling that's what Shane was hoping for." I shake my head at him.

"Would you rather, Shane?" I slap his chest.

"I'm hungry. What do you want to eat?" I ask. He licks his bottom lip, and amusement shows in his eyes. I look at the receptionist, who has been listening to us, and walk toward his office. He follows me for a few steps, then gets beside me.

"You walk around here like you own this place," he says, placing his hand on my back. I stiffen at his touch.

"Maybe I will one day." His office is similar to Grant's, but has his touches all over. He has a few baseballs in a glass case and pictures from the past on his bureau.

"So what do you want to eat?" he asks.

"I don't care. You want to order in or go out?" I wait for an answer.

"We can stay in if you want." When I nod, he calls his assistant and orders sushi.

I lean back into the couch as he sits next to me.

"So what's new, Hannah?" He is trying to be casual, but I can see right through him.

"Why don't you tell me, Aiden? Was this an ambush to talk to me?" I see him grin and shift to face me. I tuck my legs under me and face him.

"I had nothing to do with it. I think Shane wanted us to talk."

"About what?" I play stupid, but it has been eating at me.

"He thinks we have unfinished business." I touch his arm.

"Do we?"

"No. Not anymore." He is so matter-of-fact as he says this. "I heard a saying once and never understood it till you walked away from me on the dance floor."

I'm biting the inside of my cheek. "What is the saying?" I ask. He takes my hand.

"If you love something, set it free. I have to do it. You're with Grant. The faster I accept this, the faster I can get on with my life, and you can get on with yours." I don't know how I feel about this. I face away from him and lean my head against the couch. He loved me. I have to set him free too. I want to be with Grant.

"I'm sorry about everything." I look back over at him.

"What are you sorry for? I messed it up." He tucks my hair behind my ear and runs his knuckles along my cheek.

"Thank you." I kiss his cheek, and he hugs me. We hear a knock and separate.

We eat at the small coffee table in front of the couch like two old friends. We catch up on what's been going on with Annie and with Grant's work in Rome. He tells me more than Grant does.

"He comes home next week. I want to surprise him and pick him up." I look at Aiden to see what he thinks.

"I don't think it's a good idea."

"Why?"

"Grant doesn't like surprises." I think about it and ignore his advice. I think it will make him happy.

"We will see about that." I see the time and get up. "Thank you for lunch, Mr. Grace."

"Anytime. I enjoy your company." We hug, and he walks me out all the way down to the front doors. I don't even have to ask him.

As I drive home, I feel good about the outcome between us. I know he won't get in the way anymore, and Grant and I can focus on us. I decide to call Grant and tell him about the lunch. I don't want to keep anything from him. Honestly is the best policy. It rings a few times before he picks up.

"Hey, babe, I was just thinking about you." I smile and marvel at his words.

"Really? What were you thinking?"

"Nothing I can say at the moment. How is Annie?"

"Good. I visited her, then headed over to have lunch with Shane. He invited me yesterday."

"He's in San Francisco." I hear his tone change.

"I found that out after I got there."

"What the fuck is Aiden up to, Hannah?"

"No, it was Shane, but I did have lunch with Aiden." He starts to interrupt me. "Hear me out. He knows I love you and only you. There is nothing to worry about, Grant. I mean it. I'm yours and only yours." I wait for his response.

"I don't like that you went behind my back."

"I didn't. I was ambushed by Shane."

"I will talk to you about this later." And then I hear a dial tone. Why is he so mad? I let it roll off me.

CHAPTER THIRTY-SEVEN

That night I wait for his call, but I never get it. I have Shane to blame. I get up early and wait until ten to call Shane's cell. I hate time zones.

"Hey, Hannah." He sounds all happy.

"Fuck you, Shane, you set up this whole happy intervention between me and Aiden, and now Grant won't talk to me. I hope you're happy." I hang up on him and put my phone on silent when he calls back. I walk around my room, trying to pull it together.

Three days pass before Grant finally calls me.

"Hello." I keep my voice monotone.

"I'm sorry I overreacted." That's it? What the fuck? I don't deserve this. I don't talk.

"Hannah, I'm sorry. I just don't like the thought of you and Aiden in the same room." I still remain silent. "Say something, Hannah."

"Like what? I told you I had lunch with him. I didn't lie to you. I was honest, but you ignore me for days. It's like you want to punish me every time I do something you don't like."

"I'm sorry, baby." I'm so angry, I stay silent. "I was mad, and needed some time to think. I know you would never do anything Hannah. I'm sorry. I come home on Thursday." I can hear the smile on his face as he reels me in. "I want to see you. I miss you."

"I miss you too." I try to stay mad at him, but I can't. I miss him too much, and I want to see him. I think about how I'm going to surprise him, and smile.

"When do you land?"

"Sometime in the morning. Not sure yet."

"OK."

"I got you something." He's playful. I like playful Grant.

"Good. I deserve it after the way you acted," I reply.

"Yes, you do. I'm a lucky man to have you."

"Don't forget that, Mr. Grace."

"I won't. I love you."

"I love you too."

"I will call you later."

"OK. Bye." I wait for him to say bye, but he hangs up. I try to figure out how to get in touch with Derek. I should call Aiden and see if he will give me his cell. It's worth a shot. When I pull up my contacts, Aiden is the first one. I press Send and wait for his voice.

"Hey, you." His voice is sexy as always.

"Hey. I have a favor to ask you."

"Anything for you." I hear him rummaging through papers.

"I need Derek's number."

"What for?"

"My surprise." I hear him hesitate.

"You sure you want to do this?"

"Yes. I can call Shane for the number, if you don't want to give it to me." I give him the option of saying no, knowing I'm lying because I have no plans to call Shane.

"I'll text it to you."

"Thank you. It's always a pleasure doing business with you, Aiden." I flirt with him, not meaning to.

"Yes, it is, Hannah."

"I'll talk to you later."

"I hope so." I hear the flirting back and feel bad for starting it.

"Bye." I wait for his text and like promised, I get it in under a minute. I call Derek right away.

"Derek."

"Hi, Derek, it's Hannah."

"Hello, Mrs. Winterfield, how can I help you?"

"I was calling to see if you could pick me up before you pick Grant up on Thursday. I want to surprise him." I wait for his answer. Would he say no?

"That will not be a problem. I will call you tomorrow with a time."

"Can we keep this between us? I want Grant to be surprised."

"Yes, of course, Mrs. Winterfield."

"Please call me Hannah, and thank you. I'll talk to you tomorrow."

"OK, Hannah. I'll call you after Grant calls me with the details."

I sit and enjoy my small surprise.

I take the kids to my parents' house for a barbecue. Summer is in full swing, and the kids finished school today. We celebrate the last day of school with a swim in my parents' pool. My parents can tell I have found my way again, and I enjoy feeling like myself again. I sit on the steps and watch Hunter jump off the diving board. They are like little fish. My dad is swimming with them, tossing them around. I see my mom make her way over to the steps with her famous daiquiri. I take a small sip, trying to avoid the brain freeze that comes with it.

"So, what are your plans for this weekend?" she asks.

"Nothing. Grant comes back Thursday." I can tell she likes that I'm talking about him.

"That's nice. Do the two of you have plans?" I shake my head no and take another sip.

"If you want, I can take the kids away with us." I think about it. I never would have before Grant, but I think I could use some alone time with him.

"When are you leaving again?"

"Thursday morning. They can sleep here tomorrow night." She looks hopeful.

"When are you coming home?"

"Monday. We just want to check on the house and get it ready for next month." I think about it.

"You sure you don't mind taking them?" She is glowing with excitement as she bumps me.

"No, they are terrible kids. Of course I want them. We will have fun."

"OK," I agree. I secretly get excited. I can have Grant to myself for five days. It makes me want to call him and tell him, but I'm sticking with my surprise. I start making millions of lists in my head. I pack for the kids and pack for myself after the kids go to bed. This is going to be good for us. We can stay in the city or go up to the Cape. Either way, I get to spend time with him, and I can't wait.

CHAPTER THIRTY-EIGHT

Wednesday flies by. Derek calls to let me know he will be picking me up at eight. I drop the kids off and stay to tuck them in and help my parents load the car. Before I know it, I'm lying in bed, feeling like a kid on Christmas Eve. I can't wait for tomorrow to come so I can see Grant and surprise him. The pills don't work as well, because I am too excited, so I get up before my alarm goes off to get ready. I'm fully dressed and ready at seven, and I pace the kitchen while drinking my morning tea. I want to call Becca, but I would wake her up if I did. I pace and wait until I see the car pull into my driveway. I nearly jump for joy when I see it. I straighten out my new sundress; it's way too short, but I want to give him something to look at on the car ride home. I slip on my sandals and meet Derek at the front door.

"Hello, Hannah. Let me get this for you."

"Thank you, Derek." I hand him my bag and lock the front door.

I feel the excitement build the whole way to the airport. I think about how I should surprise him. Should I wait in the car and surprise him when he gets in? Or should I be leaning against the car when he gets out? I think about both and decide on outside the car. This way I can jump on him and kiss him, rather than doing that in the car. I want to feel him against me again. I start to realize how in love with him I really am. It didn't take long to fall for him; I smile when we get to the airport. I watch as Derek pulls in, but I don't see Grant's plane yet.

"They're taxiing around," Derek says. "He should be here in five minutes." I look out the window for his plane and finally see it coming. I want to jump out now, but what if he is looking out the window? I wait until I see the stairs open. I start to get out of the car, but then I freeze. Grant is with someone. I see a woman appear next to him, and I watch as they kiss. He takes her hand and holds it down the stairs. I'm frozen in time as I watch them. I can hear my heart shatter on the ground and lose my breath like I have been sucker punched in the gut. I know Derek is seeing this. I have to act fast.

"Derek, take my bag out when you put his in. Please don't tell him I was here." I slip out the door facing away from the plane and tuck myself next to the tire. I want to cry, but I don't. I can hear Grant's voice laughing with this woman. Derek greets them. I think he is making sure Grant doesn't walk around the car.

"I'll get that for you, sir." I listen to him get them in the car, and I move around to the back. Derek walks around and sees me. I feel pathetic. I'm hiding behind the car like a pitiful person. He opens the tailgate and puts all the bags in. He takes mine out and closes the door.

"Hannah, I will call Sam to come get you."

"Don't, please. I can get myself home. Just please get out of here."

"I'm sorry," is all he can say.

"Me, too." Derek gets into the SUV and pulls away. I stand there in the middle of nowhere with nothing but my suitcase.

I'm in shock, just watching the SUV as it disappears out of sight. I begin to walk off my anger to the nearest building. I notice a car pull in, but keep walking. I start to feel uneasy when it pulls up next to me. As the window slides down, I see it's Aiden. I stop and look at him, and I see red. When he steps out, I attack him. I run right up to him and start slapping him and hitting him with my fists.

"You knew. You fucking asshole! You knew and didn't tell me!" I'm screaming now; he doesn't move as I hit him. He takes every swing and just lets me get it all out.

"I hate you. I hate you both." I stop and fall to the ground. He takes me in his arms and holds me while I cry.

"I didn't know," he whispers.

"Yes, you did."

"No, I had a feeling but was never able to confirm it."

"Then why are you here?"

"I had a feeling. I didn't want to see you get hurt. I know how Grant is."

"Who is she?" I watch as he hesitates. After a deep breath, he begins.

"Ava, my ex that cheated on me with him." His voice is bitter, and I feel the same way. I move closer to him and he pulls me in. We sit on the ground while I wrap the last ten minutes around in my head. What a fucking asshole. I think of last week when I called Grant in the middle of the night, and I thought it was the TV I was hearing. It was her; it had to have been her.

I grab my bag and walk over to Aiden's car. He opens the trunk, and I see his suitcase. He places mine next to his and opens my door. I sit in his car and feel so many different emotions at once. I feel angry towards Grant. How could he do this to me? Was he just stringing me along? Was this some kind of sick pay back for me sleeping with Aiden? I trusted him with me heart and he shattered it.

"Catch up to him," I say. "I want to see if he brings her back to his apartment."

"Does it change anything if he does?"

"No."

"I'll take you home." His eyes are soft as he says this.

"No, take me anywhere else. I don't have to be home until Monday." He nods. I stare out the window, and before I know it, we are heading north. I replay seeing Grant and Ava. He looked so happy with her. He kissed her. As I think about it, I hear my phone ring. I take it out of my bag and see it's him. I turn my phone on silent and throw it in the backseat. I look over at Aiden.

"Let me disappear until Monday. I don't want anyone to know where I am, OK?"

"If that's what you want. No one would ever find you at my house."
I adjust my seat back so I'm almost lying down. I can see the sky this
way, and I get lost in the clouds.

To be continued...

Hannah, Grant and Aiden's story continues in
Letting Go of Grace.

ACKNOWLEDGEMENTS

I once heard it takes a village to raise a child, and I believe that to be true. I have a village of people who I love and adore, that have helped me make this dream come true. Without you I don't think Falling into Grace would have ever seen the light of day.

I would like to thank my Hubby. Have I told you lately that I love the shit out of you? To my monsters, you are my everything. My heart would not beat, or be complete without the three of you.

Mom and Dad, thank you for letting me be me. I know I'm the favorite, but don't worry, your secret is safe with me! To my favorite sister, you do realize you are my one and only? To my favorite brother, you two dunk it out.

My girls, I can't even find the words to describe what you mean to me. Lisa, Norma Jean, Aunt Betty, you are my cheerleaders! Mindy, you are the bung to my da-lung. Chrissy, I adore your honesty and encouragement. Michelle, you are the only person who I can tell the absolute truth to, even if it makes me sound like a horrible person, you just get me. Trish, sometimes I wonder if we share the same brain, but really, get out of my head already! Erin, my favorite teen mom. Thank you for letting me vent when things get stressful and for always having my back on the playground. Diana, thank you for our late night dance parties. Jacky my oldest, and most cherished friend. We always pick up where we left off, even if it's been months in between. Ellen, thank you for hopping on the crazy train! *Becca* is a culmination of all you wonder woman in my life. Without you all, I would be a hot mess!

I would like to give a HUGE thank you to Marilyn, my wonderful editor. You gave me hope again. I don't know what I would have done without you!

And finally THANK YOU, to you, the reader, for taking a chance on me.